W9-CBB-889

CHASE BRANCH LIBRARY
17731 W. SEVEN MILE RD.
DETROIT, MI 48235
313-481-1580

JUL 17

CH

# HUNTER

## MERCEDES LACKEY

HYPERION
LOS ANGELES • NEW YORK

If you purchased this book without a cover, you should be aware
that this book is stolen property. It was reported as "unsold and
destroyed" by the publisher, and neither the publisher nor the
author has received any payment for this "stripped" book.

Copyright © 2015 by Mercedes Lackey

All rights reserved. Published by Hyperion, an imprint of Disney Book Group.
No part of this book may be reproduced or transmitted in any form or by any means,
electronic or mechanical, including photocopying, recording, or by any information
storage and retrieval system, without written permission from the publisher.
For information address Hyperion, 125 West End Avenue,
New York, New York 10023.

First Hardcover Edition, September 2015
First Paperback Edition, August 2016
1 3 5 7 9 10 8 6 4 2
FAC-025438-16176
Printed in the United States of America

This book is set in Adobe Devanagari
Designed by Marci Senders

Library of Congress Cataloging-in-Publication: 2015008778

ISBN 978-1-4847-2543-6

Visit www.hyperionteens.com

To the loving memory of my mother,
Joyce Ritche, who was always there for me,
and was from the first my biggest fan

1

YOU COULDN'T SEE outside the train windows at night; the
conductor had opaqued them. Most people probably wouldn't
want to see out anyway. I looked around at the rest of the passengers in the car—I'd noticed when I got to my seat that I was the
only one there who was under thirty years old. I'd seen flashes of
fancy railcars like this in vids, and while waiting for track clear-
ance at the Springs station, when I'd been down there with my
Master. Stepping into the sleek silver tube with its rows of heavily
padded blue-gray seats had felt unreal. As I covertly examined
the people around me, in their clothing that was obviously not
handmade, I wondered if they were trying to figure out why I had
invaded their expensive, important world. They'd been studiously
leaving me alone in that way that said they were curious but didn't
intend to actually say anything, while I stared at the reflections in
the dark windows and wished I were back in my little room. Or

maybe they already knew what I was. Master Kedo had told me on the drive down to the Springs station that all the personnel on the train were told about me, so maybe the passengers were too.

Now I was the only one still awake. Pretty much everyone else had their seats in the recline position, their cocoons on, and their privacy hoods over their heads and shoulders. It looked like a scene out of one of the drama-vids we watched now and again, the ones that turned up in the weekly mail. I didn't care for them much, but my best friend, Kei, loved them, so I always sat through them without a complaint. That's what friends do, right?

Well, okay, maybe some of them were watching their own selection of vids in there, but you couldn't tell; they'd have their buds in and their glasses on. There was just row after row of reclined seats, skewed so no one *quite* had his head in someone else's lap, each person bundled up tightly like a swaddled baby, with soft black mounds over the top halves. The cocoons were made of some fabric I'd never seen before, soft and plush, like kitten fur. I'd watched as they settled in for the night, and a lot of them had asked for Nightcaps. If something bad happened now, they would all die without ever knowing they'd been in danger.

All but me. My seat was reclined, of course. I didn't have any choice in that; all the seats had reclined and swiveled for night at the same time. The conductor did that for the whole car. But I hadn't fastened down the cocoon, and I wasn't going to use a hood. I certainly wasn't going to have a Nightcap. My Masters would have a litter of cats if I even looked at a Nightcap.

Well, no, they actually wouldn't; my Masters didn't do that sort of thing. But they'd give me that *look* that said *You know better than that*, which actually made you feel a lot worse than if they'd had a litter of cats.

I wanted to look out, even though I knew the view would be no different from daytime. The track was safe enough—well, as safe as things ever got out here below the snow line. It was enclosed in a wire cage that was kept electrified for five miles in front of and behind the speeding train. Back when things were finally being put together again, after the Diseray, that was one of the first things the army had figured out: the way to keep the trains safe. Outside the cage, though, that was different. Some places were safe, protected. Some . . . not. Some were hell on earth.

I'd seen that hell on earth once, a small version of what could happen when the Othersiders decided there was a choice plum to pick and they were going to pick it. Two years ago; I was fourteen then. Summer, of course; in winter, *all* the settlements are relatively safe, protected by snow and cold. Anston's Well was—still is—a nice place, with nice people in it. About thirty families, big enough to have their own storehouse and trading post. The Othersiders must have decided it had reached a point where it was big enough to bother with.

The first I'd known about it was when I got woken up from a sound sleep by the Monastery alarms. My Master Kedo was pounding on my door as I was stamping my boots on. "Summon!" he'd said, so I'd summoned my Hounds, who'd joined his four that were milling about in the hall outside my room, and we'd met the rest outside in the snow. Everybody, and I mean everybody, had piled out of the Monastery. Even the oldest and youngest; and the ones with no magic and no Hounds were armed.

When we'd gotten down to Anston's Well, about a third of the houses were on fire, and there were monsters in the streets, trying to pull down people who were holding them off. There were more monsters just outside of the palisade around the town; that was where Kedo had sent me. The Hounds and I . . . it was just a blur for most of the night. I did a lot of shooting—some magic, but mostly shooting—while the Hounds kept what I was shooting at too busy to come at me. Kedo had given me an AK-47 with incendiary rounds, which the Othersiders I was up against did not much like. The turning point had come when the rest of the Hunters from the other settlements finally reached us. By dawn, we'd driven the Othersiders off. The bodies that didn't dissolve, I think they carried off with them. We lost that third of the houses that were on fire, but we were so lucky . . . just two deaths, though nearly everyone who wasn't a Hunter was hurt or burned. But like Per Anston had said, "We can rebuild. We can't resurrect."

I wouldn't show how scared I was now, like I hadn't then; I'd spent a lot of time learning how not to show it, but I was scared. Of course, I wasn't from a place that was precisely *safe*, but it was safer than most of the territory we were speeding through. And I was going to be going out there into the worst parts of it, if not now, then soon. It would surely be no more than a year before I was patrolling it.

I'm a Hunter, and that's my job. There is no more important job in the world. Hunters stand between the monsters of the Breakthrough and ordinary people. If it hadn't sunk in before, that sure had been made clear to me the night Anston's Well was attacked. I knew those people; they were my neighbors, and a couple of the hurt folks were my friends. They'd come up to dance at the

Safehaven flings, and I'd run off the Othersiders from their fields, and . . . that was when I knew for certain-sure that there was nothing more important than being a Hunter. Because being a Hunter meant I could *do* something about the Othersiders that no one who wasn't a Hunter could do. It had been the Hunters, not bullets, not RPGs, who had turned the tide that night, who had kept Anston's Well from being another one of those casualties in the war between the Othersiders and humans. This isn't a job you pick, it's a job that picks *you*—but if I'd been given the choice, I'd still be a Hunter. That morning—on the way back up to the Monastery in the back of the truck, my Master Kedo had given me this long and searching look. The measuring kind. I guess he must have seen what he wanted to see, because he'd ruffled up my hair and said, "*Now* you are a real Hunter, *chica*," and leaned back and closed his eyes, looking satisfied.

One of the stewards was making his way through the rows, checking on everyone. He had on the dark green uniform of the Train Service, which looks military, but isn't, and had a serious, square face with ginger hair. I wasn't sure why he needed to check on people, but this was an expensive and very exclusive way to travel, so I supposed the illusion of always being served came with it. No one flies but the military, of course; the skies are just too dangerous. There are other trains, not like this one, where people are packed in like cattle; they have to hump their own luggage, bring their own meals. I saw them at the station, and it looked like the old pictures of people fleeing from a war.

Not me. I was told that once I was away from my Masters and home, I would always get the star treatment, partly because of what I am, partly because of my uncle. That was another thing that felt surreal. It was hard to think *I'm* related to someone important. It certainly didn't make any difference up on the Mountain.

The steward paused at my row, and I tensed a little, expecting a rebuke, or a demand to lie down and sleep, like everyone else. But instead, he leaned over the man between me and the aisle, and whispered, "Are you really the Hunter?"

I nodded. His eyes went wide. "You're so young!" he blurted. "You're just a girl!"

I thought about telling him that I had been a Hunter since I was nine; then I thought better of it, since that didn't fit with the story I was supposed to tell, and I should start using that story right now. The Masters and the Monastery aren't even supposed to exist, and when someone turned Hunter they were supposed to go to Apex City immediately, anyway. There aren't a lot of Hunters, after all. Maybe one person in a hundred or two hundred is born with the ability to do magic, and maybe only half of them become Hunters. There's not another place like the Monastery on the whole continent, at least not that I know of. Back at the beginning of the Diseray and the Breakthrough, Hunters tried to train themselves, and about half of them died before they mastered their magic and learned how to work with their Hounds. So having Hunters report to Apex for proper training was the law; it was probably a smart law, too.

I just shrugged at him.

"Can I see the Hounds?" the steward breathed.

That took me by surprise. "Here?" I asked. "Now? I mean, sure, but ... would that be ... polite?" The Hounds are not exactly quiet about making their entrance, and I wasn't sure if even earbuds and cocoons would insulate these other important personages. Nor how they would feel about being awakened by a full pack.

Now, the Hounds would probably love it. Sometimes I think that they feed off of admiration as much as they feed off of manna. Although, maybe admiration is another sort of manna.

He glanced at the rest of the passengers, but when he looked back at me, his face was all lit up with excitement, and I couldn't help smiling at him a little. Sure, for me, I summon the Hounds, and it's just Tuesday, but even for the folks in the settlements on the Mountain, seeing the Hounds is a special thing, so how much more special would it be for someone who spent most of his life taking care of rich people in a train?

"The rec car is empty," he said eagerly. I nodded, shucked myself out of my cocoon, and edged into the aisle. I followed him through two more cars full of silent cocoons and into the rec car. We picked up two more stewards on the way. One of them stopped and whispered something into a grate at the end of the car; I guessed that was probably the car-to-car comm, or something like it.

He was right, the car we ended up in was empty. The autobar blinked its lights at us, then went back to wait mode when we didn't go get ourselves drinks. The game consoles were silent, as were the gambling tables.

There was some clear space at the back with fold-down exercise machines. That was where I went. By now I had quite an audience, and more were coming; that steward who had whispered into the radio must have spread word about what I was going to do through the rest of the train. It made me a little nervous because

I didn't usually do this with an audience; normally the Hounds are already with me when people see them. I closed my eyes and envisioned the Mandala; that opened my mind to the Otherworld.

The Mandala, of course, is *my Mandala*, the same thing that's branded on the backs of my hands. They're tattooed, but the tattoos trace over the actual Mandala. Every Hunter's Mandala is a circular diagram, and every one is different. They're really pretty, actually; if you didn't know better, you'd think they were just fancy decoration, like regular tattoos. There's an outer circle, then a circle of little signs inside that, one sign for each one of your Hounds, then another circle, then maybe a triangle or a square or a hexagon. There might be signs inside that, but there are always two squares on top of each other after that, making an eight-pointed star. Then in the center of that is a sign that's you. If you know how to read them, they'll tell you how many Hounds the Hunter has, but there are other things in the Mandala that no one knows how to read. They look sort of like the Mandalas in some of the Buddhist or Hindu god-paintings at the Monastery, but the language isn't Chinese or Sanskrit. They get burned into your hands when your magic wakes up, the first time something really bad happens to you that involves Othersiders. If you're born a Hunter—because you can't be *made* a Hunter—the Hounds will come to you then, for the very first time, and the act of them coming over from the Otherside burns the Mandalas into the backs of your hands.

With my eyes still closed, I drew the three Summons Glyphs in the air with sweeping gestures; if I opened them, I knew I would see the Glyphs hanging in midair, drawn in flames, which was something of my signature. Every Hunter uses the same three Summons Glyphs. They look like runes; maybe they actually are runes, but if so, no one has ever translated them. They tell the Hounds that the Hunter is calling them. My Glyphs, being drawn in fire and all, are very showy, which is odd, considering I tend to keep myself to myself and drawing attention makes me feel naked. I heard the group's swift intake of collective breath.

With an abrupt gesture, I cast the Glyphs to the ground, where they lay burning just on top of the carpet, and I opened the Way—and all I can tell you about that is how it feels. It feels as if I am reaching across the Glyphs with my gut and opening a door. Weird, I know. But that's how it feels. The Glyphs make the door, and at the same time, they put a kind of seal on it that nothing can cross but the Hounds. Now I opened my eyes, in time to see them bursting out of midair between me and the onlookers.

You know, that never gets old, no matter how many times I do it. There's this amazing feeling, a *Wow, these are* my *Hounds, and I brought them!* And, for me at least, there's also a feeling as if my best friends in the whole world had just come through the door into my room: an *I'm so happy we're together again!* I always have that, even if I'm summoning them right before a bad fight.

Someone gave out a nervous shriek; all seven of the Hounds turned their heads in his direction to stare with their flaming eyes. Little flickers of flame danced over their coal-black coats. Some Hounds always look the same, but mine don't. I was one of the three Hunters on the Mountain, including my Master Kedo, who had Hounds who could change what they look like. They'd chosen to appear as black greyhounds this time, which was a good choice: there wasn't much room in the rail car for anything bigger, they were intimidating without inciting panic, and there was no way that their usual forms would have fit.

"They just look like dogs," one of the stewards said doubtfully. My pack leader, Bya, looked over his shoulder at me and dog-grinned, then, before I could stop him, whipped his head back around and blew a jet of flame at the doubter. There were shrieks, but I stepped in between them, right into the flame, and let it play over me.

"Illusion," I explained, as the panic subsided. That wasn't the truth of course; Bya had merely ordered the flames not to burn anything or anyone, but knowing that my Hounds could turn the laws of physics inside out would only make these people's poor brains explode. I know it made *my* brain explode the first few times I saw them do impossible things.

After that, the Hounds went into superstar mode and graciously accepted the admiration of the crowd. Everyone wanted to touch them, pet them, and the Hounds were in the mood to accept buckets of that—probably since we hadn't Hunted in two weeks, and they were bored and hadn't gotten what they considered to be their just quota of adoration for a while. When they're in a petable form, they go all out; their coats are as sleek and soft as the antique silks I've handled at the Monastery.

In a situation like this one, I don't have to dismiss them, they go off on their own. When they got tired of it all, they went to the Glyphs still burning on the floor and leapt through to the Otherside. Bya was last. Bya seems to like people more than the rest of them. When he went through, the Glyphs vanished, and the crowd mingled around a little more, asking me stuff about them. I felt pretty awkward, but at least they were asking me about the Hounds instead of myself, so I managed not to get too tongue-tangled. The radio at the end of the car chimed three times after a bit, and they all kind of alerted on it and dispersed back to their duties. All but the steward of the car my seat was in. I guess he got to stay with me because I was in his charge.

"Would you like something to drink?" he asked, pausing at the autobar. "You might as well, the bar can mix you up just about anything." He stood there with his hand just over the keypad, waiting.

I thought for a moment. It was just a little intimidating, and a little intoxicating. Here I was, in a situation I had never found myself before, a situation where I could have absolutely anything I wanted.

Almost anything, that is. That put things into perspective. I really wanted to turn the train around and go back home. For a moment, homesickness swallowed me up. But I kept my Hunt-face on, just as I'd been taught.

"You choose. I just don't know what the options are. Something soothing, sweet, and hot with nothing like a drug or alcohol in it," I said, thinking I was going to get some sweet, hot tea, which I *much* prefer to the hot buttered tea some of my Masters like. Well, it isn't real tea—nobody on this continent can get that anymore—it's herbal tisane. But it's real butter. Cows can't live up in the mountains, but goats and sheep can, and we have both at the Monastery. Sometimes we get cow butter and milk from the settlements, but mostly we rely on our own herd for that sort of thing.

"I know just the thing," he said, and went to the autobar. He brought back something medium brown and opaque, with an intriguing smell. I sipped it; it was odd but good. Creamy *and* sweet. "Hot Chocolike," he said, and gestured for me to follow him. I did, sipping as we went.

At the vestibule to my car, he paused. "If—if something were to happen to the train—you and your Hounds would protect us, right? We'd be all right with you here, until help came, right?"

I thought about that. Thought about the likelihood that if there was an attack that involved something big and nasty enough to break through the electrified cage, the train would probably crash, and at the speed it was going, not even the crash-bubbles would save us. And that if any of us did survive, we'd be too injured to do anything, or unconscious. We'd be too far away from Apex for an Elite team to get here in time. I thought about other possibilities that didn't involve crashing, in which case the armed cars at the front and the rear of the train would do a lot more about protecting us than me or the Hounds ever could. I mean, there were machine guns with armor-piercing, blessed bullets in there, or incendiaries and mortars, and some trains were even rumored to carry small missile launchers with Hellfires loaded. I'm cursed with a very good imagination, and right then, what I could imagine was terrifying.

But my Masters had told me that when I got out here in the world, the people here would look at me differently from how they did at home. That Hunters were some sort of legendary beings off the Mountain. Not that Hunters weren't respected on the Mountain, because we were; everyone knows the job we do is dangerous, and we get the respect a warrior merits. But nobody treats us like we're minor gods or something.

We didn't get a lot of live vid on the Mountain; we were off the grid, and our electricity had to be saved for things that mattered, so mostly it was just the officially mandated stuff we warmed up the vid-screen in the community hall for, or old, stored stuff on drives and disks that you can watch on a solar-powered tablet, or things that came in the weekly mail. We don't *lack* for electricity, because we can keep the lights and the comm system and the intranet going all the time, but we're all taught to be mindful, very mindful, of waste. That kind of mindset goes all the way back to the Diseray, when no one had much of anything, and everything was being scrounged. *Think twice, act once,* is what everyone says. When kids are taught to read and write, it's one of the first things they print out.

That was when it hit me: off the Mountain, Cits—that's ordinary people who live in the cities—absolutely believed what the vids showed them. And the vids showed them that Hunters were able to protect them from anything. Then it hit me that there must be a reason for that.

I wasn't going to do him any good by breaking that illusion now, was I? I had to think about this before I answered him. Think twice, act once.

"Yes," I said simply. "So long as you forget how young I look and do exactly what I tell you to."

Enough of the Hunter mystique must have attached itself to me when I summoned the Hounds that he just got this hugely relieved look on his face and sighed. Then he opened the door for me and waved me through.

I went back to my seat and perched on it, legs crossed in lotus position, zazen style, sipping the drink. It must have been terrible territory we were passing through, for him to have asked that question. Now I *really* wanted to see what was out there, even though I had goose bumps all up and down my spine. It's what's unknown and unseen that scares me the most. That had almost been the worst of it, that night at Anston's Well. I mostly couldn't *see* what was coming at me. Flashes. Teeth, eyes, claws. I knew some of the monsters of the Othersiders, but by no means all of them—some we still don't have names for, some came out of other mythologies, ones we don't have books for. Nothing is scarier than what you don't know.

There was a lot of speculation among the folks that depended on the Monastery about just what happened to cause the Diseray— that's what everyone calls it, the time when the old world that created vids and trains and planes and all of that got turned upside down. It's been about two centuries and a half, a little more maybe, since it happened.

I looked over at the steward, who was doing something on the keypad. The lights got even dimmer. I was just a ghost of a reflection on the opaqued window.

I wondered if people like the steward ever thought about it. I do. The other Hunters tied to the Monastery don't so much, but I do.

I knew there were volcanoes and earthquakes, because the Island of California used to be part of the continent, and there's Old Yeller, a volcano where a park used to be that still sends up ash plumes that ground the Air Corps, and Olympus, another one in the northwest that took out a whole city. Every so often, when the wind blows from the right direction, we still get ash-plumes that mean everyone has to wear masks until they settle, and the ash in the the sky is the reason why there's snow on the mountains all year long.

I stared at my reflection in the window, with my dark brown hair making a kind of shadow around my face, glad I hadn't lived through those times. Bad as right now was, I could imagine how much worse it had been.

The steward came back over when he saw me looking at him. "Anything I can do for you, Hunter?" he asked. "Anything you'd like to know about Apex, for instance?"

I thought, well why not? It would be a good idea to find out some of what I should play dumb about. "What do they tell you Cits about the Diseray?" I asked. "I never learned all that much about it. And please sit down; it gives me a crick in my neck to look up at you." He gave me a funny look, but since I was curled up, he sat gingerly down on the edge of my seat, as far away from me as he could, to be respectful, I think.

"We don't dwell on it." He shrugged. "Mostly they give us a couple days on it in school, so we know to be properly grateful for being safe now. There were plagues, which we cured. Storms got worse, which we couldn't do anything about, and which is why only the Air Corps flies now and we rely on trains. The South and North Poles switched, which we can't exactly do anything about either. There was a nuke set off on purpose by Christers on the other side of the world. And the Breakthrough, when all the magic and monsters happened. That's mostly what I remember from school."

I nodded. I'd read the diaries of some of the people who gathered for safety at the Monastery; farmers, hunters—the ones who hunted for food, not my kind—craftsmen, a couple of soldiers— it had been a real mixed bunch. That was when they all pitched together and built Safehaven, the first settlement, the one right at the foot of the Monastery, up in the snow year-round. The

Monastery itself predated the Diseray; it was started by Tibetan Buddhists, but by the time things got sorted out, it had turned into a home for every kind of religious folk but Christers. Right now there were some Celtic, Norse, Greco-Roman, and shamanistic traditionalist types, several Native Americans, including my Master Kedo, some Shaolin monks, a couple of Hindus, one lone Sikh, and a couple of Shinto Masters. The one thing they'd all had in common was that there was some magic tradition in their religions, which helped them understand the Othersiders and how to fight them, and that they were all determined to work together to help each other and people who came there for safety.

"Why?" he asked. "What do they tell you?"

I told him part of the truth. "Mostly we read the stuff that the people who settled our parts left behind. Out where I'm from, those are kind of like manuals for what not to do. They don't go into the stuff that happened outside our mountains, or the *why*, or the parts about what other people did at Apex so much as the *what we did*, if you get my meaning."

I couldn't tell him the whole truth, of course, that the Monastery had probably the best records around of that time. The Monastery was a real anomaly; I don't think there is anything else like it, on this continent at least, but . . . there's a lot of continent, and even now, hundreds of years later, there are still holdouts and warlords and places where people hunkered down and survived that no one has run into yet.

"Well," he said, "the big thing that saved people around Apex was the military. Over on the East Coast, where Apex is now, there were a lot of military installations; they were the backbone of defense, and the place people went to looking for safety. When the first Hunters emerged, they naturally went there too. That's how Apex started; a lot of really smart tech and builder people, and the military, and the emergent Hunters, protecting everyone that came to them."

He didn't say anything about the Christers, other than what everybody knows, that some fanatics set off a nuke, but there didn't seem to be a lot of Christers in Apex from what I'd seen. The Christers of that time thought it was their Apocalypse, and the Masters say they were all confidently expecting to be carried up to Heaven while everyone that wasn't them died horribly, or suffered for hundreds of years. Only that didn't happen, even when some of them decided that the Apocalypse must need a kick-start like a balky engine, and set off some sort of nuke in what used to be Israel. They still didn't get carried up to Heaven, not one; they just died like everyone else, so that's why it's called the Diseray instead of the Apocalypse.

"So what do they say did it?" I asked. "The Diseray, I mean? And the Breakthrough."

"Probably the polar switch, maybe the nuke. Maybe both." He shook his head. "Maybe something we don't even know about."

That wasn't the way I'd been taught it happened. The Masters say that it didn't all happen at once, that things just got worse and worse until the bombs went off. And that, they think, is what caused the Breakthrough.

But even the Masters don't know that for certain-sure. The only thing they know for fact is that in the middle of disaster after disaster, the Othersiders came through, and with them came magic.

I sipped my drink. "Sometimes I think it was like the old story in one of the books I read when I was little, where this girl named

Pandora opened a box and everything horrible burst out of it and spread over the world."

He smiled at me. "So that would make the Hounds as Hope in the bottom of the box? That sounds about right." I smiled back, oddly glad that he knew the story too. Most of the Othersiders are monsters: Drakkens, Kraken, Leviathans, Gogs and Magogs, Furies, Harpies, things we don't even have names for. Things that belong to myths and religions from all over the world, and things that don't match anything at all. Even now, new monsters keep coming across. But when the first of them arrived, the Hounds came too. If it hadn't been for the Hounds, I don't think we'd be here anymore.

"If you could call anything Hope, it'd be the Hounds," I agreed, and then his station beeped at him and he had to go back to work.

I sighed and finished my cup of yummy goodness, and wished I could summon Bya back through again to cuddle up with. There wouldn't be room for him on the seat, though. This was a long trip; it took a lot of effort to keep trains protected, so they couldn't just whoosh across the landscape or they'd outrun the protections. I had another day and a night on the train, which was taking me from the middle of what used to be called the Rocky Mountains all the way to the East Coast, and then it would arrive in Apex City, which is the center of everything, and I would find out why Uncle had sent for me rather than one of our other Hunters. Another day and night to get used to being alone and lonely, to get used to being homesick.

It was an ache that wasn't going to get canceled out by a hundred cups of sweet stuff. I already missed everybody. And I was nervous and scared, and I'll admit it. But when Uncle contacted the Monastery, he'd said that if we went any longer without sending a Hunter to Apex for training and assignment, they'd send a team to look for one. And I understood. We didn't dare have a team snooping around the Mountain looking for Hunters, or we'd probably end up losing *all* the Hunters we had to Apex, and we couldn't afford that. I just wasn't sure why the Hunter Uncle asked for had to be me.

Now, right now, I bet you're thinking, *Well, if these Monastery people are all wrapped up in protecting and helping everyone, why aren't they in Apex in the first place? Or at least, why aren't they sending their Hunters there?* And I don't have a lot of answers, but the Masters seem to think that the government has gotten less trustworthy, and I've never known the Masters to be wrong. So we have been keeping our Hunters at home, because we can't count on the government to protect us.

The last time I'd seen my uncle in person was when he put me into the care of a yellow-robed monk at the Monastery. We must have gotten there by another train, although I don't remember it. I might have been hurt, or unconscious, or maybe sedated. The monks told me I was one of a huge group of kids that was evacuated ahead of an Othersider Incident. "Incident"—that's what they call it when monsters avalanche over your town and wipe out everything that gets in the way, like they tried to do to Anston's Well. One of the last out, they said; Uncle brought me and a handful of other kids who didn't have any family either. All the rest got adopted quick by families, but I got taken by the Masters. I know *why* now. They could tell I was going to have control of magic, and thought I might become a Hunter. They're good at being able to figure that out. I vaguely remember my mother and father from before that, but the Incident itself—nothing. The more I think about it, I was probably sedated. My bachelor uncle was probably not well equipped to cope with a hysterical toddler. But even though he left me there, it wasn't as if he abandoned me. I remember him from that night, and he wrote to me all the time, at least a letter a week, and presents every time he could think of an excuse, and I'd seen him in news stories over the years, getting grayer and balder. He's a very important man, prefect of the police, and the Hunters who aren't in the army are under his command.

The fact that he is so important is why I'm here in a train full of important people or their relatives instead of being hauled to Apex across the country in a military transport, like most new Hunters are.

As I sat there mulling over what I knew, it came to me that maybe the reason he'd sent for me was to show that his family was just like any other—that even when it was his own blood-kin that was the Hunter, then to Apex she had to come, whether she liked it or not.

Well, I didn't like it, not one bit, but . . . I could see the justice.

The warm drink had finally made me sleepy, and it wasn't private enough here for me to curl up and have a good cry about being sent away from everyone I knew. I pulled the cocoon up over and around me and lay down on the soft surface of the seat. But I didn't snug the cocoon tight. The steward might just have been a timid fellow—or he might have had a reason for asking if the Hounds and I would protect him.

I was a Hunter, and a Hunter who wants to grow old always expects the worst. So I had my seat belt on, under the cocoon, and I left my boots on too, and I didn't snug the cocoon down.

I wished I were in my little room, with the heavy stone and wood walls of the Monastery around me, and the snow between me and Othersiders. I missed my bed, even if it was a bit harder than this couch, and even if this cocoon was cozier. I missed the sounds of the Monastery—the monks and the Masters often had religious things they got up in the middle of the night to do, which all became part of the rhythm of day and night, and when you were used to them all of your life, they were like a lullaby. I really missed the smells—incense and snow and breakfast slow-cooking overnight. I missed the warm wool blankets that smelled faintly of sheep, and the faraway sound of wind whistling through the evergreens.

Most of all, I missed knowing there were other Hunters around me, knowing that I wasn't alone, and that if trouble came, there would be a bunch of us to meet it. All that missing things made it hard to fall asleep. And when at last I slept, I slept lightly.

COME MORNING, the important people around me continued to sleep, kept in cozy blackness by their privacy hoods. I came awake and alert all at once; unless a Hunter is sick or drugged, that's what we do. It's training so hard and so deep it's almost instinct. The windows had been transparented, so I finally got my look at what was outside the cage.

Flat, open fields. Flat by my standards, anyway. I know I keep talking about "the" Mountain, but that's just the mountain that the Monastery is on. I'm used to mountains that tower all around, mountains that are at least half snow all year round, mountains that take up most of the sky. So, flat . . . that was new. And kind of cool. I had never seen that much sky before. I knew where we were immediately, 'cause I'd studied the map of the train route and how things used to look there before the Diseray. We were into land that used to hold enormous grain fields and vast herds of cattle. The grain was still there, blowing in the wind, though it was mixed with all kinds of things now: weeds, native grasses, other things like wildflowers and the odd vegetable, something hard to kill and less than tasty to a cow. You could tell because it wasn't uniform like in the old pictures, where it was almost like an ocean of grain all the same color. It was all patchy out there now, patchy in color and patchy in height. I got kind of an excited feeling in my stomach; I'd only ever seen land this flat in pictures and really old vids, and seeing it in person was nothing like looking at pictures. For the first time ever I could see a flat horizon.

The cattle were still out there too, but they were feral now, never saw humans except when they were hunted the way the buffalo that had roamed here had been hunted, and looked nothing like the fat, box-shaped walking meat-sacks that used to drift around these green fields I'd seen in those history books. These were cattle like you could find sometimes down in the valleys below the Mountain: crazy-eyed, wary, and rangy as a goat, and as the train sped by, they ran away from it, fleet and agile, then whirled to stare at it suspiciously as if to make sure it wasn't going to escape its cage. There are a few of them at the Mountain that some of the folks in the settlements have caught and tamed down, but it's so hard to keep them fed properly and from running away that most people don't bother. Goats and sheep are easier to keep, and they do better if the herd has to be driven up into the snow to protect them from a monster raid.

There were things that weren't birds circling overhead. Harpies. I could tell by the shape. Huge, blunt wings, though they still shouldn't be able to fly, Master Kedo says. He says it's probably magic keeping them up. I've driven them off hundreds of times, and we've killed a few too; they're like huge vultures, but with four legs instead of two, and something that might look like a human head in bad light. The head is bald for the same reason a vulture's head is bald; they stick it right down inside the body cavity of whatever they're eating, if the thing is big enough. They have a short, blunt muzzle, and a mouth full of pointed, tearing teeth.

They were probably waiting for one of the cattle to do something stupid and get itself killed. Harpies didn't hunt; they were scavengers, like vultures, and cowards at that. Nothing to worry about unless a flock of them decided to take you on, or you were toddler size. One of the things I was really proud of was that nobody had lost a kid to Harpies since I'd become a Hunter.

But in the far distance there was smoke, a lot of it, and it had that tinge of black that told me it was coming from burning buildings. I squinted; there was some movement at the base of the smoke, and if I could see movement at this distance, it had to be something big. Drakken maybe, or Gogs and Magogs. So—I'd heard about this before I'd left. Out there was what was left of Springdale. Springdale was lucky; everyone had gotten out before the Drakken charged in and set everything ablaze. No point in going back, either; the Drakken had taken it for their nesting grounds, and you might as well think about going to the moon as think about taking back your town when Drakken moved in. And the Hunter Elite weren't going to show up and take the town back, either. Not even an Elite team could handle a flock of Drakken when they decided to settle. Since the Springdalers had gotten outside the danger zone on their own, it had been up to the army to evacuate them to a new settlement. No wonder the steward was nervous last night. One Drakken couldn't take on a train, but a whole flock could. Drakken hadn't wanted Anston's Well. There hadn't been any of them at *that* attack. I don't know what we would have done if it had been Drakken that night. Just give up, probably, let them have the town for nesting season, and only take it back when the snow drove them off again.

I'd never Hunted Drakken; I'd never, ever heard of a *single* Hunter who had. The Masters said there had been Drakken killed by groups of four or more Hunters working together, and Elite teams could do it, but it couldn't have been recently, or for sure it would have been on the official vid-broadcasts we were supposed to try to watch. Between the fire they breathed and how fast and big they were, I couldn't imagine any way to kill one down here on the flat plain. You'd need a way to pin it, and then a way to escape being turned into scorched meat yourself.

In between the cattle at the side of the tracks and the burning town, there didn't seem to be anything. I knew better than to trust that. It was just when the landscape seemed empty that it was inclined to sprout things that wanted desperately to kill you.

Now, some of this was pure, mindless, "humans are the tastiest things there are" sort of wanting to kill you. And we are the best "eating" there is for Othersiders; the younger we are, the tastier we are. If you haven't studied magic, and most people haven't, you wouldn't know why. It's because of the manna, which is raw, magical energy. Everything makes it, but humans make more of it than animals, plus we're born with a huge honking reservoir of the stuff, so young humans are extremely tasty indeed. The manna is one reason why the Hounds work with me; together we can take out very manna-rich targets, and they get to eat it all, since I don't need it.

But the most dangerous of the things, and the rarest for humans to see, are the brainy ones. The Folk. They kill humans for reasons of their own, and we don't know what those are, because they don't speak to us, except on very rare occasions, and then it's usually a challenge or very cryptic. They live on—they *own*—the Island of California, among other places. Most people never see them. Of those that have, almost all are Hunters, and they lived to tell about it because they killed the Folk before the Folk killed them. Are the Folk in control of the other creatures? Sometimes. Were they the ones that caused the Breakthrough, or did they just take advantage of it? No one knows.

Cits never hear about the Folk because the government really does not want people to know about them. That's what my Masters told me, anyway, when I was picked to be sent to Apex. They warned me to be careful about talking about them out in the rest of the world; they told me before I left that unless and until someone important actually said something about the Folk, I was to pretend they didn't exist. Us on the Mountain know, all of us, because of the Masters, who don't believe in holding back information. Master Kedo told me that he reckons that the military and the government that's based in Apex would rather regular Cits didn't know there were creatures out there that were that smart and in control of things.

As I looked out that window, I got one of those *feelings*, a goose-bump moment combined with a certainty. It's not being a Psimon, because I'm not. My Master, Kedo, says he thinks it's that I'm sensitive to the magical presence of things, and sometimes I can tell what they are, if they're powerful enough.

Anyway, that was how I knew that there was one of the Folk

out there. Maybe more than one, I couldn't tell this far away. Springdale had fallen because *they* wanted it to. And I was very glad we were speeding past it. We were going fast enough that they probably wouldn't notice us. Incidents are horrible enough without having the Folk involved. But that explained why the Cits of Springdale had managed to escape. The Folk *let* them, holding back the monsters until everyone was out. Why? Heck if I know. The Folk do things all the time that make no, or little, sense. And maybe that was another reason why the government didn't want ordinary Cits to know about them. It's hard enough knowing there are monsters outside your protections that you can at least predict. But smart monsters that are completely unpredictable? That's enough to put people into a panic.

I quickly directed my thoughts to concentrate on my token, One White Stone. This is my Core, the object I have learned to think about exclusively when I am worried that something might pick up my thoughts. This is a trick the Masters taught me, and so far as I know, I am the only Hunter who does this, though most of the Masters of all sorts do. Before the Breakthrough, I think the Masters must all have been Magicians along with being religious personages, even if they didn't call themselves that, because how they teach us to use magic is from books or traditions hundreds and hundreds of years old. My Master, my special mentor, for instance—his name is Kedo Patli, and his magic is all from what used to be Mexico. There's Dineh Masters, who've taught the Way of the Monster Slayer to two of our people, and Ivor Thorson, who knows all about Norse things and taught Rennie Clay, and Lady Rhiannon and her group, who do Celtic magic and taught old Mary, Hudson, Big Tom, and Little Tom, and—well, like I said, it's a big mix. Even the carvings and paintings, the weavings and embroideries that are all over the Monastery are a mix of all sorts of art styles.

The Hounds know that when my thoughts are full of One White Stone, there is danger around me. They would know, on the Otherside, that something was up and be ready for a summons.

It's just not wise to talk or think about the Folk. Some people believe it can summon them right from the Otherside. I don't know about that, but I do know that thinking about them certainly gets their attention.

The smoke dropped behind us, and I relaxed a very little bit. Enough that when the steward brought me breakfast, I was able to enjoy it. Some of the Masters are vaygen: they only eat plant-stuff, and animal-stuff that doesn't involve killing, like butter and eggs, but most of our people up on the Mountain are omnivores, so the smoked bacon and eggs weren't new to me. Except that I suspected this bacon at least was clone pig—vat-grown meat a couple of cell generations down from the sample that had been taken from a living hog. It had a kind of uniform taste and texture I wasn't used to, and I missed the "wild" taste and leanness of bacon that comes from a pig that's raised outside of a confining pen. But there was some orange-colored juice that was really nice and more of that Chocolike. We have coffee—it grows on mountains, and people managed to get it to grow on ours—and I like coffee a lot, but I could get used to this other stuff pretty quickly. There was toast made from bread of a sort I wasn't used to. Ours isn't wheat bread, it's half lupine flour and half other stuff, depending on what got ground into flour lately; it's dark and dense. This was hardly like bread at all. It was all right, especially with butter, kind of delicate.

Like cake that wasn't sweet. Our jelly is a lot better than Cit jelly, though, so I skipped that. Cit jelly is insubstantial, sweet without having an actual flavor.

I think of "us" and "Cits" as being different, which we all do where I come from. Up on the Mountain, even though we're *technically* Cits, we never use that name for ourselves except with outsiders. Cit means "citizen," which everyone is except outlaws or preps or vivalists or militia, or anyone in the army. Back in the early days, when it was the Armed Services that were protecting everyone they could gather up over in the East, that was how they divided folks up. You were either a soldier, or a Hunter, or a Cit. When Apex got built, they kept those divisions, 'cause it was easier. But we use "Cit" to mean "person who lives in a city."

Except when we're talking to Cits. You never want to go out of your way to make people think you think differently from them. No one wants to give the army a reason to come snooping around the Mountain. We don't want to lose our Hunters, and we don't want people who haven't the right to know about it find out about the Monastery. My uncle knows, but he's different. He was fifteen years older than my father, and he was raised in Safehaven. The monks told me that when he was fourteen, his parents took the family to Apex because they wanted him to get more education than you can get on the Mountain. Apex was where my father, his baby brother, was born.

My breakfast was long gone by the time most of the others started waking and queuing up for the 'fresher. I'd used it as soon as I'd gotten up; it was . . . okay. It was very, very strange, to strip down to your skin, hang your clothes in a glass box, step into another glass box, and get you and your clothes vibrated all clean.

It just doesn't *feel* really clean, even if your hair is all silky and your skin tingly when you get out. I'd sniffed my clothes over, but they smelled . . . not at all. And even one much-faded old stain on the bottom of my pants had gotten vibrated away, but it still didn't seem right.

When Uncle wrote us to ask for me to be sent to Apex, the Masters had taught me all about how to use 'freshers and other tech so I wouldn't find myself at a disadvantage, but on the whole, I like a real bath or shower better.

I didn't stare at the others as they lined up, but that didn't stop them from staring at me.

I was wearing the same clothing I wear for Hunting at home, because I don't have much else. I know I had to look odd to them. They were all done up in what I guess must have been the latest fashions, a lot of light, shiny or soft matte fabric, and the women were in colors we don't see very much, because we can't dye things those shades with the dye we make ourselves. It was pretty, and I guess it was all right for being in buildings all the time, but it was stuff that wouldn't last half an hour in the woods. And the women were all in shoes with heels that must have caused a million back-aches. I was in sober dark brown linen, a hooded wrap-coat and pants tucked into real leather boots with sensible flat soles (elk hide, if you want to know), and a knit wool tunic the color of oatmeal. I heard whispers but politely ignored them. Besides, I had my exercises to go through.

You don't become a Hunter without knowing magic. The Masters told me that a lot of Hunters off the Mountain don't go much beyond the summoning, though, and they couldn't see the point of that. So like all the Hunters the Masters train, I knew a lot of magic, and magic is a slippery thing; it doesn't like to be controlled, so you have to practice all the time or you lose it. The spells and Glyphs just slip out of your mind and are gone if you don't keep it up. Like I said, the Masters were Magicians before magic was so easy to come by in the world. You should see their books; beautiful things, drawings and designs in colored inks and paints on every page. Some are one long piece of paper—scrolls. Some are paper folded back and forth and held between two covers tied together, and some are real books. Everybody with even a tiny little bit of magic gets taught at the Monastery; there aren't many who have as much as me, but it seems like everyone has a little bit. Master Kedo says that's normal, but most people are too lazy to learn how to use it or keep it in their heads. On the Mountain, though, we use everything. When we butcher a pig, every bit of him becomes something. And when we have magic, we keep it sharp, even if all it's good for is to throw your voice to the other side of the valley or light the fire. So every morning, right after breakfast, I ran my exercises.

You're probably wondering what that feels like. It's like pulling a bow without an arrow in it. All this tension, this pent-up power builds up in you, and you take it as far as you can, but instead of releasing it all at once, the way you would if you were shooting an arrow, you relax back down again and let the magic flow back into you. A little like doing kata, the moves of martial arts without the strength behind them that turns them into attacks. If I were home, I'd go through spells properly, with gestures, fully visualizing the lesser Glyphs, then sketching them in the air. But that's not the sort of thing you can do in a place surrounded by people who don't know you, so I just ran through them all in my head, visualizing them.

It's all fighting magic, of course, except for things like lighting a fire, drying wet clothes, some kitchen magic. Blows and counters, tricks and traps, and, most of all, shields and defenses. It takes concentration, and the Masters used to bang drums and set the kids to playing around me and do anything they could to break that concentration, so the stares and whispers didn't really bother me at all.

The *screams*, however—

I snapped out of my little world, and I was on my feet with my knife in my hands instantly, drawn out of the sheath in my boot, since it was the only real weapon I had on me. No need to look farther than the windows for the reason for the screaming; I was looking right into the glittering gold eyes and arm-long ivory fangs of a Drakken. It was just a flash—the train was moving *fast*—mostly an impression of huge teeth and angry eyes and dark green scales streaming by the window. But every Hunter knows what a Drakken looks like.

I wanted to scream, but I held it in. Hunters don't scream. Not when we're startled, not when we're terrified, not when we're hurt. Not when we're dying. Though in our case, the dying usually happens too fast to scream. Screaming only brings more trouble, and if you feel the urge to scream, you probably already have too much trouble to begin with.

The steward opaqued the window a second after I opened my eyes, but I'd taken it all in, like a camera, and now I *remembered* past that initial flash of impression and I knew we were in very deep trouble. There wasn't just one Drakken out there; it was an entire flock. They had been raving at the cage, trying to cling to it and being flung off by the electrical charge. They *couldn't* have seen the train from where they were at the ruins of Springdale, we hadn't blown the whistle (which would have attracted them), and in any case, this was nesting season and they'd taken that town for a nest. They wouldn't leave a nesting site on their own. So there was only one reason why a flock of Drakken would be attacking the cage around the train.

They'd been led here by one or more of the Folk. Had to be.

I wasn't even consciously aware that I was up and running until I hit the door to the car. It opened just a hair before I reached it, and I saw that every single door all the way to the armed car at the front was open. The steward must have been quick-witted enough to have registered what I was doing, and slapped the controls to open them all. I went into a full-out run down the length of the moving train. It might not have been my best sprinting time, but it was right up there.

The door to the armed car was closed and locked, of course, but I'm a registered Hunter. I was registered from the moment my uncle sent for me, and my palm on the door-plate opened it to me. I was confronted by another sealed hatch and a metal ladder welded to the inner hull. The engineer would be below in his sealed pod; I wanted the top deck, where the gunners and their commander were. I really don't remember going up the ladder.

The three gunners reacted predictably to my sudden appearance, whipping around in time to see me presenting both hands, backs to them, with the round Hunter Mandalas with their intricate designs tattooed there. The Mandalas identify us *instantly*; nobody in his right mind would dare try to counterfeit them, because he'd either be found out quickly or he'd be sent out to Hunt and . . . well . . . that would solve that. "Joyeaux Charmand," I said. "Registered Hunter. And yes. Niece. What's the situation?"

Part of the situation was obvious; the monitors at every gun station linked to cameras on the exterior of the car were not blanked. The Drakken were keeping pace with the train, throwing themselves over and over at the electrified cage. Drakken don't fly, but they can leap enormous distances, and their size utterly defies the square-cube law. But then, most things from the Otherside defy the laws of physics. If you've never seen a Drakken, well, see if you can find the Tenniel illustrations of the Jabberwock from *Through the Looking-Glass*. Like that. Only about 150 feet long. Like some deep-water horror of a head married to a snaky body with a row of spikes down the back and a whiplike tail, perched on thin birdy legs with wicked-long talons at the end of them. They're usually various shades of brown and green. Their eyes are gold and the size of bushel baskets, and they have fangs as long as my arm and as sharp as knives. I wasn't, at the moment, concerned with them. They were the distraction.

It isn't practical to keep the cage electrified for more than five miles in front of and behind a train. Most beasties don't bother to try to break through the cage when a train isn't there; why should they? They can see for themselves there's nothing in there, until there is, and by the time they see the train, it's generally sped past so fast they haven't a hope of catching it. And they aren't bright enough to realize that if they could get inside the cage well ahead of the train, they'd have it.

Ah, but when the Folk get involved . . .

And I knew it, I knew it when I saw this, that one or more of the Folk was behind this. Drakken just don't act like this on their own.

*One White Stone. One White Stone. One White Stone.*

"*Psi-shields!*" I snapped at the soldiers, because they probably hadn't yet figured out that one of the Folk was out there. The Folk aren't like us humans; we can have magic, or we can have Psi, but we can't have both. They can. Psi-shields are tech, and I don't know how they work, I only know they block thoughts. They're only on the armed car, and they aren't nearly as effective as something a real Psimon can put up, but they're better than nothing. It would be nice to have a Psimon on every train, but . . . they're more rare than Magicians, and the army gets first call on them. Psi-shields would do, and I didn't need these lads pulling their sidearms on me in here because the Folk took them over. The armored car has plating of Cold Iron so the Folk magic couldn't get inside, but that meant my shielding magic wouldn't work right in here, and the Masters hadn't taught me how to dodge bullets yet.

"But there's—" began the one with the most stripes.

"Don't argue with her, you moron. *Do it*," snapped one of the other two, then, without waiting for orders, reached out a long arm and snapped a series of switches over the ranker's head.

"Full zoom ahead," I said, and the same fellow scrolled a wheel that zoomed out the view on the front monitor more than a mile, two, five, out to where the electrification on the cage ended, out to where—

—part of the cage was missing!—

—and someone was standing there, sparkling like a queen's tiara in the sunlight, with another shimmer all around him and a Drakken waiting like a dog beside him.

The ranker knew what to do about that. He slapped a signal that told the engineer below to hit the emergency brake, because if we hit that shimmer at speed we'd flatten like a tortilla on it, and there wasn't a damn thing the Cold Iron shielding could do about it. And he hit something else at the same time as I was grabbing a stanchion to keep from going arse-over-teakettle, and six Hellfire missiles streaked away from the front of the train. They all hit at once, in a burst of flame over the track that made the front-facing monitor white out for a moment. But when the monitor cleared again, he was still there, standing casually behind his Wall, although the Drakken had fled.

Trains take a long time to stop. Two miles for us, plus the amount we'd traveled when we'd spotted him. Cheeky bastard could see we were stopping, and lifted up and began levitating toward us, floating along with his arms crossed casually over his chest.

Oh, this was so not good.

*One White Stone. One White Stone.* I kept my concentration on my Core. Maybe this Folk Mage couldn't get past the Psi-shields . . . but maybe he could. If he could, it would only be enough to read thoughts, but the most important thoughts in this car right now were mine, and I didn't want him snooping. A cautious Hunter stays a living Hunter.

He couldn't get the Drakken to come in the cage with him, though, so we had that much going for us. We'd only have to face him and whatever else he could summon.

We came to a full stop. He was still a mile away. I made a lightning decision.

"I'm going out," I announced. "Can you creep the train behind me at a walk?"

"Are you—" the ranker began, then snapped his mouth shut. "Yes, Hunter, we can do that."

"I need to get out to summon, and I don't want to do that when

I'm trading eyeball-glare with him," I explained. Wordlessly, the smart one handed me a headset. It was . . . well, ridiculously tiny compared to the ones we have on the Mountain, but I knew what it was. I stuck the ear-carrot in the right place and adjusted the threadlike mic boom.

"If you see a chance for firepower, give us a sign," he said.

I thought about it. The Hounds could and would protect me from nastiness like blowback and shrapnel. "The sign will be 'Zapotec,'" I said. He gave me a weird look, but nodded. I wasn't surprised. Most Hunters have never heard of the Zapotec, and I'd be shocked if a Cit ever had, but one of their old men is the most important one of my Masters, my special mentor, Kedo, the very first one who helped me learn my magic. His people were the Zapotec, and he'd turned up at Safehaven right after I did. My Hounds were Zapotec too, and I don't think that his turning up was an accident.

With a whoosh of hydraulics, a hatch above me opened and a ladder dropped down. I climbed it to find myself at the top of the engine, which was hissing and popping and making heat sounds. It took a moment to find the ladder that took me to the ground, but as soon as my feet were on earth, I used the field summons.

The regular summons takes too long in an emergency, and I was horribly, horribly vulnerable every nanosecond I was out here without my Hounds. So, I used the field summons—which, ironically enough, is both instinct for a Hunter, and the first summons you ever do. I held my hands over my eyes, shouted the words that were the vocal equivalent of the Glyphs, and felt the Mandalas on the backs of my hands light up. I mean that literally, it felt as if they were etched in red-hot wire.

There's always a price for everything a Hunter does; the price for fast is pain.

I felt the Portal open up in front of me, the door to Otherside in the air that is fast and dirty, and unlike the Glyphs, can't be held for long, and heard the scream of defiance as my Hounds, who already knew how bad things were, rushed up and out and to my side.

And now they had their true forms.

The smallest, Bya, was the size of a horse. The largest was the size of the shed you'd keep the horse in. And they looked like something out of a peyote dream, things people had once thought were only the hallucinations of an artist in a high fever. Uh, no. They were real enough that when that artist, a man named Pedro Linares, caught a fever and saw into the Otherside, *they* were what he saw.

Take just about any animal. Now add spines, wings, horns, whatever you like. Now paint it in eye-watering psychedelic colors and crazy patterns. Now make it horse-size or bigger, give it a *lot* of manna and the ability to use it, and add the physical offensive weapons: the stingers, the claws and poison fangs, and fire-breath. That's an *Alebrije*, the Zapotec version of a Hound. And they like us, they like humans, and near as I can tell, they hate the Folk. Which is a damn good thing or Pedro would never have come out of his fever dream. Heck, the *Alebrijes* might even have been the ones that cured him.

I'm the only Hunter I know with *Alebrijes* as Hounds. Most of them have things that look like dogs, some get slightly more exotic, but only Master Kedo—and maybe the Zapotec Hunters, if there are any—and I have *Alebrijes*. Somehow, Master Kedo had known I would, and had drifted up to the Mountain just in time to teach me—although now he says he's never leaving, he likes it there. Master Kedo is . . . not exactly like a father, and not exactly like a brother to me. Maybe like a grandfather? I don't know how old he is; like most Masters once they get past about fifty, he looks aged and ageless at the same time. When it comes to magic, he is all business. Outside of magic he's funny, and warm, and he made sure every minute of every day that I knew he cared about *me* as much as he cared about the Hunter I was becoming. All the Masters care about their students, but I think Master Kedo and I have something special.

Having Hounds like no one else was another damn good thing, because there was a chance that the Folk Mage ahead of us might not recognize them or know how to fight them.

Bya, as usual, glued himself to my side as we walked out to meet the Mage, the huge engine barely crawling along behind us. The rest ranged to either side of me, carefully not touching the cage.

Outside, I looked calm, cool, indifferent.

Inside, I was a screaming mess. I'd never faced one of the Greater Folk alone before, and when I had seen one, and only one at anything but a distance, it had been one that a Master—not Master Kedo, but Master Shinji—had faced down before, and Master Shinji was with me at the time. Scared? I was glad I was dry and empty, let's just say that. And my mouth was parched, and my stomach a cold, hard knot, and my heart going like a fancy-dance drum.

Because not only was I going up against one of the Folk, I was going up against a Mage. The ones I'd seen in the distance, and the singleton I'd run up against were all feral; hair down past their knees, but all dreadlocks, braids, and straggles, with feathers and carved stones and bits of bone braided in, dressed in skins with the hair still on, decorated with beads and trinkets and whatever other odd bits take their fancy. They hadn't been Mages; all their control of magic was at the level of instinct. Babies in their control, when compared to the Mages. But even so, on the Mountain, to keep from triggering some sort of blood feud, the policy of the Masters was to drive them away rather than kill them. Off the Mountain, it was general wisdom to kill any Folk you saw before they saw you. Either way, you just do not take chances with the Folk.

This one was nothing like that. This one was something far more dangerous. This one was *civilized*, highly trained, and even more unpredictable.

But my hands were steady, my vision clear, and so was my mind. So. It was time.

*One White Stone. One White Stone. One White Stone . . .*

# 3

SOON ENOUGH I WAS trading eyeball-glare with the Mage, him hovering in midair with his arms crossed, me on the ground surrounded by the Hounds. The Folk . . . well, we don't know what they *really* look like. The one thing they can do better than any human is illusion, so the truth is we don't know if what we see are their true forms, if they're shifters and can change form and shape for really and truly, or if it's all illusion. But I can at least tell you what they let us see. There's some differences among them—hair, skin, eye color, and definitely costume—but they all share certain things.

For starters, they are *beautiful*. Even the wildest, most feral of them is gorgeous enough to make you gasp if you aren't ready for it. They all have pointed ears about as long as your forearm, and eyebrows like antennae, and thin, sort of pointy faces. They're tall, usually seven or eight feet, with thin bodies to go with the faces.

Since he was floating there, his long, long silvery-lavender hair, perfectly groomed and smooth as ice, ended a couple of feet past the soles of his shoes. His hair was done in some sort of elaborate style with strings of sparkly beads behind his right ear. He had a silver headband stretched across his forehead, with a lavender stone in it that matched his lavender eyes. I couldn't even begin to describe his costume. It was all of some soft, shiny silvery-lavender stuff, with floaty sleeves, and lots of layers, and every visible bit of it was covered in silver embroidery and more sparkly beads. The sphere-shaped Wall around him glimmered like the surface of a soap bubble, all transparent and faintly iridescent, like oil on water, but I had just seen that six Hellfire missiles wouldn't dent it, so I wasn't fooled by how fragile it looked. Besides, Walls and Shields always look like glass bubbles that are only *barely* there. Looks are always deceptive in magic.

He and I stood there staring at each other for a while. My Aki-Do Master taught me that the one who makes the first move sacrifices his advantage by putting his energy out there, so I had learned patience. Behind me, the train thrummed quietly; I knew the soldiers in there keeping the cam on us also had the long-range pickups going on the external mic. I wondered what they were making of the long silence. Finally the Mage spoke, and his voice was just as beautiful as his face. A low tenor, with lots of over- and undertones to it. He had a voice that sounded like the lower registers of a harp.

"I see you, Hunter."

There it was, the traditional opening of a battle. But not a duel. Good, that meant I could cheat, and I intended to.

"I see you, Magician," I replied.

"What have you to do with the sheep behind you?" he asked in a conversational tone.

"I am the shepherd of these sheep," I responded, taking responsibility for the train and everyone on it.

"Then the shepherd can spare a lamb ... or two. Or more."

Now *that* surprised me. I hadn't expected him to try to bargain. I concentrated on my One White Stone, however, and kept my face as smooth as the stone itself. "Not an option," I said flatly. "You must look elsewhere, Magician." There were people who would sell their fellows to the Folk. Where I came from, you earned a rope necklace doing that, but there were scum and lowlifes who would do that and not think twice about it. There are always people who aren't human, who think the only thing in the world that matters is themselves. The kind of people who caused the Diseray in the first place, and no, I didn't need the Masters to tell me that, that's just plain sense. If you don't look after your fellow man, if you think that what you want is always more important than what anyone else wants or needs, you're not human, and that's that. There is no virtue in selfishness, not one bit.

Slowly he tilted his head to the side. I was *not* wearing a Wall or a Shield.

Now ... let me put you straight here. Remember how I said that magic costs. So where I was taught, I learned to do the most with the least, which is kind of how everyone on the Mountain lives. Do the most with the least, everyone has enough, and there's something to spare in an emergency. So, yeah, I could have put up a Wall to match his, but why? The Hounds could do it too, and they were faster than me; if Bya felt something coming, he'd snap up his Wall to deflect what was coming before it hit us. *Then* I could invoke my better, stronger one, and meanwhile I wouldn't be bleeding manna. And *he* wouldn't be reading my strength from my Wall.

So he was puzzled, because I wasn't doing this the way the Folk would, and maybe the way any other Hunter he'd met had, and he was studying me, trying to decide if I was just stupid or if I was a lot stronger than he could guess.

And while he was studying me . . . let's just say I wasn't being idle. Most with the least, right? I had a little tiny bit of magic going, slowly grinding through his Wall, so subtle, so inconspicuous, it was happening right under his nose and he wasn't even copping it.

"You have no Shield, no armor," he said conversationally, "and yet your mind is smooth."

*One White Stone. One White Stone.*

"So they say." I shrugged. "Of a courtesy please unencumber the way, Magician. I would take my sheep to their pasture."

*There, I asked you nicely. Go away.*

"You could," he replied thoughtfully, tilting his head to the other side, "take them to mine."

*Say . . . what?* Had he just—

"We have shepherds tending our flocks," he continued, confirming what I thought I had heard. "You could be one, take seisin of me, take *me* as your lord, and forsake the lords of the city. You would find a more pleasant life, I do assure you. Your sheep would be tended. You could tend them yourself, if you wish. They will even prefer their new life."

Okay. *This* was new. I stalled for time. A little more and my magic would have scoured my part of his Wall very thin indeed.

"The Folk have no love for my kind," I retorted. "Why would you offer such a thing?"

He laughed. It sounded like bells. "You interest me, Hunter. You are not a sheep. You are more clever and patient than a wolf. You are braver than the lion. You are a new thing. You might prove to be a weapon in my hand. Or . . . something else." He leaned down, his eyes glittering at me. "You are partly incorrect. Not all of my kind consider yours to be the enemy. And my kind do not find yours . . . uncomely." He straightened. "Properly groomed and garbed of course," he added, with the arrogance that was natural to someone who was sure of his own superiority. "And your Hounds, they interest me too."

Bya's back vibrated under my hand as he growled.

"They are new to me as well," he continued. "What are they?"

His Wall, at the point where he faced me, was thinner than paper, and he had just handed me what I wanted on a platter.

"Oh," I said. *"Zapotec."*

And I flung myself to the ground and the Hounds flung themselves on top of me as I flung up a Wall of my own around us.

And a hell of ordinance blasted into his Wall at point-blank range.

I didn't see it, of course. I was buried under the Hounds and under all of our Walls. But I certainly heard it, and I felt the concussive force and some of the heat, and I made myself as small as possible and thought of my One White Stone, kept up the process that was the Wall, and felt energy pouring out of me like blood out of an open wound until I was dizzy.

The Hounds were fine, given that they had their Walls and mine too, and reverted to their doggy forms when we walked back to the first of the passenger cars and got back on the train the easy way. I—well, I was shaken, I was starving, I was exhausted, what I wanted was to lie down and not think, but I knew that I needed to debrief with the military types. If this had been the Mountain, I would have to report first to the Masters while everything was fresh in my mind, and the military men on this train were the equivalent. But the Masters warned me that pretty much everything out in the Cits' world had a zillion spy-eyes on it, so I was pretty sure that every bit of the encounter had been broadcast up the line to Apex and the authorities. After all, if we succeeded, there'd be a record of something important—an encounter with a Folk Mage—to learn from. And if we'd failed, well, they'd have a record of what not to do.

The Cits in the cars would want to know what was going on, and most of them were of a high enough status to demand and get information, even if they didn't get all of it. They knew about the Drakken. They knew about me running like the wind to the armed car. They knew about the train coming to a stop. And they'd have seen the glare of the Hellfires ahead—twice—and now they would presumably have at least been told that there'd been a confrontation with Othersiders and we'd (obviously) won.

I was right about that, and the stewards were having to hold people back from the door of the first car. It wasn't like a riot or anything, but there was a lot of excitement there, and they were crowding up the aisle. I figured the Cits needed to make a fuss over *something* to occupy them for a while, so I left the Hounds to be fussed over and went back into the armed car.

Now ... I wasn't nearly as cool as I looked, way down deep inside, but for now, I would be all right. Once I'm in Hunter mode, I'm kind of in a Zen state where nothing much bothers me. I figured I couldn't afford to let Hunter mode slip right now. I was going to pay for that later by having a proper little meltdown in private, but that would be then, and this was now, and right now I needed to make people think I had known exactly what to do all along. That's part of a Hunter's job.

I wasn't sure what I'd find up on the gun deck, but I was actually kind of pleased to find it full of sober faces rather than whooping and hollering as the train shuddered into motion and began to pick up speed again.

"Did we—" the officer began.

I shook my head. "No telling. Can you show me the playback on crawl-time? I was busy kissing dirt at the time you made the big bada-boom."

The playback showed me pretty much what I expected on slo mo. The Folk Mage had just enough time to realize what was going on and *poof* out before the barrage got through his Wall. I wouldn't be able to play that trick on him again, and possibly not on any other of the Folk, but then, I'd expected it was a one-off. Heckfire, the whole encounter was a sort of one-off; I'd never heard of one of the Folk talking to a Hunter sensibly. Nor of any of the Folk offering—what had he offered? A job? An alliance? To be his pet?

Then again, if any Hunter had taken up such an offer, no one among us humans would ever hear about it, would we? He'd just vanish, presumed dead.

I dragged my thoughts back to here and now. "There—" I said, pointing to the telltale flash of light *inside* the Wall that wasn't quite obscured by the stuff blowing the Wall to bits.

The officer said something rude, then sighed. "He *bamphed*."

I nodded. "Yes. But getting him dead wasn't the point, or our job. The point was to get him gone, and our job is to get these people safe inside the city."

Well, they didn't like it. That didn't surprise me. My Masters had explained to me in detail the difference between the way a soldier thought, the way a Cit thought, and contrasted both with the way a Hunter thought. Our people, of course, were not like Cits or soldiers, more like Hunters in their outlook. Cits—the city folk sort of Cits—they want victories. They want to win, or cheer the winner. Soldiers want things to end neatly, they want victories too, and win or lose, they want things *ended*. But up on the Mountain, we're much more pragmatic. We know what seems to be an ending rarely is, that victories don't last forever, and you take what you can get and make the most of it for as long as you can. I had to have all that, the way Cits think, the way soldiers think, taught to me. It wasn't natural for someone raised in the Monastery to think that way.

Short form: for these soldiers, anything that wasn't a victory was a defeat unless someone managed to spin it as a victory. Which, the officer would do as soon as I left, because that was *his* job.

"My guess is they won't bother *this* train, and maybe will think twice and three times before they tackle *any* train for a while," I said, to give him something to work on. Then I smiled on the surface, because I really needed to go be truly by myself, or with Bya, for a bit. "You men were ace. All I was good for was to be the bait and the distraction, and the mouse that ate into his Wall. No way

I could have taken him; best I could do was make a hole for you to shoot through."

Which of course wasn't true, but it fed more into their mind-share. They looked a lot more cheerful. I could almost see the thoughts spinning up behind the officer's eyes.

Then I left.

The first car was all private compartments, 'cause if the train had to drop cars and put on emergency speed, guess who'd get saved? The friendly ginger-haired steward surprised me by waiting at the door of the car. "There's a lot of people that want to thank you," he began, then gave me this odd little smile. "But I wondered if you wanted to let them just yet. . . . You look like you could use a short break."

I didn't break down in front of him, but . . . wow. He must've been a borderline Psimon. "Actually . . . I . . ." I began, and before I could say anything more, he'd whipped open the door of the first compartment and kind of gently shoved me in. It was small, but there was a tiny 'fresher in there, a little bitty sink with water taps in the wall, and a bed, a real bed, turned down and waiting. And some snacks and drinks.

"Push that button when you're ready to come out and mingle," he said. "I'll come get you." Then he shut the door and I was finally alone.

Not for long, though. Bya ghosted in through the closed door (yes, they can do that when they are on this side) and was all over me. And that was when I cried, and shook, and cried some more. All of the ways that could have gone bad went through my mind in vivid detail. I could have died, and everyone in the train could have died, or the Mage could have made me his prisoner and made me watch while everyone died, or he could have used me to get at my Masters and the Mountain or . . . lots of things. Lots of things, and not a one of them was any kind of happy ending.

It took me a while to calm down, let's just say.

Then I washed my face, put a cold cloth on my eyes until they stopped looking so red and you could tell they were hazel instead of scarlet, ate something that looked like a tiny artwork made of food, drank a lot of water, and went out to get fussed over.

I don't like fuss. I don't like it when it's people I know, and I like it less when it's people I don't. But the Masters and Uncle both made it very clear to me that part of my job now was to accept the fuss and take it as a gift, even when it made me feel a little sick inside.

The fellow I was coming to think of as "my" steward was watching at the end of the car, and stopped me before I went on. "The Company would like it if you could do a walk-through on all the passenger cars," he said.

Well, things had just gotten more interesting. "Uh . . ." I said, deciding to play turnip again. "What company?"

"The one that owns all transportation that isn't military," he told me. "Like this train." I actually knew that, the Masters had explained all that in school when we were kids and getting our current history lessons.

"I thought the Armed Services—" I began, still playing dumb.

He shook his head. "The military does one thing well: fighting. They don't run Cit things."

Which I knew.

"Not even the trains?" A logical question for someone who didn't know, because transportation is a big thing to have control of.

"Only military transport. And the Company would like you to make an appearance."

But there was a little more nuance this time; when he said "the Company," he really meant "the people right on top and in charge of the Company." Which told me, as I had figured, someone had already relayed what had happened upline, and orders had come downline. This wasn't a "the Company would like it." This was a nicely phrased order. I didn't know why they wanted me to do this; maybe I could figure it out later.

"Right, I can do that," I said. I could hold off more hysterics and then have the usual post-Hunt collapse for a while. "Then let's get to it, shall we?"

He just nodded, and opened the door for me. People crowded around, as best they could in the narrow car. I smiled gravely and nodded and said soothing things; the Hounds eeled their way through the legs and to my side, packing around me to give me more space. I made sure to say something to everyone, but the first person who thrust a piece of paper and a pen into my hand and asked for my autograph kind of threw me. For a minute, I didn't know what she wanted; "autograph" just wasn't a word we used up on the Mountain very often. But it happened over and over, not just in the first car but in all of them. So I scrawled my name and added a version of my Mandala with a lot of symbols left out, and they seemed to like that.

It was draining. I'm not used to spending that much time with that many people after a Hunt. Neither are the Hounds; they slipped away from me one by one, leaving only Bya. And it wasn't just working *down* the train, I kind of had to go through a shortened version on the way back up.

When I got to my car, though, "my" steward was waiting. "The Company has authorized you to have that first compartment," he said. "The one I opened for you. They want you to have plenty of rest."

I could have kissed him. I wasn't sure I was going to be able to do anything, much less sleep, with the people in my car staring at me and pretending not to stare. "I would really like that," I said with feeling. "Thank you. And thank you for opening it in the first place."

He blushed a little. "Just push the call button if you want anything. There's just a short interview for you to go through, and they'll leave you alone."

Oh, someone else wanted to debrief me; probably the officer, alone, without his men listening. The thoughts of that were completely drowned out by my growling stomach. I was starving; I felt hollow. There is kind of a feeling of warmth where magic energy is when you are really fully charged, and when that's drained, there's a hunger there too, and you feel a little too cold, and a little too light. Not light-headed though, more like the opposite, as if your head is too heavy for your neck. Working magic does that to you. I was already contemplating a great big slab of meat and some greens as the steward showed me to the compartment, where the bed had vanished and a bigger table and two seats were at the window. But what was waiting there was not what I thought it would be.

I was expecting the officer from the armed car again, this time with more detailed questions from upline. What I got was . . . a vid-screen, and someone in a uniform looking at me out of it, and a cam-eye glowing at me.

He was very sober-looking. "So, you would be Joyeaux Charmand, the prefect's niece."

"Yes, sir," I said, not sitting, but taking that formal stance I always did when standing before a Master.

"Sit, please. I just want to ask you some questions."

I schooled my face into a pleasant but sober mask, and sat.

The steward showed up as if I had summoned him, and brought me a glass of water. I smiled at him gratefully, which made him blush again. Bya pressed in next to me but didn't make any other moves, although by the way he eyed the vid-screen, it was clear he understood I was talking to the person on the other side. I sipped the water, just enough to buy me a little time while he phrased his first question and I thought about the answer.

He asked me careful questions, except he didn't mention the Mage. Instead he talked about a cluster of Drakken and a Gog. Warning tingles ran all over me when he did that. I didn't correct him. For some reason, this man or his superiors wanted a... What did the history books call it? A "sanitized" version of what had happened. Something without the Mage in it.

A version that the Cits would be told...that had to be it. I sipped water. It tasted flat; definitely recycled.

His next question confirmed what I'd figured out. "How do you think those Drakken and that Gog got inside the cage in the first place?"

"Hunters have seen Drakken and Gog working together in the past, so I would guess it was the Gog who figured out he could tear the cage apart ahead of the train if he got the Drakken to help," I said. Now I was thinking really, really hard. I had to spin this, somehow, and I wasn't used to spinning anything, much less being a spin doctor. Gog were smart-ish. Not like the Folk, but you could talk to them, even if all you got was "Shut up, lunch."

To explain Gog, I'll have to go back to Greek stories again. They're a lot like the Cyclops that Odysseus tricked. About that smart, which is to say, not very. The other critters, the two-eyed Magog, we don't see as much, and some Hunters think they're Gog mates and are the smarter halves of the pairings. You might not actually *see* them together, but where there is a Gog, there will be a Magog somewhere around. The names are from the Christer Bibble, and that's all I know about where the terms came from. "Obviously we stopped when we saw the Gog, and when the first round didn't take him down, we knew he had a Wall up. I got out because I had to keep the Gog distracted while the shot got set up, and I had to weaken his Wall," I said. "Gogs can only concentrate on one thing at a time, and while he was having a standoff with me and the Hounds, he wasn't protecting himself, and his Wall was getting weaker as I worked on it."

"So, besides creating a hole in his defenses, you got out and made yourself a target so the creatures would concentrate on you?" He didn't look approving, he didn't look disapproving. He was . . . waiting for something. I just didn't know what it was he expected to hear.

So I'd give him honesty.

"I'm a Hunter, and our job is to protect the Cits," I pointed out. "This wasn't even a real Hunt, not with an armed car full of Hellfire missiles backing me up. Really, all I did was get warning out in time to stop the train, then I managed to rig things so the soldiers could save the day." There. More spin for the military. He was military; that should make him happy.

"Thank you, Hunter," he said, and finally produced a very small smile. "You made my job much easier than I thought it would be."

"Uh . . . you're welcome," I replied, but the vid-screen shut off, and a shutter closed down over the cam. I thought for a moment, only now allowing myself to feel all those things I'd put off. Exhaustion, mental and physical. And that raging, roaring hunger. Right now hunger was stronger than exhaustion. Bya pressed into my leg. I thumbed the call button.

"Is there any way I can get a steak and greens and beans?" I asked when the steward came in person to see what I wanted. "Please?"

4

WHILE I WAITED, I sat and thought for a while, running over everything I'd learned in school when we talked about how things were run off the Mountain.

See, back in the Diseray it was the military that sort of took over, learning how to fight off the Othersiders and gathering up survivors as they hunted for a really defensible place where they could make a fortification and restart civilization. They *never* left anyone behind. It was what became their motto: *"Modo ad pugnam paulo durioribus"*—"We just fight a little harder." It was a good thing they did, too, because they picked up and protected the very people they needed most, the techs and the makers and the smart people, the kind of folks who are not obviously useful when what you are doing is mostly fighting, and are not real good at protecting themselves, usually. They picked up some of the first

Hunters, who helped with the defense. Anyone who wasn't military or Hunter got called a "Cit." When they found a good spot that was defensible and had a lot of stuff that was still intact and could be looted, they dug in, and the Cits started figuring out what to do about the Othersiders besides throw lots of ordinance at them. Someone invented the first Barriers, and then they all started building Apex. The general in charge was really smart. He knew that the military excels at doing military things the military way. But. It's really bad at doing civilian things. Eventually, Apex was the sort of city that was safe to live in, and once that happened, there started to be hard feelings between the military and the Cits. That's when he sat down with people who were starting to become leaders among the Cits, and they divided things up. Premier Rayne is the guy in charge of the Cits, and the general is the guy in charge of the military. When something needs to be done, the side that is best at doing that sort of thing does it. So there are private, for-profit entities that handle the stuff that isn't military, like trains for civilians, and food production, and power and water. When you're working for one of these entities and you say "the Company," you mean the one you're working for. By choosing what I said carefully, hopefully I made whoever was in charge of the Company happy, *and* I made the military happy, which was definitely a bit of a juggling act. It was crystal clear that what my Masters had told me was right: Company, government, or military, the powers above did *not* want anyone to know about the Folk. I had been a good little Hunter and kept my lip zipped.

My steward brought me a cute square bit of meat and some other things. I looked at it, then at him. "You've never fed someone just off a Hunt, have you?" I asked. Before he could answer, I continued. "I've burned a zillion calories. I'm starving. It's like running a marathon. Uphill. Both ways. With a backpack full of bricks."

He blinked at me, then picked up the plate and came back with a proper Hunter's meal, the kind I would get after a Hunt even if it was a lean year. Because you don't starve your guard dogs, and you don't short a Hunter who is protecting you. Not that we ever, ever let anyone starve on the Mountain. That's not our way. But if the year is bad, Hunters get the bigger shares. Usually we can make up for it by doing regular hunting, and bringing home meat when we are on our patrols.

Now this was where I truly missed real meat, as opposed to cloned. But they made up for the lack with the seasoning, and anyway, it's bad manners to complain. And there was wine! I like wine, though as an underager I didn't get it often, only a glass on Holly Days.

I pretty much inhaled the meal while my steward pulled the bed out of the wall (so that was where it was!). Bya, my beautiful, sleek boy, got bits, nibbling daintily, unlike a real dog. The Hounds don't need to eat our food, but some of them like it. I could rest my eyes on him forever in this form: silk-sleek black fur as soft as the sleep cocoon; long, narrow muzzle; pointy ears; whiplike tail; lean and all whipcord muscle, with only his glowing eyes showing he wasn't a real dog. I was concentrating on the food so I wouldn't have to think about anything else. My brain needed a cooldown. The steward went out into the hall and came back with my smaller bag.

"I thought there might be something in here you'd want," he said a little awkwardly, and smiled, then showed me all the gizmos in the compartment. "Ah, you'll be on after the news from Apex City in about thirty minutes if you want to watch."

*Huh* . . . I didn't know what to say. In fact, I wasn't quite sure what he meant, so he took that as a "yes" and turned on the feed. "Remember, if you need anything, press the call button," he said as he left, taking my polished plates with him, and leaving me in a darkening compartment with brightly colored people nattering away on a holographic display between me and the window.

I knew I should have been paying attention to what they were saying, but my brain was still trying to process everything when the Apex Prime Vid logo came up, with a fanfare, and then a splash-screed of "SPECIAL REPORT! ATTACK ON THE PHOENIX FLYER!"

Well that would be me, I guess.

There were the usual sorts of announcers that sort of blend into each other—for me, anyway. They seem interchangeable. Mostly I was interested in what they were going to *say* happened, because that was what I was going to have to answer questions about in public. And sure enough, the footage had been tampered with. I studied it hard to get all the little details right. Interesting that they'd left in the Mage Wall, though; could be Cits didn't know enough about Gogs to know they weren't Magicians.

Bya watched too, staring intently. He'd seen other Hounds on vid before, but never himself and the rest of his pack. "You look gorgeous," I told him. "And *dangerous.*" He gave me a grin and went back to watching.

Then things got even more interesting, because there I was, staring at the camera. It was parts of the debriefing I'd done right here in this compartment!

No wonder the officer had said I had made his job easier. I'd responded to all his cues in such a way that he hadn't had to edit out the Folk Mage. That meant he could not only play it for those people who demanded the debrief but weren't allowed to know about the Folk, but he could release chunks of it straight to the news feed.

"Well, the new Hunter is quite a change from Ace Sturgis, wouldn't you say, Gayle?" the announcer man asked. "He won't have to worry about a fashion challenge, but if I were Ace, I'd be watching over my shoulder, because with this intro, she's definitely trending!"

"Oh, you never know what's going to happen to Joyeaux when she gets to the city, Johnny," the woman replied. "I have the feeling there are a lot of unplumbed *depths* to this new Hunter. I think she hasn't even begun to show us everything she's got."

Uh, what? Why were they discussing me as if I was some kind of vid star?

"Only time will tell," said the man, with a solemn nod.

"Well this reporter can tell you one thing," the woman said, and leaned toward the camera. "No matter what the rumors were about her, now that I have seen her myself, I say Hunter Joyeaux would be a contender no matter who her uncle was! Hunter Ace had better keep sharp if he wants to stay on the leaderboard!"

"And with that, I'm Johnny Night," said the man.

"And I'm Gayle Pierce. And that's *your* Hunters on the job! Keeping Apex and the Territories *safe!*" And there was a sudden bit of fanfare, and a brightly colored Allied Territories symbol with the *A* for Apex superimposed over it, and the program changed to something else.

I shut off the vid-feed, feeling not only every bit of my exhaustion, but now confusion as well. Rumors? Oh . . . great . . . and wait, what—what was a leaderboard? And what was I going to do about all this? When the Masters said I would be treated like a star, I didn't think they meant this! This was all turning out way more complicated than I had ever dreamed.

Before I could even begin to start fretting about any of that, Bya gave me the shove with his nose that told me *he* knew I was about to have my real post-Hunt meltdown. So I made the vidscreen go away, climbed into the bed, and made room for him. He radiated warmth and a soothing sort of comfort, but still tears stung my eyes. I wanted home and the guidance of my Masters so bad I was *sick* with it.

I wanted the Mountain, where I had lived for as long as I could remember, not all this flat land. I wanted snow and the knowledge that there wasn't one of the Othersiders, not even a Folk Mage, that could stand that much cold for very long. I wanted my little room in the Monastery, no bigger than this compartment, but so much homier, so much warmer, all glowing, polished wood and feather bed and thick down comforters. I wanted people I didn't have to watch my words with. But most of all, I desperately wanted my Masters, I wanted Kedo, I wanted someone to tell me what to do. . . .

But they wouldn't. They hadn't been telling me what to do for a couple of years now. Like the time when I was trying to figure out how to make the spell for a magic net work. I didn't know then that Kedo was teaching me how to take two different spells and combine them to make something new. *I* knew he knew how to make a net, because I'd seen him do it. But he wouldn't tell me. He'd just looked at me in that way that said, *You have all the information;*

*you need to find the way for yourself.* That's what Kedo, or any other Master, would do now, and inside, I knew that.

Which, of course, only made me feel worse. Then I shook with the fear I hadn't let myself feel out there, then—and this was new—with anger that those mindless vidiots were making me into some sort of... of... *entertainment.* Then finally the fatigue hit like a sack of hammers to the head, and I went straight into no-dream-time.

I woke up at dawn, as always.

Bya was gone, which I expected. There's only so much time they can spend on this side, I think. Or maybe it's just more comfortable for them on the Otherside, I don't know. I don't even know if the Otherside they come from is the same as the one that the Folk and the other strangelings come from. What I did have when I woke up was a head full of questions.

No way to answer them, of course. It would have been nice to be a Psimon and just *talk* to my Masters whenever I needed to. Psi and magic don't go together except for within the Folk, though. But... yeah. Millions of questions.

Again, I used the 'fresher and, since I had my little bag with me, I went ahead and changed out of Hunting gear. It still wasn't anything like the Cits were wearing, but it wasn't quite as somber and monklike: a tunic my best friend Kei had embroidered for me over soft leather trousers. The tunic was golden brown linen, embroidered with red and yellow flowers, and it had this nifty wide leather belt that matched the pants and had pockets sewn into it. I pulled my hair into a tail, and thought about my friends back on the Mountain.

Right now, Kei was milking her family's goats, and I knew exactly what *she* was thinking. Not about me even though we'd been friends ever since I beat a Harpy to death for trying to carry off one of the nanny goats. No, she was thinking about Big Tom, and scheming to get him away from Ramona, even though she didn't have a chance in hell of doing that, and anyway, if she had any sense at all she'd wake up and realize that Dutch down at Silverspring was crazy for her. Right now the other Hunters at the Monastery, Caleb and Rory, Andi and Luce, Big and Little Tom, and Shen and Aci, were all doing *their* morning exercises, first kata, then the magic ones.

I wanted to be there, with the Monastery perched on the side of the Mountain in the snow looking exactly like the big Buddhist Monastery at Lhasa did in old pictures, except for solar panels covering the roof and part of the mountainside. It was beautiful, with the thick concrete walls painted a mellow tan and the concrete roof dyed red, instead of tiles. Tiny wind generators along every roofline, each of them with a shaft that was actually a prayer wheel, because, why not? Until you got up there, though, you'd never know you could only see a third of it. The rest of it, including lots and lots of storage, was actually dug into the Mountain. That sort of excavation is something that has to be done very slowly and with a lot of labor now. Back when the Monastery was built, it had all been done by machines.

When you went around doing your jobs, everyone greeted you, even if they didn't like you. And with those who liked you, there would be brief touches, pats on the back, hugs. Back home, we're a touchy bunch. Everyone hugs, everyone kisses, even some of the monks and the Masters, like Kedo. I never, ever lacked for that. It's not that everyone loves everyone else, but where I come from everyone is loved by *someone*, and knows it. Now all that was far, far away; nobody had touched me once since I got on this train, and I felt all the more isolated.

But right now, the world on the Mountain was going right along, counting on me to satisfy the needs of Apex and the Territories and keep them secret and safe.

And I would.

So I closed my eyes, tried to be with them even though I wasn't, and did *my* exercises. Then I rang for the steward.

He brought me the same breakfast as yesterday, and looked a little surprised at my change of clothing. "Is this going to be better than what I had on for the city?" I asked him a little anxiously. "I know it doesn't look like—fashionable stuff, but—"

"You'll be fine," he assured me. "You're trending. By tomorrow, people will be figuring out how to fab clothing like yours, and in three days, there will be as many people dressed like you as there are people dressed like Ace or Bree or Daze."

I blinked at him, not sure what he'd said, but *he* thought it was reassuring, so I figured I would let myself be reassured. "Uh . . . who's Ace?" I asked. "They were comparing me to him on the news."

"Hunter Ace is very popular," the steward told me. "Don't worry, they compare everyone to him."

"Popular?" I repeated. "What's *popular* got to do with anything?"

"People love watching him Hunt," said the steward, sounding

puzzled. "Don't you—oh. I guess you don't watch much vid out there—"

"We're kind of busy," I pointed out dryly. "We have to hunt and grow our food for ourselves. And make our own clothing from wool, hemp, linen, and ramie. And cut the wood to heat our houses. And—"

He laughed, cutting me off. "Never mind, I get the idea. I wish I had the time to explain it to you, but I'm sure they'll tell you all about it when you get to Hunter headquarters. Now, they've cleared the line for us," he went on, "and we've been putting on speed all night. We should pull into Central Station just after lunch, and I have more requests from upline."

I blinked again; you *never* clear the line for any train other than one that carries mega-VIPs. That's just how it is. That was crazy. . . .

"Prefect Charmand doesn't want the vid-hounds to get at you, so he's sending someone for you. We'll stop a little short of the station at the same platform that the premier uses, you'll get off there and be met, and then we'll go on." The steward grinned. "I can't wait to see their faces when they realize what happened."

Wait, what? I was going to use the premier's—

Well, Uncle *is* pretty important. And it wasn't as if the premier was going to want it on a spur of the moment thing. And it meant I wouldn't have to—wait, what?

"What about vid-hounds?" I asked, feeling stupid.

"Gayle Pierce on channel Apex Prime got the exclusive last night—your interview—and now every station wants you covered. There'll probably be twenty or thirty vid-hounds at the station wanting interviews. Not just the majors, there's the foodie channel that will want an interview about what you eat, and the hobby channel that will want to know if you do anything besides Hunt, the fashion channel, all four movie channels, the book channel—well, you get the idea." He nodded as if I *would* get the idea, when all I knew about was Apex Prime. It was about all we could get. Here I had been thinking that all those vid-dumps that came once a week from the city by mail were all coming from Apex Prime—and I had been wondering how they *fit* all that stuff in twenty-four hours every day.

"Oh . . ." I said in a small voice.

"But the prefect is seeing to it you won't have to talk to any of them until you are ready," he continued, as if it was a given that I would *want* to.

Suddenly my palms were damp and I was more nervous than I'd been facing down that Mage. After all, the only thing *he* could do was kill me horribly. These people . . . they could make me look stupid.

The train slowed. The vid-screen popped down, and words scrolled along with an announcement in a female voice that sounded artificially generated. "This is an unscheduled stop. We have not yet reached Central Station. Please remain in your seats. You will arrive on time. This is an unscheduled stop. . . ."

We'd been rolling through protected lands for some time before that, and the difference between them and the unprotected plains could not have been more graphic. People and machines moved freely through fields so mathematically precise I doubt there was a millimeter of wasted space. Some fields were covered with black vinyl, through which the food plants protruded, to preserve the moisture in the soil and cut down on the weeds. Some supported racks of hydroponics trays. Some were real grain fields, more or less like what I was used to. Not that we didn't use the vinyl or the hydroponics—the hydro was fed by our tilapia pond—but we didn't do it on this scale. There were probably *some* animals out there, because real meat, eggs, and dairy were luxury items that the high and mighty still wanted, but most meat was vat-grown, and eggs and dairy were completely synthesized from vegetable oils. I was pretty sure that the eggs and dairy I'd gotten on the train were real. I was also pretty sure that once I was off the train I wasn't going to see the real thing again unless Uncle took me to dinner.

The thing about the protected lands was the Barriers. You could see them in the distance as a shimmer between huge pylons that stretched a thousand feet up. The Barriers were tuned somehow—don't ask me how, it's a big secret, and probably involves both squints—that's what the military calls scientists and technicians—and Magicians. Whatever it is they give out lets ordinary stuff pass without a problem, but let one of the Othersiders try, and it'll end up ash. Of course, that doesn't stop anything that can fly *over* the Barriers, but if something tries that, there's helichoppers, planes, and stationary guns to shoot it down.

The closer we got to the city, the more little towns there were, and the more powerful the Barriers got. Finally about a mile out, we passed a really powerful Barrier, one I *felt* as we went through it, like slamming through jelly that tingled. And then we were in the city itself. Or the burbs, anyway.

After the Diseray this all was rebuilt, because it pretty much got stomped flat, burned, or just erased. So the city is laid out in a wheel-and-spoke pattern, cut into quarters by the two big rail lines, north–south and east–west. The eastern terminus is farther than I would go, at the Port. Now that we didn't have to travel inside an electrified cage, there were several tracks here. I counted five more on my side.

We were clearly going to stop well short of the Hub and Central Station. In fact, we got switched over to the farthest track on the line, passed through a physical fence, the sort that I was used to, about twelve feet of chain-link with razor wire on top, and inside the fence was a complex so precise, so gray, and so purposeful, it could only be military.

We pulled up to a platform. I was already standing up, with my bag in my hand, when the steward opened the door. I was too nervous at this point to keep sitting down. He took my bag before I could say anything, and made a waving motion with his free hand. I went to the end of the car and got off, feeling just about ready to bolt like a feral cow at the sight of a wolf.

There were actually two people there, both guys, both a couple years older than me. You know, army-recruit-age. One was a dark-haired, dark-skinned soldier in a pristine khaki army uniform. The other—

Blond hair. Black-and-silver uniform, sleek black trousers that looked like something molded, not sewn, dull silver tunic that buttoned to one side, with a tiny stand-up collar, also with no visible seams. Mirrored one-piece sunglasses that looked more like a visor. I knew the uniform of course, though I had never seen anyone in it before in person. This was a Psimon—someone who had psionic powers rather than magic. He was, almost definitely, a telepath. He might be other things too, but telepathy and mind-reading were the most valued Psimon powers. Psimons were rarer than Magicians, about as rare as Hunters. We'd never had anyone born a Psimon up on the Mountain; or at least, if anyone had been, they kept it to themselves and told no one but the Masters. There was a reason for that. Psimons made people uneasy. You can guess why. How many things running through *your* head would you like someone else to know? Not very many, I bet. Because that's what Psimons do; they read your thoughts. *Supposedly*, they aren't allowed to go snooping in your head unless you're a criminal; they're only authorized to be like a radio, sort of a passive receiver that gets the really strong stuff that is associated with a lot of emotion—like a robber thinking about a robbery he's going to do, or a would-be murderer about his victim. *Supposedly*, everyone has a kind of filter in their head made up of all the random stuff they think about all the time that only lets those strong, emotional thoughts get through. That's *supposedly*.

As soon as I saw the uniform, I had my One White Stone up in my mind. I didn't want some random Psimon getting even a single stray thought about the Mountain, the Monastery, and the Masters.

The soldier took my bag from the steward, who didn't even get off the train. The door slid shut and the train accelerated out of the station. We hadn't been stopped for more than a few seconds.

"Joyeaux Charmand." It was the soldier, and it was a statement, not a question. "Psimon Green and I have been instructed to take you to Prefect Charmand."

I put my Hunt-face on, and nodded gravely. "Thank you, soldier," I said. "And Psimon. I appreciate the courtesy."

It was obvious where I was supposed to go, because even though I had never seen one in person, the gray transpod was familiar to me from vids. There's really no good way to say this—it looked exactly like a gray roach egg, a sort of rounded rectangular box with windows in the top half and a door in the middle. It waited at the side of the platform—a curiously bare slab of concrete, although I expect when important people use it, there are all manner of temps put up to make them comfortable. The soldier, looking so stiff I thought he was going to shatter inside his crisp khaki uniform, led the way. The blond Psimon followed me as I followed the soldier. He stowed my little bag in the cargo hatch of the pod. My other bags, I assumed, would catch up with me. The Psimon opened the door of the pod for me, and I climbed in.

There was a rear-facing seat, a front-facing seat, and a pilot seat. I took the front-facing seat, leaving the Psimon with the other. I hoped he wasn't prone to motion sickness. The soldier took the pilot seat, and a moment later we pulled smoothly away. He was guiding it manually for now, as we wove our way through the streets of the complex. Soldiers and military vehicles everywhere.

The Psimon pushed the glasses up on the top of his head and gave me a cocked eyebrow and a little quirk of the lips that wasn't quite a smile. His eyes were an intense blue. "So. You're probably wondering why a Psimon came for you. Call me Josh, if you like."

"Um," I said cleverly. "Actually this all happened a little faster than I was ready for. I hadn't gotten to the wondering part yet."

He laughed. "I'm Prefect Charmand's personal Psi-aide. That

means I do things like ensuring that if he doesn't want people to know where he's going, I can keep Psi-sniffers confused. So I'm here to make sure no Psi-sniffers figure out where you are, once the texers on the train start spreading the word that you got off here. On base, no one is going to probe us. Once we match up with traffic, we'll just be one more transpod in the stream to them." He did something to the window controls. The view outside darkened just a little, but not much. "And now if any face-rec is running, it won't pick you up through the window."

It was a little like he was speaking a completely foreign language. I puzzled through it with difficulty. So he was Uncle's personal man, so . . . could I take a chance on dropping my concentration? No, better not. He was going to make sure no one could find me telepathically . . . which they could, even though I was thinking about the One White Stone. That just meant they couldn't read my thoughts, not that they couldn't find me. But how could vid channels hire telepaths? "I thought everyone Psi-sensitive was supposed to be in PsiCorps," I said, after a moment.

"Marginal talents are of no use to us," he replied with the casual arrogance of someone who *knows* he's good. "Maybe in the past, before there were physical Psi-shields and when even the least bit of Psi could be put to use, but not anymore. But a lot of the channels use them as chasers. We're green. Thoughts of you ended at the train; with me running interference, this transpod will sniff as holding three ordinary Cits."

"Oh." Well what else could I say? "Ah, thank you . . ."

He cocked his head to one side, looking at me thoughtfully. "For someone trending, you really are awfully vid-shy." He put two fingers to his temple and closed his eyes for a moment. "There, the prefect knows you're confused and concerned. I expect he'll have someone who can advise you."

I felt, at that moment, totally helpless. "I'm . . . from this little village in the Rockies," I said. "We get vid from Apex a couple times a day when they punch the signal through all the Othersider chaff and we have electricity to use to run the community receiver. Everything else has to wait for the weekly mail. One block of this base probably holds more people than my whole village." Of course, that didn't count the Masters' Monastery, or the people brought there to train, or all the other settlements on and around the Mountain . . . but it wasn't a lie.

I expected a superior smirk, but what I got was a look of sympathy. "When'd you pop Powers?"

The lie was so ingrained it slipped smoothly off my tongue. "Six months ago. The village waited to make sure it wasn't going to fade, then contacted the prefect, and it's taken this long to arrange things."

"And how long have you been Hunting?" he asked, looking a little surprised. "Because that standoff was ace."

"Every day since I popped." That was pretty much the truth, although as a precocious ten-year-old Hunter, I wasn't allowed to Hunt *much* except the gremlins in the fields at first. "Well, with Powers. Without Powers, everyone Hunts, we can't afford not to, so . . . since I was old enough to use weapons. Too many of them, too few of us."

"It shows," he said, now with some respect. "I bet you were already used to driving off the strangelings without Hounds before that, too."

"Not as much as you might think," I replied. "We keep the village up above the snow line. They can't go there, so the village itself is a haven. But the farm fields? The grazing meadows? Every day. I got a *lot* of practice in six months, and plenty before that with weapons."

He shivered. "I've only ever seen Othersiders on vid," he replied slowly.

We passed through a set of gates and out into the main traffic; the soldier engaged the auto, and the traffic stream took control of the transpod. He turned the pilot seat to face me and relaxed visibly. "I want to thank you personally, Hunter," he said with a lot of the same look in his eyes that the Cits in the passenger cars had had. "My brother is second gunner on that train. You saved his life."

"*We* saved everybody's lives," I corrected. "I did my job, they did theirs."

He had this *My brother tells it different* look on his face. "Figure I was the hand and the brain," I said. "The soldiers in that armed car were a hammer. Without me, they wouldn't know where to hit, when, or how hard. Without them, I had nothing to hit with."

The guys exchanged a guy-look. Finally Psimon Josh opened his mouth. Actually, he snickered first. "Can you imagine Ace saying something like that?"

"Glitterboi? Never in a hundred years," the soldier replied, with a disgusted look on his face.

"Can *someone* please tell me about this Hunter Ace?" I begged. "They talked about him on the vid last night like I should know everything about him."

The soldier laughed. "He's a Hunter, and I'll admit he's really good, and he's fantastic to watch when he Hunts seriously dangerous Othersiders. It's even better watching him and his brother, Paules, Hunt together. But he thinks he's king of the world, and acts like it."

"I heard they had to build a second Hunter HQ just for his ego," Josh deadpanned, and the soldier laughed. "His admirers think he's very good-looking. He's certainly very flamboyant. I don't follow his channel, but you can't help getting bits of him on the news feeds, because he's on all the time."

"Wait—" I said. "Channel? He has his own channel?"

"Every Hunter does. They'll explain it to you at headquarters." I wanted to push for more info, but Josh was turning those intense blue eyes back on me. Measuring. What was he looking for? I thought about my stone.

Meanwhile there were a lot of other uncomfortable but exciting things tying me up inside. This was the first time ever I had been alone with two guys around my age that I hadn't grown up with, and both of them were, as we say back home, *keepers*, though in different ways. The soldier was as chiseled as a heroic statue, while Josh was kind of baby-faced and sweet-looking when he wasn't giving you one of those gimlet stares. He had an easy smile, with one dimple and crystal blue eyes. I prayed he didn't notice my cheeks flush every time he looked over at me. I wanted him to keep looking, but I wasn't sure how to get him to do that without being obvious about it.

This was all really, really different. It was one thing to be joking around and mock-flirting with boys you'd known all your life, especially when most of them were interested in someone other than you. It's fine to be twirled around at a Satterday dance by a

Hunter you'd worked with for years, with both of you knowing you just need to let loose and work off some steam.

But to be sitting with two *yummy* strangers, alone, and wishing you could get one of them in particular back to that Satterday dance and show off a little for him to see where that went?

Let's just say I was glad I had the stone to hold in the front of my mind, because I sure didn't want Josh to pick up on any of that, either, and it sure was emotionally loaded. What would he think of me?

Not that it mattered, in the end, which was depressing. I knew I was supposed to go right to the training quarters and I would probably never see him again.

Still...

"My girl is all fangirly over Ace," the soldier grumbled. "All that lone wolf business."

"And his *tragic past,*" Josh said, smacking his forehead with the back of his hand and putting on a pose, like the hero in a melodrama.

The soldier grinned. "I had to keep him from sniffers once," Josh went on. "He acted like I was something he was going to scrape off his shoe as soon as he was alone."

That was when I saw it happen: Josh went from "scary Psimon who can see inside your head" to "one of the guys." The soldier relaxed and they started in on guy-talk, and left me sitting there not understanding more than a quarter of what they were talking about. Which was kind of good and kind of sucked, cause it would have been nice to have them both treating me at least a *little* like I was a girl, if not a nova star.

But...on the other hand, Josh *was* a scary Psimon that could see inside my head, and I had a head full of things I didn't want him to see. So, Uncle had sent him for me, all well and good, but no matter how cute he was, I didn't dare drop my guard around him.

So I looked out the window at what could be seen of the city. Pretty much what it looked like in vid, clean and shiny, lots of buildings that went from three to eight stories tall, in various inoffensive pastel colors. Hard to tell as we zipped past in the regulated traffic stream what they were. Not like you were allowed to have things like, say, strings of wash hanging outside your house in the big cities. It wouldn't be practical; all those people crammed into one building, where would all the wash go? And not like you'd need to, with the way people can live in cities, I guess.

Traffic slowed as we got into the Hub, and here were all the shopping places, the lighted-up signs, vid-boards two stories high, some people dressed like the Cits on the train, all looking like they were in a hurry to get somewhere and do something. But there were also lots of people dressed quietly, too, stuff in very subdued colors, and nothing radical about it. Except for the heels on the shoes most of the women wore. How could they *walk* in those shoes? A couple of times I actually caught my own face on one of those vid-boards, and the footage of the Hellfires going off, which was a jolt and just seemed completely unreal.

The soldier turned his seat around and put his hands on the controls, although he didn't use them. It was quiet in the transpod, but if I put my hand on the glass, I could sense the vibrations of noise outside.

As we got to the center of the Hub, the crowds thinned to almost nothing, though pod traffic was as thick as ever. Buildings loomed above me, steeper than the mountains, blocking off the sky. It was exactly like being in a deep, deep canyon. And *nothing* like the pictures in old books and vids of how cities used to look. Because, of course, Apex Hub had pretty much been built in about a decade, and all by the same people: the Army Corps of Engineers, mostly, with some of the Cits that had gotten rescued and protected. There wasn't any real variation in the buildings— there were three models, actually. There was the rounded tower, the stepped tower, and the straight tower. They were all made of the same cream-white stuff. That made sense when you knew the army had done most of the planning and construction. After all, when the army has something that works, they just make a lot of it. They were all smooth, without any ornamentation, with row after row of recessed windows. About the only way in which they differed was by height. All at once, I realized what it was Apex Hub reminded me of—one of those big model cities that had been built to show "the city of the future" that I'd seen in old vids. And as soon as I realized that, I had to wonder . . . had the builders actually seen one of those old pictures, or old vids, and deliberately copied it? That sounds like something the army would do too. If it works in a model, it probably works in real life, right?

Abruptly the pod made a left-hand turn, and we whisked down a ramp into a lighted cavern underneath one of the buildings. A moment later, we pulled up next to a glass door, with blast doors open to either side of it, and stopped.

"Good luck, Hunter Charmand," the soldier said formally, with a little sketch of a salute as my door opened. "Pleasure serving you."

"Thank you," I told him, and didn't have time to say anything else as yet another soldier came around to the side of the pod and stood at attention, clearly waiting for me to get out. So I did, and discovered that Psimon Josh and I had an escort of four soldiers in fancier uniforms, dress uniforms, to take us to my uncle.

This was getting more intimidating by the moment. But I stiffened up my spine and nodded like this was all my due, and followed them into a building that swallowed me up and probably wasn't going to spit me out any time soon.

# 5

I HAD NEVER BEEN in a building like this in my life.

The Monastery was big, but it was all wood inside, and beautiful. We didn't waste anything, so even dead, bark-beetle-killed trees got used in the interiors, where the flaws and bug-tunnels were transformed into a zillion works of art. When the monks weren't doing spiritual things or training, they were generally doing something with their hands, and a lot of them were wood-carvers. So door frames, beams, window frames, door panels, wall panels—anything that could be made ornamental either was, or one day would be. And if it hadn't been carved yet, it *had* been polished until it glowed. The regular houses in the village were also wood, with plenty of ornamental touches on them, too. After all, when winter came, and you were a farmer, you had a lot of time on your hands, and what better use to make of it than to make your house a little nicer?

This building was Purposeful, like that, capitalized. The floor was something smooth and gray, the walls were a different, lighter gray, the ceiling was lighting panels, and there was no ornament anywhere. I wasn't sure what the floor and walls were made of, but it wasn't anything natural. Here, it was *really* obvious that the army had built this place. If something was useful, had an actual purpose, was functional, then it went in. If it didn't, then it got left out. Or, more likely, it was never even considered in the first place.

Of course, since we get vid, I'm not a complete turnip, I know an elevator when I see one, and that's what Josh was herding me toward. There were two more soldiers at the steel elevator door, one on each side, and they got in with us, flanking us. Josh pushed the top button, and up we went. Feeling myself rising, moving . . . that was unsettling. Once, we'd had a little earthquake up at the Monastery, maybe caused by some of the Othersiders that had gotten into the old mines. It had made my insides go, *No, the ground shouldn't move!* just like this elevator did. I was just glad I wasn't claustrophobic.

Of course, a Hunter can't be. Like the time Kedo and I had doubled up to chase some Tommyknockers out of a mine the Rock Knob settlement was trying to reopen. There'd been barely enough room in some of the shafts for us to go single file, and we'd been forced to use the hand-tap code because we didn't want to alert the little horrors by talking. I had never been so glad to have my Master and mentor with me than that day; he kept reaching back, not just to "say" something, but to give my hand a squeeze, 'cause that's the sort of thing he did. I needed every squeeze. Dark, close, and quiet beyond *anything* I'd ever experienced before . . . and the only thing telling you that you weren't alone down there was the tap on your wrist from your partner, and the sense of your Hounds ahead of and behind you. . . .

More gray corridor ended in a closed gray double door with more soldiers. My soldiers saluted those soldiers, who saluted back, and opened both doors.

The reception room inside was a relief from the gray; it was still Purposeful, but the floor was covered in brown carpet, the walls were a warm yellow-beige, and the receptionist's desk at least had a wooden top, even if the rest of it was metal. Wow, this place even looked like vid I'd seen of an army office! You'd think that since Apex got stuff from all over, Uncle's own office would be fancier . . . but no. The receptionist smiled brightly at us—she was wearing a jacket just a little darker than the walls. "He's cleared his schedule, Psimon; you and Joyeaux can go on in," she said.

There were two more double doors in the wall behind her desk. My soldiers went ahead and opened both for us, and Josh and I went on past them and in. The doors closed behind us.

Uncle was standing at a huge window that took up the whole wall, with his back to us and his hands clasped behind him, but he turned as we entered. It was a little disconcerting to finally see the man I'd only seen in vids all this time, to be in the same room with him.

He was taller in person than you'd think from vids: about six foot four. He wore a modified police uniform, blue and gray and tailored, with gold stuff where the police had silver, and a little gold braid at the shoulders. He was going bald on top and gray on the sides, and had a mustache. Basically, he looked like someone who should be running a butcher shop or a bakery, not the Prefecture. He smiled when he saw me, and it was a real smile; it reached up into his eyes.

"Joy, at last." Josh moved back a couple of steps as my uncle stepped forward and took my shoulders in his hands, kind of holding me at arm's length so he could study my face. "You have your father's face, and your mother's eyes."

I have to say that if I had not been holding myself completely in Hunter discipline, what happened next would have startled me so much I probably would have jumped and yelped. Because one finger of his right hand moved on my shoulder, pressing it in something I recognized almost at the level of instinct. The tap code we Hunters use when Hunting together and keeping silence. Just like Kedo and I had, down in that mine.

*Love to hug you, little one, but dangerous for both. Vidding here. Show you understand.*

Vidding? In Uncle's own office? But—why? And why was he afraid of it? Never mind, I could try to find out later. Right then I just needed to follow his lead. But this was the first time I had any idea that there was something seriously amiss.

Then I scolded myself. Because I had studied *The Book of Five Rings* and *The Art of War,* and Master Price, who was in charge of the Hunters' schooling, had insisted I read Machiavelli's *The Prince.* So I knew where there were people, there were politics, and politics could get dangerous. All I could think was they'd gotten dangerous for my uncle.

"So I *understand,* Uncle Charmand," I said steadily, and put my own hands just under his elbows, tapping *understood.* "Or—I beg your pardon, sir. Prefect Charmand."

"I can be Uncle for an hour or so," he said, tapping *Good* on my shoulder before letting go. "You understand, of course, that once you leave this office, you are only Hunter Joyeaux to me. I cannot and will not countenance favoritism among the Hunters, especially not my niece."

So . . . if there was vidding going on, maybe he was trying to send a message that doing favors for me wouldn't buy favors with him? Or . . . was it the other way around? That *hurting* me would leave him unmoved?

"Sir," I replied truthfully, "I would not want favoritism. Being made a favorite spoils a Hunter, and a spoiled Hunter is pretty quickly a dead Hunter."

"Well said." He took my elbow and steered me to the window. "I thought I might be the one to give you your welcome and a little tour of Apex City before you went on to Hunter HQ. Given your unexpectedly exciting trip here, I thought you might appreciate the breathing space."

"I do, sir," I said, and then I realized that it was not a window we stood at—or rather, it *might* be a window, but it was also a giant vid-screen, one that was giving us a chopper-eye view over the city.

Uncle kept his hand on my elbow, and as he pointed out each of the City Center buildings, Hunter HQ, then the vast expanse of hydroponic and fish farms, then the acres of vat-meat, vat-veg, and algae farms, his finger kept tapping, warning me that it was not safe to talk openly. I was glad that all I had to do was nod and murmur politely, because that made it easier to concentrate on what he was saying.

"The Psimon was kind enough to let me know that you are—" He paused.

"Not quite a turnip," I said truthfully. "But I don't understand so much of what's been thrown at me. Vid channels? For Hunters? And—"

He nodded. "The Hunters need to work to reassure the citizens of Apex that they are *safe*. We can't rebuild the world if people are constantly looking over their shoulders." But his fingers tapped something different. *Hear what I don't say.* "We found that allowing the citizens to see what the Hunters were doing reassured them that there was nothing inside the Barriers to fear." *Hunters are as much entertainment as protectors.* "As a consequence, they became very popular, and there seems no harm in allowing that to continue." *Ask the armorer.*

"I . . . I think I understand, Uncle," I replied. I didn't, not yet, but maybe when I had a chance to think everything through and remember what he was saying and what he was tapping, I would. Or maybe this armorer would actually explain *everything.* I hoped so.

"You're a very intelligent young lady, Joy." He laughed. "I'll be egotistical and claim that the only reason your part of the Territories ever produced such a good Hunter is because of your genes. Eh?"

I laughed dutifully. This part, I got. So I reinforced it for whatever was recording. "I have to admit, most people back home haven't got a lot of interest outside of their sheep and goats. Half the time they sleep through the vids from Apex." Was that what Uncle wanted?

*Good girl,* he tapped. *Keep your head.*

"Obviously, then, there's no need for a search."

"Search? Nothing to find. Unless you're talking about our

homemade whiskey. The fumes alone would probably knock an Othersider sideways." He laughed with me.

My blood ran a little colder when he said that, though I laughed as though the very idea was ridiculous. The Masters were right; he had just confirmed it. If I hadn't turned up, a search would have been scheduled. And a search would almost certainly have turned up the Monastery and all the Hunters we trained there. And all those Hunters would almost certainly have been sent back to Apex, stripping my village and all the rest around the Mountain of their protectors.

Now he was pointing out the schools. One for Meds, one for Techs, one for Psimons, one for scientists, and one for all the other Cits, who might become anything that wasn't one of those. *Be like the others. Blend in,* he tapped.

He pointed out how all the roofs were green—algae-based solar-cells, so if the grid went down there would still be enough power for a building to seal itself and hold out against attack. I nodded as if we didn't have those at home.

Why would he want me to blend in? I didn't know, not yet, but it had to be important or he wouldn't have said to do it.

He also pointed out the anti-flyer guns on all the roofs. "We haven't had an incursion by flyers since before you were born, but even if a Wyvern somehow got past the bounds, he'd be lacework before he got a hundred yards. Between our defenses and the Hunters, our Cits are as safe as they think they are."

*Camouflage safer for us both,* he told me silently.

*Understood,* I tapped back, feeling hollow and forlorn. Don't take what I look like on the outside for what's going on inside. Outside is Hunter discipline, which isn't how I feel. Somewhere along the way I had gotten the idea I would be living with Uncle, that I might finally have something like a blood family again. I'd been unconsciously assuming at that no matter what, at least I'd have some family again with Uncle.

Evidently not. It took all my will not to show what I was feeling. The Masters all said Uncle was a kind, smart, and honorable man, and that he cared about *me*. Master Kedo had said the one thing I need not worry about was my uncle. They had never lied to me about anything, and I didn't think that was a lie, either.

Well, he was important. And if people thought he was fond of me, maybe they'd use me to work against him. Now maybe that was just a manipulative sort of thing—or maybe it was uglier than that. It could be—give me presents so I'd say good things about them to Uncle. Or it could be—tell Uncle they'd make things hard for me if he didn't do something they wanted. As prefect of police he could overturn arrests, lessen charges, all sorts of things. Or maybe—politics again!—maybe there were even stresses between the Hunters and the Prefecture, and there were people who were thinking he'd brought *me* in, his blood kin, so he'd have a Hunter on *his* side if the stresses turned into a break.

*I'll be careful,* I signaled back. And that was when the whole room rang with a soft chime and he made a gesture with his free hand and the window became a window, looking down on City Center. "And I am afraid that is all the time I can give you, Hunter Joyeaux," he said formally. "I am proud of you. Your parents would be prouder." *We'll talk again the next time it is safe.* "Before you go, I have a welcome gift for you."

Then he let go of my elbow and turned to reach for a little box on the top of his desk. He opened it and handed me what looked like something I knew very well. It was a Perscom, a very fine version of a wrist device that did just about everything a micro-comp could do, and although the one I'd used back at home was a chunky thing that was about half as long as my forearm, this one was no bigger than a watch. Basically, it's a voice-controlled tablet computer that's generally linked into a citywide network. Back home, our clunkier versions were still linked into the network hosted up at the Monastery, and that wireless net is one of the few things on the whole Mountain that gets 24/7 electricity from solar and wind. The ones back home were too big to take out Hunting, which was a pity because they'd be awfully useful. This little one was a jewel. That's not just better Apex City design and engineering, because I had seen people on the train wearing ones almost as clunky as my old one. That's *money.* He held out his hand, I gave him my nondominant wrist, and he strapped it on, and immediately I felt something else.

It's hard to describe, but it felt as if my brain had been wrapped in a warm, soft blanket, and I knew what else that Perscom could do.

There wasn't a word for it in Hunter code, so I improvised. *Head-protector?* I tapped.

*Yes,* he tapped back, and directed my fingers to a little stud on the underside before letting go of my hands. So . . . a Psi-shield. "Uncle, I can't take this!" I said, sounding shocked. Well, I *was.* "It's too expensive a gift!"

He snorted politely. "This is not favoritism, this is fifteen years of missed birthdays. And it's not all that much better than the one you would have been issued at Hunter HQ." He turned, and instinctively I turned to face the room and Josh, echoing his moves. "Psimon, if you could escort the Hunter to HQ, I would very much appreciate it."

"Very good, sir." Josh touched two fingers to his temple, and signaled to me to follow. I did. I didn't look back.

As I had seen from Uncle's "tour," Hunter HQ was one enormous building out on the Edge, right up against the Boundary and the innermost layer of Barriers. The tall buildings of the City Center were like toy towers in the distance, and the HQ was a three-story tall sprawl of a place. Which made sense. Hunters needed a lot of real estate to train in.

Josh delivered me to a door—but before I got out of the pod, he stopped me. "If you need anything, my contact will be on the Perscom that Prefect Charmand gave you. I can probably help you, and if it's more urgent than that, I can relay a message to the prefect. Just call." Then he smiled again. "And I might just call you, once you're not up to your eyebrows in training or working. Now hop, your CO is waiting."

I hopped, because there was someone heading for the pod with an expression that promised impatience or worse if she was kept waiting. The door closed, and off the pod sped, leaving me and my little bag on the pavement. *He might call me?* I thought. *But how would he know if—* Then I remembered. Uncle had said cameras would be on me everywhere. Josh would probably know more about my schedule than I would.

By this time, the woman had reached me.

She was taller than me by about a head, and easily old enough to have been my mother, but there was nothing about her that was motherly. Her brown hair was aggressively short, there was a scar cutting through her right eyebrow and down the cheekbone, and her face was lean and chiseled and looked very Native, with prominent cheekbones and a jut of a nose. Actually she could have been a sister or a cousin to Master Kedo, except her hair was lighter. She wore black and silver leather with silver buckles and straps everywhere, and she looked at me hard, sizing me up.

So I stood to something that was nearly "attention," and nodded my head respectfully, as I would have to one of my Masters. "Beg pardon for lateness, Senior Hunter," I said, choosing a respectful-sounding title at random. "Prefect Charmand wished to interview me."

Her eyes softened from that glare ever so slightly, and one corner of her mouth came up a little. "Good answer," was all she said. "Follow me, and hop."

She entered the building, and I grabbed my bag and followed at the same fast walk. The minute we came in the doors, I caught a flash of movement and turned like lightning, going into a protective stance.

It was a camera. I flushed. The Hunter had stopped, looking amused, but also just a bit approving. "Good reflexes," she said shortly. "But get used to it. They're everywhere." Then she took off again, and I had to move fast to keep up.

This was just like the government building, same floor, walls, and ceiling, same doors. More army construction. Evidently this Hunter was not inclined to chatter. We had covered a lot of corridor before she finally said, "I'm Hunter Karly; I've been assigned as your mentor. Understand, we don't take anything for granted here, we can't afford to. People have died in the past because we accepted that someone from outside Apex was properly trained, and he wasn't. Just because you stood up well at the train—well, sorry, girl. It could have been a fluke. You could have gotten lucky. We need to know your skill set, we need to know you're sharp, and we need to know you can handle yourself solo all the time."

"Yes, Senior Hunter," I said. Really, this just made sense. I mean, I resented it, of course, because I had been Hunting solo for years, but I couldn't exactly say that now, could I? So . . . I'd show them what I could do. It would just take time.

"I'll be your mentor in the field until you prove yourself out. And right now, we're going to your intake interview and orientation."

I nodded as she glanced at me.

"And after that, you go to refitting with me. When you're done, I'll take you to quarters, or to the mess hall, whichever you'll need first." She glanced down at my arms and added, "I see the prefect gave you a Perscom. A floor plan of HQ will be on it—"

*Aha!* Before she continued, I twisted my wrist so I could look at the faceplate and said "Map." Instantly the map came up, with the rooms we were passing labeled, a little dot representing me moving along the corridor.

"Good. You're not a *complete* turnip," she said with more amusement. I decided to test the waters with a little comeback.

"No, Senior Hunter," I replied. "I fell off the truck a month or two ago, not yesterday."

I got the reaction I was hoping for, a barked laugh. "We'll get along," she said, with enough warmth in her voice I felt able to relax a little. "And—here you are."

She stopped beside a door with a nameplate beside it. *Rikard Severn, Senior Analyst, Personnel and Human Resources.* Ugh. It sounded like one of those pre-Diseray office things. She nodded at me. I reached for the doorknob and went in.

The office looked like that of my uncle's receptionist, only smaller. Severn sat behind a similar desk with a single chair on my side of it. He looked like any of the office-dweller Cits I had seen on the train; relatively subdued suit in shades of muted blue, and a face that looked like it had been homogenized by software, with nondescript, mousy hair. I remained standing until he looked up and said, "You may sit down, Hunter Candidate."

*Hunter Candidate, hmm?* That was interesting. I took the chair.

"This is mostly a formality, given your rather impressive impromptu display on the trip to the city," he said, making notes on a cyberslate. "How long have you been Hunting?"

"With Powers or without, sir?" I answered politely. Time to repeat what I'd already told others.

Now he looked up. "Excuse me?" he said, blinking at me as if this was not what he had expected.

"We're all alone out there on the Mountain, sir," I said politely. "We don't have all this . . ." I waved my hand to indicate everything around me. Then I explained just as I had to the steward on the train. "So, with Powers . . . about a half yearish."

"Everyone . . . Hunts . . ." He stared at me and shook his head. "And who taught you the use of your Powers?"

"Should be on your register, sir," I said. This was a safe answer; the Hunter assigned to the region where the Monastery was. Of course, the truth was the poor beggar was as mad as they come; within days of showing up, one of the Folk had turned his brain inside out, so the monks never got a chance to convert him to the Mountain ways. He never even got as far as our village before they had to take him in and put him in a nice padded little room where he was drooling and playing with his toes even now. We send back his reports for him, of course. "Hunter Pieter Sanders." I sighed. "He wasn't...very good. I learned more on my own, once I had the basics." Of course he wasn't very good. That was why he'd been sent to us in the first place, and why the Folk had melted his melon for him. We knew that much out on the Mountain. When allotment quarterlies came, we always got the fourth-hand equipment, the stuff and people no one else wanted. Good thing we didn't care, and really didn't need it.

Severn's lips twisted a little wryly, but he said nothing.

"We understand, sir," I said humbly. "Apex City is a lot more important than we are, and the Othersiders can't go above the snow line for long, so it isn't often we have to worry about direct attacks." Now I raised my chin a little. "After the attack on the train, I understand that even better, sir. I'm proud you sent for me, and I hope I can live up to your expectations." That was truth. I didn't like it here, I did want to go home, but home had a lot of Hunters and it had the monks and the Masters. I wasn't at all sure *why* Apex needed to be the central location for all the best Hunters, if they hadn't had an incursion in years, but...maybe Karly would answer that later. In the meantime, the best thing I could do for Uncle and the Mountain was play along. "I'm ready to serve and protect."

He laughed. "There are no cameras in here, Hunter Candidate. You can save—"

Then he really *looked* at me. "You mean that, don't you?" He sounded...shocked.

"I do, sir." I was baffled. *Of course* I meant it! There is nothing—*nothing*—that is more important in a Hunter's life than protecting the Cits without Powers. And that wasn't something that had just been drummed into me by the monks and the Masters. That was something I felt just as bone-deep as I did my love for my Hounds and theirs for me.

"Wait here a moment," he said, and got up and left the room by a door behind his desk.

I felt eyes on me.

No cameras? Well, maybe not public ones. But there were cameras in here. And something I had just said had thrown him off. Karly said there were cameras everywhere; now I would bet there were plenty of cameras that weren't visible. I kept my Hunt face on.

I stilled my breathing and listened, hard. There were voices in the next room, and I thought one was Severn's. It didn't sound exactly like arguing, but something had gotten them worked up.

A moment later Severn came back. "All right, Hunter Candidate, I'm passing you on to the next phase." He opened that same door and waved me through. As I passed him, he called into the next room, "Armorer Kent, she's all yours."

# 6

A MOMENT LATER, I was facing the stranger from flat on my back on the floor. Before I could blink, he'd come at me. I'd been caught completely off guard.

He was sitting on me, laughing.

I lost my temper, but I hadn't lost my training. And he was slightly off balance, leaning over. I grabbed his neck with both hands and pulled, while I kicked myself into a back somersault with my legs. I managed to send him sailing over my head, and I kept my momentum going to get back to my feet. He was as quick as any of my Masters, though, and I wasn't balanced when he came at me again. This time since I knew he was coming for me, I moved as far off the line of attack as I could, and with his attack instead of against it. The momentum he gave me let me roll out of the way and get to my feet again. Then it was really on.

All I can say is, it's a good thing there wasn't any furniture in the room; it had a slightly padded dark gray floor and four light gray walls with a couple of metal cabinets set flush into the walls. Now, hand-to-hand is not what I'm good at; pretty much everything I have is primarily defensive and designed to get me *away* from my attacker. Aki-Do, mostly. I mean, really, back home, if I was in a position where I was close enough to a monster to need hand-to-hand, and my Hounds were nowhere around to help, I was pretty much in the deepest kind of trouble possible and aggressive hand-to-hand wasn't going to save me. There wasn't a lot of space in this room to get away, so I was kind of stuck in a fight I was definitely going to lose. We traded advantage back and forth for a little, but he was infinitely better than I was, and eventually he got me pinned, face in the carpet, arm twisted behind my back in the most painful of hanari holds. I banged on the floor with my free hand, and he let me up.

"Not bad," was all he said, as I stood up and pulled my clothing back into a semblance of neatness, then got my little bag from the doorway. As I did, I finally got a good look at him.

His outfit was half-purposeful—knee pads, elbow pads, shin guards, kidney belt, shoulder pads, and bracers all of scarlet and yellow—and half-fanciful. The clothing under the padding was scarlet and yellow, and another one of those odd, asymmetric styles; one long sleeve, one short, slashes of yellow through the scarlet, a shirt with an uneven hem, one boot that went over his knee, the other that ended at the ankle. He had a craggy face with heavy eyebrows, bright green eyes, and red hair that was cut short on the sides but long on the top and back. There were feathers attached to it at one side—long, thin feathers banded in scarlet and yellow. I'd guess him to be physically at late middle age, still a prime fighter, though his years? No way to guess that.

"Thank you, Senior Armorer," I said immediately, giving him the full bow I would have given one of the Masters. He laughed. His voice was dark and smoky.

"Nice. I could get used to being bowed to." He beckoned to me. "Come on. Your hand-to-hand is passable enough. Let's find out what else you can do."

The first thing he did was take me down another set of long corridors to a real armory, one that was a lot bigger than anything we had at home. Some of the weapons hanging on the walls or on racks didn't even *look* like weapons anyone sane would actually use. I couldn't identify what they were, even, just what they kind of looked like. There was a set of things with the hilts of swords, but with one to five long, flexible blades like whips. Seriously? How could you even pick up something like that without hurting yourself? There were not one, but *two* objects like very large knives that had three blades. One was more like a cross between a huge knife and a short spear, but the positioning of the blades was just really strange. The other had three blades in a sort of fan. I mean, *why?* There was a whip made out of chain—again, *why?* And things that looked like animal claws. And a circle of metal with the outside edge sharpened...

I couldn't even imagine how some of these could be used without doing more harm to yourself than to whatever you were trying to fight off.... Granted, they were all apparently made of what we call "Cold Iron"—which is iron forged with carbon and not much else in it, which messes badly with magic. So I suppose if you were stuck face-to-face with something that used magic, they might be useful. Maybe. But the way I was taught, the last thing a Hunter wants is to be up close to anything from the Otherside.

He waved at the racks. "Tell me what you recognize and what you know how to use, and how good you are with each one."

I was a little nervous, but mostly confident. I've been using weapons for years, after all. Mostly I wanted to make the senior armorer pleased with getting me. So I told him, in detail. Knives—both hand-to-hand and throwing—a sling, a sling-shot, a spear, a bow, a revolver, a shotgun, a hand crossbow, and a rifle. "I know how to use an automatic pistol, of course, both semi- and fully automatics, but what I am used to is a plain old six-shot revolver. We save the automatics for times and places where nothing else will do. The six-shots are easy to maintain, easy to make reloads for, and can be dropped in the mud and still work after. And to be frank, if you are facing off a single target that you can't drop with six shots, you are either in a situation where no gun will help you, or you have no business holding a gun in the first place."

He nodded. He didn't say anything, but it didn't seem as if he was unhappy about what I had told him.

"Does every dirt-digger up there know how to use what you do?"

I shrugged. "Pretty much, Senior Armorer. We start kids as soon as they want to learn, which can be pretty young. I was four when I picked up weapons. I was seven when they let me Hunt."

Truth, of course. Even though being above the snow line keeps the Othersiders off, it doesn't entirely stop them from trying to make lightning raids, especially the ones that can fly.

"What would have happened if I'd come in here without knowing all that, sir?" I asked after a moment.

"A lot of time spent in here, with instructors, and with me, learning how to use basic weapons," he replied.

Well. Uncle had said to ask the armorer. This seemed like the moment to do just that. "Sir? This ... I don't understand some—a lot—of what I saw on the train and I've been hearing about. Everyone getting vidded, all the time. Channels for Hunters. Trending? I just—" I waved my hands, helplessly.

He waved at me to follow, and I did, into another little office just off the armory. There were two chairs, one behind a desk and one in front. We both sat down.

By this time, I was getting hungry and thirsty. Breakfast had been a long time ago, and Uncle hadn't offered me anything to eat in his office. I've gone days without food, though, so I didn't say anything.

He opened a white cabinet in the wall next to the desk, and pulled out two bottles, then tossed me one. It was metal, cold, and full of icy, tasteless water. I was awfully glad of it. Hungry I can deal with; thirsty is harder.

"We have thousands and thousands of people all crowded together," he said. "Just to arm and train them all would be impractical. To keep them trained would be impossible."

That didn't seem to answer my question, but I kept my mouth shut and nodded.

"Imagine what all those people with arms right at hand would mean! Disputes between neighbors could turn into massacres."

Okay. I could see that. It was bad enough on the Mountain where everybody knew each other and fights got broken up real quick. All those strangers . . . it would never work. And that assumed that what got in across the Barriers was actually something that a hundred ordinary armed Cits could take down without someone, probably a lot of someones, getting hurt or killed. Our own folk on the Mountain make plenty of mistakes when they gang up on Othersiders. People get caught in cross-fire. People do stupid things. People try to be heroes. And *they* are used to working together, and it's never more than twenty or thirty at most.

"So that's why we do what we do and let them watch," he continued. He waved his hand at a camera up in a corner. "We're on camera most of the time, and each of us has a vid channel. We aren't the only ones who are, of course, you'll see."

He looked over my head for a moment, and I guessed he was thinking. "You're a smart girl. I think you'll understand this. When you put something dangerous on vid, it does something to the way people think about it."

I had to shake my head at that. I didn't get it, not yet, but I wasn't getting much time to think. "So," he said. "In the old days, there were sporting stars. Do you ever remember reading about those?"

"Uh . . . vaguely?" I replied. I did remember . . . something. Not much. Just that people were as famous for playing games as actors or musicians were.

"Well, we're sports stars. So we have . . . fans. People who follow what we do."

I gaped at him then.

"Trending means you are going up in popularity, like a sports star." *Just accept it,* I reminded myself. *Apex isn't the Mountain.*

"But what happens if things get really bad?" I asked. "What if a Hunter gets hurt, or even killed?"

"That doesn't happen too often," he replied. "But first of all, you aren't on a live feed, you're on a delay. That gives the controllers time to decide if what's happening should go out on your channel. It also gives them time to decide if you are in over your head. If so, they splice in footage of another Hunt, and send in the Hunter Elite."

I know my eyes went big when he said that. The Elite—the people who *could* take on a Drakken, or even a Folk Mage. The people who got shuttled to all the hotspots, to escort and protect refugees. The Elite were . . . well, epic. I hoped I'd get to meet some.

He smiled a little. "If you hit something you can't handle, or something entirely unexpected, you'll get pulled off the Hunt and the Elite will be sent in. Yes, there are Hunters who are hurt; it happens, people accept that. It's part of what keeps things *just* real enough that they don't turn around and demand that the government stop spending money to support us. But for a flat-out crisis situation, it's dealt with by the best of the best, and completely off camera unless the takedown is so smooth that it's to our advantage to show it."

Well . . . okay. That seemed sensible. Even if all the rest of it wasn't.

He spoke into his Perscom. "Ping Karly, the girl's ready for outfitting."

*Outfitting?*

Karly came in about a minute later and crooked her finger at me. I got up, bowed a little to the armorer, who again seemed amused by it, and followed her out. We went down another corridor to a room with a half dozen desks and computers in it.

"Now, don't take this the wrong way, but you can't wear—that stuff," Karly said, bringing up a screen that said *Outfitting.*

"This isn't my Hunt ge—" I began, but she interrupted me.

"No, listen to me, don't jaw. We're on vid. You see what I'm wearing, what Armorer Kent wears. Each of us has to have her own colors, and her own signature look. That's so people can tell, immediately, who it is they're looking at. And you need to wear outfits that look professional. Like the other Hunters wear, not like . . ." She didn't finish the sentence, but I got the picture. I wasn't supposed to look as if I just got brought in from the backwoods, even if I *was.* "Got that?"

If Armorer Kent hadn't just given me that talk, I don't think any of this would have made sense. As it was . . . well, it still didn't make *sense,* but I knew I had to accept it and go along with it.

She took my silence as agreement. "Right. First thing we need to do is pick your colors."

Well, the color combinations on the first, second, and even third page she showed me were . . . no. No way would I ever, ever have wanted to wear *anything* in those colors, *especially* not to Hunt. But finally, on the fourth page—

*"That!"* I said, stabbing my finger at the monitor.

"Charcoal, light gray, and silver-gray. Good choice." She tagged the combination, and moved it to a folder. "Now we pick some styles."

That got . . . ugh. Okay, please don't get me wrong. I *love* pretty things. I love new clothes. But . . . I'm used to getting maybe one new outfit a year, now that I've stopped growing. "Eat it up, wear it out, make it do or do without," is one of the sayings people back home live by. I wasn't used to being presented with page after page after page of Hunting gear, something called "casual wear," dresses . . .

It was bewildering and began to make my head hurt, or maybe that was hunger. Karly glanced at me, took pity on me, and said, "That'll do for now. I'll get you an outfit so you can get changed, and I'll show you the mess—that's where we eat."

All I heard at that point was "where we eat." Karly went out and came back a minute later.

I nearly lost my jaw when she presented me with one of the new outfits to put on. I mean, when had they had the time to make it?

It was more or less based on my old Hunter gear; I must have just picked it instinctively. I had a hooded tunic with a pointed hem dipping halfway to my knees, front and back, and long sleeves that had points over my hands. There was a very wide belt—I would have said a kidney belt, and it was made for use and protection, not just for show—that went over it, and an amazingly soft shirt that went under it. The tunic seemed to be made of suede leather, the belt of glove leather. Both were gray, but there were designs of stylized leaves in charcoal, edged in black, from the hem to about four inches deep on the tunic and two inches wide on the center of the belt. Then there were pants of the same suede with the leaves running up the outside of the leg, and boots that matched the belt.

Karly pointed me at a washroom to change in, and turned up just as I was pulling on the boots. I stood up quickly, stamped them into place, and gave her the nod of respect. "Senior Hunter," I said.

She said nothing, just walked around me. Even though we were both in leather, we couldn't have looked less alike. When she came back around in front, I could see she was smiling.

"You look good, kid," she said with approval. "Those are good colors on you."

I flushed. "I don't like bright colors," I said, faltering. "And . . . how could anyone ever Hunt in things like that?"

"Field gear is muted, and they 'hance the colors on the vid-feeds," she explained, and when I looked baffled, she elaborated. "What we wear to Hunt is just grayed-out versions of our colors. The editors in the vid-studios make the colors brighter before they send the feed out to the vid sets."

"Oh . . ." For a moment I felt foolish. Then I shook it off. It didn't matter. There was no way I wanted to wear things like the armorer did. "And this is all for the cameras?"

"Exactly. You're going to be on vid a lot, and it's important for your standings that you not be confused with anyone else." Karly looked at me as if she expected me to say something, but I just looked attentive. "Anyway, you are probably starving, I *am* starving, so let's go to the mess and I'll introduce you to your fellow Hunters." She snickered. "Good place to do it, since they'll have to choose between stuffing their faces and hazing you, and they'll likely pick stuffing their faces."

"But what about—"

"All your things were taken to your quarters," she said, anticipating me. "Don't worry, no one threw anything out."

Well that was a relief. I had the feeling that, nice as these things were, I would be wearing my comfortable old familiar stuff when I could.

# 7

THE MESS, OR MESS HALL, was a lot like our communal building in Safehaven, except this was clearly used only for eating, and
our community hall was used all the time, for anything where a
lot of people needed to get together. Schooling, quilting, sings,
dances, pretty much anything where more people wanted to gather
together than would fit in someone's house.

At the back of the room was something I recognized from
a couple of pictures in history books as a fancier version of our
food lines. When we have a communal dinner, everybody brings
dishes, they all get put on a counter, and you go along and help
yourself. This was the same, except that the food was all in steel
containers that were the same size, and the containers all fit into
a counter made for the purpose. Steam rising above it all told me
that the counter kept hot things hot, and probably cold things cold.
It looked like the same arrangement as at home: serve yourself.

Karly led me over to it, and I imitated her, getting a bright blue tray and some plain white china (all uniform; a lot different from our handmade stuff) and steel silverware, looking over the almost *obscene* amount of food on offer.

Hunters eat a lot. We burn a tremendous amount of calories. But there would have to be a couple hundred Hunters here to eat all this. And already I missed home food. Still, it was food, and there had been times when I would have eaten a brick if someone had buttered it first.

Karly was waiting for me at a table for two over at the far side of the room, against the wall. We had a good view of the room, without being out in front of everyone. Once we were seated, and I started eating, I noted the dozen or more cameras covering every angle. I was going to have to figure this out somehow. Were people just so bored that watching Hunters eat was entertaining?

"Why do they vid all the time?" I asked. I wanted to hear this from someone other than Armorer Kent. Maybe Karly would have an explanation that added something.

"So they make sure to catch it if anything interesting happens," Karly replied, and chuckled. "About ninety percent of it just gets chucked out. You'll get used to it. After a while you don't even notice the cams."

I was not at all sure about that.

There were a few people already here, and I tried to look them over without being obvious. I was pretty sure they were doing the same to me. "What are the others like? Are there Elite here?" I asked, my voice urgent. "I've—" Here came the lie. "I'm not used to being around other Hunters."

"Don't worry, you'll be fine." She chuckled, amused at my anxiety. "You'll see. Just relax, be yourself, and everything will be all right. And yes, the Elite live here too, but we don't see them too often, except for Kent."

Armorer Kent was Elite! I restrained myself and concentrated on my questions. Everything the armorer had told me seemed to be accurate so far, but I still had more questions. I bombarded Karly with them; what did it mean that she was my mentor? How long would that go on? Were there any other candidates here now or was everyone a full Hunter? After Karly had gotten about halfway through a big slab of what looked like vat-beef, she started talking in a low voice about the other Hunters that were here, eating. "Red, white, and blue: Hunter Lars. Lars is a practical joker but he means well. Purple, black, and red: Hunter Bendel. If Bendel weren't a Hunter, he'd probably be out doing something else stupidly dangerous. Blue, light blue, and gray: Hunter Garent. Garent is always trying out new magic spells, sometimes they work, sometimes they don't. White, gold, and silver: Hunter White Knight. He's a Christer, and we tend to use that name for him rather than his real one."

Hunter Knight stood out in the room, not only because of his colors, but because he was a very tall and muscular man despite the fact that he didn't look much older than me. He sat alone, and his white outfit featured an enormous gold and silver cross on the front and back. "Subtle," I said dryly. "I would never have guessed."

Karly smothered a snicker in a bread roll. "I've got no problem with him. Does his job, never shirks, and if he wants to harbor the delusion that his Hounds are Angels and it isn't magic he's doing but wielding Holy God-power, well, whatever gets the Othersiders dead works for me. He's not real popular with most of the others, though."

I could understand that. The Christers I knew only grudgingly accepted the protection of the Mountain, and they all seemed to cherish a bitter disappointment that the Diseray *hadn't* been the Apocalypse, and they hadn't gotten sucked up to Heaven. Kind of hard to blame them, when the world fell to pieces like they'd been told it would, but then none of the "good" parts happened like they'd been told they would, and they were left to stew with the rest of us unbelievers. The monks had pointed that out to me a couple of times, after I'd saved the Christers' bacon only to get sniffed at and looked down on. And also my own mentor had remarked that, given that no one had gotten whisked away by angels, that left them with two equally unpalatable conclusions: either all their prophets and books had lied to them, or they were *all* just as unworthy and sinful as us unbelievers. No good choices there, either way, for a true believer.

I didn't have to wonder which camp Hunter Knight was in. He'd be in the "unworthy" camp, or he wouldn't be here, wearing that cross. This was probably his idea of penance, or maybe of making himself worthy. He didn't look more than two or three years older than me, maybe less, very blond, and very uncomfortable in his own skin.

"And here comes trouble," Karly breathed as five Hunters entered in a group, with one of the tiny hovering cameras I'd heard of, but never seen before, and a reporter who was wearing a screaming red outfit.

The Hunter talking to the reporter wore gold, red, and white.

His white-blond hair was very long, and threaded with gold, red, and white feathers on one side. He even had a gold, red, and white starburst painted around one eye on the same side as the feathers. Not even the paint and the feathers could hide the fact that he was stunningly handsome, and I realized I had been seeing him, off and on, on the news feeds from Apex for the last several years. And here I had thought he was some sort of rockster, and not a Hunter at all.

"... not what I would call a *rival*," he was saying to the woman in red, who wasn't *quite* simpering at him. "She said herself it was all the doing of our brave soldiers in the armored car, that all she did was distract the Othersiders until they had a good shot. That's not exactly *Hunting*, now, is it?"

I realized, of course, that this was Ace and he was talking about me. Presumably cameras were even now trying to get my reaction to his words. I kept my expression bland, and looked at Karly rather than Ace. "Who else is in his pack?" I asked.

She smothered another snicker. "Pack. Good one. Rose, pink, and white is Hunter Cielle, who would very much like the world to think Ace adores her. Yellow, brown, and cream is Hunter Raynd. Green, blue, and silver is Hunter Bithen. Green, pale green, and yellow is Hunter Paules, Ace's younger brother, practically his shadow. See one, the other will be somewhere around. Orange, brown, and black is Hunter Tober."

Cielle was as pretty as Ace was stunning, her hair dyed pink to match her colors. Raynd was a haughty-faced, dark-haired, dark-skinned woman. Bithen was dark, bald, and sardonic, but I suspected that bald was a choice rather than genetics. Paules was a faded copy of Ace. Tober's hair might also have been dyed black to match his outfit; like Ace, he had feathers of his other two colors threaded into his hair.

Ace concluded his interview—which he had very much dominated—and sent the woman in red off with a wink that made her simper even more. Then he turned and scanned the room. And spotted me.

Oh great.

*Don't make any enemies,* I reminded myself. *Or, at least, don't make any that haven't already made up their minds.* This wasn't my first go-round with bullies. Even in the Monastery, kids turn up who are bullies, and sometimes it takes a while for the monks to weed them out or teach them civilized behavior. So even though my insides tensed up and I could *feel* adrenaline start buzzing through my system, I defaulted to my training when it came to situations like this. Don't be the one that acts. Be the one that takes that energy and turns it against the attacker.

He headed straight for us. No point in pretending not to notice. I sat up a little straighter and put on the blandest expression I could manage.

"So," he said sarcastically. "This is the new nova-star that's going to knock me off the number one spot. And what would be your name, now, turnip?"

I blinked at him mildly. "I'm very pleased to meet you, Senior Hunter Ace. My name is Joyeaux."

He tapped his chin as if he was trying to think of something. "Joyeaux, Joyeaux... something. Oh yes. *Charmand.* Nepotism, much?"

I clamped down on my temper. If I got too angry, my Hounds just might decide to cross on their own... which would be painful and inconvenient at best, and which Ace could decide was aggressive behavior at worst. "I don't think so, Senior Hunter," I said, truthfully. "I'd really rather not be here. Until today, I hadn't seen the prefect since I was four or five. And Apex City is amazing, but I'd really rather be at home. In fact, I told Prefect Charmand that I would rather stay and Hunt for the folk I've lived with most of my life, but he made me understand it was important that I come here."

He stared at me for a moment as if he couldn't quite believe what he was hearing. Then he barked a laugh. "I think you actually *mean* that!"

"I do, Senior Hunter," I replied very quietly, now holding back a surge of horrible homesickness instead of anger. "But since I'm here, I don't want to knock anybody anywhere. I just want to Hunt and get on."

He brought his face down to mine, snarling a little. "Well, if you want to *get on*, you'd better start talking about how you took out that Folk lord. Nobody's ever done that but a full Elite team." He nodded at my start. "That's right, the rest of the world thinks it was just Drakken and Gogs, but we got the real feed here. We know what you did—"

"Ace," Karly said, warning in her tone. "This isn't the time or the place."

"No—wait!" I interrupted, holding up my hand. "I guess it wasn't obvious from the feed. It's not that big a deal. The... Othersider wasn't dropped, he ran off. I told the truth: it wasn't *me* that chased him off, it was the Hellfires. And if you want to know what I did, I'll show you right here and now, but I don't know if the trick is ever going to work twice."

Ace was completely taken aback, which was something of a relief—and by this point everyone in the mess hall had started to gather around us. Good. Now he'd have a harder time trying to bully me. "Trick?" he said suspiciously.

I nodded. "Trick," I replied. "Where I come from, we don't have Hellfires or anything techy, so we have to learn how to use the least magic to get the most result. Look, I said I'd show you, and I can do that right now. Can one of you make a Wall or at least a Shield? It doesn't have to be Folk-strong, just enough for me to show what I did."

Ace looked around at his friends, but it was Knight who stepped forward. "I'll make one," he rumbled. He bowed his head for a moment and muttered something prayerful under his breath, and a good, strong Shield rose up around him.

"Right," I said, and stood up. "Look, this is what I did. Only I did it fast. This time, I'll do it real slow so you can all see everything."

I sketched out the Glyphs in the air that I would normally form only in my mind, and set that abrasive little spell to grinding away at Knight's shield. "You see? Just a little, little magic. Slow, subtle." I deliberately glowed it, to make it more visible, so you could see that there was something like a spinning disk right at belt-buckle level to Knight, and that it was etching its way through his Shield. "The Folk have got so much power that doing something small never even occurs to them, and this kind of thing just gets right in under their noses. If I'd tried blasting at his Wall, he'd only have made it stronger, or deflected what I was doing, or just kept making new layers of Wall under the old ones. Instead, I just nattered for time, and let this grind away until I had a hole for the Hellfires.

Then we all ducked." I shrugged. "Not exactly heroic, diving for cover under a pile of Hounds."

They were all gaping at me as if this approach was something that had never even occurred to them, either.

"Like I said . . . I wouldn't count on this working twice, or at least, not in the same way. It depends on if the Folk Mage figured out what I did, and if he tells someone else," I continued apologetically.

But at this point all the others were crowding in close, wanting to see it again. Knight stepped back, obviously uncomfortable now, and Ace took over the situation, ordering someone else to give me a Shield to grind. I let him. This allowed him to be the boss and get center stage again. If he wanted it that badly, I'd let him have it.

I repeated the spell more times before everyone was satisfied. Ace was now grinning as if I was a pet that had performed a particularly clever trick. When everyone had gone back to their tables (and I was hungry all over again) he reached out to me in a way that I read as non-threatening. I was right, he just mussed my hair a little, like you'd do with a youngster. "Not bad, kid," he said patronizingly. "Not bad at all. Thanks for the tip."

Like I said, I know bullies. Deflect, deflect, make them think they got their way even when they didn't, but never *actually* give in to them. Become innocuous, not worth tormenting or thinking about. *Become the landscape,* so Kedo put it. "My pleasure, Senior Hunter," I said deferentially as he walked away, heading for the serving line. I waited until he'd gotten what he wanted, then went back for something to replace the energy I'd expended.

Karly came with me, though all she got was a sweet of some

kind. When we sat back down, she was looking at me with a skeptical expression. I shrugged. "Deflection is more efficient than opposition," I said, quoting Master Kedo.

Surprisingly, she smiled. "All right. I was just hoping you weren't a coward."

I felt a little smoldering anger again. "If he ever actually picks a fight with me, I'll gladly assist his energies into a Folk-forsaken wall," I replied shortly. "I'd just rather not have to waste my time."

Now she grinned. "Finish up. I'll show you the way to your room. Your Perscom can take you from there."

It seemed there was something called a "residential section," and that was where we all had rooms. Well, I had expected a "room," but when my Perscom unlocked the door for me, it looked like what they gave us were what used to be called "apartments," a set of rooms for one person. A lot more than what I was used to.

I wandered around it for at least thirty minutes, marveling. It was . . . oh, more luxury than I had ever seen in my entire life.

I even had my own bathroom, which was the first thing I'd seen so far that made me like being here.

The three rooms were all decorated in the same shades of gray, and finally it dawned on me that these were *my* "colors," and how had they managed to *do* all that? It baffled—and in truth kind of scared me a little. People just weren't supposed to devote that much care and attention to any one person.

I'll admit it, though, it was really seductive. The shelves in the bathroom were loaded with all sorts of scents and lotions and cosmetics. There was a cool-unit in the same room that had the vid-unit, a couch, a couple of chairs, and a couple of little tables with some vaguely abstract objects on them. The cool-unit had bottles of chilled water and fruit and sweets, and over it was a cabinet with wasabi peas and nuts and things in jars, a thing that gave me instant boiling-hot water, and some canisters of herbal teas and a brown powder that I tasted and discovered was the powder they made that Chocolike out of. Nice.

There was a second vid-screen in the bedroom; the bedroom itself was much, much bigger than my little room at the Monastery. My bedroom back home was just barely big enough for my bed and the chest that held my clothes. This room was not *quite* big enough to feel too big. The bed was large enough for two people—or four, if you were a family trying to sleep warm that night. There was plenty of room around the bed to walk, and there were little tables on either side of the headboard. The vid-screen was mounted on the wall across from the foot of the bed. The bed itself looked like a futon, but it was made of something else entirely. I didn't know what it was, but it yielded to me, then supported me, just like that chair had, and there was a charcoal-gray blanket made of the same soft stuff that the cocoons in the train had been made of. Obviously no one would actually need a blanket here, since this was a building where the temperature never varied, so the only reason it was there was for the look and feel. The closet (which was about the size of my old bedroom at home), to my intense relief, had all my old clothes (including the outfit I had changed out of in the washroom, all cleaned and hung up), but in front, to my discomfort, there was three times that much in brand-new stuff in my colors—some obviously Hunting gear, but some . . . well, it looked as if someone had decided I needed a whole lot more clothing than I remembered choosing. More unease. More feeling of wrongness, of *Koyaanisqatsi*—"life out of balance."

The first thing I did was take a good long hot shower, and while I was doing that, carefully sampled the soaps and scents, ending up rejecting most of them. Hey, I like smelling nice; I just want to smell the way *I* want to smell. I found a lotion I liked: simple, herbal. The makeup kind of tempted me—who doesn't like to look pretty?—but I didn't know how to use it. I'd figure it out later. It wasn't anything like the homemade stuff we had back home.

This was an upside-down version of what my evening would have been at home. There would have been a very simple meal with the Masters and the monks and the other Hunters, and we'd all eat the same thing. Everyone but the Hunters took turns cooking and cleaning up; even if you hadn't run into any Othersiders that day, patrolling was hard work, and in winter, it was harder still, so we were let off from doing most chore work. Then we'd all go down to the community hall to see if there was vid we were supposed to watch, and if not, there'd be some music, maybe, or someone would pick an hour or so of programming, or we'd play one of the old vids from the library or new ones from the mail. I'd talk with my friends, or we'd play a game. A lot of the girls brought fancy-work with them, since the lights at the community hall were better than the ones in most peoples' houses. The Hunters would mostly leave early; we needed sleep as much as we needed food. Since the Monastery and our village, Safehaven, is above the snow line and it was always cold, I'd pick up a warming pan and get some coals from the fire at the entrance to the cells and stick it in my bed while I got undressed. In winter I tended to go straight to sleep, but in summer, sometimes I would lie awake a while, and look out my window. Sometimes there was a moon and stars. Sometimes there was a storm. Always there was the snow, that promise that nothing much would dare come up here.

But, like I said . . . upside down. I turned off all the lights in the other rooms, pulled on the pair of soft pants and top that had been waiting for me on the bed, got a bottle of water, and turned on the vid. Even though it felt really, really strange to be watching vid all alone, and to be watching vid and not have to think about how much power it was going to use. Because I wanted to get to the bottom of something.

I started scrolling through the channels. Channels and channels . . . it was crazy how many there were. It was when I got to *H* that I felt absolutely stunned, because . . . okay, there was a Hunters channel, which was what I had expected, given what I'd been told. But there was also a channel for each and every Hunter I'd seen today and a whole lot more. I picked Ace's, and was assaulted by loud music. He was somewhere dark, but with a lot of flashing lights, and a lot of people, dancing. A little message at the bottom advised me this was a live feed.

The cameras *did* follow us everywhere.

I had to; I picked my channel. I mean, who wouldn't, right? I was almost expecting to see myself on the bed, but to my relief, it was just the interview I'd given to the military debriefer on the train, followed by when I was showing the other Hunters how to grind down a Shield. Not much of that; you couldn't really see the magic unless you had the Eye, and that went with being a Hunter, so it would be really boring to someone who wasn't a mage. Then it cycled to the edited encounter with the Othersiders. That's when I found out I was already number nine in the top ten Hunters.

No wonder Ace was annoyed.

I cycled through some of the other Hunter channels. The main one was a summary with clips of what everyone had been doing, and some sort of rankings thing, and some talking heads talking gossip. The individuals had live feed if they were doing something interesting, like Ace was, or interviews or dockues or old feed if they weren't. And always, so often it was starting to sound like a mantra, there was that little fanfare, followed by the AT and Apex logos, and the same voice saying, "And that's *your* Hunters on the job! Keeping Apex and the Territories *safe!*"

I remembered something another of my Masters had once said. *Be careful when someone repeats something too often; things that are repeated often enough can start to seem to be true, even when they are not.* So . . . this was getting repeated over and over.

Meaning? That we had to convince the Cits that we could always keep them safe. To do that . . . maybe that was what the sports-star stuff was all about. It would trivialize what we did, sure, but it would make the Cits feel everything was all right, when not only were the Cits not safe outside the Barriers, but they weren't all that safe inside them, either.

Did Uncle know? He had to. He was in charge of all the Hunters that weren't with the army. Was this something else he'd been trying to warn me about?

Apex was *full* of more people than I could imagine. Lots and lots of people, all crowded together. And if they were constantly on edge, waiting for something to get in over the Barrier and attack—

I closed my eyes a minute, trying to think it all through. All right, think of them like a—a herd of deer. Deer are always on edge, always ready to be attacked. Just crack a stick when walking, and *poof*, they're gone, in a panic. And all those Cits, on edge, all the time . . . if they even *thought* there was an attack, they'd go running off in all directions. Running into danger, getting in the way of Hunters, throwing whatever was supposed to be going on into utter chaos.

And then, well, then they'd exhaust the fear, and *not* react when there *was* danger. The only way to prevent that was to make them feel everything was under control. But if you made Hunting seem more entertainment than it was protection . . .

Gladiators. We were gladiators. To make the Cits forget that Apex was under siege. To make them think that defeating things was . . . well, not *easy*, but a sport. Like a shooting contest where occasionally someone got a little bloody. To make them think that the things that did get past the Barriers were trivial, and no more dangerous than a bad dog. So if they happened to see a Hunter out there in their neighborhood, taking down something, they wouldn't run screaming for the nearest shelter and scare everyone else around.

I turned my attention back to the feed. It boggled me to think how much time was spent just putting these feeds together. And how many people watched them? Everyone? It couldn't be everyone, there were too many channels. But evidently, it was a lot of people.

The . . . strangeness, the intrusion of it, hit me at that point and made me feel all cold inside. This *thing* that we Hunters were here for . . . this wasn't clear-cut and simple, the way it was at home. At one level, I was still a Hunter, but on another, I was supposed to deceive all those people, make them think something that just wasn't true. I wasn't used to lying. And to have my life itself be a lie . . . not all the private bathrooms in the world could have made me want to stay here if someone had given me the chance to go. I wanted to curl up in a ball of misery and cry, and there was no reason why I shouldn't, but there was also no reason why I had to do it alone.

I drew the Glyphs and opened the Way, and Bya walked slowly through it in his dog-shape, gave me a long look, and then jumped up on the bed with me. I put my arms around him; of course, the moment I did, he knew everything that was wrong and settled down. I cried into his silky fur and finally fell asleep with my head on his shoulder.

When I woke up, it was in complete, black dark. That alone would have told me where I was, if I wasn't always aware of my surroundings. But nothing could have hammered home the difference between here and there more than that darkness.

I lived in a box with no windows now. Like a toy someone had carefully put away until wanted.

# 8

I SLEPT AGAIN. Then, same as ever, even though the bedroom didn't have a window to the outside, I woke up at dawn, or close enough to dawn as made very little difference. Bya was gone, of course. I was always on dayshift on the Mountain, and waking at dawn was something that was as much a part of me now as the Mandalas on the backs of my hands. The black dark was a little off-putting, and it took me a minute to fumble my way to the light switch in the headboard of the bed, but after that I got back on track. It didn't take me long to get ready, and once I had, I checked my Perscom. "Schedule," I said, assuming there would be such a thing. I was right. The Perscom obliged, showing me that I was supposed to report to the armory in two hours. Just then a soft chime went off in the whole suite, followed by an impersonal female voice. *"Hunter Joyeaux is due in the armory at oh eight hundred hours,"* it said. Well, so this was the equivalent of the Monastery bells. At least I wouldn't oversleep.

I reminded myself that I was still a Hunter. I still had the same job, and maybe what I was doing was even more important, since the Cits didn't have a clue.

I followed the map to the mess; there was almost no one in it. Only me and Knight. I decided that an ally wouldn't come amiss, if he'd unbend to me, so before I got my rise-meal, I went over to him. He nodded, then looked surprised when I didn't head for the food line.

"I didn't get a chance to thank you for helping me out yesterday, Senior Hunter," I said, with just a touch of formality. "I apologize for my poor manners."

He looked at me as if I had grown a second head. "You're welcome. Is everyone so mannered where you come from?"

I smiled. "We'd get smacked if we weren't," I said.

He laughed. He looked entirely different when he wasn't dour. He actually looked like some of the pictures in the King Arthur book I read once. "Well, you probably shouldn't be polite to me," he said. "I'm a ranker, but not very popular with the other Hunters."

I shrugged. "The other Hunters probably never had much to do with a Christer, but there's three villages of your people in my old Hunting territory. We got along. I don't see any reason why you and I shouldn't. Besides, where some of this comes in, I *am* a turnip, and I reckon you'll be more inclined to explain than Ace."

He regarded me thoughtfully for a long moment. "All right," he said finally. "Go get your breakfast and come ask your questions."

I did. Thanks be, there was stuff there I knew. Eggs were good, and real, and so were fried potatoes. I filled my tray and came and sat down across from him. He put his own empty tray aside, folded his arms, and waited for me to ask something.

"Rankers, trending, all the Hunter feeds on the vid," I said as I sat down. "The armorer explained how we're supposed to be making the Cits feel safe. So what's a ranker, and what's trending, and how can anyone watch all those channels?"

He snorted. "Rankers. We're all ranked by popularity, and that's determined by how much our channels get watched. We're gladiators of a sort. You know what gladiators were?"

I nodded, my mouth full.

"Trending means you're going up in the ranking. Some other cities have Hunters showy enough to get some feed here as well. They have a channel for each Hunter, and for anyone else who's popular: musicians, artists, dancers, actors." He shook his head. "Other channels come and go, but they always have one for each Hunter, and one channel for the Elite teams. There's an entire industry just built around making things to put on the individual Hunter channels."

"That's—crazy—"

"It's not as hard as you think. If you watch, unless there's a live feed, there's generally no more than two hours' worth of actual stuff, then the channel repeats. I'm fairly sure it's all designed to keep regular working people—not ones with money, who could go places and do things—inside and watching during all of their free hours. They actually *are* safe if they do that, and watching is passive. Passive people don't ask questions. Passive people don't even think of questions to ask. They just accept that they are perfectly safe, no matter what, and that all the fighting Othersiders they see is something that could never endanger them, even if they recognize the area." He took a bite. "Mostly, though, they won't. Only rarely do things get as far as sectors where people are actually walking around outside, and you'll discover that most people think that some or all of it's fake."

I had to blink at that. Knight was *smart*. I don't know if I would have been able to work that out for myself.

"There are about a hundred Hunters here, not counting the Elites," he continued. "Sometimes more, never less. We run on three shifts, and there are about two dozen of us that are popular enough to be called rankers."

*So—that was what that word meant.* "And they vid everything?" I said faintly.

He made a face. Mind you, it wasn't really noticeable, but I'm trained to catch little things. "Everything. And when there isn't something juicy, the talking heads will speculate and hint. So watch what you say and do, or the next thing you know, they'll be turning you and Karly into a couple."

I wanted to face-plant into my eggs. "Oh god," I groaned. "It's worse than back-fencer gossip...."

"It's back-fencing on a big, anonymous scale, because everyone doing all the gossiping on the 'puter net hides behind IDs, and no one's accountable for what they say." He shook his head. "It isn't just Apex that gets the feeds, and it isn't just the Hunters at Apex that have channels, but Apex is..." He searched for a word.

"The Apex," I supplied. "Like Holly-woods was before the Diseray."

"*Dies Irae,*" he corrected with a slight frown. "You unbelievers always get it wrong."

"The Diseray? That's what everyone calls it—" I looked at him askance. "Except you Christers? What'd you say again?"

"*Dee-es Ear-ray,*" he replied, sounding it out. "It obviously wasn't the Apocalypse since not one person got Raptured, so it had to be something else. *Dies Irae* means 'Wrath of God.'"

Well, this was news to me. Of course, even though I Hunted for the Christers, they were all pretty closemouthed around us "unbelievers." They didn't like to talk about their religion *at all* to outsiders. Especially they didn't like to talk about it to the folks from Safehaven and the Monastery. Maybe because their Big Moment had turned out to be such a letdown, and we Hunters and the army were the ones that had pulled their bacon out of the fire.

"See, now, that's one reason why people don't like you," I said mildly, and took a bite of apple. "That 'unbeliever' business. It's very unfriendly. You Christers act as if the only people in the world that believe in anything is you. Other people believe. They might not believe in the exact same thing as you do, but they still *believe*, and telling them they don't is unmannerly, not to mention wrong." I waited to see if he was going to take anger at that. It was something I had been dying to say to a Christer's face since the day I'd first met one.

He stared at me as if every word that had come out of my mouth had been so completely unexpected that he didn't know how to respond to what I'd said. Finally he began to chuckle. "You're very blunt, Joyeaux Charmand."

"A Hunter who wastes time in beating around the bush generally becomes a dead Hunter," I pointed out. "Is it true you call your Hounds 'angels'?"

"Only to annoy people like Ace," he admitted. "And make the home-folk happy. Although they have wings, and they are mightily handsome."

I was envious. "Yours *fly*? Mine don't. I've asked them to, but Bya says they don't do that."

"Yours *talk*? Mine won't. I wish they did. Every time they want to tell me things, we have to go through a game of Twenty Questions." He traced crude Mandalas on the tabletop with a wet finger. "Given a choice between fly and talk, I'd take talk."

"Good point." I thought over my first day, and wondered how his had been. A whole lot harder than mine, for certain-sure. "Why are you here, anyway?"

"Same as you, I got told to come. Or maybe not quite the same as you, my people were told that either I came or some of their shipments were going to get delayed." His face darkened. "But we're closer to Apex than you are, out there in the west, so we already had a good idea that I was going to get that sort of *encouragement*. Preacher did some negotiating, so I guess my people got a better deal than just bending over for the blackmail whip."

"I'm sorry," I said softly, meaning it. "But why would they do such a thing?"

"Because my Hounds and I are holy terrors on the Othersiders, and even if most of the Cits think of us as entertainment, Apex *needs* the best Hunters." He wiped out his tracings with the flat of his hand. "If you didn't get it from the armorer, I'll tell you now. It's a constant state of siege outside the Barriers. The Othersiders never forget that Apex is the target to take down if they want to conquer the whole continent. Don't you forget it, either. No matter what people outside these four walls think, not all the Hellfire missiles in the arsenal will keep them safe without Hunters. The Elite take out the big stuff, but there aren't a lot of the Elite, and often as not they're handling things Cits aren't supposed to know about. We're needed as much as they are, if not more."

"But what about the—" I sensed someone approaching from behind.

"Morning, Knight," said Karly. "You want me to answer that?"

Knight spread his hands. "Morning, Karly. She's your responsibility. Be my guest, unless you think I'd do a better job."

Karly put her tray down at our table, and it didn't look like she'd taken offense. "Did you warn her that unless she's into that, she'd better go all young and innocent-eyed and sexless as a baby doll, or the flacks will pair us up?"

I blushed. Knight got a little lopsided smile. "Something like that," he admitted. He turned to me. "What the Cits haven't figured out yet, and no one is saying out loud, is some of the really deadly but smaller Othersiders can get through the outermost Barriers, the ones way out there at the edges of the farming fields. Actually *through* them. Then they find ways over and under the Prime Barrier."

I felt my eyes go wide, and I felt my insides go to ice. "*What?*" I blurted. Because . . . well, that was supposed to be impossible! I mean, I knew there were ways of sneaking *around* the Barriers, or getting under or even over them, but *through*?

Both Knight and Karly nodded. "That's why we have the army out on the farms and patrolling all the perimeters. And there are the Elite Hunters too. Things go down bad, now and again the Elites get scrambled *inside* the outermost Barrier as well as outside of it." Knight was sober-faced. "They get vidded, but it doesn't always get shown, and when it does, it always gets reported as being shot outside all the Barriers."

No wonder the government was so worried about people being sure they were safe.

"There's not been any drop in the numbers of kills," Knight continued. "Not since I've been here. Granted, it's not Drakken and Gogs but the ones that are horse-size and smaller—"

"They're the smart ones," I finished for him. "That's not good."

Knight picked up. "And the Psimon are always scanning for things that have gotten in and might be hiding, and there's a special cadre among the APD that's always looking for signs of Othersiders in hiding. And there's us. Because our Hounds can sniff the scent with no problem, so we're encouraged to go out and show ourselves—"

I was startled yet again. The Psimon were scanning inside Prime Barrier for Othersiders? Could that mean they were watching for . . . Folk? *Inside* the Prime Barrier?

Knight glanced up at one of the corner cameras. "I've been here as long as is reasonable if we're going to pretend this is just the only three up at this hour sharing an idle chat over Caffeelike. Good Hunting to you."

*Pretend?* Then, well, it made sense. They were editing everything we said and did, so yeah.

Karly tendered me a sympathetic look as Knight sketched a formal salute and marched out of the room. He really lived up to his Hunting name. His outfit somehow suggested armor, and he never seemed to just *walk* anywhere. I sighed again and looked down glumly into my juice.

"I hate all of this," I said. "The vidding, the star stuff, and the secrecy. But I hate being away from home, and I expect I'm just going to have to get used to all of it. People need to be protected, and that's what we do."

"Good attitude." Karly nodded. "And now you know why your first several shifts are going to be inside the Prime Barrier. What're your weapons?"

"When I can choose?" I thought about that. "Any need for silence?"

"Sometimes." She watched me. I sensed this was another test.

"Hand crossbow for silence, nine-mil auto if we aren't going anywhere dirty, six-shot revolver if we are, couple of throwing knives for backup, shotgun with deer slugs for anything the hand-gun won't take down." I regarded her steadily.

She nodded. "That and the ammo is a reasonable load-out. I'll let the armory know; they'll make up our day packs. When you solo, you'll check your assigned territory, make your weapon deci-sions, and do the same for yourself. You ready?"

I stood up. "As I'll ever be."

Our assignment was inside the Barriers, in the area that Uncle had pointed out to me from his office: the part of Apex that held what the Cits here called the "city farms." Nothing like farms, of course; big hydroponic greenhouses with tilapia tanks, big blank buildings where they built cloned meat and vegetables in vats. Vat-grown was what most people got, and there were grades of that, because as the parent cells aged, the quality and flavor degraded. First run off the cow or the carrot was best; by the time you got to fifth or sixth run, everything had to be enhanced with artificial flavors and colors. That was why the vat-farms kept the real things on hand, in protected conditions that were nothing like what I would call a farm, so they could take samples for new batches all the time.

"This makes this part of Apex a big target, though," Karly pointed out, as we stood on a little platform that gave us a good view over the small pastures that held a few cattle, sheep, pigs, and fowl.

"Easy kills, for things that eat meat," I observed. "No place for the critters to run or hide."

Karly nodded and hopped down off the platform. I followed. The Hounds were milling in that sort of restless pattern around me that meant they were alert but didn't actually sense anything yet. They'd reverted to the greyhound shape for now. Karly's Hounds— she only had four—looked like wolves carved out of a block of shadow. Somehow they didn't quite look three-dimensional. She directed them with little hand signals.

"How spooked would these meat-sacks get if I sent the Hounds among them?" I asked.

Karly snorted. "Not. They're used to Hounds in the first place, and in the second, they're about as bright as bricks."

I nodded. Bya looked up at me, mouth open a little in anticipation.

"Search," I told him and the others. "Stay in range." That meant they weren't to go farther away than a bullet would reach. A lot of the Othersiders just laugh off bullets, but a lot don't. Rule of thumb is that if it's not one of the Folk, the smaller an Othersider is, the more likely it will be that a bullet or at least something made of ferrous metal will end it. All our bullets have steel jackets, shotguns have steel slugs or steel shot. The Othersiders get badly hurt by anything with iron or steel in it. Back in the Diseray, people discovered that by accident, and then found old folk tales and books that said the same thing about "supernatural" critters. That was when the army started *seriously* hunting for libraries and looting anything that was folklore, traditional tales, myths, and fantasy. A whole lot of it proved out true, too. It all got incorporated into Hunter and Magician training.

The Hounds spread out across the neat patchwork of enclosures, quartering the fields as Karly and I moved along, all their senses alert for Othersiders. We were alert too; the Hounds are awesome, but the Othersiders are crafty, and some of them can pull all sorts of tricks of popping in and out of our real-space. *Bamphing* is what we call it. My Hounds can do that too. Not all Hounds can, but mine do.

All the time, in the back of my mind, there was this thought: *could* the Folk get in here, inside the Prime Barrier? I had to keep reminding myself that even if they could, this was absolutely no different from Hunting at home, where there were no Barriers and the Folk could *always* get to us if they cared to.

We quartered over the pasture-pens without any more incident than scaring up and putting down a few Hobs. That was predictable; Hobs are like roaches, you never really get rid of them. Hobs look like little shrunken people, bent over and hairless, about the size of a rabbit. They wear clothing, which a lot of Othersiders don't—pointed hats, leather pants, wooden shoes, and shabby linen tunics. Every so often I'd see some movement in my peripheral vision and turn quickly only to realize it was a hovering cam. I was never going to get used to that.

When we had covered the pastures and gone over every inch of ground between the buildings, Karly waved me over to a round hatch in the ground. "Storm sewers," she said. "Don't worry, nothing worse down there than runoff water. And lighted so the cams can see. But if there's anything that got under or over the Barriers last night, it'll have ducked down here to wait out the day."

I eyed the hatch dubiously. At home, the only underground places big enough to prowl through are our own basements and some mines. I never liked Hunting the mines.

Still, I didn't have any choice, since that was part of the assigned territory. With more than a few second thoughts, I waited while Karly hauled the hatch open, then followed her down the ladder inside.

I didn't know what to expect, but to my surprise, it was a big sort of cement tunnel, about nine feet in diameter, with just a runnel of water in the bottom. It smelled like stagnant water, but no worse than that. And it was lit really well. I hadn't in the least expected that.

Karly caught me staring at the lights and nodded wryly at them. "Hard to fly a cam down here. And hard to vid in the dark."

Well, of course, that made sense. This was all part of Hunting, and those weren't just lights, those were light and cam rigs, all for the benefit of our audience.

Once we were in the tube, our Hounds came down. Karly's jumped, but not mine. They just apported. *Bamphing*. "They'd never give Knight this territory," Karly said as we started our patrol. "His Hounds wouldn't work well down here. Good in the open air, though."

I was about to ask what Knight's Hounds looked like, when Bya growled and I felt a sort of warning tingle all over. And then I heard the little *tap-tap.*

"Knockers!" I shouted, "Shields!" I threw my own up, and as it snapped into place, saw the egg-shaped distortion in the air around Karly that told me she had gotten hers up. The Hounds went on alert and down the tunnel toward us poured a gray-and-brown flood of wizened little humanish things about knee-high to me, like mostly naked, bent-over old men, scraggle-haired, ugly as broken concrete, and all armed with flint-tipped weapons, nasty stone hammers, and needle-sharp teeth.

"The *hell?*" Karly yelped, which told me she'd never seen Knockers before. But I had. The Hounds and I had fought them so often I didn't even need to give orders.

The great lighting down here gave us *way* more warning time than we'd have had in the mine tunnels. With our primary shields up, we couldn't be knocked silly by the paralyzing *fear* that the Knockers induce. I didn't like to think what would have happened to some poor Cit doing maintenance, or Apex Police Department down here. My Hounds flattened themselves against the wall of the tunnel, and, taking their cue from mine, so did Karly's. I unloaded the shotgun, reloaded, and unloaded it again. The entire front rank went *splatter* as the heavy slugs hit them, the next rank or two got bowled over, tumbling into the horde behind, and they all tangled up for a few precious moments in a tumble of blood-spattered nasty. Bya and Dusana *bamphed* to a point just behind the pileup, and the rest spread themselves between me and the Knockers. I shoved Karly against the side of the tunnel and threw up stronger shields around us both. Then, as one, my Hounds belched out fire.

This wasn't the pretty stuff they'd played with on the train. This was great, roaring gouts of hell-mouth just like the stuff that comes out of a flame-thrower. Caught between fire in front and fire behind, the Knockers screamed in a thousand voices. Some tried blindly to run, but there was nowhere to run to; the ones that the fire didn't get, Karly's Hounds and our guns did, and it didn't take long for them to stumble and fall onto the concrete with the others, writhing horribly and screaming until they died. The backwash of heat was enough to scorch your skin, which was why I had shoved Karly against the wall and shielded us both with magic.

It was over in maybe two minutes. The Hounds snapped their mouths closed, cutting off the flames. Dusana leapt over the black-ened corpses to join us. Bya lifted his leg and pissed on one before doing the same.

Karly, of course, was already poking at one of the Knockers, seasoned Hunter that she was. "The *hell* are these?" she asked, looking at me.

"Knockers, or Tommyknockers. They live in caves and mines," I said briefly. "And they just can't keep from giving themselves away by tapping on the walls with the hammers before they attack."

Karly shook her head. "I probably read about them in a brief-ing at some point . . . but I have *never* seen these things before, not in person, and not in vid. The hell?"

"I'm from the western mountains," I reminded her. "Some have old silver mines with enough still in them worth looking for, some copper, and lead."

"Not a lot of mines around here," she pointed out. "Please tell me these things don't make their own tunnels. . . ."

"Not that I ever heard," was all I could tell her. "The only time I ever saw them was when we were asked to go in and clean them out." As Othersiders went, they weren't dangerous to a Hunter who was forewarned, but a swarm of them could be lethal if you weren't prepared for them. But for anyone but a Hunter, like a regular Cit, or even a heavily armed policeman? Toast. Because like many Othersiders, the Knockers have a weapon that is magic *and* psionic in nature—in their case, the ability to induce terror. Other sorts of critters have seduction; some can make you giddy, or laugh hysterically. You get hit with one of those psionic or magic offenses, and they can easily get the drop on you.

A Psimon would be able to shield against the psionic weapons—but not the magic and certainly not the teeth, the claws, the numbers. And a Psimon has another little problem; a Magician, like me, can start the spell going and forget it. A Psimon has to constantly concentrate on what he's doing to keep his defense active. That's why Psimons never go Hunting without at least a squad of regular military.

"So they're only in mines?" Karly asked, poking one with a toe.

"Or caves. Definitely tunnels underground," I told her. "We've never seen them in the light of day."

Of course, hardly anyone mines anymore. If you need metal, you go get it from a Diseray ruin, or a pre-Diseray junkyard or trash site. There's precious metals in our mines, though, and gold and silver are something you don't usually find in ruins unless you come upon a jewelry place that somehow escaped a couple centuries of humans and Othersiders looting. "They swarm like bees,"

I added, and poked at one of the smoking corpses with the tip of my shotgun barrel. "The queen was in there, more than likely, and more than likely this was a swarm that was looking for a home."

Karly made some notes on her Perscom while I was talking. When she finished, she swung her shotgun off her back into a position where she could use it. "You'll have made your rating today, kid," she said wryly as we both stepped around the edges of the pile of bodies. They smelled like baked algae and hot rock. "And, thank you kindly, you'll have raised mine. I can put in for that bathroom upgrade now."

The rest of the sweep was not nearly as eventful as the swarm. Our Hounds sniffed out some giant bug things and killed them with claw swipes, adamantly refusing to bite them. We shot a couple more Knockers, strays or scouts, maybe. Eventually there was no sign of any more Knockers. I could see Karly starting to relax as we doubled back and climbed the ladder to the surface.

Part of me wanted to follow her lead and relax a little too. After all, we'd already swept the area above before we came down here. And anything we'd missed—or anything that might turn up— would be no more dangerous than a wild dog or a cougar. Right?

But the rest of me never, ever relaxes unless I am in some deeply warded or otherwise protected place like the Monastery or the Hunter headquarters. And even then, there's a tiny bit that is still alert. Maybe that's the difference between Hunters who were trained as I was, out there in the boonies, where we can't ever take safety for granted, and Hunters who were trained here in "civilization." It's not a fun way to live, but at least you *stay* living.

So when Karly stopped moving, I reacted immediately.

"Hounds! Catch!" I snapped. Then I reached up, grabbed her belt, and yanked her down.

She fell off the ladder and landed soft on a pile of Hounds, hers and mine. I ducked my head and didn't look at what was up there.

9

KARLY'S HOUNDS dragged her away and began licking her face. I skittered down the ladder and joined her, and after a minute or so, she came around. The second she did, she grabbed my shoulder and pointed down-tunnel, and we both scampered farther away from that open shaft.

"Gazer," she said. I sucked in my breath. Gazers would paralyze you with a look, and you couldn't use the cute trick of a reflection to shoot them, either; a reflected look worked as well for them to paralyze you as a direct one. Shields didn't work against the Gazer paralysis; I don't know why. They looked like nothing so much as giant floating eyeballs inside a forest of hair with fat pink tentacles below, and the only way I could think that one had gotten across both Barriers was that it had floated up, floated across, and floated down. Dangerous for the Gazer, since at any point in that process it might get spotted and shot down. "It must have seen us when we went into the sewer, and it's been playing cat-at-a-mousehole waiting for us to turn up again."

Well, now this was bad. Gazers almost never were alone, they generally ran with a pack of a different kind of Othersiders we called Jackals, and if the Gazer didn't paralyze you, bake your brain, and flay the flesh from your bones, the Jackal would harry you until you ended up looking at the Gazer and got caught anyway.

Then again . . . if it had floated over, maybe the Jackals hadn't been able to come with it.

"Did you spot a Jackal?" I asked, and Karly shook her head. Well that was one in our favor anyway.

"It's going to come down here if we don't come out," she said flatly. "How good is your combat magic? Can you do more than etch something's shields? Or do we need to call for an Elite?"

I gulped, because I wasn't sure. Gazers can make their own Shields, and they are very strong. The first, last, and only time I'd ever faced a Gazer I had been with three other Hunters and most of the village. We'd dazzled it with flash-bangs from the villagers, and while it was confused and blinded, we'd all hammered it at once from a safe-ish distance with levin bolts and other magic. I don't honestly know which of us took it out.

But everyone back home said my combat magic was the best. And everyone swore I'd been the one to take the Gazer down. "I've got full combat magic," I said, hesitantly. "But—"

"Then, my call. We can't wait for an Elite. No telling if one's going to be available this minute anyway, and we don't want that thing to get bored and go looking for other prey. We have to keep the Cits safe. I play bait," she said flatly. "My magic is limited to shields and some illusions." She turned around, pulled out her Perscom, and pointed it at the lights overhead, then tapped something in. The lights went out. She trotted quickly but quietly down the sewer and did the same several more times before she came back to me. "HQ will already know we've got a Gazer, and *if* there's an Elite free, they'll be on the way already," she said as she returned, and nodded at the cameras. "But we can't wait for help. It only knows that *I'm* down here," she pointed out. "I'll go over in the lighted part of the sewer; you stand here in the dark. I'll get its attention and shield, and you take it out. Hopefully you'll do that before my shields go down and it turns my brain to mush."

Before I could say anything, she was slipping away down the tunnel and into the section just past the manhole. There she stood, her pistol out, her Hounds around her, waiting. My lot dimmed everything down to shadow and crouched against the side of the tunnel as we did the same.

The tension was horrible, and all that was going through my mind was that my combat magic wasn't nearly as good as the monks said it was, that it wasn't nearly good enough to take down a Gazer solo, and that we were all going to die unless my Hounds could do what I couldn't. And we waited. And waited. You couldn't hear anything but a faraway drip of water and a very, very faint, somehow unpleasant hum that the Gazer made. Running away down the sewer to another exit wasn't an option. The Gazer was up there where there would be people at shift change, and by my Perscom's reckoning, that wasn't far off. By the time we legged it to another exit and back to here, there would be a slaughter. And Karly was right. Even if there was an Elite free, they still had to get dispatched and get out here. No one was going to get here to help us any sooner than fast transport could bring them.

This was our job. We had to be up to it.

Even if I was shaking all over and felt like I was going to scream.

The humming changed, ever so slightly, the pitch edging upward. The Gazer had gotten impatient. It was moving.

The dangling tentacles inched down through the hole first. No use even trying to shoot those; Gazers regrew those the way lizards regrew a shed tail. Ugh! The sight of those pink, dangling things, like ugly, slimy worms, just made me nauseous. The Gazer's Shields looked like soap bubbles made with dirty water; there were little moving specks in the shields and the color was a slightly cloudy off-white. What were those specks? No one I'd ever talked to knew, and Gazers weren't in any mythos that the Monastery knew about.

When we'd smashed the last one, that was exactly what we'd done, just hammered it into the ground with brute force. I had to be smarter than that.

More tentacles, then the start of the hair—that marked the bottom of the Gazer proper. Still, Karly held her fire. The Gazer paused; by now it could see that part of the tunnel was dark, and part in the light. Was it smart enough to figure out that someone could be hiding in the shadowed part?

That must have been what was going through Karly's mind too, because at that moment she unloaded the full mag into the bottom of the Gazer.

The bullets evaporated in little puffs of fire, and the Gazer dropped into the tunnel like a stone, turning its single eye on Karly.

She wasn't being stupid, though. She had already squeezed her eyes shut, was reloading blind, and shouting to her Hounds as her Shields flared into life. But she had to open her eyes to shoot, and that was when the Gazer got her.

Her mouth dropped open. Her face became a mask of terror. Her shields started to fluctuate.

My Hounds and I hit the thing with everything we had.

I went for cracking the Shields wide open, with magical hammer-blows to the top, because I thought they were a bit thinner there. Unless you could see magic in operation, all you would see would be the shields bowing and snapping back, but what I was doing was using magic to beat on the Shields with actual, physical force, literally as if I had a giant invisible hammer and was trying to crack a geode open. The two biggest Hounds leapt in and started raking the shields with glowing claws, while the smaller ones poured fire out of their mouths on it. All my muscles were hurting, exactly as if I were using that giant physical hammer for real. And there was that draining from the pit of my stomach, telling me I was pouring out magical power as fast as I could. For a horrible moment I *knew* it wasn't enough, that it was never going to work.

And then—it did.

The Gazer screamed as I shattered its Shields, thanks to the damage those Shields were taking from my Hounds. Then it was engulfed in fire, and it stopped screaming aloud. I covered my ears, although that did nothing, as the screaming in my head went on for far too long.

When it did stop, the Hounds didn't stop hosing what was left of the Gazer down with their fire. They kept pouring flame over it until there was nothing left but a slightly greasy, charred mass on the floor.

I ran to Karly. There was blood coming out of her nose and her ears, but there was sense in her eyes as she tried to sit up from where she had fallen. I was crying a little and made her stay put. I still couldn't quite believe I'd done it.

"My . . . leather's getting . . . ruined," she managed as my Perscom and hers beeped and said, *"Medic unit dispatched."*

"I'll buy you a new outfit," I said, feeling drunk with relief, as I smeared the tears out of my eyes. "Fires of Hell, I'll buy you two."

I must have stood in the shower for a good half an hour, just letting the hot water pour over me and trying to empty myself of thought and emotion, like the Masters taught me. Karly was going to be all right, but getting hammered by a Gazer meant she'd be out for at least a couple of weeks, and I'd get assigned another mentor. I wondered who it would be.

*Powers, please, not Ace . . .*

So *this* was the sort of thing they were having to deal with here in Apex? No wonder they needed Hunters! I—wasn't exactly glad I had come here, I still wanted to be home, but at least now I knew that hauling me in hadn't been some sort of way for Apex to show its power over the Territories, or for some stupid reason I couldn't even imagine right now because I couldn't think like they did. No . . . no, all I could think about was the people who had come out of the buildings at shift change, after I'd helped Karly up the ladder and let her lie back on the ground with the Hounds around us, guarding. Ordinary Cits, wearing the uniforms of whatever place they were working at—tunics and pants in various colors, with name badges and insignia on the chest and back. One of the girls who had ventured closer and brought us bottles of water had looked almost like Kei. That was when it hit me: these people weren't any different from my friends and all on the Mountain. Not where it counted. The only difference was they weren't allowed to have anything to defend themselves with. I couldn't leave now. I *couldn't*. Their faces would haunt me forever if I did and I found out something had gone bad.

When the medic team picked us up in a helichopper, they hadn't paid any attention to me, and the little cams had all been pointing at Karly, who looked pretty dramatic. I tried to be inconspicuous. But once we landed, I got grabbed by someone important-looking, who ran me through a ruthless debrief in front of at least a dozen floating and stationary cams right there on the landing pad. Only when he was satisfied was another medic team allowed to hustle me inside and run a quick check over me. They asked if I wanted a sedative or a calmative and I said no. They asked if I wanted dinner in my room and I said *yes*. The cams followed me as I practically ran for my room, and I was so grateful to be able to shut them out. Then I showered and showered and showered, and showered some more until I finally felt light and empty and more or less peaceful again.

I was bundled up in a soft robe thing and combing out my wet hair when there was a tap at the door. I opened it, and there was a cart, all by itself, standing in the hallway. On top of the cart was a covered tray. I took it, and the cart rolled away.

Someone had been taking notes on what I ate.

And... damn it all, I was *starving*. We'd done *two* lots of Othersiders today, and normally when that happened, it was all with conventional weapons, not magic. Whoever had put the tray together for me was well aware of that, too.

I ate. Then... I couldn't help it. I turned the vid on and tuned to my channel.

It came up right at the point where Karly was saying she'd be bait. I wasn't sure I would be able to watch it, but I did. It was too bad that the vids didn't show the Shields or the magic... although you could kind of *infer* the Shields based on where the bullets burned up on them and the fire wrapped around them. I managed to keep to my Zen-space and analyzed what I watched. Although I had to wince a lot... I hadn't realized I'd been screaming the whole time I was pounding the Gazer with magic blows. I sounded like a little girl.

There were some cursory shots of Karly being evac'd—this was my channel, so I guess Karly didn't figure as importantly on it—then the cut to the debrief. I was a mess. There was mud and soot smeared all over my face where I'd brushed my tears away, my eyes were red and swollen until you couldn't tell that they were hazel, there was ash and mud and stains all over my clothing, and my brown hair was nearly black at the roots with sweat and was coming out of the side-tail. It made me glad, in a way; the girl who badly needed a shower looked and felt a lot more like *me*. Hunters shouldn't look like vid stars. Hunters should look like that....

Then the talking heads came on and started yammering away, but the only interesting thing was that they *implied* that all of this had taken place outside the Prime Barrier. Why only the first one?

Maybe the Cits already knew things got through the second . . . or, to them, only the first was important.

There wasn't much else they were saying that mattered, and I turned over to Karly's channel. And I was *really* happy to see how much footage she was getting, with the cameras zooming in on her like in an old movie when she said, "I'll be bait."

I switched to the news. We weren't the only Hunters who had had encounters today, it seemed. The news was full of it. Ace had run into another, much smaller swarm of Knockers, though he'd been taken by surprise and hadn't handled them as quickly as my Hounds had. White Knight got three Redcaps and a Wailer—some people called them Banshees. Paules and Tober had both taken down Ketzels—kind of miniature versions of Drakken; although they had brightly feathered wings and could fly, they weren't nearly as much of a danger as Drakken were, and my villagers Hunted them without Hunters on a regular basis. But if you were a soft Cit here in Apex and saw one of them diving at you, it was probably thoroughly terrifying. Paules did a lot better with his Ketzels than his brother, Ace, had with his Knockers, but then, he hadn't been taken by surprise.

The news was full of the "outbreak," as they called it. Once again, it was implied that most of this was outside the Prime Barrier, and the talking heads were yammering a storm about how there were theories that sunspots had weakened the Barriers or some of the generators needed replacing.

It was the way they talked about it all that was striking. They weren't excited, they weren't concerned, and I got the impression that they'd show the same kind of interest in just about anything else. They were actually *more* animated talking about the person who was responsible for keeping the Barrier generators in repair, suggesting he was someone's crony and not up to the job. So... they were trying to keep people from being afraid. But was that such a good idea?

I suddenly felt horribly tired. Also something I was used to after a fight.

"Tomorrow's schedule," I said aloud. But instead of getting a schedule, the image of the two news-twerps on the vid-screen was replaced by the armorer.

"Uh—sir?" I stammered. He looked up, as if startled by my voice. Then his mouth twitched a little, in a shadow of amusement.

"Hunter Joyeaux," he acknowledged. "Evidently you said something that your suite AI interpreted as needing my intervention. What was it?"

"I asked for my schedule for tomorrow," I explained. He nodded.

"Do you feel the need for a day off?" he asked. "If you feel rocky, you get one off, after a fight."

I shook my head. This time what I got from him was a real smile, one of approval.

"Right, then, I was just looking into who I might assign as your mentor." He looked offscreen, frowning a little. "Do you have any objection to being mentored by a Christer?"

"Oh, White Knight? Not hardly," I said, actually feeling a lot of relief. "I think we ... established boundaries this morning. There's Christers in my—I mean, in my *old* territory. We'll get along."

"Good. Follow today's schedule; meet White Knight in the mess. As you know, he's another early riser. He'll brief you on his territory." Before I could say anything, much less thank him, the screen went back to the news. They were showing me and Karly again. I didn't really know what to think about that—though at least they weren't trying to make us out as lovers.

But before I could switch it off, someone else appeared in the screen, a Hunter I hadn't met yet. "Hunter Joyeaux?" he said. A little older than Knight, midtwenties. Stocky, brown-haired, and friendly-looking.

I pulled the robe a little tighter in reflex. I mean, this was a strange guy staring at me in a robe I was naked under! "Uh, yes?" I said, not at all cleverly.

"I'm Hunter Trev. We thought you might not know that some of us gather up after dinner in the main lounge, and that you are welcome to join us," he said. Then he winked. "There's popcorn: caramel, cheese, buttered, sugar-cinnamon..."

Now, if he hadn't said that, I probably would have politely declined. But . . . popcorn! I *love* popcorn. We have buttered popcorn as a treat back home, and although I had never tried the other kinds he'd just mentioned, my mouth was watering at the thought of yummy, hot, buttery, salty—I could find room for a bowl of popcorn.

"I'll be right there," I said.

I hurried into a pair of soft gray pants and a baggy charcoal top, pulled on some equally soft indoor shoes, and told my Perscom "main lounge." I wondered for a second if there was any chance Josh might be there—I glanced in the mirror to make sure my hair was all right.

But then I told myself I was being stupid. Why would Josh be there? This was a Hunter thing, not a Psimon thing, and anyway, he was Uncle's personal Psi-aid. He was probably working.

Once again, the headquarters seemed oddly empty. I only saw one other person in the halls, and that was at a distance. Where were the people who cooked the food, cleaned the rooms? You were always running into someone at the Monastery—

But then again, all the people at the Monastery were awake at the same time. No one ever Hunted at night, unless it was a tearing emergency, like a child had been snatched down in one of the settlements. Three thousand people lived at the Monastery itself and the village of Safehaven around it. Here, were there five hundred at most? Probably not even that.

Of those, since there were three shifts, a third would be asleep at any one time. And another third would be out on patrol, or if they were on an Elite team, handling something big.

The main lounge turned out to be not entirely unlike the community hall back home when we had the vid-screen up. There was a *huge* vid-screen at one end, a lot of really comfortable, heavily upholstered and padded chairs and sofas, and low tables with bowls of popcorn on them. The chairs and sofas were full of people, all of them dressed comfortably, the way I was.

When I came in, the image on the screen froze, and everyone turned to look at me. "Uh, hello," I said into the silence. "I'm Joy."

It was the one who had spoken to me on the vid, Hunter Trev, who got to his feet. "Come join us!" he said with enthusiasm. And everyone began talking at once, introducing themselves, suggesting a seat, showing me where all the snacks and drinks were. I ended up in a big chair that swallowed me up in a good way, with a bowl of popcorn and some cold, spicy tea. And then I found out why they were all together.

They were going over the unedited vids of their hunts. And

not, like, being mean to each other. I mean, they picked at each other, but it wasn't harsh. "Regi, for pity's sake," someone groaned, when all one guy had to show for his day's work was a single Redcap. "*That's* what you're calling a Hunt?"

"It was a big 'Cap!" the other fellow said forlornly. "It came up to my shoulder! It had a knife!"

Everyone (well, not me, but everyone else) threw popcorn at him.

For the Hunts that had been more serious, they'd stop the vid, sometimes every few minutes, break down what was going on, ask questions. Or make fun . . . one of the girls got caught with a really silly expression on her face, tongue sticking out of the corner of her mouth, as she hosed down a swarm of huge bugs with a small full-auto.

Then . . . my vid came up, and I froze with my hand halfway to my mouth. *What are they going to think of me?* was all that was in my head. These were all friends, clearly—I was the outsider.

By this time the vid had run forward enough that Karly and I were shielded and the swarm of Knockers had just come into view. And someone swore.

"What in—what *are* those things?" someone else said with a gasp. Then the scene froze and everyone looked at me.

"Uh—Tommyknockers," I said, my voice going up in a squeak. And when I said that, the view went split screen and a wik-entry for Tommyknockers came up on the right side, with a picture.

"Mines and caves," Trev read aloud.

"Fear radius? That's not good news for Cits!" said Sara, the girl who'd made the funny face, with some alarm.

They all turned back to look at me. "They never leave underground," I said with more authority. "Our miners even tried to bait them out, and they won't come up. They don't make their own tunnels either, so they're not going to dig into basements."

The vid started again, and they all watched it avidly, stopping it at times to ask me questions. A guy made a *very* crude joke about Knocker naughty-bits (which were kind of obvious under those excuses for loincloths), and I went hot and red all over. I went even redder when Sara teased me for it, and dared to throw a piece of popcorn at her, which she caught and ate with a grin, and suddenly we were all friends. It was like being with the other Hunters up on the Mountain, only . . . only somehow, less serious.

By the time the vids came round to our second encounter, the one with the Gazer, I realized I was somehow coming to feel—at home? At home enough to feel comfortable answering questions about what we'd used on the Gazer until that vid was done and we were on to the next.

"Do you do this every night?" I asked Trev, who had plopped himself down in the chair next to me so he could monopolize the bowl of sugared popcorn (too sweet for me).

He nodded. "Some people would rather watch themselves alone, some would rather not watch at all. We happen to like the company while we pick our performances to bits." He regarded the scene on the screen, which was Paules being dive-bombed by the Ketzels while people laughed and yelled at him to swat them. I hadn't noticed him until then. Maybe he wasn't as full of himself as Ace was. He just made a face and didn't protest. "It's normally not this exciting, though. This was a helluva day."

I just nodded.

When the vids were done, a few people started a card game. Some settled down to conversations. The card game got an audience. Paules waved good-bye and left. Some people put a vid-game up on the vid-screen that they played with their Perscoms. The thing that had brought them all together was over. I found myself yawning and got up to leave, realizing that bed sounded very, very good. I'd be coming back every night unless something got in the way. It was a nice mix of people in the rankings, which made me feel comfortable; I was happy that not everybody was as competitive as Ace and his friends.

Trev intercepted me before I left the room. "Enjoy yourself?" he asked. "Going to keep joining us?" I nodded, and he grinned. "Good! Just come down when you feel like it, it's not an obligation or anything, but you'll always be welcome. Good Hunting tomorrow!"

"Good Hunting," I wished him, and went back to my rooms.

Then I got into bed, blacked the lights, and tried to get straight to sleep. I was suffused with relief that no one had died today . . . and that my mentor wasn't Ace.

◄◙ ▷

Knight was already in the mess when I got there, and I had taken pains to be up early. He'd already gotten food for me, and I noticed what he had gotten was identical to what he had for himself. He nodded at the tray as I sat down. "Try it. I think you'll like it," he said. "It's a healthier version of what we eat where I come from."

I made a face at him. "I like sausage biscuits real well, thanks,"

I replied, and picked one up and bit into it. The biscuits were too fluffy, but like I said, vat-meat makes a good ground base, and the good, fresh herbs and spices more than made up for the fluffy biscuits. There was that, and fruit, and yoghurt, and Caffeelike. He drank his black. I put in lots of cream and sugar. "Briefing?" I said after I swallowed my first bite.

"We'll be outside the Prime Barrier. And there are places where the Second Barrier goes over water at that point, so it's a slip-in zone. They call that part of Apex 'Spillover.' People who have come here without getting jobs first live out there. Or people who have been here all along and haven't gotten jobs inside the Prime Barrier." His face was neutral, but there was a faint tightness in his voice that gave me the notion he didn't much like this. Well, I didn't much like the notion that people were kept outside the Barrier either, but I kept my Hunt face on. "You see . . . there are Cits . . . and there are Cits," he elaborated while I listened. "Apex only has so many jobs and so much room. So unless you have family here to take you in, you have money, or you came from someplace else with a job offer in hand, if you turn up at the Barriers, you don't just get to come inside and set up house. You have to wait outside, make some kind of place to live in the ruins, and keep seeing if you can get a job. That will get you inside, and make you an actual citizen of Apex. But they *are* Cits, and they *do* get Hunter protection."

I didn't say anything, but I wondered if his people did the same as mine. Because people do turn up, looking for a settlement, out of nowhere. And what we do when they turn up is test them. The first test is whether they pass by the Hounds—both to make sure they aren't Folk in disguise and to make sure they aren't thieves or troublemakers. I've never seen any of the Folk try to pass as human, but we've turned our share of troublemakers away. Then we test them to see if they're lazy—and by "we," I mean all the settlements on the Mountain do this, having learned the hard way in the past that the lazy make as much trouble for you as the actual troublemakers. We give them a spot to build a home and the instructions, and *some* help and the start of the materials. If they don't have a skill, then they had better learn one fast, work for other people, or become a farmer. We'll supply some seed and help, but after that . . . unless they fail through no fault of their own, they'd better get used to working for other people because no one is going to feed them for free.

And I could see how random people showing up all the time wanting to live in the city could be problematic here in Apex.

"Having people out there attracts the Othersiders," Knight said, and shrugged. "But the choice is to have a bunch of people squatting in shacks inside the Prime Barrier, or squatting in slightly better and more defensible ruins outside. Either way, they're going to be attracting trouble, and possibly making it. Those in charge decided if they were going to make trouble, it should be outside the Prime Barrier. Someone has to patrol it, so this is my regular territory. Mostly what turns up there is mobs of small stuff; not so bad individually, but a mob can pull you down, easy."

"Like the Knockers. Load-out?" I asked.

"Magic and iron or steel," he replied. "A lot of the small Othersiders that turn up in Spillover are only affected by magic or ferrous metal."

I nodded. "Same crossbow as yesterday," I said. "Shotgun with steel-shot loads." A pistol probably wouldn't do me much good.

"Pair of long knives, set of throwing knives. And do you think I can get about two pounds of these?" I held up one of the little cubes of sugar I'd used in my drink.

He blinked. "What for?"

"Bait," I explained. "A lot of the small, stupid Othersiders can't resist sweets. If they won't come out, we might be able to lure them in."

He gaped at me a little. "Where did you learn *that*?" he asked. "I mean, how?"

"We have silver birch up where I am. You can boil down the sap to make a sweetener. Little Othersiders were always stealing the sap before we went to steel taps and buckets." It was one of the places we taught kids to Hunt in. The little monsters were always hovering around the birch trees, longing after the sweet sap being collected, repelled by the ferrous metal, and paying no attention to anything else. Worked as good as luring in Death-Moths with a flame.

He tapped all that into his Perscom. "Right. Soon as you finish, then let's go. It's a long ride out there."

We got our load-out and there was a pod with an army driver waiting for us at the entrance. Knight didn't seem surprised, so I figured this was not anything special called up just for me, which was fine so far as I was concerned. Knight stayed quiet all the way to the Barrier, which was where the driver left us.

There are doors in the pylons that create the Barrier. Although going through the Barrier itself outside of a pod or a train car isn't lethal to a human, it's not fun and hurts a lot. Not that I've done it, but the descriptions were pretty vivid—feels like your skin is on fire, and all your muscles start twitching. Of course, it doesn't kill a human, though it does kill an Othersider. We used the door in the nearest pylon; just an ID check at the door in, another at the door out, and then we were in Spillover.

And I was shocked.

There hadn't been any of this on the part I had come through on the train. Maybe the authorities cleared Spillover away from the train routes, which wouldn't surprise me. But Spillover looked like nothing so much as the pictures from just after the Diseray. Tumbledown buildings, some empty, with window holes like sockets in a skull. Most buildings were abandoned, but some had little signs of life, like clean windows with shutters that could be pulled closed in case of attack. The nearest of those had a guard stationed at the door, an old man with one leg sitting on a piece of rock with a crossbow on his lap. He and Knight nodded at each other. A strange smell hung in the air; I finally identified it as the scent of mildew and damp and rot that hangs about abandoned buildings. Not something I'd sniffed much in the mountains.

There was an army guard on the other side of the door, and a line of people starting to form at the base of the pylon. I looked at it quizzically. "What's all that?" I asked Knight as we walked away, deeper into Spillover.

"They're lining up for a day pass into Apex," he said, voice flat. "A couple are going in there to shop or trade, but most of them are going in to apply for work. Remember what I said earlier? If you have a job, you can live inside. A job gets you a voucher for a small apartment right away."

The people lining up hadn't, for the most part, looked hopeful. Their clothing was shabby, faded, and, from the look of it, never had been made from stuff as sturdy as we make up on the Mountain. Our stuff doesn't look shabby until it's been handed down at least twice. "Does that happen often?" I asked. "Getting a job, I mean."

He shrugged. "Two, maybe three a day."

I looked back over my shoulder. The line was already fifty or so people long. "Why so few?" I asked.

"Because most jobs are skilled. Unskilled stuff is all done for free by prisoners." His face was absolutely expressionless. "It's not hard to get enough prisoners when you can get thrown in for years for things like going into debt, talking back to police, being suspected of sedition or fomenting discontent or having ties to someone who has. The people who are lining up there and *will* get jobs probably had them before, ran out of money or got tossed into jail, and rather than getting tossed in again for homelessness escaped to Spillover. They can at least keep getting day passes to apply for work from here."

I didn't need him quickly seizing my hand and squeezing it to know to keep my lip zipped. With cameras hovering around and catching everything I said or did, even an *expression* could be considered grounds for getting a stern talking-to from someone like the armorer. Knight might be able to get away with speaking his mind, but anything I said or did wrong could come around to bite Uncle. So I just nodded, kept my Hunt face on, and kept walking. Then there was what Knight had said about "sedition" getting you thrown in jail. They surely wouldn't do that to a Hunter, but I couldn't think of anything I could say about what Knight had just said that didn't have the potential to buy me and Uncle some trouble, so I changed the subject. "What's the most likely thing we'll need to take down today?" I asked as a woman hanging up worn and frayed clothing under the protective eye of a young boy with a lethal-looking slingshot spotted Knight and waved to him. He unbent enough to smile at her and waved back. The boy waved too, but didn't stop scanning the sky and places where trouble might rush out.

"Lately, it's been Ketzels, but that could only mean I'm due for a change," he said.

I reckoned up seasons in my mind. "Actually maybe not. You've been getting parents hunting for the young in the nest," I said. "Down here on the flat you should be getting parents taking the young out to hunt now."

He made a face, but didn't contradict me. "Time to call the Hounds, then. I'm interested to see yours."

"Likewise." We stopped on the cracked and broken asphalt of what had once been a street. There didn't seem to be anyone living in the nearest buildings, which looked as if they had been two-story apartment complexes. I drew the Glyphs and cast them down, and opened the Portal, and my Hounds came bounding through in all their eye-watering glory.

They circled Knight and stared at him. He stared back. "Blessed saints. I thought those colors had been enhanced in the studio."

I had to laugh at that. "Oh no, that's all them. They even glow in the dark."

He looked a little pained at that but said nothing. He only drew and cast his own Glyphs, and when his Portal opened, what bounded through it were four pure-white winged lions. I knew they were lions, because I've seen pictures of lions—but of course, no real-world lion ever had wings.

"Gabriel, Michael, Raphael, and Uriel," he said, nodding at them.

"Bya, Dusana, Begtse, Chenresig, Shinje, Kalachakra, and Hevajra," I replied. And please do not ask me why, if they are Zapotec, they have the names of Tibetan deities. They picked the names, or were created with them, or just decided to *tell* me those were their names to mess with me. Maybe they chose those names to honor some of my Masters. Maybe the Tibetan Othersiders and the Zapotec Othersiders are actually the same. I just roll with it.

Knight sketched a salute to my Hounds as his hovered in midair. They were blindingly white. I bet they glowed in the dark too. I nodded to them, with respect, one Hunter to another.

"I'll bet they blind the little Othersiders just on looks alone," he said, with one of his rare smiles and even a hint of a chuckle.

Bya snorted, turned, and trotted off straight ahead, as the rest fell into their usual pattern, quartering and cross-quartering the territory in front of us. Even though they'd rarely Hunted in an urban setting before I came here—only once, actually, and that was to clean out a set of ruins—they took to this landscape as easily as if they had Hunted through it all their lives. Knight's Hounds arrowed off, doing the same from the air. Those wings were never big enough to support the weight of a full-grown lion, but then, Hounds didn't exactly need to obey the laws of physics.

*We like him,* I heard in my head, in Bya's voice. This was something of a shock, since the warmest feeling they'd ever had to Christers before was a studied indifference, and plenty had evoked pure detestation. On the other hand, since Knight was my mentor until Karly was better, it was a good thing they did like him.

*Well, good,* I thought back. We didn't waste words, the Hounds and I.

They chased up a lot of little stuff, but they took care of it themselves. Knight's Hounds quickly figured out that mine would flush the winged things for them to take down, and they could harry the running things right into the jaws of mine. We only had to take out a couple of little horrors, me using my hand crossbow with steel-headed arrows, Knight wielding a more lethal slingshot than the boy at the entrance had sported, with steel balls for ammunition. It was very satisfying. Actually, it felt a whole lot more like being at home. This was the sort of Hunting I was used to doing, and I was good at it. "I'd like to talk to the armorer about having us do this together once a month when you're running solo," Knight said, his voice sounding more relaxed and much more like himself now that we weren't treading on potentially dangerous ground. I wonder if he guessed how appalled I was by what he'd told me about the Spillover. "My lot can't go after the runners the way yours can."

"I'd be open to that," I replied. And I knew, now that I'd actually worked most of the morning with Knight, that'd I'd enjoy it too. Hunting as a duo is more efficient. And not as lonely. I was only just beginning to realize how lonely Hunting solo was. Three Hunters lived permanently at the Monastery, the rest all went to their home villages once they were trained, and there was a lot of ground to cover, so we all hunted solo once trained.

Now I wondered, as we Hunted the landscape of ruined buildings ... what would it be like to know you would never have to Hunt alone again?

Then again, it would be terrifying to Hunt all the time with someone you cared about. You'd not only have to worry about yourself, you'd have to worry about them, too. I thought of how awful it had been to watch Karly set herself up as bait, and I only *liked* Karly as someone who had been friendly and helpful. *That's why Hunters don't marry Hunters, if they marry at all,* I decided.

# 10

I KNOW I'VE SAID this a lot before, but Hunting is very hungry work, so we'd brought food with us. You see, it's not just the physical stuff. Magic is energy we use, but to move that energy around takes *more* energy, and that has to come from someplace. That someplace is the Hunter herself, so you burn through a lot of calories. Knight called a halt around noon so we could rest and eat. The Hounds, of course, were quite satisfied with their quarry, and just dispersed themselves around us with a couple on guard while the others rested. We found ourselves some high ground on the roof of a gutted building that was still sound and ate while the Hounds kept watch.

"What's your home like?" Knight asked out of nowhere.

"Mountains," I said, my attention caught for a moment by a glint among the ruins, but nothing came of it. "Really tall ones. Snow all the way down into the deepest valleys half the year, though warm enough to grow plenty of stuff in the other half. For some reason the worst of the Othersiders don't much seem to like the cold, so we can always retreat to the snow if we have to. What's yours like?" I figured the best way to avoid more questions was to get him to talk.

"Mountains, but low ones," he said, and his mouth turned down a little. "Part of it is lush and green, part is poisoned and ruined by mining. Othersiders don't like the poisoned parts, so we have the option of living where it's safe and dying slowly from the poisons in the earth and the water, or living where it's clean and green and getting killed quickly by Othersiders. My people live in the poisoned part; the Othersiders absolutely will not go there. Most of the people still mine, since the cities all need some raw materials; the mining itself isn't that dangerous. I suppose that the miners reckon if your life is going to be short anyway, you might as well get a good job out of it that pays well. And I will say, mining does pay well. We're not poor."

There was nothing in what he actually said that could be taken as seditious—and anyway, I would bet that Hunters were allowed to get away with saying things most Cits wouldn't dare to because we're a scarce resource. But the deep bitterness, and the darkness in his tone when he spoke made me think there was a lot of built up rage in there. I was slowly beginning to understand why. I don't know if the Masters had sheltered me from this knowledge, or if they genuinely were not aware of it themselves, but I was beginning to get pieces of what might turn out to be a very ugly picture.

"The poisoning," I said. "That's from before the Diseray?"

"Most of it; they used to mine coal and bring gas out where I come from. You can't get coal and gas out of the ground cheaply without bringing out poison with it, and before the *Dies Irae*, they flattened whole mountains and filled in the valleys with the debris, and the debris itself was poisonous. We actually mine the debris for things like arsenic." There was no doubt of the bitterness there. "Those Knockers you took on yesterday. They turn up in mines, you told Karly?"

"I'll bet you never see them in your mines because of the poisons," I replied. Mining metal ore isn't inherently poisonous, though if you aren't careful (we are) extracting and smelting it out can be. But we work small, and slow, and careful, and to be honest, there is a use for anything, even poison, if you look for it, so why not capture everything? Like they say when we butcher a pig: "Use everything but the squeal." We use some of the poisons we get in smelting on weapons against the Othersiders, and in tiny amounts, some poisons are also medicines, things like dyes, or, with careful application, insecticides and rodenticides.

Besides being as gentle as we can on the land, working small, slow, and careful means we never send enough to the capital to get them excited and interested in us. Just enough to pay for a few things we can't make for ourselves, and that they won't send us as part of our support.

"Have you got relatives back home?" Knight continued. "Or is it just your uncle here?"

"No one, just friends." I began telling him about my friends—omitting the other Hunters, of course, and concentrating on Kei. "My grandparents are gone, but they would have been really old by now anyway. They moved from the Springs to Apex to get Uncle a better education. Then they got a surprise, my father, and when he was grown, he met a girl from a town called New Bana who was visiting cousins, and he married her and moved there. Then New Bana got overrun. It was too far from Apex for an Elite team to get there in time to save the town. I was just a toddler, and I really don't remember that. Uncle got me and some other kids that were orphaned and took them to families in the Springs who offered to take us. My best friend Kei was one of them too. She's really pretty, black hair down to her waist when she combs it out. She's probably going to have her pick of every boy in the Springs, because she's not stuck on herself even though she's pretty, and she's as good with a gun as she is with a needle." I told him a lot more about Kei, some of the funny stories about the trouble we used to get into together, just harmless stuff, pranks that made even the victim laugh, then tilted my head over. "What about you?"

"Ma and Pa are still doing all right, but . . ." He shrugged. "You get to know what the signs are that the poison is getting to people, and the early signs are there. I've got a girl; they fixed us up back when we were little, and we suit each other. Her name's Verity. Verity Clark." His voice softened when he spoke the girl's name, and I smiled a little. "I'm hoping I get a high enough ranking I can get double quarters eventually, so I can bring her here, though I don't know if she'd like it."

I nodded; a couple of the Christer settlements on the Mountain do that too; arrange matches for kids from families that are friendly with each other. Then they marry them off quick once they get past sixteen or so. Given he *had* a girl, I was kind of surprised he hadn't married her already. By my guess, he was about eighteen, nineteen. But maybe his people didn't marry off as quick as the Christers I was thinking about did.

It made me a little sick, though, to think of Knight's people, dying by inches because they lived on poisoned ground. I resolved to think on that for a bit and tucked it in the back of my head. It was time to get moving again. Knight and the Hounds and I had a lot of ground to cover.

And we hadn't gone far before we ran into another something I hadn't seen before.

Knight's Hounds alerted, and came zipping back to us, and began going through a little dance. Mine coursed back through the ruins right after them, and I got the word from Bya what was up before Knight puzzled out what his Hounds were trying to tell him.

"There's a flock of little things with butterfly wings out there on about an acre of tumbledown," I said. "Bya says they look to be flitting around something that looks like a celebration or a fair or—"

"Goblin market," Knight identified grimly. "They use it to catch children—the ones that don't know any better and get drawn in are never seen again."

Bya gave me details on how the market was set up. Several dozen Othersiders, all child-size, all with butterfly wings and clothing that looked as if it were made from flowers, were playing music, dancing, and playing games amid displays of what looked like choice fruits. They hadn't put out any outliers, so evidently they didn't know we were in the area yet. I recounted all this to Knight.

He nodded. "I don't usually get this far. It's a lot of ground for just me and the Hounds to cover. They might have been doing this for . . . well, weeks, months even." He looked me over shrewdly. "Can you put a dome over the place to catch them all?"

Mentally, I calculated size from what Bya had shown me, and shook my head regretfully. "Too big. Half that size, maybe—" But

I was thinking fast. "I could do a net, though. Same amount of energy, just spaces between the energy strings. Only problem is they'll escape it by stretching the holes sooner or later."

"As long as you can keep the escapees to four or fewer at a time, that'll do. With all our Hounds, we shouldn't have any trouble taking them all down." He looked over the Hounds, who all looked up to him as to a pack leader. "You Hounds spread out all around the perimeter," he ordered. "I don't want anything escaping if they manage to squeak out of the net. It'll be your job to get what does."

Bya nodded, and mine ghosted off . . . which kind of surprised me in a pleasing way, since they hadn't shown any indication to accept anyone but me as a leader since the last time one of the Masters Hunted with me. I'm not the sort of person to take offense if there's a team Hunt going on and someone else is alpha. It's about the Hunt, not who the leader is.

I concentrated for a moment, and sketched out the right Glyphs in the air, forming up my net, while Knight watched, sober-faced. It didn't look very impressive; in fact, it looked like a transparent ball of yarn, glowing a little, hovering in the air in front of me. Well, that was because it was all packed down tight. I remember the first time I finally managed the net spell; it took me *so* long to figure out I needed to make a magic weave, then combine it with the expansion spell, that I think I plainly exasperated Master Kedo. I'm not usually that dense, but it was my first combination, so . . . *I* think I had an excuse. I reached out and plucked it out of the air, and hung on to it with my left hand. I wanted it ready to throw the moment I needed it. I *could* have spread it all out and floated it over the top of the Goblin market, then dropped it, but I thought they would probably see it if I tried that.

Knight and I slipped up on the open area surrounded on all four sides by roofless, ruined four-story buildings. It looked as if these buildings had all been part of the same thing, with a grassy courtyard in the middle. Another apartment complex? Probably. It was a good place for the Othersiders to set up their Goblin Fair; if you didn't know there was something going on here, you likely wouldn't see it, since they were screened by the buildings.

And when we got there, we saw a dozen of them swarming around their prey. They'd got themselves a kid.

Too young to know better, or maybe nobody had ever warned him about these things, or maybe just too curious for his own good, the raggedy, dirty-faced, half-starved-looking boy had a dazed and dazzled expression on him as he stared at the pretty things. And what kid would be suspicious of something that had big wings like a butterfly, a sweet and innocent face, and the chirping voice of a bird? No matter how many times you told him, in his heart he would know that nothing that pretty could be bad, right?

And especially when it looked like he hadn't had a good meal since he was born, and they were holding out big, shiny fruits to him, breaking them in half to show the succulent flesh dripping with juice. He was reaching for one when I fired the crossbow at the creature holding out the fruit to him.

In an instant, they whirled to face us and showed their true nature.

They were still winged but had the wings of bats, wasps, and flies. Their limbs stretched and thinned, they lost all but a few tattered rags of clothing, their skin darkened to leather, their hair to a few patches on their skulls. Their faces stretched and developed muzzles, with yellow eyes and huge mouths full of rows and rows of needle teeth. They opened their mouths to hiss or snarl at us, and as the child screamed and ran off in terror, I pulled back my arm and threw with both natural and magic strength, and the net expanded as it flew through the air. As soon as it was in place, I dropped the net of magic over them. Then I pulled all the edges in tight and held on for dear life.

Something that big is hard to hold. I could feel energy and strength draining out of me, and I had to physically *hold on*, exactly as if I had a half-acre net full of goat-size, fighting animals that I was trying to control. One escaped into the air almost immediately and was taken by one of Knight's Hounds, who flashed down like a hawk on a bird. Another got away, this time scrabbling off into the ruins; Bya got him. Then I was too busy trying simultaneously to keep the damned things off me while keeping the net around them to pay any attention to what Knight and the Hounds were doing. Those fangs were dripping with *something*, and I didn't want to get bitten to discover if it was spit or poison.

They did escape, by ones and twos, but never more than that, and I got the impression from the fire-gouts, the figures running and flying around in my peripheral vision, and, above all, the ear-piercing, high-pitched screams that the escapees never actually got away. And Knight kept firing into the creatures still in the net, taking them down one at a time while I closed the net tighter and tighter around the ones that were left. An odd thing happened while I was doing that; it felt as if something—not the camera—was watching me, with intense concentration. And maybe there was, but the Hounds didn't alert, and I didn't have the attention to spare for anything other than what I was doing. I had to make sure the horrors didn't escape more than a couple at a time.

Then nothing was escaping. My Hounds surrounded the netted things that finally realized their doom and stopped struggling and began to scream.

All the Hounds, Knight's and mine, leapt on the remaining creatures in the net; there was a lot of thrashing, a lot of shrieking, and then it was over.

I let the net dissolve, and happened to look down at a body. "Ick," I said, half in disgust and half in fascination, as I watched what was left of the Goblin dissolve into blackish-brown goo.

Knight came over to me and looked where I was looking. "Yeah," he said. "Goblins do that. You've never seen it before?"

I shook my head. These flatlander Othersiders had a whole new flock of types that were new to me. Othersiders I'd killed before either just stayed dead bodies, or evaporated.

"If you just *kill* one, it'll stay whole for a while, but if the Hounds are around to eat their manna as they die, they go to goo right away." He crossed the battlefield, picking up our spent ammunition, shaking the goo off it. "Thanks, Joy. I've never been able to take out a whole market before. My magic isn't that strong, or that versatile, outside of a really, really good Shield." He glanced over at me and smiled grimly. "This'll be a lesson they won't forget. When the rest of the swarm shows up to find out what happened to the marketers, they'll know it's not safe for them to set up here anymore."

"And there's one kid who won't trust a pretty Othersider again," I observed. I glanced around to see if there was any sign of the boy we'd rescued. There wasn't—I felt those eyes on me again and thought for a moment I saw a hint of movement and a flash of pale purple out of the corner of my eye, but there was nothing in the empty window where I thought something had been when I turned to look at it fully. Light can do funny things in ruins. Just a bit of old rotten cloth or a shard of glass in a window, and you think you see a spook. The Hounds still hadn't alerted, so I put it down to that. I fought off the creeped-out feeling and cold hand of fear down my back and reminded myself, yet again, that this was *no different* from Hunting at home, where Folk could show up any time. "You say you don't know what they do with the kids they take?"

"I've never found bones or other remains." He handed me my crossbow bolts. "Once, I managed to get there just as they were leaving. They'd opened up a kind of door in the air, like one of our Portals, and the last of the kids was just going through."

I couldn't help but remember how the Folk Mage who had addressed me as "shepherd" had asked me to hand over some of my "sheep." Had those kids been spirited off to join such a flock? What happened to them when they were? Did they become slaves or playthings?

Or did they become something else entirely: walking, portable sources of manna or life-energy to be drained whenever one of the Folk felt like it? Human milk cows . . .

Right about then was when the fatigue hit me and I went a little unsteady; it all must have shown in my face. Knight didn't touch me, but he picked up my pack and his and nodded. "That's enough for anyone's day." He spoke into his Perscom. "Hunters White Knight and Joyeaux, heading back to base."

"Roger, Hunter," the Perscom replied, and that was what we did. I was already thinking of jokes I could make on myself with the others when I hooked up with them after supper.

That night in the lounge was the best time I'd had since I got to Apex City. I felt comfortable with everyone, and they were easy with me. We had a different sort of snack this time, two kinds of what they called "pretzels," which I'd heard of but never seen before.

And Karly turned up! She looked pale and shaky, but everyone was really happy to see her, me especially. It was pretty obvious she was a regular in the lounge meets. She turned down the snacks but accepted spicy tea and sat down next to me on a two-person couch.

"Well, everything they say about a Gazer-head is true," she told me as she moved very carefully. "Tell you what, kid, I think it is all kinds of not fair that I am having the worst hangover of my life without a good time to show for it."

*Everyone* laughed at that, but sympathetically. "I got the edge of a Gazer-stare once," said Trev, as he settled in next to a girl with green stripes dyed into her black hair and put his arm around her. "I don't even want to think about what your brain bucket feels like now."

And then we went over the vids, and I got a couple of good tips about how to hold my net spell and not have to get as close to the net itself as I had when I was holding the Goblins. Tonight there was even some vid from an Elite team, taking down a really huge Drakken, and I got to see how it was done. Basically, it was pin the wings, then the tail, then the head on the end of that long, long neck, then they chipped away at him until he just collapsed. It was crazy impressive, and the Drakken was so big that to get him all in frame you never saw the Hunters except as tiny little figures around him. Each one of them was about the size of one of his talons.

Karly left early, but so did I. I was *tired*, and besides, I wanted to see what one of those channels for "Cits who are famous for being famous" was like. It was like watching a party where I didn't know anyone, didn't know any of the jokes, and didn't much care for the music. But it surely was pretty. I thought maybe if I ever got a chance to go to a party like that . . . well, it might be fun if I knew some people there. We could never match all that gorgeous stuff in a million years, back home.

That was when my Perscom chimed, and the vid-screen in the outer room lit up. "Incoming call," said that impersonal voice, "from Psimon Josh Green. Accept?"

"Yes," I said, and immediately regretted it. I should have said "voice only" because I didn't know what I *looked* like at that moment and—

But it was too late. Josh was on-screen, and presumably so was I. I forced myself to leave my hair alone and sat down in a chair. "Hey," he said, grinning. "That was quite a performance yesterday. Thought I'd call you to see how you were doing."

My heart rate took a little uptick. "I wasn't the one playing bait for a Gazer," I pointed out, then realized that had come out wrong, or could be taken in a way that I hadn't meant, and added, "but, thanks for checking!"

If Josh took it badly, he was better at covering it than any guy I'd ever known. "I can't even imagine trying to face off against a Gazer," he said. "The prefect said you'd be fine, that you probably Hunted worse than that before breakfast, but I knew I wouldn't be able to think properly if I didn't check for myself."

"Uh . . ." I felt myself getting really hot. "That's awfully nice of you. I mean, you don't even know me."

"Yeah. But can we fix that?" he said, and his expression seemed so genuine . . . but he was a Psimon. A Psimon! He could so easily just be angling for a chance to tiptoe through my head! Of course, I wasn't going to say that. Luckily, he either noticed things were on the verge of getting awkward, or that I was running out of things to say. "Right now, though, I'm pretty sure you have an earlier morning coming than I do, so now that I know you're okay, I'll say good night. Sleep well!"

"Night—" I said, and then he rang off.

I was so flustered I had to do three full reps of my Aki-Do exercises before I had worked it all off. Because when I wasn't trying to keep from acting like an idiot in front of him, now I had time to think . . . and wonder if he had some other motive in calling me than the one he'd said. What if he was trying to get close to me to get at my uncle for someone? What if he was trying to find out how much Uncle had warned me about?

But Uncle had told me to blend in, and a lot of the other Hunters seemed to have pair-ups and romantic interests that their channels showed. So shouldn't I try to do something like that? And if Josh was trying to get close to me for some sneaky reason, and I was already thinking about that possibility, couldn't I blend in *and* maybe find out his real motive at the same time?

But . . . oh, this was making my head hurt. Why couldn't things here be simple?

The next morning my vid-screen came to life as soon as I brought the lights up in my room. It was the armorer.

"You are off today, Hunter," he said. "That's policy. Two big Hunts in two days nets you a full day off. You'll Hunt again with Knight tomorrow." Before I could answer him, the screen blanked out.

Well. *Now* what would I do?

The question was answered before I got to do more than get myself up, clean, and dressed, when there was a little chime, and a mechanical voice said, "Incoming call from Psimon Josh Green. Accept?"

"Yes?" I said, assuming that since this was during the working day, it was something from my uncle. Official congratulations for high ranking or something. Josh's head and shoulders filled the screen against a blue background with the PsiCorps logo on it. I put on my best manners.

"Psimon," I said, nodding formally.

He raised an eyebrow and smiled faintly. "No need to be formal, this isn't an official call. I've free time tonight. Want to come with me to a couple of places? Your schedule has you off today."

It took me a minute to parse out what he was saying, and it surprised me so much that I blurted "yes" before I actually thought about it.

His smile broadened and again I felt my cheeks flush. "Good! Be ready and at the front at seven. I won't keep you waiting to eat longer than that, I know you Hunters get testy if you're made to wait too long for dinner. Green out."

The screen blanked. I sat there in shock. I'd just been asked on a date. A date! I hadn't had a date in ... well ... a long time, and I'm not sure those meet-ups at the village Satterday and Holly Day dances constituted what anyone would call a "real" date. I was kind of half excited, and half supernervous. Nothing that Josh had said when I'd met him had made me think he was being anything other than polite when he said he'd keep track of me—and not even that first call yesterday had made me think he was going to make a second one. Oh, if only Kei was here! She was *so* much better at the boy stuff than me. It all came so naturally to her; she could be flirting with three guys at the same time, with them in front of each other, and it all was cute, and each one of the three would be sure she was flirting only with him. She was almost as good as a Psimon at knowing what boys were thinking. And what kind of a *date* would I have here? He'd be taking me out in public! Wasn't he worried I'd do something wrong?

But wasn't this exactly what I'd been thinking about? That he was a Psimon, that he might be trying to get closer to me to read what I was hiding behind my Psi-shield and my One White Stone?

Or again . . . he hadn't said anything last night. Could this have been Uncle's idea? Was there something Uncle needed me to know that he couldn't explain directly? If so, what was it?

Thank goodness Karly turned up at my door, or I wouldn't have known what to do. She still looked really pale and shaky, but also really determined.

"Shouldn't you be in bed?" I asked.

"Remember I told you everything is vidded, or at least public record?" I nodded. "Your date tonight is already registered on your public schedule. Since I'm still officially off duty, I'm going to help you get ready for it."

I gaped at her like a real turnip, kind of in shock. I mean, yeah, intellectually I knew I was being watched, but . . .

"The Image Center isn't that far," she said. "And this is likely to take all day. But you're going to need me or someone is going to bully you into something ridiculous."

We went up an elevator to the third floor—I could have run up the stairs, but I didn't want Karly to stress herself. The Image Center turned out to be this all-white room with a man standing in it, waiting impatiently, next to a big white chair. "Sit!" he ordered, and gave Karly the stink eye, but Karly folded her arms over her chest and didn't budge, so he just heaved a big sigh and muttered something to his Perscom, and a panel rose up, and a second big white chair that had been behind it rolled by itself into the room and parked itself next to mine.

We both sat down.

I hadn't believed Karly when she'd said it was going to take all day to get ready for my date, but it turned out, I should have. I'd forgotten completely about the vid-star aspect of all of this, and I was informed that not only was Josh taking me out on a date, he was taking me out to something vid-star rank. *Much* bigger than that fancy party I'd watched on the Cit channel last night. Dinner was just the start of it. The rest of the evening would be spent at the Strauss Palais.

Karly explained it all to me as this strange man was having my whole body scanned all over again.

"It's a new trending thing," she said. "There are the sorts of clubs that Hunter Ace goes to—"

"Loud, crowded, and dark." I nodded. We call that mash-dancing, and we replicate it as well as we can, given we don't have three-fourths of what we'd need. But what we do have is bonfires, and that sort of formless dancing goes well there.

"Exactly, and you've already been given outfits that would have fit there. This is different. This is a club where you wear a very specific sort of costume. It looks like a ballroom out of a palace, and all you do is waltz. It's called Straussing; the club is the Strauss Palais."

"Wait, what?" I said, bewildered. I *thought* I knew what a waltz was, but I got the feeling that what I knew and what this was were as different as my old Hunting gear from my new stuff.

"Don't worry, that's why you're here early. They'll start designing the gown now, and while it's fabbing and until they can fit it and the accessories to you, someone will teach you how to waltz." The man turned off the scanner, I stepped off the platform, and a tall, willowy blond man with arched eyebrows came through one of the doors and took me by the hand. I looked uncertainly at Karly.

"That's why I'm here, kid," Karly said. "I'll make sure he doesn't turn you into something idiotic."

Well, if I couldn't trust Karly, who had already helped me once with the clothing they wanted to put me in, who could I trust? I let him draw me away.

And for the next couple of hours I worked harder learning how to dance than I had any time outside of a hard Hunt. When we stopped for lunch, I was as hungry as if I had been Hunting all morning. I didn't go down to the mess; I ate with the designers as they showed Karly and me the designs.

I didn't object, since they also showed me some vid-capture of Straussing, and what they made for me was nowhere near as ridiculous as some of the enormous foof-things that the girls in the vid were wearing.

"I wouldn't let him put you into one of those—cake dresses," Karly said. Now I was so grateful she had come along to help I could have kissed her.

What they'd made for me was restrained in comparison. "Edwardian," was what the chief designer said it was. Two gowns, really, one kind of a coat over the other. The one underneath was a dark gray that faded up from the bottom into a pale, pale gray. It had a tightly fitted top with a high waist and no sleeves. Over that was a dark charcoal gown with the same high waist and fitted top, cut low, with short sleeves, and heavily done all over with embroidery of silver peacock feathers. Silver peacock feathers in my hair, and a silver peacock-feather choker, and my Perscom hidden under a little bouquet of flowers on my wrist. It was still . . . a lot. Though nothing nearly like as much as what Karly called a cake dress. I just hoped I wouldn't look too silly.

"I think you'll be safe enough now," Karly said, when I'd finished approving everything. "I'm going to go put a bag of ice on my head." I grabbed her hand when no one was looking and mouthed, *Thank you,* and she managed a grin, gave me a thumbs-up, and left.

Then it was back to the dancing practice with the instructor, then to be worked all over like a prize sheep at judging time. And it seemed I wouldn't have to learn how to use all that makeup on short notice because I wasn't allowed to touch so much as a brush. They did it all, then told me to hold my breath while they sprayed something on me. Then they messed with my hair until they were happy, and only then did they put me into the dress. And I mean that, I was *not* allowed to dress myself, which was just as well, because I don't think I would have known, quite, how to put it on right. By that time it was close to when I was supposed to go, and Karly *and* Trev and Sara and Dazzle and a couple of others turned up to see what I looked like "cleaned up," as we'd say at home.

So . . . finally . . . they let me look in a mirror.

And I honestly, truly didn't recognize myself.

I *looked* like a rockster or a vid-star.

Karly laughed as I gazed into the mirror, dumbfounded. The rest applauded.

"Your expression says it all," Trev said with a chuckle, and mock-bowed at me. "You're a credit to the Hunters." One of the chimes I had gotten to know so well rang through the room.

"And just in time," Karly said. "That's your fifteen-minute warning, and since you had better *not* run in that dress, it should take you about that amount of time to walk to the entrance and meet the Psimon."

I didn't so much *walk* as drift in a kind of daze. And somewhere deep inside me I was still thinking that this wasn't *me*, that I was going to feel ridiculous, that I was going to make a fool of myself.

But . . . oh . . . the look on Josh's face when he stepped out of the pod and I stepped out of the shadows to meet him?

Priceless.

Dinner . . . well, it was pretty clear that either Josh came from a much more important family than I'd thought, or someone else was paying for it, because not one bit of it ever saw the inside of a synther or a vat. He'd taken me to some place that was made to look like it was outdoors even though it was in, and the lighting was all twilight. There were "stars" in the ceiling, and you could hear crickets and frogs, and every little table was in its own little foliage-surrounded alcove, with candles on it.

But after that first burst of dumbfounded shock, Josh redeemed himself. He made me feel comfortable and he didn't spend the time showering me with stuff about how beautiful I looked or anything like that.

"Is this anything like where you came from?" he asked, once he'd ordered for both of us (Karly had warned me this was how it was supposed to go, so I had just sat back and let him).

"Yes. No. Both," I said, as the fellow he had ordered from came back with little fancy bites of something. And wine. If they were giving me wine at the beginning of the meal, I had better be careful. "Sometimes, when it's safe, we have dinner on the porches, where we can see the stars. But we can only do that because we're above the snow line, so everyone is all bundled up, and there's no frogs or crickets, and even when its safe, everyone has a gun or a bow near at hand. And I think our food is better than here—yours is fancier, but ours is . . . more real." I ate one of the little bites, and then had to say in honesty, "On second thought, I take it back about the food."

He laughed.

But I wasn't going to sit there and let him ask all the questions. The more I learned about him, the better off I was. He might let something slip that would help me figure out his game. Or if he had one. "Have you lived here all your life?" I asked. "Did you always know you'd be a Psimon?"

"Yes to both, at least as far as I can remember," Josh replied, sitting back in his chair a little and sipping his wine. I nibbled at one of those bites. "Psi talents usually show up very young, if they're going to show up at all. I can remember hearing thoughts and projecting them before I could actually speak. They had to put a Psi-shield on me so I would learn to talk—thinking what I wanted into my parents' heads was so much easier than talking!"

We both laughed. And funnily enough, hearing about him as a little kid, seeing that Psi-powers were, to him, no different than being left-handed or a natural singer, made his being a Psimon less threatening, somehow. Weird, I know, but it was like this was something he couldn't help, and now he was just doing what he could with it. I asked him to tell me about living in Apex City. It didn't take a lot of prompting. And I wanted to hear about Apex from someone else besides Knight. Because there is always more than one side to everything. By the time the main course came, I'd learned that the Psimon school was run by one of the premier's oldest friends, who hand-picked the assignments for every strong Psimon that graduated. From the way he talked and the things he didn't say as much as the ones he did, I gathered that this was a live-in school and you basically didn't see your parents much once you were in, that while the kids were encouraged to think of themselves as a kind of family, they were not encouraged to get *too* close to each other. And that the attitude of people outside of PsiCorps toward the Psimons tended to make them feel very divorced from the Cits. That was less so in the army, but then, rarely was a Psimon ever called on to go snooping inside a soldier's head for sedition.

Then he started telling me stuff about what other Psimons did, the ones not in the army. I knew about the Psimons going with the army to take out Psi-strong Othersiders. I knew now that some of them scanned constantly for Othersiders. And I had known that they could pick up unshielded thoughts casually, which was why I'd kept my own mental shield up when I met him—and still had my guard up even now.

But this was the first time I had heard that a lot of them would spend shifts sitting in an observation post letting open thoughts drift through their heads. That made me mighty uneasy, and mighty glad of the Psi-shield in my Perscom. Even if Josh wasn't snooping, how would I know who could be? Some of what Knight had said seemed to be weighing pretty heavily on the truth side.

Josh wasn't the sort that got that kind of assignment, though. He had gotten assigned to my uncle extremely young.

And, from everything I could tell, my uncle had proceeded to treat him as if he was kin. "I think Prefect Charmand taught me how to be a human being again, as well as a Psimon," he admitted over dessert. "Sometimes I wonder if that would have happened if I'd been assigned to him later, and looking at some of the other Psimons . . ." But he didn't finish that thought. Instead, he looked at my face, then my empty plate, and said, "I think we need to work off that dinner, don't you?"

# 11

THE POD DROPPED US at the front of a building that was like every other building: tall, utilitarian. But the front was all lit up, and projected on the flat front was something I had never seen before, ever. It was a façade of a palace, only a fanciful one, made to fit the expanse of the building itself, and so convincing you would have to touch it before you convinced yourself it wasn't all carved up in ornamental leaves and swirls and creatures. And over the door of the place, words a full story tall were apparently carved. STRAUSS PALAIS.

Kind of hard to miss.

There were lots of people coming out of pods pulling up to the place, all of the men in formal suits like Josh was wearing, some of the women in gowns even more fantastic than mine. But at the moment, we were the only ones surrounded by hovering cams, and I was forcibly reminded—because the cams hadn't been so obviously present in the restaurant—that people were watching everything I was doing.

That's just downright spooky, and I felt more than a tad bit on edge. And just plain . . . way, way, way out of my depth. There was more wealth in one of those dresses than any of the settlements on the Mountain saw in a year! And I felt unsettled. Except . . . nothing ever came out of nothing. People didn't get *given* things like this, unless maybe they inherited money, and even then, *somebody* had worked for it. Right? Even I had worked for the gown I was wearing.

But I couldn't help thinking about that raggedy little kid in Spillover. . . . How many years of meals would he get for the price of one dress?

It was hard to think when there was all of this around me, and maybe that was the point. Maybe all this was *supposed* to distract people like me. Seductive. Like my bathroom . . .

We went in the door, and it was a big hall, about two stories tall, with stairs at the back, and what I figured were refreshment bars on either side of the stairs. Josh slipped his hand in mine and squeezed. We went right up the stairs and stood for a moment at the top, surveying and being surveyed.

The music was coming from everywhere; they must have had a wizard speaker and projection system. I literally could not have imagined anything like this, and had to fight another wave of feeling like any second someone was going to spot me for a phony and throw me out.

Gilded arches ran along all the walls except for where the sweeping staircase came down, and framed by the arches was a landscape of an amazing formal garden at twilight, all lit up, right out of a pre-Diseray vid. The ceiling was the starry night sky. There were seats and tables of various sorts around the edges, just under the arches, but most of the floor was reserved for dancing. Right then, although this was incredible, I was feeling just as tense as if I was staring down something as dangerous as that Folk Mage. They'd told me things were different here. But did they know how different?

The music that was playing now was for a medium-speed dance, and the partners rotated beneath us like pairs of flowers gyring and floating in a slow-moving stream. Some were better than others. So many things to worry about!

"Shall we?" Josh asked as the cameras hovered.

He must have done this a lot, because he just flowed us in, and before I could squeak we were safely circling around our mutual center, going with the clockwise flow of the greater dance.

At first I was really busy counting in my head, making myself *feel* what Josh was about to do rather than trying to anticipate it. That's harder than it seems for a Hunter; we are all about anticipating what the Othersiders are going to do next, and planning five or six steps ahead of them. I finally got myself in the right headspace, and it all snapped into place and I could relax and pay attention to what else was around me. I managed not to be overwhelmed by all this . . . glittering, gleaming *stuff*. And then I started feeling light-headed again, because of Josh. His arm around my waist was nothing like the instructor's—it felt warm, and sort of . . . personal. My hand on his shoulder was cold; the one in his hand was warm. He smelled clean, and a little bit like cedar.

The dance we had joined ended, and another one began immediately. Now, I am in pretty superb shape, but I had to wonder about how well Josh was going to hold up. There was no way that he was in as good shape as a Hunter. *No one*, not even a message-runner, is in as good shape as a Hunter. I could probably dance for hours; this was nothing like as hard as running my territory back home from dawn to dusk with my full load-out on my back.

But I should have realized that these things were designed to exhaust mere Cits, many of whom probably never walked more than fifty yards at a time. After four more dances, the music ended with a chord that everyone but me seemed to recognize, the couples separated, and the men bowed and the women did this thing called a "curtsey," with their skirts spread out around them. My skirts were narrower, so I did this dip with my arms out instead of spreading out my skirts. Then the floor cleared, all of us going to the little tables around the edge. The light dimmed, the lamps on the tables came up, the scene playing out behind the arches turned to a garden at night illuminated by fireflies and candle lanterns.

I couldn't help but keep half an eye on it, waiting for a swarm of Othersiders to invade it, even though I knew it was just a projection.

Girls in black-and-white outfits with really short poufy skirts, white aprons, and big foofy white bows on the tops of their heads came around, and I realized these were more "waiters." Josh ordered something while I scanned around us. He didn't seem to notice.

Light came up in the center of the room, and a couple who were so beautiful they didn't look real swirled into the middle of the floor. She was wearing a dress with a train about three yards long, over another skirt with row after row of ruffles, and a built-up behind, all in gold satin. He was wearing a matching gold satin outfit, but it wasn't a tuxedo; it looked something like a military dress uniform, only there were fanciful things up the front and lots of loops of braid at the shoulder and platelike epaulettes with fringe on them. She picked up her train and fastened the end to her wrist in an incredibly graceful, sweeping motion. The music started and they danced. I had to stop myself from staring at them with my eyes as big as saucers.

Professionals, of course. We knew about professional dancers at home; their performances were one of the things we liked to be sure to catch. But, wow, this sort of thing is *so* much more impressive in person than on a vid-screen. I forced myself after a while to just half watch with a look of admiration (I think) on my face, while I half watched everything else. Most people were only paying cursory attention to the dancers. A lot were talking. A lot were furtively eyeing us and the other Apparently Important People. The people who had cams hovering over them were . . . well . . . acting. Just like they'd been acting when they danced. The dancers didn't seem to care. Probably even when a Hunter and a Psimon weren't here, people didn't pay that much attention to the professional dancers. This was mostly a reason for people to catch their breath, drink, and rest a little.

I wished I had suggested something else, something more like what a regular Cit would have done, something to make me blend in better. But I was here now, and I had to make the best of it. This was part of the job, right? Because if things were really, really dangerous, no Hunter would be wasting time at something like this. This was all part of making the Cits feel safe. And I was with Josh, who was better-looking than any boy I knew back home, and who seemed really happy to be with me, and even if he had some other motive for getting close to me, at least right now he was good company. And if Kei ever saw this, I knew she'd be talking at the screen, trying to give me advice I couldn't hear, mostly about flirting.

But on the other hand—this was all so amazing, it was all I could do to keep from gawking! There was a little girl inside me who wanted to run around the room, peering and poking at all the fancy dresses, running to see how they made the garden scene look so real, asking questions of the professional dancers.

What Josh ordered had come. It was fizzy; my sensitive tongue caught a bit of alcohol in it, but not so much I was worried about it affecting me. It tasted like a lot of things, nothing I was familiar with, and was acidic and faintly sweet. I gave him a look of enquiry. "Sham-pane," he said. "It's a kind of wine."

So, some sort of fizzy wine. I would have preferred mineral water, but I guess that is hard to come by here. I sipped it carefully. He leaned over the table to speak.

"The dance periods are called 'sets,'" he said. "Now, every other set, it's expected you are to dance with whoever comes to ask you, and I am expected to go ask other women, until the last dance of the set. Then I come claim you."

"I only dance with boys?" I said. He nodded.

"Or, rather, you only dance with people dressed like boys. There might be some lizzes here, but they'll be in proper partner outfits, and only the one in trousers will ask you to dance." He shrugged. "This is all as formal and regimented as an army drill."

I nodded. That would be all right. It wasn't exactly egalitarian, though. I mean, back home, a girl can ask a boy to dance as well as a boy can ask a girl. And why couldn't one of the girls-dressed-as-girls ask me to dance if she wanted to? And the business of the man being the one to lead in the dance. You'd think it would be the better dancer, whichever partner it was. Things felt out of balance again. But then I thought about those huge dresses, like bells, and pictured what would happen if two women wearing those tried to dance together, and I had to stifle a giggle. No . . . that would not work, not at all.

The professionals finished their routine and bowed out to a spattering of applause. The lights came back up again, and as we put down our empty glasses, there sure was a rush of people to get to our table. Quite by accident one older man, who had gotten up just as the rush began, got shoved to my side of the table, and, a little annoyed at the rudeness, I touched his elbow to say I would dance with *him*.

He looked shocked, then delighted, then embarrassed, then delighted all over again, and the lady he was with practically clapped, her face a big grin. This was one of the couples that just seemed to be here because they wanted to be, which made me feel good. If I was going to be the prize catch, well, someone who deserved it should hook me.

So, much to the jealousy of the others, he led me out. The music started with a big chord, which I now recognized meant we were supposed to bow and curtsey, then we positioned ourselves, and we were off.

He wasn't as good as Josh, but he was having so much fun that it was fun to be with him. *He* was enjoying himself so much I didn't feel so stifled by everything around me. It even felt a little like being in the community hall on a Satterday Night. When he made missteps, I just echoed him so it looked like it was on purpose. When the dance ended, he thanked me, squeezing my hand. "Hunter Joyeaux, that was wonderful! You made me look like—"

"A *gentleman*, which you are, and it was fun—" was all I managed to get to say before I was claimed by another eager . . . well . . . sycophant. This one chattered through the whole dance, which was all right, he was doing such simple steps it was easy to follow him and answer him at the same time. Didn't I love Apex? Wasn't it a huge difference from the mountains? Did I—would I—did I think—

I have to say it was rude and intrusive by home standards, but I suppose this was one of the people who'd started to follow my channel, and I guess watching practically everything I did, at least in public, made people think they're somehow part of your life and entitled to know more about it. I just kept myself calm, tried to look like this was as much fun as dancing with that older fellow, and talked to him nicely and remembered how the Masters would answer when there was something they didn't want to discuss, sliding away from the topic the way they slid away from the blows people tried to land on them. And as soon as I got the chance, I curved him to talk about himself, which he wasn't at all averse to doing.

That pretty much repeated itself until Josh got me for the last dance of the set, and a different quartet of professional dancers took the middle—this time the women danced on the tips of their toes, which kind of made me startled, since I didn't even know that was possible, and it looked like they were defying gravity.

Josh saw my face and chuckled. "I was going to chat with you about White Knight, but it's sheer curiosity on my part and I can see you want to watch the ballee dancers. At least, I think that is what they're called. Ballot dancers? That can't be right. It's not a social dance, it's a watching dance. Usually they do whole—plays, I guess you'd call them, only it's all in dance. This just started getting resurrected from a vault of vids and books someone found about four years ago."

Well they were dancing a little play right out there in the middle, and all I could think was that I couldn't imagine how anyone could balance on the tips of their toes, let alone dance on them, without magic. I even figured out what the play was, before too long—it was from Shakespeare, *Othello*, which of course ends badly, but it ended badly in such a gorgeous way that you couldn't feel the same sad you would if it was the play. He let me watch in peace, and then came a set when he was my only partner. Having had all those other fellows made me realize how good he was, and I said so. And oh, it was so wonderful feeling his arm at my waist and his hand holding mine—but I didn't want to tell him that. I didn't want him to think I was thinking all this meant more than *he* was thinking it meant, and . . .

Oh why couldn't I have been Kei?

And why did I have to keep second-guessing all this?

"When did you have time to learn to dance like this?" I asked finally.

He made a little face. "I cheated," he told me.

I giggled, and then tried to cover my mortification that I had giggled. "How do you cheat at learning dancing?" I asked.

He let go of my waist and briefly tapped the side of his head. "Psimon, remember? I mind-rode one of the pros. With full permission of course."

I was astounded. I had no idea you could get *physical* memory that way, but I guess you can. It was creepy actually—and made the stories I had heard back in the mountains about how a Psimon can imitate you so well your closest relatives can't tell the difference seem more plausible.

I felt as if I ought to say something, but I couldn't think of anything to say, so I changed the subject slightly. "Would you want to do this again?"

"The question is, would you?" he responded, throwing the ball back at me.

Well what was I supposed to say? I didn't want to make him feel bad, if he'd chosen this to entertain me. But . . . all this . . . Had this really been his idea? Was it Uncle's, and was *this* the sort of thing that was supposed to make me blend in with the other Hunters? "It's fun . . ." I managed, thinking of what it would be like a second time, when I might not be so intimidated and self-conscious and maybe I'd have a better idea about Josh's motivations. When I might be more sure about him, be able to think more like Kei and manage to say all the right things that would make him think of me as someone he wanted to get to know a *lot* better.

"Then we'll do it again." He consulted something somewhere over my head, or at least seemed to. "However, I am reminded that a Hunter's day begins early, so this will be the last set of the night I am afraid. All your fans will be disappointed." Again the reminder of how many people were watching. I could never get away from it.

"I can't stay out too late," I agreed, feeling the unseen pressure of those cameras on me. "I'm ready to get back." Although I wasn't, not really. I wanted this to go on until I was too tired to make one more step. I wanted to get a chance to hear more about him. Most of all, I wanted to get relaxed enough that I might be able to read him a little better. I wondered if he'd been given some sort of signal, or if that stare over my head had meant another Psimon was talking to him. It could have been either.

A pod was waiting for us when we left, and we got into it and sped away. But then Josh put the privacy screens up on the windows, and kind of dropped his air of smoothness. "I have to apologize just a little if you felt like I was overdoing things. You know, the Palais, the fancy dinner..."

"It was fun..." I repeated. "But I kept thinking about the people where I patrol, and the ones back home, like my friend Kei. They never even see anything like all that. *I've* never even seen anything like that. We didn't know people lived like that here." I bit my lip a little, and my eyebrows furrowed. "Kei would go insane. She'd say it was like Sleeping Beauty's ball." I was confused. I only could think one thing. I was *not* going to "get used to this." I never wanted to be the sort of person who looked at an expensive dress or a fancy meal and thought *yawn*, instead of how many poor families could be fed with that money, or how many rounds of ammo could it buy to protect people outside the Barriers?

"Well, this is what you do," he told me firmly. "Remember your image. Remember you have to have and keep an image. If you are going to fit in, you have to keep your head down and your ratings up."

I nodded. He had *not* been privy to what Uncle had tapped out for me, yet here he was using practically the same words. So maybe Uncle trusted him enough to tell him some of our secrets?

He dropped me at the door to headquarters, bending and kissing my hand as he handed me out of the pod, which made me blush, and then he got back in the pod and sped off and I went up to my rooms. When I got there, I stripped off the gown, sent it down the cleaning chute, and got into the shower. As the hot water sent all the makeup down the drain, and I went from being the exotic thing I'd seen in the mirror to being *me* again, it felt as if I could think more clearly. More like myself.

I looked into my eyes and told myself that I wasn't going to turn into a female copy of Ace. I'd never see *myself* in the mirror again, if I let things change me like that.

"We'll split up for the morning. Stay close enough that if one of us runs into trouble, the other can get there fast," White Knight said over biscuits and gravy, "but far enough that it counts as Hunting solo. It's the next step of your assessment."

I nodded, though I hadn't expected to be doing any solo Hunting quite this fast, once I'd been told what was what.

"The other thing is that because there are two of us, we're going to be going deeper into Spillover than I usually patrol," he continued. "Truth to tell, I'm not sure what to warn you about, because I haven't been out there in over a year."

Now ... we have some smart people up on the Mountain. I mean book-smart, not just survival-smart. When the Diseray happened, we ended up with a mix of both, and that's kind of the way it stayed. So something that one of my teachers—as opposed to my Masters—taught me was how to look at numbers, as in where things are changing over time. That's a lot easier here, the computer does it all for you, so I'd asked my Perscom to show me some stuff. "Whatever it was like then, it'll be worse now," I said. "This morning I asked the computer to show me Hunts over time for the last five years. Everything stayed pretty flat for four, but this year is getting worse month by month. It's very gradual. Like, it's not as if things have doubled from this time last year. But there is a slow and steady increase in the numbers and the hazards."

That sent both his eyebrows shooting toward his hairline. "I knew it *felt* that way," he said slowly. "But you're telling me it wasn't just me?"

I nodded my head.

Knight sucked on his lower lip. He tapped his own Perscom. "Reasons for increase in Otherside incursion over past six months?" he queried aloud.

"Population pressure: probability fifty-four percent," the Perscom said. "C and C orders: probability fifty-two percent. Personal vendetta: probability forty-nine percent. All other probabilities twenty percent or less."

"C and C?" I asked.

"There's some indication that at least some of the Folk actually work together, with something like a Command and Control structure of their own, like we have in the army," Knight replied, and scratched his head. "I've never seen anything to make me think they were . . . but I never thought to ask the Perscom if things were getting worse around here either."

"I want some grenades this time," I said finally. "If we need anything bigger than that, we need an Elite, or artillery or air support and at least another Hunter. *Can* we get artillery or air support?"

"Not in Spillover, unless we actually see a force trying to knock down the Barrier," Knight said truthfully. "Or something equally nasty that could get inside."

The pod dropped us at a different part of the Barrier this time, and if my memory was correct, it was nearly to the spot where we'd routed the Goblin market.

This time the door we went through didn't have a guard, and there was no one lined up to come into the safer zone. The safer zone was utterly unpopulated; what looked like huge window-less buildings, maybe for manufacturing, surrounded another huge windowless building. Knight nodded at it. "Prison," he said briefly. "Factories around it. Underground tunnels to the factories. Humans are all tucked behind a lot of concrete and ferrous metal. That keeps the Othersiders from even bothering to roam here for the most part. And as for the prisoners, no prison is escape-proof, but who'd try to escape when you'd be as visible to anything that *was* here as a laser dot in a coal mine?"

Good point.

We passed into a landscape even more devastated than before. There were no signs of human habitation. That didn't mean that there weren't any humans here, it just meant there were no signs of them. Anyone who lived here was deeply in hiding.

I was conscious of the grenades on my belt; even at home they weren't part of my usual load-out, and when I carried them, it meant there was probably going to be something serious to deal with.

Or I might have to start an avalanche, but usually we use sticks of home-brewed TNT for that.

They were smaller than I was used to, but that meant I could throw them farther, which was probably a very good thing. "Close" counts with a grenade. . . .

Once inside, Knight and I split up. He directed me to go back in the direction we'd patrolled the last time; he went out to "new" territory. I cast the Glyphs and called the Hounds; we took our usual solo pattern. Six of the seven ranged out around me, with Bya beside me. I scanned the sky; he scanned the ground, with senses much keener and more varied than mine.

I found the site of the Goblin market; it was deserted, with no trace of the puddles of goo the Goblins had turned into when they died. The wind whistled forlornly among the buildings; I thought about the half-starved kid I had seen. And when I saw a bunny peeking around a lump of broken-off cement, I didn't even think. I sent Bya after it. Bya ran off and dispatched it, then fetched it, like a retriever. He knew what I was thinking, of course—he always did—and with a toss of his head he flung the limp body of the bunny into thin air. Well, apparently thin air. I knew where it had gone, because when we didn't Hunt, my Hounds and I just hunted. Bya had a place Otherside where he stored what I killed. I guess nothing Otherside found dead game at all interesting.

So while we scouted for trouble, I did what I did at home; I had the Hounds keep an eye out for game. Twice more we got something, a squirrel and a second bunny. I was watching for something else too. That kid.

I figured, scared as he was, he'd had my face and Knight's branded into his memory as people who had helped him. And I figured he would be watching for us. So after covering a fair amount of territory and coming back to what you might call the "neighborhood" where the Goblin market had been, I spotted one eye under a shaggy shock of hair peering over the corner of a broken window at us.

I didn't say anything. I just pointed right at him, then at my feet.

The eye widened. The tuft of hair vanished. Bya looked at me and dog-grinned; he could hear the kid coming. I couldn't, yet, but I knew he wouldn't be grinning at me otherwise. I looked away for a moment, peering in the direction the kid would be coming from, and when I looked back, the game was at Bya's feet. You know, I never can figure out how he does that.

It was about that time I sensed Knight moving in behind me, but he didn't say anything, so I ignored him for the moment.

The kid edged nervously around the corner of a building and paused. "Come here," I ordered, in a quiet, but carrying voice. He sidled over, but his eyes were on the game. And I was right about him being half starved. "You got folks?" I asked, figuring not.

He shook his head. That explained why he'd fallen for the Goblin ploy. No adults to warn him.

"You got friends?" I asked.

This time he nodded.

"Come get this, take it with you, and share it," I ordered him. "And from now on, don't trust anything that's not a Hound or a human. Got it?"

He nodded so hard I was afraid for a moment his head would come off. Then he scuttled the last few feet between us, snatched up the game, and ran off with it.

"I never thought of doing that."

"Plain old hunting, or feeding the kids with it?" I asked, turning to face him.

"Both." He looked off in the direction the kid had vanished into. "I thought about bringing food out here, but—"

"Don't bother, there's food all around here, and your Hounds will probably be willing to drop at people's feet whatever you shoot or they snatch out of the air." I absently ruffled Bya's ears—or what passes for ears. "I know a bunny here and a squirrel there might seem like next to nothing—"

"You forget, I'm a turnip too," he reminded me. "One bunny can mean the difference between getting by and not making it. That was a very Christian—I mean, compassionate thing you just did."

I half smiled. "And likely it will be cut from the vids," I said. "So let's go find something to keep the ratings up."

# 12

IT LOOKED AS THOUGH taking down the Goblin market had put a good scare into anything else that had been prowling the area. Knight's Hounds and mine decided to liven things up by herding everything they could find toward us in one large mob. All mere nuisances to fully armed Hunters with good magic; the main challenge was putting them down before they could get away. There were a couple of Black Dogs, a lot of Piskies, a few Goblins in their natural shape, and a single big Redcap. Redcaps are vicious buggers. They look like those cute little statues that used to be in gardens: little, old, bearded dwarfy things in pantaloons and jackets, that stand from knee-high to maybe chest-high. They wear pointy red hats that give them their name. They carry knives as long as your arm, they've got skin that can turn away small-caliber bullets. And they like to dye those red hats with the blood of their victims.

Of course, Redcaps are no match for a Hunter and a Hound or two. Even a mob wouldn't have been a match for me and Knight and our pack. At least it gave the hovering cameras something to broadcast.

I waited until we were in the pod taking us back to headquarters before bringing up what I'd been thinking about, off and on, for the last couple of days. "Can I borrow your Perscom?" I asked. He looked at me oddly, but passed it over. I typed in how he could contact one of the least obnoxious of the Christer leaders back home, Brother Vincent. I passed the Perscom back to him.

"I don't know if your people would be willing to move," I said slowly. "But that's an option. There's plenty of work, and no poison in the water or the soil." I nodded at his Perscom. "They're Christers, one of the settlements I used to patrol. Actually most people are around that part of the territory, but some of them don't much get along with others of them, and I'm not sure what faction your people would belong to." Truth to tell, the stuff the Christers argued about always made my head ache. Whether water had to be splashed on you or you had to do a full-on ducking, whether it had to be when you were just born or when you were old enough to understand things for yourself... and those were just the *easy* things they argued about.

Well, at least the folks thereabouts knew better than to tell about the Monastery on the Mountain. If there's one thing that they all have in common it is a deep understanding that if they reveal the Monastery is there, they lose the protection of the Hunters that would be co-opted by the government. Even the most hostile might not much like us, but they like being eaten, overrun, or otherwise turned into easy prey a lot less. Something the Diseray taught them was not to depend too much on being right and righteous to save them from bad things.

Brother Vincent at least has a decent attitude. *"God defends our souls,"* he'd say. *"He leaves our bodies to us."*

Knight nodded. "You know, you would have a true understanding of that if you—"

I held up a hand. "White Knight, you are my mentor, but I'm old enough to know my own mind, thanks. I've been around a fruit salad of Christers all my life, and none of them made a dent and neither will you. Truce?"

He looked a bit annoyed but nodded. I figured on the annoyance. I have never yet met a Christer that liked being told I didn't want any part of his religion, thanks. Oh well.

"I don't know if your people will get along with this bunch. I don't know if they'd want to move. But we have mines—mostly for metals, and mostly boarded up, and there are Knockers in them, but ordinary folks can kill Knockers with fire and bullets, and your people ought to be able to get some metal out to make a living. At least they'll be able to drink the water safely, and grow food they can eat on clean land, and there's plenty of land and never enough farmers." I shrugged. "Like I said, it's an option. And if the Cits have to replace your miners with machines because they've moved, well, that's their option too."

About then the pod pulled up at headquarters. I was hungry, so I was out of the car pretty quick, while Knight was still sitting there looking like he was thinking hard.

After I left my load-out at the armory, so was I.

As in . . . what was I thinking, sending someone I didn't even know all that well in the direction of the Mountain?

But the Hounds liked him. And the Hounds are pretty darn good judges of someone. And...well...I just hated to think of anyone trying to live on poisoned ground. That just added one more lead weight to the stack of misery anyone outside the Barriers has to cope with.

But then I thought about what the Masters would say about compassion.

And about putting yourself in others' shoes. Which, truth to tell, I hadn't done when it came to the Christers. There was Knight, with his burden of guilt, and maybe they were all like him, laboring under the burden of feeling they deserved to be punished, and even looking for that punishment. Maybe that's why they were so unpleasant. Guilt and self-loathing tend to make you cranky.

I ducked in and out of the shower fast, because I have to say, I was starving, and I wanted to get to the mess quick. Then, before I went to dinner, I took a moment to look at the ratings and I nearly passed out in shock.

I was—number two? But—why?

Then I remembered what else I'd been seeing when I checked on their Hunts, Ace and his pack, and I realized that even our mass drive of pathetic nuisances would have been more exciting than what Ace was probably doing today. I felt my mouth twisting in a cynical sort of grimace.

*Ace, you can only coast on being spectacularly handsome for so long when people tune in to see something die.*

Which gave me a little pause. How often did they tune in to hoping to see the Hunter die?

I shivered. But I let it pass. Right now I was hungry, and right now

I wanted to get in and out of the mess hall before Ace and his crew turned up. I didn't want a confrontation right now. I would probably get one sooner rather than later, but I didn't want one right now.

Much to my *happy* surprise, though, the first person I saw when I cleared the door was Karly.

She looked a lot less shaky. She spotted me as soon as I came in, and started to tentatively raise her hand, as if she wasn't quite sure if I would acknowledge her or not. But I ran right over, of course, forgetting how hungry I was, and plunked myself down in the chair across from her.

"How are you feeling?" I demanded. "Did you overwork yourself, helping me with the date? Do you still have the headache? Are you even a little dizzy? Numb anywhere? Having muscle control problems?" Those were all signs of persistent nerve and brain problems after suffering a Gazer attack. And when she'd been walking me through all the stuff with the designers and the gown before my date, she'd been pale and very shaky, though I hadn't said anything in front of the non-Hunters. You kind of don't do that. Especially if we're supposed to be making Cits confident about us. "Are you actually feeling *good* yet?"

"Not bad, no, yes, no, no, and no," she laughed. "But the headache's easing off and is almost gone. They'll clear me to hunt tomorrow, or the next day, or at least they think so. You forget, we get the good tending here. No trying to guess whether or not you're healing up when we have machines that can tell us."

I didn't snort and tell her the truth, which is that some of the Masters are so good they are better than any machines. I just nodded, didn't hide my relief, and went to grab something from the line before returning to her table.

"So, watched your Hunt today—you did good," she continued, as I slid into the seat and began on my food. "Smart to herd all those little monsters into one pack; that made it a lot more impressive."

"We just do it that way at home because it's more efficient," I said, telling the truth. "One Hunter, one set of Hounds, big territory. You waste a lot of time and energy chasing vermin all over the landscape, otherwise."

Karly nodded and took a drink from her glass, and that was when Ace and his gang chose to materialize.

I saw from the look in his eye he was going to start something, and I braced myself. But he turned toward *Karly.*

"So, Hunter Karly, I hear you figure you're ready to go out and rack up some more ratings points already—" he began, and sneered. "I reckon you think hanging out with this one is gonna help you out big time. Hunting with her—"

"Seriously, Ace," I interrupted, "You sound like you've been chewing loco-weed. Nobody is hanging out for ratings, and nobody was glory-hounding. If there'd been an Elite free to take that Gazer, we'd have waited. But it was almost shift change, there were Cits coming into the danger zone, and we didn't have any choice."

He turned and stared at me with his mouth hanging open before shutting it with an audible snap.

"You just use that head of yours for something besides holding up your hair," I continued. "You just ask your Perscom to show you how things have been getting worse, and more and more Othersiders are getting past the Barriers over the last six months." He had a pole-struck-ox look on his face. Evidently it never occurred to him that someone would figure out he'd been coasting. Sure, the Cits in the richer districts deserved protection, but they were so well insulated behind layers of Barriers that whatever got that far could be taken out by police with a shotgun loaded with blessed salt and iron shot. "I've seen your old Hunts. You were *hot* good. You earned every point of your rating. You got whole rookeries of Ketzels all by yourself! You got entire clans of Redcaps. You got most of a Goblin market. You could do that again, anytime you wanted to! Hunt Spillover. Hunt Warehouse, Industrial, Farm. Hunt Northside. Check the stats for the last week or so to see where things have been the worst, where stuff's cropping up the thickest. What's outside the Barriers is getting in and it's about time the Hunters put a stop to it."

"More than time," Karly seconded grimly.

Now everyone in the mess hall could hear this. I wasn't making any effort to keep it quiet. By this point Ace had gotten over his shock and was starting to get mad, and was about to lay into me—verbally at least—when his brother, Paules, interrupted the tirade before it began by poking him hard in the ribs with an elbow and jerking his head sideways at the rest of the room.

Ace turned a little and saw what I'd seen. Those very few that weren't staring hard at their own food were nodding at what I said. All my friends from the nights in the lounge were nodding hard. Especially those who had hard districts to patrol and, like Karly and Knight, had been finding worse than the usual nuisances lurking. Ace took a second look around, and I could see the moment that he realized this was not the time to force a confrontation, by the way he lost all expression.

He didn't answer me, though. He just turned and left, with his friends following him. I went back to my dinner, and after a moment, so did everyone else. I wondered how much, if any, of this would turn up on the vids.

Probably none. Fighting among ourselves over ratings was not something I expect people running the vid-feeds wanted Cits to see. I resolved to skim over the channels again, though, and see if I could figure out what they *did* want the Cits to see besides Hunting and Hunters playing in glamorous places. Though I still couldn't quite wrap my head around why they'd want to see us cavorting around in the first place. Wouldn't they rather go do the cavorting themselves? Maybe they couldn't afford the clubs that Ace went to, or that restaurant and place that Josh took me to, but having a little shindig with friends in your own street is more fun than watching someone else have a good time. Isn't it?

Well, at least Ace had been put on notice now, and so had his friends. I'd fibbed about looking at his old Hunts, but I reckoned he *had* to have been a fine Hunter or he wouldn't have gotten that rating in the first place. I wondered why his own Hounds hadn't gone at him before I did. My Hounds sure give me notice when they think we haven't been working hard enough. Rightly so— they get the manna from the stuff we kill, and if we don't kill, they don't get the manna.

Then again, Ace only had two Hounds, so maybe a few Piskies was enough manna for them.

"Daydreaming?" Karly asked, interrupting my thoughts.

"Kinda." I smiled a little sheepishly. "Was just thinking about how surprised I was when I got my Hounds and there were seven of them." I stopped myself before I added that pretty much everyone up on the Mountain either got a lot of Hounds, or three or so really big, powerful ones. I mean . . . bigger than draft-horse big.

"I don't know how you control them all," she replied.

"I don't. We're a team." I shrugged. "I guess it's easier when your Hounds talk to you."

"Mine . . . *feel*, I guess you'd have to say, more than talk. Though mostly what I get from them is this impatient *I'm hungry, let's find something*." We both laughed. I've gotten that often enough from Bya.

"Well, if they're hungry and you're worried, call them through and ask them if they want to join my pack," I offered.

Karly had this expression on her face as if this was something she had never heard of. "Wait. They can do that?"

I stopped myself just in time from saying we did that all the time on the Mountain when a Hunter was hurt or sick. No point in the Hounds going hungry, after all. "Did that when my teacher was down," I said. "Bya will take charge of them." He would, too. He loves being alpha to a huge pack. "We worked fine, down there in the sewer."

Her face lightened. "So we did. They're telling me a few more days before they'll let me Hunt, and I can feel my boys getting anxious on the Otherside. It'll ease my mind to know they're getting manna."

"Well, good. How long have *you* been Hunting?" I asked, curious now.

She ran her hand through her hair. "Not as long as you might think. I popped late. I was an agro-squint, if you can believe it, and

I was out alone in the fields past the Fourth Barrier checking on an experimental run of beans when I heard the worst sound I'd ever heard in my life and spotted a full pack of Black Dogs heading for me from where they'd dug under the Barrier."

Black Dogs look exactly like they sound. Big, heavily muscled black dogs with fiery yellow eyes, like the breed they called Rottweilers in the old days. They're probably related in some way to Hellhounds, which we don't see nearly as often, and are about twice the size of Black Dogs. One of their weapons is their voices— when they howl they can rupture your eardrums.

"I stuffed my fingers in my ears and ran for my pod, but they were overtaking me too fast, so I jumped up onto one of the robo-tillers, grabbed the wrench always stowed up there, and was about to take out as many as I could when my hands started burning." She shrugged, with a rueful smile. "And suddenly I was a Hunter."

"Happened almost the same for me," I told her, the whole truth this time. "I was out with a shotgun"—which was almost as big as *I* was back then—"and instead of the Piskies I was supposed to chase out of the field, I ran into a clan of Redcaps."

"And how'd your boyfriend take to finding out his girl was a Hunter?" Karly asked. And the way she said it sounded... weighted.

"Didn't have one." Again the truth. "But I don't think, if I'd had, he would have liked it, since obviously I had to come here. I don't know how Knight manages with his girl back home."

Karly sighed. "Well, my wife had a meltdown. We'd only been married a couple of months, and she couldn't take it, couldn't take that I'd be in danger every day. She hadn't signed on for that, you know?"

I did know. I'd seen the same thing happen to old Mary and to Big Tom, and they'd been married to their spouses a lot longer than a couple of months. "I'm sorry," I said, and meant it.

Karly must have heard as much in my voice, because she smiled a little, ruefully. "I keep telling myself it was only a matter of time, all things considered. Sure, it was a huge, big stress that broke us up—but little stresses over time can do the same thing if what you've got isn't strong enough. Nobody's at fault; we were both just mistaken. When I manage to be philosophical about it, I can say that this way at least we didn't end things in fighting and bitterness. Something bigger than both of us ended it for us, so there was no blame on either side."

"Oh, bull hockey," I said. "I bet you swore the air blue and broke things."

That got a laugh out of her, and I prompted her to tell me what life had been like for her at Apex *before* her powers popped.

We chitchatted a little more, and then I went straight on to the lounge.

Nobody said anything about me facing down Ace, but they didn't have to say anything. The approval was there, in the way they jibed at me for herding a bunch of little stuff together and calling it a Hunt. Even though I was by far the youngest Hunter there, I got treated like an equal, someone they'd be more than willing to have at their backs.

When the vid-critique was over, Trev had a different idea than the usual card games and so forth.

"We haven't done face time in two weeks," he announced. "Who's with me for Flannigan's?" Then he turned and pointed at me. "You need to see how to do this, Joy."

"Do what?" I asked, but Karly, who had come in about halfway through the vid-viewing, just chuckled.

"Face time," she said. "Let's head for your room and we'll get you fixed up."

We went back to my room, and she picked out one of the showier outfits for me, like the sort of thing Ace and his crew wore at those clubs, which was when I got the vague idea we were going to one. The outfit was one of the suedelike charcoal tunics and a gorgeous soft pair of black trousers, but the wide belt and all of the appliqué work on the tunic was in a metallic silver fabric instead of gray leather. She helped me pick out some cosmetics and showed me how to put my hair into a tail under my right ear and string beads on strands of hair to hang in front of my left ear. "There, you look ready to meet your fans. Meet the others at the front entrance," she said. "I'm too tired for face time, but you go and show them what a Hunter is made of." She grinned and left, and I changed, did my face simply and quickly, and went to meet the others. There were six in our group, including me, and we all piled into a big pod that Trev called.

We ended up at a place that smelled of beer and food—not in a bad way, mind. But what nearly made me turn and run for the door was that the whole room was covered in Hunter things. Pictures, posters, what looked like someone's tunic with a claw slash across it in a frame. Like . . . the place was a shrine to Hunters. And when we got in the door, the Cits in the place were like the Cits on the train had been after I'd helped chase off that Mage. I stuck close to Trev, but the Cits were really excited to see that I was with the group.

There were vid-screens in the four corners of the room, and all of them were playing live feeds on Hunter channels. It was time for the night shift to go out, and I got a look at what they did. You might think that night Hunting is inherently more dangerous, but it isn't. A lot of the things that are bad and small are strictly daylight prowlers. Gazers aren't out at night, for instance, and if you think about it, that's logical, since they require their prey to be able to see them. The stuff that *is* nocturnal has no advantage over us, since our Hounds can see in the dark and we have night-vision goggles. In some cases we have an actual advantage, since light hurts or even kills them, and you can take them out with a focused-beam flashlight. Vampires, for instance, are just pathetic, except when they've got an ambush set up. Light in the eyes, *bam*, they're blinded and it's all over. Being stronger than five men and supernaturally fast doesn't do you a lot of good when you can't see.

The others explained things to me as the place emptied and refilled, emptied and refilled. This was a "bar," which I remembered from old vids and books. Specifically, this was a bar where people who were fanatical about watching particular Hunters went. Trev's loose group of friends was popular here, it seemed. There were . . . a lot of these bars, and every week or two weeks, Hunters were expected to turn up and make the Cits happy by being able to get close to them. These were "fans" and this was "face time" or "fan service." It was overwhelming on one hand, and kind of touching on the other. I overheard a couple of Cits arguing about how much of the Goblin market Hunt Knight and I had done had been "special effects" and how much of it had been real. It seemed the Cits understood that the feed was being tampered with, but they thought the vid editors were making the Hunts look *more* dangerous than they really were, not less.

But how could you not feel friendly toward someone who so obviously wishes you to do well? Because most of these Cits did, even if they thought it was more sport and acting and less danger than it actually was. "But you're so *young*," was what I kept hearing.

As Trev had led us in, he led us out again, and the big pod was waiting for us as we wormed our way past the crowd. When we all piled in, he turned to me. "So. Mostly we do this in groups. Two hours, at most; if you stay past two hours, too many people see where you are on your vid-feed, and it can turn into a mob, and a mob can get impossible to handle."

I nodded.

But then he added something else I had not expected. "Too many random, uncontrolled people in one place makes a tempting target, too," he stated with a warning sort of tone in his voice. "Two hours or so, it's safe; after that you want to leave so the gathering breaks up."

Tempting target? For *what*? Was this a hint that the Folk actually *were* getting inside the Prime Barrier, or did he mean something else?

But before I could ask, he had already changed the subject. "You did good, kid," he continued with approval. "Always remember, even if they get drunk and obnoxious, they're on your side. And—well, drunk and obnoxious is why we do this in groups."

We all piled out and went to our rooms. That was when I got a text on my Perscom from Josh. Seemed like he must have been watching my channel, then timed his text for when he figured I was back again.

*Would have been fun to surprise you at that bar.*

I'd have been surprised, all right.... *Why didn't you?* I replied.

*On duty,* came the answer. *Boring party, but I need to be here. At least someone left a vid-feed on.*

I was going to say something, but then I got the beep of another text coming through. *And I am summoned. Later.*

I felt a wave of disappointment, even if I still couldn't shake my suspicion of his motives, and yet—grinning like a right old idiot. Because he texted me. And he'd been watching me at the bar. For once, I was glad of all the cameras.

I was tempted to watch my own channel as I got ready for bed, but I resisted.

I did watch Knight's, though, and I was glad to see he looked pretty good. I hoped the folks back at his home ground were happy with what they were seeing. It might make them more receptive to moving. The more I thought about it, the worse I felt about those folks living on poisoned land.

I mean, I could understand the big cities needing more Hunters than turnip territory, just judging by the amount of nastiness *I* had run into since I got here. So I could understand them demanding most Hunters be sent here.

I could even understand now why, out where we were, we didn't get a lot of equipment. That stuff has to be paid for, and it wasn't as if we were chipping in to what the cities need. It's easier to collect taxes from all the Cits in a city than it is to collect 'em from folks out where we are. We can say "no," and make it stick, so they don't even try. Sometimes they send us stuff, most times we pay for it.

But more or less forcing people who're providing something you need pretty bad to make the choice between living unprotected and living poisoned, just so you can get what you want . . .

That was just wrong.

Why, at least, weren't they getting enough from their coal that they could build bunkers to live in and machines to tend *their* crops?

Maybe that was why Knight didn't do the "fan service" stuff—not because he was a Christer and objected to it, but because of how horribly his people back home had been treated. If that was so, I couldn't blame him, not one bit. He was the kind of guy who would do his absolute best on the job, but why should he go out of his way to do more once he was back at Headquarters? No, if I had been in his shoes, and I didn't have to worry about putting on a show to help Uncle . . . I'd probably do the same.

# 13

"YOUR RANT SEEMS to have worked," Knight said by way of greeting, as I brought my breakfast tray to his table.

"Uh, you mean Ace?" I sat down and started on my meal. Around Knight you needed to eat efficiently, or you'd have to run off with half your food still on the plate when he got up to leave, which was a criminal waste.

"He traded territories with Karly. Good thing too, since at the moment Hunter Jade is covering her own territory and Karly's." Knight ate eggs methodically. So did I. "I'm pretty sure Ace is going to find plenty to Hunt today; Jade posted something on the message boards yesterday about needing more help out there."

"Well, good, and may he pull so far ahead of me that he's a speck in the distance." I said that and meant it, since I was finding the fact that I was number two pretty uncomfortable. You know that feeling when you *know* something is sizing you up for an attack? Like that.

Knight gave me a look as if he suspected me of sarcasm, then shrugged. "We'll be splitting up again today, and moving farther along the Barrier. I haven't been to this part in over six months, so it could be quiet, or it could be trouble. Make sure you keep your headset on."

I nodded. This would be like working at home, really, with the Hunters working nearest each other staying in contact so that if one got into trouble, the other could probably get there in time to save him. If you had good enough control of your Hounds and could send them on ahead, that was even better.

We went a long way in the pod this time, and it dropped us off at a section of the Barrier that, on our side, was row after row of bulky things under tied-down covers. "Military storage," Knight said with a shrug of disinterest as he saw me staring at them.

The Spillover side of the fence was like the day before. Ruins. Only today, it was overcast and starting to drizzle. Didn't matter, I've Hunted in blizzards and pouring down rain. Only time I take cover is when there's lightning. I'd dressed for it, discovering there was gear in my closet marked "waterproof." It was, too, and *way* better than the waxed and oiled canvas, with patched-together outer shells of bits of vinyl and plastic too small to use in the fields, that we normally use at home. Buying waterproof fabrics is a pretty low priority for us. After all, you can always get dry when the work is over. Ammunition for the guns we can't use reloaders for, though, is a different matter.

Knight went left, after summoning his pretty Hounds. I summoned mine, and looked at Bya.

"Would you tell Karly's Hounds that they're welcome to join us, if they're around?" *Around* is pretty relative to Hounds, so long as they are on this side.

Bya grinned at me, and sat down. *They're coming,* he said, and so we waited.

Hounds are fast, even when they can't *bamph,* and it wasn't long before I saw them streaking toward us, jumping from one tarp-shrouded lump to another. I went to the door in the Barrier pylon and let them through. They weren't friendly to me, but I didn't expect that; so far as they were concerned, they were there for two purposes, to Hunt and to eat, and the sooner we got that started, the better they would like it.

With our allies in the pack, we moved out.

I've heard people call the Mountain, especially above the snow line, desolate. It never seemed that way to me. But this ... this was desolate. Hundreds and hundreds of people had once lived here, in these windowless, roofless hulks of brick and crumbling cement. It had been single-family homes here, I think, though "single family" had a different meaning back then than it does for my folks. Street after street, row after row, with holes in the rows where the house had been wood or something else that wasn't as sturdy as cinder-block, brick, or stone, and was long gone. I could feel the ghosts. Not literal ghosts, just ... memories, I guess. Memories get sucked into stone and brick over time, and you can feel them if you have magic. I feel this almost everywhere there's ruins, but mostly since I got here I'd been Hunting with Knight, so I didn't feel it as much. It's when I'm alone that I can really sense it, and for me at least, the worse the weather is, the more it seems to come out.

So many of those memories were of the people who had lived

here and died horribly. The memories were thinned by age, watered down by time until instead of terror and despair, the background was a disturbing melancholy, but . . . yeah. It was spooky enough that I actually thought I saw something, pale and tall, in one of the windows, watching me. I even thought I saw something where a head would be, a little flash, like the sparkle of a jewel or a glint off of metal. Startled, I brought up my rifle to look through the scope—but there was nothing there. Maybe an odd sort of streak of light that passed when I moved a little. It rattled me, because for a moment, I thought it was that pretty Folk Mage. . . .

I reminded myself not to get spooked by memories or rattled by ghosts, if there were such things. My job was to protect the living. The silent dead have no claim on me or my time. We pressed on, through the gray and the sour-tasting drizzle.

Bya alerted about the same time that I both sensed magic and smelled something.

The sharp, metallic scent of ozone.

The others came streaking back to me, and we huddled next to a wall while I listened to them.

There was a big, sprawling, single-storied building not far from here, and somehow it had kept part of its roof. In that sheltered part was a nest of Othersiders. Ketzels.

They live in colonies, like those little green and gray parrots. From what the Hounds told me, they'd built their nest in the corner of the part of the building that still had part of a metal roof. Now, that was good, because they won't fly in the rain if they can help it, so there was a good chance we had them boxed in. But it was bad, because they can shoot lightning out of their eyes and mouth, and they wouldn't care if my magic net had them pinned down. The Hounds could take it, but I couldn't.

And for birds, they are awfully tough. It wasn't going to be easy to take them down. But for eleven Hounds and one Hunter, not impossible either; we just had to be smart.

I had a sudden thought: those Ketzels had been huddling in semidarkness all day, and if I popped off a bright light in the middle of them, there was a good chance most of them would be blinded, at least temporarily.

My Hounds were following along with my thoughts, and nodded. I explained it out loud to Karly's, who grinned at me. They liked it too.

"Right. You four get ready to jump in when I pop the light, and I'll put up the net. If you get into trouble I'll drop the net to let you out, but that will give you first shot at the kills," I said to them, then looked to my own seven. "You lot *bamph* across the net once the dazzle wears off, and I'll keep shooting to give them something to think about besides you."

Mine nodded again. We've played that game before when we've come up against something that can shoot back. I don't even try to aim, I just shoot high to avoid the Hounds. Seems to work most of the time.

Now, how not to be stupid, lesson one. "Joy to Knight," I said into my little boom mic.

*"Knight here."*

"We've sprung a nest of Ketzels. Fifty yards north of my position. Do not *think* we need backup since I have Karly's Hounds too."

"*Understood. Moving in your direction in case backup is required.*" Good; he wouldn't be coming on the run, but he *would* be moving in the right direction in case everything went sour. Satisfied that I had done everything by the book, I nodded to the Hounds and we all moved out as a group.

Ketzels are gorgeous, and that is their natural shape. It really makes me feel bad to have to take out things that are so beautiful. They're bird-shaped, about eagle-size, only bright blue and green, with two really long, flexible feathers coming down out of their tails—a lot like the Chinese Phoenix birds that are carved and painted and embroidered all over the Monastery, only blue and green rather than red and yellow. And, like I said, they can shoot lightning out of their eyes and mouth. The real, it-will-kill-you stuff, not like a spark that will just make you jump. When we got to where the nest was, I pulled out a neat little gadget from my pack and eased it up over the pile of rubble I was behind. I hoped they wouldn't notice it. It's this thing of tubes and mirrors that lets you see without poking your own head up out of shelter, and I was able to get a good look at the situation.

I was happy to see the nest only held adults; I'm going to guess about fifteen, because Othersiders tend to pack in multiples of the magic numbers three, five, and seven. I'd have had a hard time killing a baby bird. The Masters would have had me save any babies if I was back home; they were always trying to figure out ways to turn Othersiders, and make them like the Hounds. But I wasn't home, and I was pretty sure the people in charge here, from whoever was in charge of Hunter HQ to Uncle all the way up to the premier (if he bothered to keep track of such things) wouldn't much care for that idea.

Magic, however, can't be cast by mirrors. Has to be line-of-sight. So I had the Hounds all eel their way into position, Karly's Hounds closest. When I could see in the mirror that they were in place, I folded the gadget and stowed it again, then readied myself, took a deep breath, and surged to my feet. I gathered the manna, sighted on the spot I wanted, right in the middle of the birds, which had spotted me but were reacting sluggishly to my presence because of the cold. Mentally I painted a target Glyph right on the spot, sketched a couple more Glyphs in the air, and flung the power on its way.

Then I ducked, squeezing my eyes shut as I did so, because *I* didn't need to be blinded, thanks.

The light exploded through my closed lids as I dropped behind the rubble. Wow. I knew then I must have been pretty keyed up—that was a *lot* of light.

I popped back up and called the net, threw it, and slammed it in place as Karly's Hounds surged into the confined space. The birds were mostly shaking their heads wildly, but three of them had to have been looking in some other direction when the light went off, because they were taking to the air, screaming at the Hounds. Their feathers stood on end, and there were little sparks coming off of them like off of a burning pile of black powder. Before they could concentrate to zap the Hounds, I gave them a couple of shots to think about and ducked back down again.

A single lightning bolt slammed into the top of the rubble above my head, leaving behind the smell of steam, hot brick, and ozone.

I moved a little, popped up, and snapped off another couple of shots. Before I ducked back down again, I caught one of Karly's

Hounds as his jaws closed on a Ketzel. There wasn't much to see; a crunch and a poof of rainbow-colored sparks and some light between his teeth as he inhaled the manna. Ketzels didn't turn to ooze or goo.

I ducked back down in time to miss getting hit by another couple of lightning bolts. They were recovering faster than I had thought.

*How much manna have these things got?* I thought at Bya.

*Lots,* came the answer. *There's enough for all!*

Bamph *in then, I'll give you covering fire.* More Hounds in there would just add to the Ketzels' confusion, which would be good. Better if I could actually knock down to the ground some of the ones I could hear flying.

This time when I popped up, I took the time to aim and winged one. Bya was waiting for it with open jaws as it tumbled to the ground. It was chaos in there now, and nothing even tried to zap me, since the Hounds were gleefully at work like a pack of ferrets on a rabbit warren. It wasn't long before my main worry was to wing the flyers so the Hounds could get them, rather than kill them and maybe waste the manna.

When one of Karly's Hounds crunched on the last one, I dropped the net and coiled the manna back up inside me, then spoke into my mic. "Joy to Knight. Nest down."

*"Well done, Hunter,"* came the reply. I felt a little flush of pleasure, and gestured to the Hounds to pack up around me.

"Well done, pack," I told them, and looked to Karly's Hounds, who had packed up together. "Now, would you fellows like to stay with me for the rest of the day, or shall I let you back through the Barrier and you can go Otherside?"

The Hounds looked at each other for a moment, then back at me.

*They're staying,* Bya said, and I got a second flush of pleasure. It's quite the compliment when someone else's Hounds consider you a good enough Hunter that they'll pack with yours.

"I don't know enough about Ketzels to know if they've driven anything else out of this territory, so be careful," I warned them, and we moved out again.

Knight was a good judge of distance; we hit the edge of where we'd worked last time—or at least, that was what my Perscom said—just about midday. I elected not to stop to eat lunch, since I never did when I patrolled at home. I just kept on the move, good and wary, and ate with one hand. Good thing I did that, too, since we weren't more than halfway back when my radio crackled to life.

*"Knight to Joy. Got a Wyvern. On the double."*

He didn't have to tell me twice, and I wished I could *bamph* like the Hounds. A Wyvern's not a Drakken, but it was going to take both of us *and* the augmented pack of Hounds to down it. Wyverns can fly, as Uncle had reminded me. Like the Gazers, they can get *over* the Barriers, if they are sneaky and come in under conditions or places where radar and cameras can't catch them.

But how had it managed to get this *far* without radar or flying craft or lookouts spotting it? Something the size of a Wyvern should *never* have gotten past anything but maybe the outermost of the Barriers, but this was right on top of the Prime Barrier!

Well, now was not the time to ask questions; now was the time to move.

*Bya, ask the other pack to escort me. You lot* bamph *ahead to Knight,* I ordered, and felt Bya's assent. A minute or so later, all four of Karly's Hounds were running in close formation with me. They couldn't *bamph*, and neither could I, and right now Knight was going to need all the help he could get. I went into the fastest lope I could and yet still watch out for things that could send me on my face. I kept looking at my Perscom to see how far we were from Knight, and not liking the answer.

I was used to Bya and how good all his senses were. I guess I was subconsciously expecting the same thing out of Karly's Hounds, but we were no more than a few hundred yards from Knight, according to my Perscom, when we literally ran into the second Wyvern. I tripped over its tail and ran into its bony rump.

I'm not sure which of us was the more startled, the Wyvern, or my group. I sure know I was the more scared. I was scrambling backward as the Wyvern whipped his top half around and snapped for me. He actually got my backpack, and I thought I was going to die right then and there. He picked me up off the ground and shook me when I fired off the first spell I could think of—the one I'd just used, the explosion of light.

At the same time, one of Karly's Hounds gave off this angry snarl, like someone ripping a giant sheet of tin in half. And it jumped with its jaws wide open and latched onto the Wyvern's cheek where there was some loose hide.

I was half blinded by my own spell, but the Wyvern let go of me with a shriek, and I dropped to the ground. I remembered a narrow place we'd just passed, it must have been a hallway or something, two big concrete walls really close together. I scrambled to my feet, heart racing, sweating with terror, as Karly's Hound hung on for dear life while the Wyvern shook his head back and forth, the Hound dangling from his cheek. I shook my head, cleared my eyes, looked back, and spotted the hallway. Took aim at the Wyvern's eye, got off a good shot. Missed the eye and hit the eye ridge, which made the Wyvern stop long enough that the Hound could drop off and run to us. Then we all pounded for the hallway with the Wyvern right on our heels, and wedged ourselves all the way into the back while the thing raged and snapped at us from the end.

"*Joy?*" my radio bleated.

"There's two," I said breathlessly, choking back a sob of fear. "Two Wyverns." I was shaking all over, my stomach in a knot. I took a deep breath, bringing up every bit of discipline I had to get myself back under control, because if I didn't, we were dead.

"*Roger.*" No more from Knight. I just crouched there, waiting for some of the fear to ebb so my brain would work again.

I had someone else's Hounds with me, and I was facing one of the nastier medium-size critters among the Othersiders. The good news was that his only weapons were teeth and claws. The bad news was he was half the size of a house, he was faster than me, and he had a big, blunt, ugly head, with teeth as long as my finger, on the end of a longish neck. Not as long as a Drakken's, but long. And his hide was pretty armored, so unless I could hit an eye, I was only going to give him flesh wounds.

I looked at Karly's Hounds. "I think we're in trouble," I said.

Suddenly, there was a *bamph* and the small space got a bit more crowded. But I didn't care, because Bya had joined us.

*Friend is safe for now,* Bya said, staring at the Wyvern. *In a hole.*

"*We've got cover,*" Knight said over my radio at the same time. "*I sent back your alpha. HQ says no Elites are free at this time.*"

"Got him, he's here, and thanks." With Bya next to me, my head started working again. More good news, the walls were sturdy enough, and the Wyvern light enough—flyers don't really weigh much—that he wasn't making any headway in his attempt to get at me. Probably the same was happening with Knight. I made my head slow down; went into what was almost a Zen state, the way I would if I was sparring one of the Masters. There was a way out of this . . . I just had to observe and keep on observing until I could spot it.

If I shot out the Wyvern's eye, he might or might not pull back. I might even be able to get both eyes, then he *would* pull back. But he still wouldn't be vulnerable. . . . Did I have manna enough to flatten him to the ground with a good hard smack, or a levin bolt, and then hold him down while I chopped off his head?

Maybe, but then I wouldn't have anything left to help Knight with.

I had grenades, which would at least bruise him, maybe break rib bones, but to use them in this passage would be suicide.

Then I noticed that the Wyvern always lunged at me with its mouth open, and I got an idea that was either brilliant or insane *and* stupid, but I couldn't think of anything else and we were running out of time. We couldn't wait until an Elite or a team was free again; that might take until nightfall, and by then the Wyverns *would* have friends.

Bya saw what I was thinking. He whined, but *bamphed* out and back, and when he was back, he dropped a length of metal pipe as long as my forearm in my hand.

I waited for him to explain the plan to Karly's Hounds. They didn't like it either, but . . . well, that Wyvern could outwait us. And maybe all this activity would attract friends even faster. I pulled a grenade off the bandolier and pulled the pin. Then I had the pipe in one hand, a grenade with the pin pulled, and my thumb on the safety in the other. The Hounds and I all looked at each other, and the Hounds nodded. I swallowed hard and let my fear turn into adrenaline.

"Three," I counted down. "Two. One. *Now!*" And we all lunged at the Wyvern as he lunged at us.

The Hounds went for the loose skin on his lower jaw to keep his mouth open. I fired off a tiny version of the flash-spell right in his eyes, and at the same time, shoved that piece of pipe forward into the open jaw, jamming it in as far as I could. I felt teeth gash my hand, but not the pain, not yet, just a tearing sensation. When I felt the pipe stick tight, I shoved my other hand with the grenade in it as far into the back of the thing's mouth as I could.

I didn't get off unscathed; both my right hand and left arm got slashed by teeth as the Wyvern rattled his head around, trying to dislodge Hounds, grenade, and pipe. Dripping blood, still not feeling anything yet, I backpedaled into the rear of the hall, the Hounds let go and followed me, and the Wyvern pulled back, tossing his head up and shaking it, grenade either caught in his throat or—

Well, a few seconds later it went off, blowing apart the monster where the shoulders met the neck.

*Then* I began to hurt. I looked; they were good slashes and they'd need stitches, but at least nothing vital was cut and it wasn't to the bone. I'd been hurt this bad before, and finished my Hunt. I could do the same today.

Bya licked my wounds, which cauterized them and stopped

the bleeding, though they hurt like *fire* still, and we clambered over the remains of the Wyvern. The Hounds waited just long enough to suck up the manna before it escaped—not long—and we headed for Knight. Bya went on ahead and flashed an image of the sitch into my head.

Knight's four Hounds were still outside the hole, fluttering with agitation. The other Wyvern, a slightly bigger one, had its head stuck down the hole Knight and my other Hounds were at the bottom of. But now that it was two Hunters and fifteen Hounds, four of them flyers, the advantage was all on our side again. And believe me, if Knight's God was responsible for Karly's Hounds deciding they wanted to come along today, then Knight could drag me in for a thanks prayer any time he wanted.

I eyeballed the ruins and found the place where I wanted the Wyvern brought, right between two none-too-stable walls. Then I asked Bya to tell Knight's Hounds what I wanted, and I described the rest to Karly's.

"Knight, one target down, luring yours out and hopefully crippling it," I said into the radio, and before he could object, I signaled to his Hounds to start.

You can probably figure out what we did; the flying Hounds dive-bombed the Wyvern with rocks and raked him with their claws until he backed out, and made him mad enough to break off from the hole where Knight and my Hounds were hiding and come after Knight's Hounds. They lured the monster between the walls, which I dropped on him with two grenades. Got lucky too, pinned both his wings. He couldn't move then; Knight and I and the Hounds basically bit and slashed and shot at him until he was dead. It took at least an hour. It was the long way to kill something, but a lot smarter than ramming a grenade down his throat.

As Knight moved in for the coup de grâce—at this point I was too tired to do anything but watch—I caught some movement up on a wall.

Whatever was there was only there for a second. But I could have *sworn* it was . . . watching us. Watching me. It might have been a human. If I was living out here and heard a ruckus, I'd want to see what it was, but maybe I wouldn't trust Hunters enough to stick around once I saw they'd won. Just because we hadn't seen anyone here, that didn't mean they weren't there. Feral kids, maybe.

A shriek from the Wyvern snapped my attention back to the fight, as Knight managed to chop the head off. And when I looked back, whatever had been watching us was gone.

We didn't have to drag our sorry tails back to the pylon and the pod that would have been waiting for us. Given the fight we'd just had, and the shape I was in, they sent a chopper for us. Like the trains, the choppers have some sort of shield that lets them pass right through the Barrier. There was barely room for us and the field medic and all of the Hounds, even after the Hounds made themselves as small as they could, so the cabin was pretty crowded until we landed. I didn't much care, since that meant I had warm, furry bodies holding me up while the medic checked over my slashes.

I was just now feeling pretty bad about being so stupid as to run right into the second Wyvern, and must have apologized to

Knight six or eight times before he calmly, and wearily, told me to stop. "You were with a strange pack you couldn't talk to; they were with a strange Hunter they had only Hunted with once," he pointed out. "We got out of it alive. That's what matters."

"And that's two fewer Wyverns to come over the Barrier," the field medic pointed out as he finished bandaging my arm.

"That too," Knight agreed. So I shut up until we landed, and I got taken off for a better job at fixing my slashes and a debrief at the same time. A real doctor who briskly did things with sprays and gadgets while three people, one in army and one in police uniform and one in some sort of outfit I assumed was Hunter gear, asked questions. An Elite, I think. Best believe I was hard on myself. Giving myself excuses was not going to help anything or anyone, least of all me. It did seem to surprise the ones debriefing me, though, that I was basically giving myself a dressing-down before they could. It kind of left them with nothing to say except "dismissed."

"Dinner in my room," I said to my Perscom as soon as I was in the corridor, because I was feeling the effects of the painkillers now and getting a bit lightheaded. At least my arms didn't hurt, and I could move my fingers. I gave my Perscom a list of finger food, because I wasn't sure I was up to eating like a civilized creature, and by the time I dragged myself to my door, the electric cart with a tray on it was waiting there for me. It wasn't what I'd ordered, but actually, it was *better*. It was a bunch of those yummy little appetizer things I'd had at dinner with Josh, only enough to sate even the hungriest Hunter just off a Hunt. I didn't question why that was what had turned up; I was starving.

It hurt to lift the tray and carry it in, but I did anyway. I could barely stand at this point, but I wasn't going to climb into bed covered in Wyvern bits, so I showered—the bandages were waterproof—and then started eating, taking one piece at a time from the tray on the table next to my bed. The effort to chew seemed almost too much, but I knew if I didn't finish all those calories, I was going to regret it. And to waste all that deliciousness would have been a sin. It felt so good to lean back into all those soft, piled pillows. And before I was done, Bya *bamphed* himself into my room too—he must not have gone back Otherside with the rest when the chopper landed and I opened the Portal. He laid himself along the side of my bed, like another pillow, warm and soft and supporting me. He practically gleamed, he was in such good shape. There must have been a lot of manna in those Wyverns.

When I'd shoved down the last bite and swallowed the last bit of drink, I got the announcement of a call coming in, with no ID, which meant someone wasn't calling from his Perscom. "Camera off, answer," I said, because I didn't want anyone to see me just now. The vid screen came up.

It was Josh. Now I was really glad I had ordered the camera off. Before I could say anything he frowned. "Joy, I hope you have your cam off out of vanity and not because—"

I interrupted him. "Vanity," I replied. "I look like I just got dragged behind a slow-moving horse through ten acres of wait-a-minute bushes. My hair's a mess—I'm mostly okay, I promise!"

He looked mollified. "Well, all right, if you say so. I know this is what you're supposed to be doing, but—"

"No buts about it," I replied, and left a long and significant pause. Because ... as much as I liked Josh ... I wasn't going to let anything get between me and Hunting. Karly's story about her ex-wife was cautionary tale enough.

"Fair enough," he agreed, to my intense relief. "Did you get my dinner? I mean, the dinner I had ordered for you? I figured you deserved a Hero Dinner. I had it sent from the restaurant and told HQ so they'd give it to you when you asked for food."

I got warm all over and even felt a little bit of giddiness that had nothing to do with drugs. "That was you? Josh, that was one of the nicest things anyone ever did for me! Thank you so much!"

He chuckled, and his smile warmed up his eyes in a way I hadn't expected. "Glad you were able to eat it. I'll call you tomorrow when your hair isn't full of twigs, okay?" He was laughing now, a little, which I figured was a good sign.

"That'd be great," I said with real enthusiasm, and he rang off. I figured I would close my eyes for just a little bit and then watch the raw vid of the fight to see what I'd done wrong—and right. I would have been happy to hear the whole group's take on it too, but . . . I was just too tired.

Maybe tomorrow.

# 14

WHEN I WOKE UP, I didn't hurt nearly as much. And Bya was still with me. I'd scooted down during the night until I was lying down, and when I woke up, my left arm was draped over his shoulder.

"Light," I said aloud, and not only did a soft light come up, but my vid-screen came up too. The doc who had taken care of me at the debrief was on it.

"This is a recording. Hunter Joyeaux, you are ordered to take bed rest today, and you are off duty for the next day after that. You should be fully healed by tomorrow, but you've lost blood, and we'll want to be sure you weren't infected or poisoned by those bites. You are not confined to quarters, but sleep as much as you can and take the medicines that arrive with your meals. That is all."

There was a recorded—and very formal and stiff—congratulations from Uncle; it looked and sounded like something he recited from a script every time a Hunter got a particularly good kill. Only at the end did he unbend enough to give a hand signal of "well done" that only he and I would recognize. Which made me blush a little.

I flexed my arms and hands experimentally, and while stiff and a little painful, they didn't hurt anywhere near as much as they had before. Bya's spit is really good at making things heal fast, but this was even faster. I was impressed and I wasn't worried about toxins or infection; it would have taken care of that, too.

Bya grunted, and raised his head to give me a measuring stare. "Yeah, I'll be all right," I told him. "You can go on back." If I was going to have a reaction to nearly getting killed, it would have been last night—nightmares. I didn't remember any, but then, if Bya soothed them away for me, I wouldn't. I only ever get the shakes in the first twenty-four hours now.

Bya licked my face and jumped down off the bed, and I opened the Portal for him, and he faded back home. I ordered breakfast, and got another shower. I think another pound of cement and brick dust came out of my hair again. My legs were all wobbly when I was done, so I figured I had better take the doc's advice. I got my tray from the cart when it arrived, put the old tray on top, and staggered back to bed. While I ate, I reviewed the raw vid a couple of times, and finally came to the conclusion that while I should have been a lot more alert, I hadn't been as stupid as I'd thought I'd been. That wretched Wyvern had been mostly hidden from view from every angle; clearly he had been waiting to ambush Knight if Knight had found a back way out of the hole. And, of course, it showed us being *outside* the outermost Barrier, not inside it. Which made what the medic said in the helichopper make a lot more sense. He'd been talking for the cameras, of course.

With a vague sense of dread, because I really didn't want to find out I was ahead of Ace, I checked my standings. I was still number two, and Ace had opened up a bigger lead, which was a relief, actually. I called up his channel, and he had scored a very impressive series of kills yesterday. It looked as if he and his Hounds had overturned every rock and poked into every hidey-hole in the territory. He'd even routed out a Vampire and made pretty short work of the fang-face with just him and the two Hounds, and he'd done it all without even mussing his hair. After the recap, his channel showed him live, going out to another tough district. "Good for you," I said, and then the pills that had come with breakfast hit me like a hammer between the eyes and I curled up for a nap.

When I woke up again, I felt pretty good. My arms and hands were a little stiff and tender, but they didn't hurt. Unwrapping the bandages, I found there were pink lines where the gashes had been. I decided to get dressed and go to the range to practice, then to the room full of exercising machines to make up for not going out hunting. But before I did, feeling bold, I searched for Josh's number; I got it, but the little icon next to his name said he was "not available to talk," so I just left him a vid message with cam feed to the effect of "Thanks for checking on me last night, I appreciate it! And thank you again for that amazing dinner!" I actually managed not to blush while I was recording it.

I didn't do badly on the range, and the exercising machines were kind of fun, if weird. Obviously we don't have those at home; if you want a workout, you get someone and spar. I got a good sweat going, like I would have after a sparring session. I figured I would go get some dinner, meet up with the others in the lounge like we always did, and then sleep.

The exercise rooms had been completely empty. That was kind of unnerving for someone who was used to living practically in the pockets of everyone else at the Monastery, but even the solitude wasn't helping me put everything I'd learned together with what I knew and come up with an explanation for why things weren't feeling right.

Then I found something that always helped me think—there was a sauna in the exercise room! We had one at home, and just letting the steam bake me into a puddle, generally while I let my mind drift, usually shook things loose.

So I wrapped myself up in a towel and found a bench at the back and laid myself down on it. And sure enough, clearer thoughts started forming up in my head.

Apex and the other big cities—or at least, so I was thinking— were at a turning point they might not even realize was happening. At first, of course, it had been a pure battle of survival against the Othersiders; the major battle was here, where there was the biggest concentration of army and armed services people, but *especially* Army Corps of Engineers and all the tech people who lived around this spot. Then Barrier tech got figured out, and safe spots could be created, Apex first. Those safe spots quickly became cities, and inside the cities, things were "known" to be safe. So far, so good. You could expand the Barriers, at least to a point where you could actually grow food and be mostly self-supporting. Things got a lot safer.

And that was where people got complacent. They got not only all the old tech back up and running, they got better tech. You could be absolutely certain that you wouldn't get attacked by anything but maybe a nuisance like a Piskie if you were inside the most-protected zone. Life was really good. You maybe thought you didn't need Hunters anymore, at least not in and around the city.

And . . . okay, I already knew I had to keep quiet about that. But what was the pressure on Uncle, and how did I fit into it? Maybe it wasn't just that the Othersiders were getting smarter and some of them were learning to come over and under the Barriers a lot more often . . . Maybe the Barriers themselves were getting weaker, or the Othersiders had figured out a way to get through them, the way the trains and choppers did. Maybe that was what Uncle had found out, and he wanted to say something. Probably his original intention in bringing *me* here instead of some other Hunter had been to show that he wouldn't spare his own kin from duty . . . and maybe that had backfired on him when he wanted to make this new danger public. Because once . . . whoever it was . . . had found out I *was* his kin, they'd gone to him and said something like "Keep your mouth shut about the Barriers, or we'll make it hard on your niece."

I could see that happening. I mean, I've read history books from before the Diseray. There were all kinds of things that people *could* have done and *should* have done that would have prevented it. And they didn't. Because the people in power liked where they were just fine, thanks, and they stayed there because of people with money. And the people with the money didn't want to lose a single cent of that money doing the right things. Power makes you stop thinking of anything but yourself.

And just as I got to that point, I heard the sauna door open and shut, and two sets of footsteps. I was well hidden by the steam, and whoever it was stayed near the door. It seems they had come in here to have a conversation. So . . . maybe it was wrong of me, but I stayed quiet and listened.

"Nothing ever stays the same. People change, and so have the Othersiders," said someone whose voice I didn't recognize. "They're getting smarter."

"Or maybe *something* is teaching them," replied the other person. I thought it might be the armorer. "The premier can't have anyone realizing that. The Cits will just start asking *why* they aren't safe anymore and start looking for someone who could make them safe again."

"Well that goes no place good. . . ."

"Who else would they look to but General Priam?" There was a long pause. "But it goes deeper than that. I think this may have *started* happening a good long while ago. I think that's why the premier started the full-time vidding of the Hunters *years* ago."

"That goes no place good either."

"Exactly." There was a very long pause. Now I thought I knew why they had come in here. All this steam was probably very bad for recording equipment. I closed my eyes and breathed very quietly. "Meanwhile the Othersiders start getting inside the outermost Barriers. Just a few at first. But, for whatever reason, in the last six months or so it's started getting slowly, slowly worse. Smarter things are getting in, and *more* of the little things getting in."

"And no one noticed because of creep." I knew what that was. We talked about "creep," when we talked about strategy at home. When things just kind of creep up on you so gradually you don't know it's happening until someone points it out. "You think anyone besides the prefect's niece noticed?"

"It's a good thing we have room. If things are going downhill, we're going to need a lot more Hunters."

Now that things were falling into place, everything I was seeing started to make more sense. It explained why there were Hunters like Ace—they were still under the impression that Hunting was mostly entertainment for the Cits, not something serious, unless you were unfortunate enough to draw a territory outside the Prime Barrier. And internal politics explained Uncle's behavior and his warnings to me.

"So what do we do about it?" asked the second fellow.

"Stay sharp, keep our eyes open. This is all just my speculation for now." Then the door opened and closed again, and I was alone.

I waited a good while, then left, got a shower, and headed for the mess. I was keeping my expression absolutely neutral so no one would read anything in it, if they happened to be watching me on the ubiquitous cameras.

That's why my head came up like a spooked deer's when the first thing I heard was "Hey, it's Hunter Joy!"

It was someone I didn't really know, but I recognized her from the lounge—blond girl, green and pink colors, gymnast's build. She grinned at me. I smiled tentatively back.

For the first time since I'd arrived, the armorer was eating here—and he got up and left his meal to come over to me. So that might well have been him in the sauna.... "I see you took the bandages off," he rumbled, and reached for my arm. "Let me have a look."

"Uh—" I flushed a little as he rolled back my sleeve dispassionately. I mean ... he's Elite. And he was paying attention to *me*. "I heal fast. One of my Hounds has healing spit—"

"Mine does too," said the armorer, examining the scars as he turned my arm side to side a little. "This is looking good. Good job out there, by the way. Potentially stupid move, ramming your hand down a Wyvern's throat, but at least you had the sense to jam the mouth open first. I was on the way, but I wouldn't have been able to get to you two before things went bad for Knight." He let go of my arm and patted me on the back. "Overall, well done. And the teaming job you did with Knight on the second beast was first class."

I was so shocked I could hardly move, because an Elite had basically just said I'd done a good Hunt and good strat. And I stayed kind of in shock, especially when several of the others came up to shake my hand and say things like "Well done" and "Gutsy moves." I think I stammered my thanks, blushing the entire time.

They waited while I got my food, then kind of waved me over to where they had all pushed their tables together. Knight wasn't there, but Karly was, and the others were all people I knew from the lounge. There were about eight of them, including Karly, all senior to me, and we all started dissecting the Hunt while we ate. It was like the vid-sessions, only without the jokes or the vid-screen. Mostly I kept my mouth shut and listened. These people all had more experience than I did in Hunting here, around Apex. There was at least one Elite, and for all I knew, there might be more.

And I learned a lot. Stuff Karly hadn't been able to tell me before she got hurt, like how to tell where sewer tunnels were when they weren't obviously marked, that there were doors sprinkled around with a particular symbol of three triangles meeting inside a circle that meant there was a smallish bunker behind them. That Wyverns hunted by line of sight, and if I could break that, they would keep going in a straight line and I could circle around behind. This was even better than the vid-sessions; I guess since I'd proved I wasn't full of myself, I'd kind of passed the "not-a-jerk" test.

So when Ace came in with his group, and looked at the gathering with surprise, I was the first one to say, "Hunter Ace, that was awesome work yesterday."

He looked at me warily, as if he suspected I was being sarcastic. "It wasn't a Wyvern," he replied.

"And you didn't end up on your butt dripping blood, either," I pointed out. "If there'd been anything in the neighborhood that had smelled blood in the air, I'd've been rabbit on toast."

He figured out I was being sincere, I guess, and gave me a kind of grudging nod. He and his gang didn't join our group exactly, but they didn't sit on the other side of the room, either. They plunked down close enough that they could listen, but kept their conversation among themselves, which was okay. Not everybody wants to talk about work over dinner; I can respect that.

I kind of wanted to say something friendly to him, but I couldn't think of what, so I settled for being as quiet as I could and listening to the others.

When the topic moved on from Hunting and it looked like everybody had gotten really engaged in the conversation and I could slip out without anyone noticing, I did just that. I was about halfway down the hall when my Perscom beeped, and Knight's voice came out of it. "Hey, Joy, meet me at the atrium, will you?"

"Sure," I said, as my Perscom obligingly showed me the way to this "atrium." Turned out it was a courtyard, complete with a fish-pond and a Zen garden with stone lanterns so like home, it made me both homesick and happy at the same time. But it wasn't open to the sky like I thought at first; it had glass over it. Bulletproof, break-proof, probably armored glass, most likely. I sat down next to the pond, and hopeful fishes came up to see if I had anything to eat.

Knight turned up as they were drifting away in fishy disappointment. "Hey," I said.

"Hey, yourself." He sat down next to me and handed me a little bag. "Fish food. Don't destroy their faith." We both tossed some on the water and the fish came surging back, happy again. "Just wanted to let you know that my folks are talking to the ones you gave me the contact information for, and we're pretty sure a lot of people are going to relocate. Not everyone." He shrugged. "You know how it is, some people put down roots and can't be torn out. But most are pretty excited. My girlfriend is, for sure. And I'm going to feel a lot easier knowing she's going to be somewhere better. Maybe after having moved once, moving here won't seem so scary to her. So thank you."

"Oh—wow! That's fantastic," I said. "But the mines—won't whoever is bossing the mines be mad about losing the miners?"

"Reckon they'll have to send in machines, like they do for crops, and the few that are left can run 'em," Knight said with a shrug. "They can't force us to stay. We just never had a place to go to before."

He leaned over then and did something I would never have expected in a million years. He kissed the top of my head, all shy-like. He was flushing as he said, "Not one Hunter in all the time I've been here has taken thought for helping someone that wasn't another Hunter. You're really special, Joy, and not just because you're a Hunter. It's because you think about other people all the time. Put others ahead of what you want. That's—that's real rare. Makes it feel as if you were my sister."

Now it was my turn to flush. "It—it's just how I was raised," I stammered. "Any one of us up there would do the same, Knight—"

"Mark," he interrupted me.

"What?" I was confused for a moment.

"Mark. My name's Mark Knight," he repeated, grinning. "The 'White Knight' business was just a nickname that stuck. Now, you'll get to sleep in, come the morning, but I'll have to patrol, so I'd best get some pillow time. I just wanted to thank you before the cameras figured out where we went."

I nodded as he stood up. "I'm glad I could help, Mark. I couldn't stand thinking of the bad choice they were having to make between poison and Othersiders. Now the choice won't be quite so bad—live above the snow line, or Othersiders. Cold's a fair sight better than poison."

"It is that. Night, Joy." And with that, he waved and took himself off. I stayed in the garden, since it was the first really peaceful, really homelike place I'd been since I got here. It being dark and all, you got the illusion it was real nature, rather than nature-under-glass. From time to time I tossed in a little fish food, and thought about how much the Masters and monks would like this.

We actually had a Zen garden, even though it was below freezing all the time. We had two; one specifically a snow garden, just rocks and dead branches and stone lamps, and another in a greenhouse, where we grew herbs. It didn't have a fishpond, though. The snow garden was used for the sorts of meditation that are supposed to make you immune to cold. I was never that good, though I've seen some of the monks out there, wrapped in wet sheets, serenely drying the sheets with the heat of their bodies.

It felt as if something that had been all tight in my chest started to loosen up. And, hey, I'd already *done* some good. I might not have family here, but it was beginning to look like I could have friends.

There was still stuff that was uneasy-making, but like my Masters kept saying, "You don't build a bridge by throwing everything you can find at the river."

Then, as if the day hadn't already been good, when I got back to my rooms there was a message on my big vid-screen from Josh. I got fluttery feelings in my stomach as I dialed him back. Although not all of them were from how I was starting to feel about him. Dammit, I *hated* having to have all these suspicions!

This time he wasn't in his uniform or in front of the PsiCorps emblem; it looked like I'd caught him at home. There was a plain cream-colored wall behind him; he looked like he was sitting on a couch. I recognized the style of what he was wearing as what the computer had called "casual," and instead of PsiCorps colors he was wearing a sort of khaki.

"Hey!" he said, and grinned. "Well, for someone who tried to talk a Wyvern into eating a hand grenade, you're looking good. How are you feeling?"

"About healed," I said.

"Good. Healed enough to go out again?"

I checked my Perscom to make sure that I was still going to be on sick leave the next day. I was, so I nodded yes.

"Excellent—it'll be easier this time, we'll just go to dinner and see a play—" My system gave a funny warble, and he broke off whatever he was going to say. "That's another call coming in for you, I'll bet anything it's the prefect, so I'll let you answer it. They'll want his congratulations on your feed. See you tomorrow night!"

"Bye—" was all I managed, and then the screen changed. And it was Uncle, just like Josh had said.

"Joy, I am pleased to see you are looking fit," he said. But for a moment his face said *I was worried sick about you* before he smoothed his expression over. If I hadn't been looking for the change, I might not have caught it.

"I am *very* hard to keep down for long, sir," I said. "Besides, I have good people around who've got my back. People like White Knight, for instance."

There was no mistaking the look of relief on his face. "Good," was all he said, but he got my meaning, I think.

We chatted for a bit more, then he commended me for a highly successful Hunt and ended the call.

I realized as I reached for a bottle of water and drained it that I'd had more going on in the last week than I had in a month on the Mountain. It was crazy.

And tomorrow was another date with Josh. I didn't know what he'd planned on, but—well, I'd find out tomorrow.

Now, if I could just figure out how to stay under the radar so Uncle didn't need to worry about me, I might even get my life under as much control as the Othersiders would let me.

## 15

AS I EXPECTED, in the morning there was a text message from the medics authorizing me to go on the date.

It was a little creepy all over again, realizing that there was almost nothing I could do that would be private.

Once I was on my feet and dressed and limbered up, and I had a light breakfast, I did something I hadn't done since I got here. I left the building without having an assignment, and started a run around it.

Now, what I really wanted was to go back down into some part of the city that *wasn't* a factory, or a vat-farm, or anywhere else near the main Barrier. But before I did that, I needed to be able to navigate *without* a Perscom. I was pretty sure that was how all the cams found us and kept track of us. If I left my Perscom in my room, I stood a chance of being able to wander around without having people watching me. So I needed to get myself oriented, match some landmarks to the map, and memorize the map.

Easiest way to do that was to go out running.

And it was *astonishing* how fast the cams found me when I got outside. I couldn't have gotten more than five hundred yards before I had three following me. By the time I was hitting my stride, I had a swarm, because every station wanted an "exclusive" and none of them were willing to share feeds *or* use the cam for my personal channel on the chance it might get edited.

I pretended that they weren't there and acted as if I was concentrating on my run. What I really was doing was picking out the things I could orient by, and matching them to the map.

I was circling out, encompassing the schools, noting where each one was in relation to Hunter HQ, and what was around it.

Something I noticed was the lack of smell. There was a little scent from the grass, but not much else. It wasn't that different from the filtered air in the HQ building.

Off to the east was the cluster of tall buildings that was marked "Core District" on the map. That was the Hub. That would be where Uncle's office was. It looked as if it was about a half a mile away.

But for now it was time to go back. I turned around and ran the distance back to HQ as hard and fast as I could . . . catching the cams by surprise and leaving them to try to catch up.

This time when I got to the Image Center, one of the designers was waiting with that beautiful dress draped on a girl-shaped form, and he sat me down in front of it. "Now," he said, combing his hair back with his fingers. "I suppose there is no way I can talk you into a different dress for tonight, is there?"

I gave him a *look*, and he sighed.

"All right, then, I got this old thing out again so I could reassure you that *all* we are doing is altering it, so we can alleviate your allergy to *wasting resources*." He said it like it was a bad thing, but I was not hardly going to back down on this.

Besides, I *liked* that dress.

He rolled a touch screen over to me and began rapidly doing things with a touch-pen to the image of the dress. In a moment he had all the changes in, giving me long, draping sleeves and a hem that was just at my ankles all the way around, instead of the train. And a little transparent collar that would frame my neck. To me, at least, it looked like an entirely different dress.

"I think it looks *great*," I said with enthusiasm. He looked a tiny bit mollified, but not much.

"You're really handicapping me here," he muttered. I tried to look apologetic, though I didn't feel in the least like I should be. And that was when Karly showed up.

"Hi! Did you know I'm going to a play?" I asked her, as the designer whisked the dress off the form, then draped it over his arm and sauntered off with it. "Do I need to learn anything?"

"Not unless you've never been to a play," she replied, though her face said she figured I *hadn't*.

"We put on plays all the time at home," I said cheerfully. "I've been in 'em, but mostly as scenery. I'm not too good. We did Shakespeare a lot."

"Oh, well, then this won't be a surprise to you. Let's get you back to your quarters and paint you up like a show pony." She motioned to me to follow her.

Karly was pretty good at makeup; better than I was, for sure. The dress and jewelry arrived in one of the little robot carts, and

Karly helped me get assembled. I wasn't sure exactly what a *tiara* was, but it turned out to be a crown. This one was made of black metal with glittery gray and silver stones in it. It looked heavy, but it wasn't, and once Karly got done putting my hair up and fixing it in place, it felt pretty secure.

The weight had the effect of making me hold my head up very high, and Karly grinned with approval. "Keep your head up," she advised. "You want to look as if that tangle with the Wyverns didn't even leave you winded." And by that point, it was time for me to go down and get picked up by Josh.

This time, just like the last time, he came in a driverless pod. I imagine it's obvious by now that we don't use anything like pods where I come from. When *I* had to travel any distance, it was usually by horse with the Hounds around me, or rarely—like when I went all the way down to the little town where the train station was—in a vehicle that uses methane from our compost piles for fuel, and is heavily armored. We had a couple of the small ones, and one big one, up at the Monastery. I know how to drive them, though I didn't do it often.

When I sailed out of the entrance of HQ with my crown glittering and all the beading on my dress catching the last light of the sunset, Josh was already standing next to the pod door, waiting. I thought he grinned a little appreciatively. I was sure of it when he leaned over before closing the door for me and said quietly, "You look like a vid-star."

"Thanks," I said, as he got in on the other side, and I kept from fiddling with my hair by a deliberate act of will. "But I think the one who looks like a vid-star is you."

He did, too. He'd dressed to match me, in steel gray, and he looked . . . well, more than good enough to make all the girls back home jealous of me. I wondered if *he* had designers and people to help him the way I did. . . .

Oh, probably not; Psimons were supposed to be pretty invisible and not draw attention to themselves. Unlike us, *they* weren't entertainment.

"So," I finally said. "Are we going to the same restaurant again? Because that was pretty amazing."

That gave him the chance to tell me more about the restaurant. It was the same one as last time, but it seemed they had different areas with different themes, and tonight we'd be the "guests" at a "royal dinner."

The meal was interesting, though maddeningly complicated, with a different set of silverware for each thing we ate. Josh told me it was from a menu of some dinner a king of England gave around 1910, and that most of what we were getting was, first of all, faked (though you probably wouldn't have guessed it if you tasted it) and, second of all, tiny, tiny portions compared to what the long-ago people would have gotten. Really, each course was no more than a taste, which was just as well, because we'd have been hideously, obscenely stuffed otherwise. There were costumed actors playing the parts of other famous people who might have been at that dinner, so listening to them was like being right in the middle of a play instead of just watching it. There was a couple who were obviously having an affair, a couple of politicians who were having a sort of verbal fistfight, the king was eyeing women all up and down the table, and I was one of the ones he tried to flirt with from a distance.

After that we went to the *real* play.

And that was when I nearly had a meltdown. Because the

play was *A Midsummer Night's Dream,* which we *never* do. If just thinking about the Folk can summon them, what would having an entire audience full of people watching a play about Folk-like creatures do? It would not be an exaggeration to say every hair on my body was standing up, and the only reason I didn't look like I'd grabbed a lightning rod in a storm, with my hair-do like a dandelion puff, was because Karly had plastered my hair in place with stuff. It didn't help *at all* that the set was so realistic, as opposed to what we did with our cobbled-up props and effects back home. I was going half crazy trying to keep track of everyone in the theater, and kept my Psi-shield in my Perscom activated and thought hard about my One White Stone. The effects and makeup and costumes that the actors playing the fairies had made them look way too like Othersiders for me to be anything but paranoid, because I couldn't help expecting Othersiders of some sort to respond in some way. Up on the Mountain we're even cautious about just reading the play, and never do it alone. There's always someone with you to make sure you break your concentration every few lines. You know, just in case.

I never was less than Hunting-alert the entire time I watched the play, even though not one other person, not even Josh, seemed to think we were anything but ultra-safe. And I didn't dare ask him about it, not here, and not now.

The only time I got a rest from the hypervigilance was in the breaks between acts, when Josh and I went out like everyone else did for drinks in the lobby. Most people seemed to be drinking alcohol, but Josh brought me something clear and sweet and tasting of honey and mint, and no alcohol in it that I could discern. And believe me, if you even whisper the word "booze" over anything I eat or drink, I can taste it. It's just another thing the Masters trained me in—that, and drugs, and poisons. Because when you are out on a long Hunt, you end up having to forage, and the Othersiders know that and often mess with the food and water sources. And absolutely the last thing I wanted to do . . . given the context of this play . . . was to have my guard down at all.

And of course, all this time, I had to act as if everything was normal and fine. Hunting was *way* less stressfull!

We talked with some of the other people, who all wanted to meet me, and it was the usual sorts of questions, mostly about Hunts. Everyone wanted to know about Hunts. That was something I could talk about easy, without worrying about tripping myself up in a lie, so I did. I just tried to be polite and all, and not look as if I was wishing I had a full load-out on me, and finally a bell would ring and we'd go back to our seats for the next act.

But there was one thing in those intermissions that was really, really weird . . . and that was, I had the distinct feeling that there were people watching me, and not in the "fan" sort of way, but in an unfriendly sort of way. It wasn't Folk. I know what that feels like. This was just people. I never actually caught anyone staring at me, but then, I was surrounded by so many people, and there were many places in that theater where people could watch and I probably wouldn't spot them. It wasn't like the cams always on me, which was impersonal enough not to make me notice. This was like being spied on by someone who was there, in person. Had I attracted unfriendly attention somehow? Was it someone sicced on me because of Uncle? Josh didn't seem uneasy at all, though, and wouldn't a Psimon have caught people who were doing that?

. . . Unless the spies were wearing Psi-shields like I was . . .

When the play was over, we waited long past when most people had left, and now that it was over and nothing bad had happened, I started relaxing. Finally, Josh leaned over and said, "Joy? What's wrong? I was going to take you backstage to meet the actors, but you seem really tense."

Well, there wasn't anyone else around, especially not near us, and this wasn't exactly a glamorous moment. So I took a chance and probably gave the controller who was monitoring everything we said and did before it went out over the air a heart attack, and I looked Josh in the eyes and said, "Are you people *insane*? Doing *that* play? We won't even say the name of it where I come from! It's about the Folk, don't you even realize that?"

I could almost hear the censor going into overdrive and switching the view to the crowd outside or something, as Josh blinked at me.

"Uh—" he said. "They can't—"

"Do you know that? For sure? Because there is no way on this green earth that I would ever, ever take a chance on risking what they can and can't do on based what they've done in the past!" I countered. And he looked . . . blank.

"Why would the Folk come because we're watching a play?" he asked.

That was when I had to grab my temper with both hands before I lost it. "You flatlander Cits *are* insane," I said with exasperation.

"Joy, this isn't the first time this play's been performed here," he pointed out. "It's more like the thousandth. And nothing has ever happened, because we take all the precautions we need to."

And like that, all the anger and the nerves just ran out of me like I was a bucket with a hole in it. "Yeah, bring logic into it," I said sourly. "You could at least have *warned* me. I spent the entire night getting ready to fight off a Folk Mage with just my magic, my Hounds, and a handful of hairpins."

He could have laughed at me, and I had to give him this much—he didn't. And he didn't act like I was some kind of idiot for getting worked up about it. He just went to this little door by the stage and talked to someone I couldn't see. Then he let me sit there a little longer, and then, as the guys with brooms came to sweep up between the rows of seats, Josh and I left by a side door. The pod was waiting for us there, so he must have signaled for it.

"Well?" he asked as I sat back in the seat.

"Don't you dare laugh at me," I whispered. "Where I come from just *thinking* about them too much can draw their attention, and you had a whole theater full of people concentrating on nothing but."

"And Psi-shields on the theater strong enough to knock your knuckles on," he stated. "I'm sorry, I really am. I had no idea you were on edge the whole time. Please, accept my apology—and compliments, because if I couldn't tell you were upset, then neither could anyone else. Next time it'll be *Romeo and Juliet*. I just thought you might enjoy something that didn't end tragically."

"As long as there's no magic in it, whatever it is will be fine," I replied. "*I* never accidentally called to a Folk Magician, but I—"

I stopped myself *quickly* before the words "I know someone who did" came out of my mouth.

"—I've read the journals the Hunters who've been posted at my village kept," I substituted, hoping my moment of hesitation hadn't been noticed. "It's *way* too easy to call them, and you don't want to be there when they come."

"All right then. I inadvertently ruined your evening. I'm going to fix that." He learned forward and spoke at the front of the Pod. "Hub. Prefecture."

The pod changed direction, and since we were already within a couple of streets of the Hub, pretty soon we were pulling up to that underground door where I'd first been taken when I got here. Different guards were on duty, and it seemed they recognized Josh even without his uniform. "I'm just taking Hunter Joy up to see the Sky Lounge," he said as they gave him a dubious look.

Their faces cleared. Evidently this was something that was all right. One of them stayed on guard at the door while the other escorted us as far as a different elevator. We got in. There was only one button, and Josh pushed it. I'd thought my first elevator ride was wobbly-making. This one had me grabbing for Josh's arm!

He didn't seem to mind.

The door opened on what looked like a single big room that was all windows on the outer walls. As we got inside, I could see there was an auto-bar, like on the train, just to one side of the elevator column.

There were a couple of people here in uniform, and a couple in civilian clothes, but the room was mostly empty. Josh took me over to a side where no one was sitting; there were couches facing the windows, and beneath us was Apex, all lit up. "I'll get us something to drink," he said, and left me there for a moment to marvel.

He brought me more of that honey-and-mint stuff, with ice in it, and we sat back in the soft cushiony couch and looked at the lights. And finally I relaxed completely. Partly because if there was any place in the entire city that was safe, this was probably it. And partly because this was the most amazing thing I had ever seen. It looked like the cityscape from an old vid, like all the stars in the sky had fallen and were burning on the earth. "Wow," I said finally. "Just . . . wow. And you get to come here?"

"It's the off-duty and break lounge for everyone in the building," he said. "They don't like us to leave the building when we're on shift. Like it?"

"If this was how I'd seen Apex for the first time, I think I would have been in love," I said honestly.

"I think I am just now figuring out how badly I messed up, taking you to that play without any warning, and without any reassurance that we plan for things like that here. It must have been as bad as a Hunt."

I sighed. "Worse. I was trying to figure out how just two of us and my pack could protect the entire theater until the Elite got there."

"I'm an idiot. And I am really sorry. I hope this makes up for it a little."

There wasn't much I could say to that, because even I didn't know the answer to his implied question. We just sat there, in the quiet. There was very soft music playing from hidden speakers. We sipped our drinks . . . and at some point, he reached for my hand, and I was not at all inclined to take it back. We didn't say anything, but then, I guess a Psimon is used to that.

And just when I was getting . . . very comfortable with the situation, my Perscom went off. And so did his. We looked at each other, then looked at our wrists.

"Curses," I said, feelingly, because it was a reminder I needed to be back.

"Same," was all Josh could say. We got up, left our glasses at the bar, and got into the elevator. By the time we got to the door with the guards, our pod, or one just like it, was waiting.

But of course, the moment was over. Stupid Perscom.

Josh cleared his throat as the pod sped away, heading for HQ. "You handled yourself very well tonight. Really, like a veteran in the crowd."

I blushed again. "It's just being nice to people," I said awkwardly.

"It's more than that. You are a good Hunter and a good person, Joy." He gave me a long, slow smile. "You know, most people are very nervous around a Psimon, even when I go out of my way to turn on the charm. Even then, they don't want to be reminded of what I am. But you? You accepted me."

I felt even shyer at that point. And I was getting red, I could tell. "Well, I . . . You're nice, and you're fun to be with. And Uncle likes you and trusts you."

"You're a lot like him, probably more than you know. He cares about people too." It was the way that Josh said that, it made me feel all tingly good. "And both of you try to see the best in everyone. That's rare." I was blushing even harder now, and very glad that it was dark in the pod. "You make the people who are around you feel good about themselves, you know. That's even rarer."

"I . . . uh . . ." I had no idea what to say next as he gave me a long and measuring look.

And then, right out of the blue, he leaned over and kissed me.

Not on the top of the head like Mark, either, but a real, full-on kiss. I was tingling all over, so I kissed him right back, and felt his hands running through my hair and then moving down my sides. Heart pounding, I pressed closer, erasing the distance between us, when I felt him slip a little piece of paper into my hand.

Hiding it from the camera. Somehow, I doubted it was a love note.

He kept on kissing after that, so I did too, but now I was concentrating on slipping that paper into my glove. He broke it off as the pod slowed to a halt, and smiled. I smiled back, but I was kind of confused. Had he kissed me because he needed to pass me a note, or had he decided to kiss me, then remembered the note? Could he have given the note to me earlier? Or—what? He looked like he was going to say something when a speaker chimed in the pod, and a voice said, "Hunter Medical advises that Hunter Joyeaux should have been in her quarters half an hour ago." Stupid medics.

"I guess we have gotten our orders," he said as the pod door opened for me. I got out, and he caught my hand before I moved away. "We'll do this again—but do me a favor, don't go and get hurt just so you have the days off, all right?"

"I promise," I said, and then he had to let go of my hand as the pod door started to close, and the pod moved off.

I waited until I was in the bathroom before getting to the bit of paper, and read it under cover of washing the makeup off my face. It was from Uncle. I recognized his handwriting.

Josh had smuggled me a note from Uncle. Which meant Uncle trusted him completely.

Which must mean I could trust him too.

*Proud of you,* it said, which gave me a very warm glow. The rest of it, though, not so much.

Two arrows meeting each other, and a stick figure between them. That meant someone in the high political rankings was maneuvering, and he was caught in the middle of something. Then the word *sides* with a line through it. That meant that right now he was not taking sides, which could be smart but could also be dangerous. And it meant that either side, or both, could use me as leverage against him. And finally: *Be careful. Ace has powerful friends.*

I grimaced and let the paper dissolve in the water and run down the drain. And here I thought I was deflecting Ace. But if Uncle went to all this trouble to warn me...maybe not. And it looked like things were even *more* complicated for Uncle than I had thought. I'd figured there was just one person putting pressure on him to stay quiet—but this note said there were at least two factions involved and he was trying to stay out of both, and I couldn't even begin to figure out how I factored into that. I could only assume that if he'd gone out of his way to tell me this in his note, then I did.

Then there was Josh. And now that kiss was a little disappointing, and a little confusing. He'd had other chances to pass the note to me tonight, hadn't he? I was sure he had. But then, he didn't know I'd have the presence of mind to wait to read it in private.

Not for sure, anyway.

But the kiss had been the real thing.

I hoped.

# 16

I WAS *REALLY* GLAD to be back to Hunting again. I met up with Mark at breakfast as usual, and after some small talk he briefed me on the new territory we'd be working today.

Mark looked happy to see me suited up and looking ready to go. "This time we'll be working the other direction," he continued. "Mostly vat-farms and hydroponics inside the Barrier. We'll be working outside Karly's old territory." He grinned a little. "Some of the others actually got a bit jealous that we bagged *two* Wyverns and you got that nest of Ketzels, all in the same day, so we got more people who usually patrol inside the Prime Barrier who wanted to come out and work Spillover a bit. They see a chance to up their ratings with just a couple of days' worth of work."

I shrugged. "Every day someone Hunts out in Spillover is another set of Othersiders that *definitely* is not going to get inside the Prime Barrier. More power to them, and good Hunting."

We fist-bumped and laughed. Then we armed up and headed out.

It all sure looked familiar as we passed through the vat-farms, and by some of the small pens that held the animals the clonal cells came from. Well, small by my standards, I'm used to people grazing stock on huge pastures, helped out by dogs. Real dogs, not Hounds, but big ones, with a lot of wolf in them. We got out of the pod at a Barrier pylon. The difference between our side and the Spillover side could not have been more stark. Our side was all these clean rows of windowless blocks, and off in the distance, the glitter of the hydro farms under break-proof glass. Spillover was . . . well, the same bleak wreckage as the Wyvern territory had been. No one lined up at this pylon, and we passed through without seeing anything more than a wary cat scuttling away.

"When was the last time you Hunted this section?" I whispered. Somehow this place made me feel like whispering.

Mark shook his head. "More than a year. No idea what we'll find, but . . ."

I summoned the Hounds. The Glyphs burned on the ground for a while after they came through, which was often a sign of trouble nearby. "But?" I prompted.

"All that good food over there"—he waved at the buildings across the Barrier from us—"makes people desperate."

"Hmm," I replied. I could see his point. I was also not about to stop anyone who was trying to get over there just to feed himself and his family. Mark and I exchanged a look as our Hounds ranged close around us, getting the feel of this part of Spillover, testing with a lot more senses than I have.

"Well, if people are hungry . . ." I let the words trail off, and

Mark nodded. Unspoken; we would hunt as well as Hunt. Even if no one turned up, the Hounds would know if we were being watched, and we could leave the game where it would be found.

"I don't think we should split up today," Mark said as we moved out into the ruins. These seemed to have been industrial buildings; the useful machinery had long since been scavenged away, but there were still big metal frames for things between the huge buildings, and a lot of rail track embedded in what was left of the paving. As yet, no one inside the Barrier had needed that much metal, evidently. See, this is why we don't need many mines anymore; we're still mining the bones of the old world before the Diseray.

"No argument here," I replied. Somehow this part of Spillover was spookier than anyplace I had been before. Maybe because I felt dwarfed by what was here, where in the other parts, the wrecked buildings had clearly been sized for humans. These buildings had been sized for giant machines, whose human attendants had crawled all over them like ants servicing the giant queen.

Made me feel very insignificant. There might have been some parts of Apex that had machines and buildings like these, but I had never been there. My mountains may be enormous in scale, but they don't make me feel insignificant, more like I am a part of something grand and glorious. This was a new sensation, and I didn't like it one bit.

We trotted along for the better part of an hour, following one set of main tracks. There was game here, probably because there was a lot of weed patch and brush growing up in the parts that weren't paved, or where the paving had crumbled away. Mark and I both bagged a fair number of bunnies, and once a deer bounded away from us in the distance, too far for me to make the shot.

Despite these signs that no one had been this way in a long time, I couldn't shake the feeling that there was someone watching us. Someone other than the cameras following us, that is. It wasn't like the creepy feeling I had at the play. I kept expecting to see one of those flashes of movement out of the corner of my eye. Two different kinds of watchers... one malevolent, the other passive.

I wondered about Uncle's note. What did he mean by "Ace has powerful friends"? I mean, what exactly could those friends do to make things difficult for me? After all, I was being watched practically every moment from the time I left my rooms, and maybe even *in* them, though I had requested not. How could Ace or his patrons—I assumed they were something like patrons—actually do anything? They'd be caught, surely.

Unless, of course, the people on the other end of the cameras decided to make the vid go away, the way they obviously did whenever Mark and I talked about something that they didn't want the Cits to know about. Even after the fact, there could be two sets of footage, one raw, one altered, the way the Folk Magician had been altered out of that confrontation I'd had with him.

Right, then. More conciliation on my part toward Ace. Act as if I admired him.

The motive for those "friends," well, that was as easy as human nature. I could think of one motive right away. Put two bored people together and I will promise you that they will find something to bet on. Now that I knew we were gladiators, I had no doubt that people were betting on us. Ace's friends were certainly betting on him, and would not take it kindly if I overtook him.

Mark didn't seem any happier about this area than I was. By now I knew him well enough to tell when there was more edge to his usual alertness. "I feel like I'm being watched, even though the Hounds haven't found anything," I said finally.

"We might be," he said, which kind of startled me. "Not everything's been stripped out of here. This was a high-tech area before the *Dies Irae*, with a lot of security cameras all over the place. No telling how many of them are still live."

*What the*— "Live?" I repeated. "But—who would be—"

I never got the chance to finish that, because out of the corner of my eye I caught a glint of light where a glint of light shouldn't have been, and at the same time Bya shouted *Danger!* into my head. I reacted instinctively . . . because the Mountain has been attacked in the past by those who didn't come from Otherside.

I rammed into Mark with my shoulder, knocking him down and sideways, and allowing myself to fall with him. I picked a good spot to knock us into, behind a big triangular concrete thing that may have been a building once. I was glad I had chosen wisely, because a second or so later, bullets pinged off it.

I felt as if I had grabbed hold of a live wire. That is never a sound you want to hear near you. My skin went cold, and my nerves sizzled, and every time a bullet hit, my whole body jerked a little.

"*Damned fools!*" Mark swore. And immediately apologized. "Not you, Joy. And my language—"

"I've heard worse," I said, getting that little mirrored gadget out of my pack and peeking over the top of the concrete thing with it. Yep. Sure enough. I could just make out someone on the top of one of the buildings with a—

The mirror shattered and the gadget was knocked out of my hand. I yelped. It *stung*!

Sniper rifle. And someone good on the other end of it, to hit that little gadget from so far away.

I gritted my teeth, shook my hand to get the feeling back, and told my heart it had better slow down. "Who *is* that?" I asked. "Othersiders don't use sniper rifles!"

More bullets peppered our position.

"No," Mark replied grimly. "But there are people out here who do. Not everyone who's stuck outside takes being left outside the Barrier quietly. And not everyone who gets booted out, or escapes out here, likes who's in charge of the Allied Territories."

Okay, that one blindsided me. Isolated thugs, looking to pick off Hunters to loot the bodies for our goodies . . . isolated bandits, picking off *anyone* to loot the bodies . . . We got them on the Mountain, too, of course, and in the early days there had even been a lot of rival warlords fighting over what remained of civilization, and there were still a few of those around to this day.

"Separationists?" I asked in a half gasp. There were still a few settlements of them out our way, folks who hated the premier and the Territories, though there'd never been one left alive long enough when they attacked us to walk us through their philosophy. So I really had no idea what their malfunction was. Were they completely insane? Had they been spellbound? Or were they just fanatics in a different direction than religion?

"Rebels of some sort, I guess," he said, trying to get a sight on the sniper without exposing himself. "We've heard rumors about crude organization out here. Some people who think they'd be better in charge than the premier. And there are always people who just have to pee in the cornflakes, because."

I suppose in the back of my mind it had never occurred to me that the army would allow anything of the sort to exist anywhere near Apex City, and that's why it blindsided me.

Like the fact that we were gladiators, only more shocking to me—there hadn't even been a *hint* of this back on the Mountain.

Then again . . . there wouldn't be, would there? No reason why the monks and the Masters would know, not living down here, and only seeing what Apex showed us. After all, I knew there were lots of things that the government didn't want the Cits to know. This was just one more.

I heard a peculiar sound. It sounded like a bullet breaking something expensive. Then another. Then it occurred to me what it was. The sniper was taking out our cameras! I started to giggle. Mark looked at me as if he thought I was getting hysterical.

I just shook my head. "I'm okay. Can I handle this?" I asked. "Getting them off us, I mean. I have an idea."

The last of the cameras exploded before it could get out of range. "Be my guest," Mark said, and winced as more bullets pinged off the concrete, making my nerves scream too. "I have no ideas except to wait until he runs out of bullets."

*Bya!* I called mentally, and a moment later I was smothered in crazy-colored Hound. *Are there many far-eyes on us?*

*Many,* he agreed.

So, these skunks were using the old security cams, just like Mark had suggested.

*And are there more men, with or without guns?* I asked.

*Only three.*

Well, that was good news. *Make the eyes watching us sick, keep Mark's Hounds from getting shot, then bind the men. Like we do with drunks and locos. Call me when you are done.*

He plastered my face with his tongue, and the little cuts where chips of concrete and camera-shrapnel must have hit me stung for a moment, then he *bamphed* out.

See, I didn't want to hurt these guys. Not yet, anyway. It's always a lot more effective when you can scare someone into leaving you alone. And as I've said before, my Hounds are really, really special.

Mark was only beginning to see just how special.

"I take it you've sent out the Hounds?" he said.

I nodded. "I told Bya to tell yours to stay out of range. He'll let us know when it's safe to come out."

So we waited. It didn't take long, but it felt like a long time, let me tell you. It was a relief when bullets stopped hitting the concrete. It was a bigger relief when Bya said *Done. The Saints will show you the way.* "Saints." That was Bya's term for Mark's Hounds. And if you want to know if he was being serious or sarcastic, I would bet on sarcasm.

"All clear," I said, and crawled out of hiding. Sure enough, one of Mark's Hounds was flying toward us, and when he saw us getting up, he hovered until we caught up with him, then flew off, with glances backward over his shoulder to make sure we were keeping up.

It was easy enough to see the first man, once we were led into the part of the ruined building where he had taken cover. He was the thing that looked like a bundle of multicolored rope with two sets of eyes. One set was his, and one set was my Hound's.

Shinje; I could tell from the colors. Shinje is mostly purple and red. Remember, I said my Hounds can look like anything? Well . . . this is something they learned how to do when I needed them to immobilize someone without hurting him. They change their form into something like a head and a couple legs and a bunch of tentacles, *bamph* in next to him, and then, before he can recover from having a horror like that just pop in next to him, they jump him and the next thing he knows, he's bundled up like a spider's prey.

Mark's eyes bulged while I leveled my pistol at the guy.

"What do you want to do with him, Senior Hunter?" I asked, all formal. Now was not the time for me to play town sheriff.

Mark thought about this. "Right now, talk to him. "All right, Shinje," I said steadily. "Let him talk."

The tentacles peeled away from the rest of the guy's head. I half expected cursing, but I guess he was so traumatized by what Shinje had done to him that he couldn't seem to muster any words. Mark walked over and confiscated the rifle that was on the floor. Shinje moved tentacles and obligingly exposed a sidearm and a knife, and Mark took those too.

"Why?" Mark said finally. "We're *Hunters*, man! Why shoot at us?"

The man finally regained some of his courage. "Yer Rayne's lapdogs!" he spat. "Ye jump when he sez, an' bite who he sez an'—"

"Now, stop right there!" Mark said sternly, and Shinje gave the guy a squeeze, just enough to make him choke off whatever else he was about to say. "We're *Hunters*, you moron, and do you think that if we were some sort of favored pets we'd be out *here*, in godforsaken Spillover, Hunting? No matter what you think when you see these stupid outfits, we are not Rayne's to command. We are not *anyone's* to command. We serve and protect *all* the people from the monsters of the Otherside, and we are not your enemies!"

"Not unless you make enemies out of us by getting in between us and our job," I added, keeping my pistol aimed right between his bushy eyebrows.

Mark nodded. "Free up his legs so he can walk," he ordered Shinje, who obliged. "Let's go collect his friends."

Mark's Hound led the way. As I had expected, the other two were together, sniper and spotter. It took a long climb to get up to them, but not a particularly hard one, since there were still metal catwalks and stairs all over this building, even though whatever huge machines had been bolted in here were long gone. Shinje had freed our captive's legs so he could walk, and we found the spotter and sniper wrapped up by Bya and Dusana respectively, while Begtse, Chenresig, and three of the four of Mark's Hounds stood guard. Our guy was sweating heavily by the time we got to the top; after all, he was carrying his own weight and the weight of my Hound. He seemed really happy to sit down and not inclined to talk.

The other two glared at us, but I thought there might be some fear behind the glares. Mark and I confiscated their weapons, then walked a little way away.

"I know what I would do," I whispered hesitantly, "but I'll follow your lead on this. I—don't know what we can get away with. . . ."

Mark scowled. "Headquarters would probably prefer we just executed them," he said reluctantly.

"You don't want to." Neither did I. It would have been one thing to shoot them while they were shooting at us, it was quite another to kill them in cold blood.

"It makes us worse than them." I could see White Knight's point. "Anyway, until Headquarters manages to fly more cameras out to us, we're on our own, and whatever we say happened, happened."

I sucked on my lower lip for a little while. "Well . . . do you have any other ideas?"

"Wait until I get done giving them a piece of my mind."

Fifteen minutes later, after a lecture from Mark about how we were *Hunters*, damn it, and our job was to protect all Cits, even if some of the Cits were idiots, and even if some Cits had decided they didn't want to be Cits anymore, Mark and I moved away from them to talk.

It might have been a much longer lecture, but Knight was big and intimidating, and my Hounds were going out of their way to be *weird* and intimidating, and our captives stayed quiet, and it looked as if Mark was having an effect on them.

"Now what?" I asked.

"Well, I had an idea," he said. "We wait until the new cams catch up with us, then we kill them."

"*What?*" I spluttered, then felt like an idiot. "Right, of course. For the cameras. Gotcha. Think they'll go along with that?"

"Only one way to find out." He marched over to them. "Now, morons. You've got two choices. One, I call a chopper for you. Two, we fake a firefight and you die, and it had better be an amazing performance. Which will it be?"

They looked at each other. "I reckon . . . we die. . . ." the sniper said slowly.

I looked at my Hounds. *Okay, Bya, let 'em go.*

Once they were out of the tangles of tentacles, we could see that their outfits consisted of layers of mismatched tatters, and they looked pretty dirty and thin, although their weapons were in good order and the sniper rifle was really excellent. So if they were "rebels," it didn't look as if their rebellion was prospering.

"Now what?" the sniper asked.

"Now we wait back where we were until the new camera comes in. I'm sure you can spot it," Mark replied with heavy sarcasm. "Then we shoot at each other, and you die. Dramatically."

"And remember," I said darkly, "if you back out on this deal, my Hounds *will* get you again."

They looked, shuddered, then looked at each other. "We'll need some blood," said the scruffier of the lot. "A lot of blood."

Five dead rabbits later, Mark and I were back in place when the camera came zipping in. And the exchange of gunfire began. We were all damn good shots, so it wasn't hard to hit close enough to make it look real, but actually hit cover instead.

It was really impressive. So was the bloodcurdling scream that rang from the top of the building.

Mark wanted dramatic . . . well, we got dramatic. There was a lot of shouting and cursing, and I learned a whole new set of colorful words I would never be allowed to use in public. And I actually had to suppress a giggle when as a "last act of defiance," the sniper took out the *new* camera as he "died."

I decided I needed to find a way to let Uncle know how this had really turned out. I was pretty sure he'd approve.

Not that any of this would have appeared on our feeds. It was already clear that, like existence of the Folk, those in charge did not want the Cits to know anyone was rebelling against Premier Rayne's rule, no matter how shabby they looked.

Mark and I sat down for a breather while my Hounds made

sure the rebels actually moved out like we said they should. "I'm glad that worked out the way it did," I said finally.

"Me too." He blew out his breath in a long sigh. "I'm a Hunter, I'm supposed to protect people, not make them into targets."

Which was pretty much how I felt, so I nodded, and we just sat there quietly until my Hounds came back. *They run very fast,* Bya said smugly. *I don't think they wanted to be wrapped up again.*

Yet another set of cameras caught up with us when we were a good half mile from the ambush point, just in time to record us surrounding and eliminating a herd of Goblins. We gave the cameras a good show, then moved on.

Which is when we practically tripped over trouble, and only the alertness of our Hounds saved us.

I know neither of us were expecting *two* concentrations of Othersiders so close together. After all, this part of Spillover was within sight of the Barrier, and if there had been anyone patrolling the hydro side, the activity should have been spotted. A lay up of Goblins was one thing—you couldn't tell where they'd wander off to next, and it wouldn't be remotely out of the question for them to go unnoticed in the couple of days they had been nesting here.

But what we almost ran into was something entirely different. It was a long-term nesting site, and a *huge* nesting site . . . of Gazers.

The nest was inside one of the old industrial buildings, a smaller one than most of the others, maybe half an acre in size, two stories tall, and made solidly of brick. It didn't have a roof, but that wouldn't bother Gazers. It looked, in fact, as if something had come along and ripped off the top part, leaving a brick shell open to the sky. And it was a good thing that Mark's Hounds were flyers, because *they* were the ones that spotted the danger before we humans got too close, streaking back with Bya in close attendance on the ground to provide translation so we didn't have to play a game of charades with them to find out what was wrong.

"What—" Mark said, alarmed at the way the Hounds were acting, boiling around us like frightened ferrets.

"A Gazer nest . . ." I said flatly, and he blanched. I wasn't feeling any too good myself.

One Gazer was bad enough. There were at least twenty, maybe more, and about a hundred gross little eyeballs that were the nestlings. This was way, way too big for us to handle, and once Bya had finished giving me the full description of what Mark's Hound had seen, Mark opened up the com link back to headquarters, while the two of us and all the Hounds made a run for the nearest building that was tall enough to look down into the one the Gazers had taken for their own.

I was being point man with weapons hot and ready while Mark handled the call, so I didn't catch a lot of it on my own comm. This building wasn't in as good shape as the one the sniper had used. But eventually we got to a spot where there was half a busted-out window, and a bit of sturdy catwalk to lie flat on. We dug out our binocs and had a look, Mark still talking to HQ. Now that I wasn't watching sixty directions at once, it sounded as if they were talking about calling in an artillery barrage, which was sensible. We both had laser pointers and we could easily paint the spot so the Gazers got no warning. Only one small problem.

We both spotted it at the same time, as some of the baby eyeballs lofted up about a story and sank back down again.

"Cancel that," Mark said. "They're fledging." If the babies were flight-capable, we were too close to paint the target and survive what the artillery would have to lob at the nest to get them all in one go. And if you didn't get them all . . . you had a scattered nest of really angry Gazers, who tend to come back with friends. Friends like Gogs and Magogs.

Someone broke in on our freq. "We all just finished our patrols and got nothin'," said a voice I recognized. Ace. "There's twenty of us sitting around HQ, including Dazzle—she can net and flash, Noob can net and flash; that'll be good enough to hold while the rest of us give the Cits a good show. And Armorer Kent's here, that's an Elite. We oughta be able to take out two nests with all of that." Noob. That was me.

HQ didn't need any convincing, though. "Put out your beacon, White Knight," the controller ordered. "Hunter Ace is right. This is going to be sensational."

# 17

DO I EVEN HAVE TO say how bad an idea I thought this was? From Mark's face, he felt the same. But he didn't dare say anything; we were on camera, and the decision had already been made for us.

They went into the building, sneaking in from the rear, one and two at a time, and we came down off the high perch to meet them because there was no way that bit of catwalk would hold more than four.

But of course, we had the cameras to watch for us now. And we had the armorer, who, thank heavens, was the one really in charge and not Ace.

It was the armorer who ordered HQ to put the cameras up around the edge of the Gazer building. They argued with him when he said that, because they wanted as many cameras on the Hunters as possible. Evidently this was a whole new thing—a Hunting party of ranking Hunters this big—and people on the live feeds were getting excited about it.

Thanks to the cameras, we had eyes on the Gazer symbionts too, Jackals. They were nasty things, just as nasty as the Gazers, in a different sort of fashion. They looked a bit like real doggy hounds: white, with floppy hound ears as red as blood, and red eyes that looked as if they were weeping blood all the time. Small, no bigger than a rabbit hound, but fast and vicious, with a mouth full of needle teeth that could turn you into shreds in a moment.

There were lots of Jackals, at least twice as many as there were Gazer nestlings. Right now they were asleep in a big pile; they must have *all* eaten recently and well, because Gazers only get sleepy after a big feast. I didn't want to think what that meant, but of course the conclusion was inescapable. The Goblins had been sleepy too, and Gazers and Goblins didn't have any problem working together. So they had probably found a concentration of people out here, and . . . well, only Hunters could hope to survive against Gazers, Jackals, and Goblins combined.

They'd probably destroyed almost a village-worth of men, women, and children. It did make me angry, though, to know that those men who had been shooting at us must also have a sort of headquarters or encampment somewhere out here, and to know that they had tried to pick *us* off instead of sniping Gazers.

Dazzle and I huddled up as soon as the armorer got off the comm. We had our Perscom screens tuned to cameras on the opposite sides of the Gazer nest, so we could see the whole thing and begin planning our assault.

"Do you anchor your net?" I asked her.

She shook her head. "Don't know how," she confessed, and looked at me hopefully.

"Okay . . . let's try this," I suggested, and made a rough circle of broken brick and cement between us. "You float yours over, I'll slam mine down at cross-grain to yours and see if I can't anchor both." We wouldn't have to worry about the Gazers seeing the nets until it was too late; even with Mage-sight, they'd be looking up into the sun and be too blinded to catch the magic.

With a ring of interested Hounds watching—she had four that looked like wolves with rose-ash smoke for fur—we gave it a shot. The first two times were failures: the first time, her net disintegrated under mine; the second, I failed to "cup" the edges of mine, and hers slipped out from underneath, then collapsed. But the third time, we got it right, and after another three trials to refine our technique, we figured we were ready. We grinned at each other and fist-bumped, then rejoined the rest of the group.

Mark's four Hounds were going to be incredibly important, since only he and one other Hunter had flyers.

"Your job is going to be to knock any Gazers that escape and take to the air right down to the ground again," the armorer said. When Mark, the other Hunter, and their Hounds all looked puzzled, I raised my hand.

The armorer pointed his thumb at me. "Go, Joy."

"I've seen raptors do that, up in the mountains," I said, which was true, but I'd seen one of the Masters' Hounds do it too. I went on to explain, miming it all with my hands. "The flyer gets height and circles—it's called 'waiting on.'" My right hand formed a winglike thing that was supposed to represent the Hound while my left made a fist that was the Gazer. "And when his prey takes to the air, he folds his wings and fists his claws—or paws in the case of your Hounds, Mark—and dives." I plunged my right hand down on my left. "He hits it—*bam!*—right on the head, but since he's fisted his claws, he doesn't bind to it, and he bounces right back up while he knocks the prey to the ground."

Mark, the other guy, and the armorer all nodded—Mark and the other Hunter in understanding, the armorer in approval. He went back to laying out the plan.

Something I noticed was how Paules and Ace stood together, and had this kind of unspoken communication going, almost as if they were twins rather than older and younger brothers. I'd never seen them in a Hunting situation together, and it was the first time I'd ever seen Ace show anything like fraternal feelings, though it had been clear a long time ago that Paules really wanted to impress his older brother.

One of the things that the armorer was absolutely insisting on was that we each have partners keeping an eye on each other; we were going to use some light-flash spells and flash-bangs to try to blind the Gazers, but there were a lot of them and a lot of their Jackals and *way* too many fledglings, and even the little ones could get a hypnotic lock on you. So we were going to have to be vigilant about that, and make sure that anyone who got Gazed got snapped right out of it.

"Which is why I want the two of you watched over by White Knight and at least two of your Hounds, each," the armorer said. Bya bowed over his paws and whined agreement; I could tell he'd been worried about that. He wanted to fight the Gazers, but he didn't want to leave me vulnerable—well, now he could relax; he had orders.

I called over Dusana, Begtse, Chenresig, Kalachakra, and Shinje, and pointed at the armorer. "Pack with his Hounds," I said. "Bya and Hevajra will stay with me."

Dusana snorted, which is his way of saying yes, so it was settled.

Dazzle, Mark, the armorer, and our Hounds all moved out first; this could not possibly have been a situation more to the Gazer advantage. There were only two doors into the whole building, and the only other way up to the second floor, where there were knocked-out windows, was a metal fire escape. The party split up into two, except for me, Dazzle, Mark, and the armorer, and slipped up to the blank brick wall and the holes where the doors had been. The four of us and our Hounds carefully inched up the fire escape, hoping it wouldn't pull free of the brick, or creak, or break underneath us. I only breathed a little easier when we were all on the platform on our bellies, the armorer had a grenade gun out, and Dazzle and I began painting Glyphs in the air over the Gazer nest with little twitches of our fingers.

I was chewing furiously on my lower lip, my stomach in a complete knot, as the nets slowly formed up, one on top of the other. I carefully curled the edges of mine over the edges of Dazzle's, praying the whole time that the Gazers wouldn't look up and figure out something was going on. When I had Dazzle's net secure, I tapped the armorer's elbow. He glanced over at me and I nodded.

He aimed the grenade gun at the nest and counted down in the barest hint of a whisper. "Three . . . two . . ."

On *one*, he fired, and I *slammed* the net down on the Gazer nest and sealed the edges down to the rock all the way around. The flash hit them at the same time the net did.

Then Dazzle let loose with *her* flash-magic, and I saw why she had gotten her nickname. My flashes were pretty good, but hers... If we weren't Hunters, people would *pay* her to put on shows of light. It was amazing. She was throwing off light-flowers and showers of sparks and eye-watering, noiseless explosions that were exactly like the flash grenades except there was no *bang*. And they were coming every few seconds. There was no point in me wasting any manna in adding to all that; I just hung on to the nets like grim death and tried to feel where they were weakening or stretching.

Meanwhile the rest of the Hunting party, having gotten the flash-bang signal, came pouring in through the doors, spells and weapons hot. Almost immediately the flying Hounds began knocking escapees to the ground, just as I had showed them. The fledglings and the Jackals were both small enough to slip through spots in the net. Of the two, it was those red-eared, bloody-eyed devils that were the most immediate danger. They were wicked, wicked fast, and I heard someone's high-pitch shrieking as some of the Jackals got through the heavy cross fire.

The armorer had scrambled down the wall on the inside to join the rest of the Hunting party on the ground, so it was just me, Mark and Dazzle, and the Hounds. Mark was methodically picking off fledgling Gazers in midair with the sniper's rifle. My Hounds were studiously looking away from the melee and staring into my face. That was smart—no Gazer was going to get a lock on them if they were looking away.

Sweat was pouring down my back, and I dug my fingers into the crumbling brick at the edge of the window. I didn't dare close my aching eyes, because I needed to *see* the net through the flashing lights. My arms burned, muscles clamping down hard, as if I was physically holding that giant net full of surging, struggling Gazers and Jackals and fledglings.

And some were getting out. We knew they were going to; just like when Mark and I had gone after those Goblins, some were going to stretch the invisible fabric of the net and get loose. Dazzle and I had to keep that to a trickle. Gazers were harder to kill than Goblins, just shooting them once wasn't going to take one out. Half the party concentrated on the Gazers and fledglings getting loose, half on the Jackals. There was a lot of screaming down there, but so far I hadn't felt that horrible, gut-wrenching surge of manna followed by emptiness that meant someone had died.

The barrage of flash grenades was getting ragged, but Dazzle was more than making up for it. I have *never* been so glad to have someone on my side than I was to have her in that fight.

And I could feel the steady drain of manna out of me that it took to keep the net strong.

Which told me that pretty much everyone was in the same shape as me or worse. Certainly the ones who had gotten needle teeth embedded in their legs were worse off. But none of us were dead, and the Gazers and Jackals and Gazer young were thinning.

Now the net was tight enough that not even the gross little eyebulbs were getting out. I was about to let myself have a deep breath when I spotted something coming in like an angry hornet over the wall opposite to us.

A Gazer. A big one. Probably the bull of the nest. I let out a wordless, high-pitched scream; Mark followed where I was looking and immediately flung the rifle up and began sighting in.

But Ace's brother had already seen it. And he and his Hounds were heading for it.

Without backup.

I tried to throw a light-flash at it, but I was spent, and all I got was a little *poof* of sparks. I didn't dare distract Dazzle.

Hadn't Ace ever taught him better? The stupid kid was looking *right* at the thing, firing a pistol wildly at it—like he was going to be able to *hit* it while running, and in seconds, the Gazer had him. He suddenly froze like a statue. His Hounds froze. The Gazer never stopped coming. Blood started pouring out of the kid's ears, looking from where I lay like macabre and festive ribbons of scarlet, and even though I couldn't see his face from here, I knew his mouth must be open in a silent scream of agony.

*That* was when some of the others finally noticed there was something wrong, that the kid wasn't with them, and spotted him.

By then, of course, it was too late.

He dropped dead to the ground before the first of their bullets or spells touched the damn thing.

Ace went insane.

He unloaded both his pistols into it, and arcing bolts of electricity, like miniature lightning, followed the trajectory of the bullets. Even a Gazer didn't have time to recover or counter, or survive a barrage like that. It collapsed like a punctured balloon, and Ace tossed away his guns and ran for his fallen brother, screaming at the top of his lungs.

The armorer stood over him, protecting him, while he cradled his brother's body, oblivious to the mayhem still raging around him. The rest of us had no choice. Half the Gazers and a couple dozen of their Jackals were still alive and needed all of our attention. And I had to hold those nets, if I didn't want to see a repetition of the tragedy. I held, and held, until I didn't think I could hold any longer, then I held some more.

Finally it was over. The last little nestling popped. The last Jackal died running, but not fast enough to escape a bullet. I let go of the nets with a gasp, and they faded into nothingness. Dazzle looked at me, her eyes rolled up into her head, and she passed clean out. Mark caught her as she fell over sideways.

"I'll take care of her," he said. "You go down to the others ahead of us."

I didn't want to. I felt like a wrung-out dishrag, and I didn't want to look at poor Ace right now. But one of us had to rejoin the group to report, and one of us had to take care of Dazzle, and Mark was probably better at carrying her down that metal ladder than I was. So I climbed down and made my way to the closer of the doors.

I walked pretty slowly—thinking hard the whole time— because what the hell was I going to say to Ace? "I'm sorry" didn't sound like nearly enough. On the other hand, the other thing that I *wanted* to say, which was that his brother had been an idiot and nearly gotten more of us killed, was not exactly...kind. But the decision was taken right out of my hands when Ace charged me as soon as I cleared the door, shouting about how it was all *my* fault and *I* had somehow let the Gazer out of the net on purpose.

I don't know what anyone else was thinking, or even if they were thinking at all, but he was giving me plenty of time to get ready as he ran at me like a maniac, and I traded swift glances with the armorer—who nodded, ever so slightly, and just as slightly stepped back.

So when Ace closed with me, I didn't try to placate him and I didn't try to run away. I stood my ground, and as he got within a couple of steps of me, I moved smoothly off the line of attack, closed one hand on the wrist that was nearest me as he swung, and flipped him over my shoulder, sending him face-first onto the ground and getting his hand and thumb stretched out behind his back in the most painful possible hanari hold I could manage. He was not going to get up from that position without breaking his wrist. And I wasn't going to let him go until I was sure he wasn't going to attack me again, or the armorer ordered me to, whichever came first.

It all happened in an instant, so far as everyone else was concerned. They all looked dumbstruck.

"I didn't let that Gazer go," I said slowly and patiently as Ace gasped with pain and tried to get back the breath that had gotten knocked out of him. "That was the nest bull, and he came over the east side of the building nearest your brother. I didn't see him until it was too late, and your poor brother started charging him."

I looked over at the armorer then and said, out loud and boldly, "Hunter Ace is understandably upset and not himself, sir. Requesting permission for the last five minutes to be erased from the public record."

There were a couple of gasps at that, though I couldn't tell whether people were gasping because I actually *said out loud* that I knew the vids were tampered with, or because no one expected me to give Ace this easy out—at least as far as the public would be concerned. But the armorer just nodded and said quite loudly, "Erase the last five minutes. Freeze and hold."

I took that as my cue to let go of Ace's hand and step quickly away from him. At that point, before he could get up and renew his assault on me, all my Hounds quickly surrounded me, practically glowing with manna. One of his friends helped him up. He brushed them aside, and stumbled off outside the nest building.

"Resume public vidding," the armorer said. "Send the choppers."

I was rather glad that the choppers could only hold four at a time. I sent my Hounds back, and Mark, Dazzle, the armorer, and I all crowded into one; I didn't see how the others sorted themselves out.

We were the first chopper on the ground, so to avoid any chance of further contact with Ace, I got Dazzle's elbow and ran her inside, taking her straight to the docs. They already knew she'd passed out, of course, so they hustled her off for a thorough checkout, gave me a cursory once-over, and sent me off to debrief.

That was easier than I'd thought; since I hadn't passed out at all, and since my part of the fight was considered relatively "easy" and I hadn't gotten wounded, it was just a quick review of the vid—which, of course, showed quite clearly that *I* hadn't let the bull Gazer out. It also revealed something that I hadn't heard at the time; that Ace's brother made no attempt to alert any of the Hunters nearest him when he spotted the thing. He just went charging straight at the monster, shouting something.

I didn't say anything about that, and they didn't say anything to me, except, "Could you have sent out a second net spell, Hunter Joyeaux?"

"No, sir, I could not, sir, and I did explain that at the planning, sir," I replied. Which I had; it was on the vid. "One net spell at a time is all I can manage."

"Very good," was the reply.

Early bed sounded very good indeed, and I was just glad that the Gazer takedown had been a group effort, and that my part in it was *very* small.

But I hadn't even gotten two steps into the hall when my Perscom pinged me.

It was the armorer. "Hunter Joyeaux. Main lounge, now," he said.

"Yes, sir," I said, and made for the room on the trot.

When I got there ... it was full. All the regular crew, plus everyone who'd been on the Gazer Hunt, including the ones who had needed medical and debriefing (except Ace and his girlfriend). And in addition, some other Hunters who I only knew from the channels. At a quick count, there were about fifty people here ... so all the ones who just came off duty, plus some from the other two shifts?

The armorer was standing next to the vid screen, waiting. A couple more people, including Trev, came in after me. They must have been the ones he was waiting for, because as I found an unobtrusive place to stand, he spoke, and everyone got instantly quiet.

Not only was the crowd subdued, there was a sense that most of them were in a state of shock and disbelief. Paules might not have been exactly popular, but he was one of *us*. Heck, there was a kind of cold emptiness in me, that *life out of balance* thing again, and I didn't even know Paules.

"What's the rule?" he demanded.

"Make sure the Cits feel safe," several of us murmured.

"I can't hear you." He glared.

"Make sure the Cits feel safe, sir!" we all shouted raggedly.

"And it's only the 'casters doing some fancy dancing on the channels to concentrate them on the tragic sacrifice young, handsome Paules made for the sake of the mission that is keeping them from feeling very *unsafe* right now." He didn't lose an atom of his stern expression. "There's also some fancy work on the part of the editors, pulling out anything that identifies how close we were to the Barriers."

The room was so quiet I could hear everyone breathing now.

"We very nearly had an unmitigated disaster," he said. "And I'm at least partly at fault for that. I should have silenced that young fool Ace as soon as he started spouting about getting all of you out there. I should have overridden the 'casters when they started agitating for a big Hunt. I did neither, because it was out in Spillover, so I reckoned there was no harm. Give the Cits a big Hunt. Show them how the Hunters work together even on the spur of the moment. That was a job for a full squad of the Elite, and it should have been done at night when Gazers are at their most vulnerable, and my own judgment was faulty. But I am going to make damn sure that no one else's was before we leave this room." He tapped his Perscom and the vid started.

I guess the reason why I was there was just so that it was clear I wasn't being excluded from the possibility of having messed up, because he stopped the vid of our attack every minute or so and took everything we were doing apart, including barking, "Joy. Dazzle. Why did that eyebulb get out?" or something like that as he pointed to an escapee. We'd always answer that it got out through the mesh, or squirmed under the net, or something reasonable—I was actually really glad to see, with all the vid angles, that we'd done a *good* job of holding those nets. Better than I'd thought.

When the vid was over, I was sweating, and so was everyone else in the room, I think. The armorer turned the vid off. "New rule," he said. "No one jumps in on the main frequency and suggests a mass Hunt. *Ever.* You get a situation like we just had, you report it, and let us handle it.

"Officially, this was a tragedy. Paules was a fine Hunter with years of protecting the city ahead of him. No, you don't know if he had ever encountered a Gazer before, and don't let anyone lead you into answering anything except how sorry you are for his brother and family and how, thanks to his sacrifice, the Hunt was completely successful and the Cits can rely on us to keep them safe. No speculation. No elaboration. Got that?"

There were nodding heads all over the room and some murmured "yes, sirs."

"Good. You're all dismissed." He stalked out of the room before any of us could get up or otherwise move, and we all obeyed him, drifting toward the mess hall or our rooms. Everybody was pretty somber. I ate without really tasting anything, and went to bed without watching any vid.

We'd been successful, wildly successful, in fact. We'd protected the Cits from a danger on their very doorstep that no one had been aware was there. Despite losing Ace's brother—it should have felt like a victory.

Instead, it felt like I needed to watch my back, and like no good was going to come of this.

# 18

THE NEXT DAY, people were still rattled. There wasn't much talking going on at breakfast. But no one was really grieving, either. Paules was the first fatality they'd had (not counting Elites) in a while, and they couldn't figure out how to feel about it. A gutwrenching *could that have been me?* Then the certainty that no one else would have been that criminally stupid . . . then the relief that it wasn't them or anyone they really knew well. It'd make for an unsettling mix of emotions.

I learned that the group effort was deemed my final test, and I was given my own territory. *Not* Spillover, but not one of the easy ones in the City Center, either. I got another industrial territory, another one of blocks of windowless buildings centered on an equally windowless residential building. Not a prison this time, I was told, but what was called "public" housing, where the people who were brought in from Spillover for permanent, but tedious and low-paying, jobs could live.

They *could* try to find a place to live elsewhere, of course, but then there would be the lengthy travel time to and from the job. Some did anyway; they had family or friends in nicer parts of the city, farther from the Barrier, who were willing to share space and rent. But most opted to have their earnings siphoned away for the privilege of living in a box and never seeing the sun, in order to be close to a job that would make me open a vein.

Of course, to an extent, *I* lived in a box. There were no windows in headquarters. And instead of half of what I earned, everything I might have been paid to Hunt belonged to the Hunter Corps... so, I suppose I was just as much an indentured servant as they were. I got much better food, and got waited on like a wealthy Cit, and by any standard I knew my life was ultra-plush, but with the exception of what I had brought with me, I didn't actually own anything, and none of my time was really my own.

But I had this much freedom still, in that I could elect to walk out with my Hounds and never come back, and if I did, there would not be one damn thing they could do about it.

One of the writers from before the Diseray who I liked said in one of his books, "Freedom is just a cage where the bars are farther away than you care to fly." I guess for the Spillover folks lucky enough to get a job in the city, their little boxes were as luxurious as my fancy suite was to me. It makes sense that when you're living in a wrecked building with a leaky roof and nothing but a fire for warmth—and where at any moment you can find yourself sharing your space with an Othersider—one of those living-cubes was downright heavenly.

I reported to the armory for my new assignment, and Karly was there at the same time. We grinned at each other and fist-bumped, then Armorer Kent came in with a piece of paper in each hand. "Originally you were supposed to get Karly's territory, and she was supposed to go to F-22," he said. "In fact those are your assignments, but we've overridden the computer assignment and switched you."

Karly scratched her head a little, then shrugged. "That's all right with me, if it's all right with Joy," she said. "I don't mind going back to a territory I know."

The armorer nodded. "Normally someone just marked to go solo would get an older territory someone's been working regularly," he said to me. "But you have more Hounds than Karly, and aside for that one slip with the Wyverns, you and your pack have proven that you're seasoned and ready to work a tougher territory alone."

"We're both on perimeter territories. It's a long way back to HQ. You know what this means, don't you?" Karly asked me.

I shook my head.

"It means you're going to have to fight me for the last fish taco every night." She kept her expression perfectly deadpan right up until that moment.

Even the armorer laughed.

◄ ►

Well anyway, there it was, I had my own territory, and the Hounds and I fell back into our old and well-rehearsed pattern. The only difference between this and home was that I took a pod out to

District F-22 instead of walking out there, or riding a horse, then called the Hounds after it rolled back to the pod-station. Then we arranged ourselves in our usual formation: me and Bya at the center, the rest ranged out around us. I like the pattern of working the perimeter of a territory, then moving inward. Generally if something is trying to hide, that drives it toward the center, rather than out into someone else's territory. That's how all of us worked at home. Mark didn't do that—but then, he generally worked Spillover alone, so I suppose it didn't matter.

F-22 had plenty of places for nasty things to hide. You wouldn't think it, looking at it from the road, where everything was all blank buildings and lawn. But that was just the façade you saw from the single road that went along one side of it. Actually since no one but Hunters ever ventured between the buildings, no one had bothered clearing away more of the pre-Diseray wreckage than was needed to build the factories and the housing blocks. In fact, a lot of the rubble just got dumped on top of the other rubble. There were trees and bushes growing out of the piles, and weeds almost as tall as me. Lots and lots of places for things to hide. I'd checked, and before I got it, F-22 was only worked about one day every two weeks since it wasn't anyone's assigned spot. It was right up against Spillover, and as I now knew, that meant that there were probably several ways for Othersiders to get in besides over the Barriers like Gazers did.

Or under them. Just because we had never seen Othersiders digging tunnels, that didn't mean they couldn't, or wouldn't. I was beginning to have my suspicions about those storm sewers too. How hard would it be to figure out where the hatches were and break into them from the Spillover side? It might take a good long while, but if the Barriers didn't go down as well as up . . . or didn't go down more than, say, six or eight feet ... it would just be a matter of the Othersiders figuring out that they could get in that way without being detected, then doing the work.

Maybe I couldn't find anything, not because it wasn't happening, but because it wasn't happening in the open. After all, in old books we had up at the Monastery, prisoners of war escaped by digging tunnels all the time, and *they* did it with guards watching them day and night.

Truth to tell, while I missed working with Knight, it felt good to be on my own. I only had to look out for myself, not anyone else, and if I thought of the buildings as rocks or cliff-faces, this wasn't too unlike being home.

And like home, in between sweeps, there were a lot of little nuisances to be herded up—all of them flyers and small enough to miss being detected as they zipped over the Barriers. There were the Fay, smaller and lighter versions of the Goblins, about the size of butterflies. Really cute, until they bit you and the wound started blistering and festering immediately from their poison, and even their spit was toxic. If I saw one Fay, I knew there were dozens within a few feet of it, so I just made a net over the area and tightened it down. It didn't have to be strong, so I could spread the magic thinner than I did the net I used on the Gazers—the same amount of magic, but more like a spiderweb than a fishing net. Fay like to torment things, and I got lucky; I saw a flock of them torturing a rabbit before they saw me. I cast my net over them and tightened it down before they had any idea I was there, and I let Dusana have them.

I cleared out six more flocks of the little terrors by the time I was done with the surface of F-22. Then it was time to check those storm sewers. Honestly? I was expecting worse than I found. I was expecting Knockers. Instead, I got Kobolds. Like Knockers, only smaller, weaker, and cowardly. A tribe of them might be able to hurt a child—and children were their favorite prey, because it was easy to scare kids, and they seem to get a kind of high off of human fear. But they were no match for us. The Hounds herded them like sheepdogs, got a good group rounded up, then went to work. I didn't shoot so much as a single bullet all day.

But we covered a *lot* of ground, though by no means the entire territory, and I was pretty weary by the time I sent my sated Hounds back and called the pod. F-22 was a lot bigger than I had thought, and to be absolutely honest, I don't think we got to more than a quarter of it. Working our way through those overgrown piles of rubble was tough. It was easier to work through a forest!

When I got back, it was late—pretty much everyone else had already eaten. But Mark was still in the mess hall and he grinned when he saw me. And so was Karly. In triumph, she waved the last bite of a fish taco at me and popped it in her mouth with a grin. I rolled my eyes, then put together dinner from what was left, and went over to join them. My Perscom pinged as I sat down and I checked it reflexively.

"Well, that's a pain," I said, irritated. "I thought everything here in Apex was supposed to be flawless."

Mark laughed at that. Funny thing, he was laughing a lot more since he and I had partnered up. "They'd like the turnips to believe that, yes. What's the matter?"

"Nothing big." I nibbled what had looked like a square of cornbread. To my pleasure, it *was* a square of cornbread. Cornbread and chili . . . It really was feeling like home today. "Just there's some glitch that they can't track down. They told me to work F-22 today, and now they want me to keep doing it, but the actual schedule still says Karly is supposed to be there, and I'm supposed to be in Karly's old territory. They just told me to ignore the schedule." It was countersigned by the armorer, so I didn't see any reason to doubt it. Karly checked her Perscom. "Same here," she agreed. "Probably some Tech punched in the wrong code somewhere."

Mark nodded and sipped at his drink; clearly he was not at all averse to keeping me company. I was glad; even though it had been good to solo, it was always better to be around people when you got off patrolling. "That happens once in a while. About six months ago, the schedule showed Dazzle and me with switched territories. Can you imagine Dazzle working Spillover?"

I pulled up her vid-feed from today on my Perscom, which showed her going over pages and pages and pages of outfits. "At least she'd look good doing it," I said as I showed it to Mark, who rolled his eyes but smiled.

"How tired are you?" he asked out of the blue.

Well that got me curious. "Not very. Walked a lot, but I'm used to that. Why?"

"I just wondered if you'd had a chance to try out the swimming pool yet," he said diffidently. "And wondered if you could swim, actually."

Swimming pool? I swam in ponds at home, of course. And I vaguely knew what a swimming pool was—a sort of artificial pond. "No, and yes," I replied.

"Well, would you like to? It's one of my favorite places to relax. At this time of night it's popular, but not crazy." He glanced over at Karly. "You too, taco thief."

"Sure!" I said with enthusiasm because, really, who doesn't like swimming? I didn't worry about if the designers had supplied me with a bathing suit, even though I hadn't picked one out myself. I hadn't picked out underwear or nightshirts either, but I had a ton of both. By now I knew that the designers, given the option, would have supplied me with twenty. "Should I meet you there?" I asked, knowing my Perscom would show me the way.

"Absolutely." He seemed very pleased. Well, yeah. I had myself a good little chuckle over that one. Because, after all, Knight was a Christer, and most of the Christers I knew were practically body phobic about showing anything. Except, of course, it was perfectly all right to show some flesh if you were swimming.

We both turned to look at Karly. She shook her head. "I'm bowing out," she stated. "I swim just well enough to keep from drowning and I do *not* consider it a pleasure. I like my water hot, in good long baths and showers."

I left the mess hall and trotted back to my room. Sure enough, there were not one, but three swimming suits in the closet, all charcoal and silver of course. I picked the one that would cover up the most, just to spare Knight, although I toyed for just a little bit with the notion of wearing the one that was mostly straps. . . .

But I liked Knight and I didn't want him to be so embarrassed that he went and drowned because he was trying so hard not to look at my boobs and butt.

I threw the suit over my shoulder and trotted off down the hall. My Perscom took me to a whole other part of the building marked "Recreation." It puzzled me for just a second, when I read it as "re-creation" and tried to figure out what swimming had to do with re-making anything. Then I realized what it was. We didn't call it "recreation" on the Mountain, we called it "having fun," or "playing games." But hey, we're turnips.

They had a whole two rooms, male and female, just for changing clothing. Funny. The Masters and monks teach us all *not* to be body shy, and half the time when we're soaking in the communal baths, we're all naked, being too tired and sore to take the time to do more than strip down and get clean before we soak our bruises in hot water. When you've just been beating back a pack of Black Dogs, trust me, getting sexy even with the best-looking guy on the planet is the last thing on your mind anyway.

So I came out of the changing room into this big, echoing room under enormous light panels, with a huge rectangular cement tank full of water in the middle of it. It was the *cleanest* body of water I had ever seen in my life—that was what struck me most. Our ponds were nice, and they were clean and the water smelled good, but they weren't crystal clear like this was. It was very artificial, and very inviting. Knight was already there, in a pair of baggy white trunks. I have to say, he was nicely muscled all over. Made me glad I had at least something to show in my suit, instead of the two little bug bites I'd had for a chest a couple of years ago. I padded up to him in my bare feet and grinned.

"That looks like one fancy see-ment pond there, mister!" I said, trying to really *sound* like a turnip, and he laughed. "Is it cold?"

"Jump in and find out, and I'll race you," he offered.

I snorted. "If you're going to race me, we have to do it right. Diving start." I wasn't worried about it being too cold. Remember where I'm from. The only way we get hot water on the Mountain is from the one hot spring where the Monastery is, or if we heat it ourselves in big boilers for baths. The only way water's too cold for me is if it has ice floating in it.

He seemed game enough, so we did a proper race. Mark was bigger and stronger, but there was less of me to push through the water, so we came out pretty close, me touching the wall just a little behind him. After that we just swam lazily back and forth for a while, then took turns diving (which I *love* even though I am no good at it), then swam some more until we were both getting wrinkly hands and that kind of good, lazy tired that means you're going to sleep really well. There were some other people there, most of them not Hunters, which was interesting—I mean, I knew in theory that there were other people living and working here, and obviously things like the food weren't coming out of thin air, but this was the first time I'd seen any of them. Most of them seemed to know each other, and organized a game at one corner of the pool that involved a ball and a net. It looked like fun, but I was tired, and I felt kind of odd about just joining them.

Something occurred to me at that moment—it was almost as if nothing whatsoever had happened out there, when Paules got himself killed. Why was that? Had Ace, and by extension, Paules, made himself so disliked that none of the ordinary folks that worked here felt any sense of loss at all?

I remembered what Josh had said about Ace . . . that Ace had treated him like something beneath him. So maybe it wasn't so much that Paules had made himself disliked, but that his *brother* had, and people just transferred what they felt about Ace to his brother.

*Karma*, I thought, and reminded myself sharply that no matter how mean Ace had been, no one deserves to see someone close to you die. Especially not like that.

Mark and I parted at the changing rooms, and since he hadn't said anything about wanting to see me back to my room, I didn't hurry in changing. But he was waiting when I came out.

Okay, I have to admit, I was happy about that. Even though all he did was quickly hug my shoulders and say, "Good Hunting tomorrow, Joy."

I managed to hug him back before he strode away. "Same to you, Mark," I called after him. "And thanks!"

It was beginning to feel like I had a new best friend in Mark and a big sister in Karly. I went back to my room grinning like an idiot and feeling good all over, and went straight to sleep without even bothering to check my channel.

So, by the third day, I had figured out it was going to take me four days to work all of F-22, which gave me a rough idea of how I wanted to cover it. Obviously I didn't want to fall into a predictable pattern, or any smart Othersiders would just move to stay one step ahead of me. I did have maps of the storm sewer system, which helped when we went underground there, but I had the feeling even though I was trying to be unpredictable, I wasn't so much Hunting the sewers as just chasing what was down there elsewhere down the line. That was irritating. Even more irritating was the growing suspicion that *somewhere*, there was a way into these sewers from the outside. Maybe it wasn't a big opening, but that was enough to let a lot of nasty stuff in. By the time I got to the fourth day, I was pondering ways of temporarily closing off parts of the tunnels so I could at least chase things into dead ends that they weren't expecting. Could I convince headquarters to put in some sort of gate system down here?

I could do that in a mine—but this was a sewer. The problem with a gate was that stuff that got washed into the sewer would get hung up on a physical barrier, which would mean sending someone down here periodically to clean it out, which—no, that was no solution.

The problem was, to me, it *looked* as if Apex had near-infinite resources, but that surely couldn't be the case if we still had people exiled in Spillover. So I wondered, as Bya and I nosed through a rubble pile, looking for little nuisances hiding among the roots, just how much energy and materials that would cost. And how would I persuade someone else that it was something needed if I couldn't even persuade myself?

And that was when the alarm on my Perscom went off. It had never done that before—and even as I was turning my wrist to look at it, a mechanical voice came out of the speaker.

*Hunter down, FF-12. Hunter down, FF-12. Hunter down, FF-12. Nearest Hunter respond. Nearest Hunter—*

FF-12? Factory Farm Twelve? I knew that territory number! That was *Karly*!

I wasn't the nearest Hunter, I was miles away. Forever far—but I started running anyway, because I wasn't going to just stand there when my first friend here was in trouble—

Then Dusana came out of nowhere and literally blocked me. I ran into his side and bounced off. Before I could *scream* at him in fury to get out of my way, Bya shoved his nose between my legs and boosted me up to the top of Dusana's back. Like I was mounting a horse!

Dusana was bigger than a horse, and I had never, ever ridden him before. He'd never offered, I'd never asked. But with Bya's shove, I scrambled aboard and grabbed at the spiky, bristly neck-crest that passed for his mane, clamping my legs around his torso.

*Hold on!* he said in my head. This might have been the third or fourth time in our lives that he'd talked to me—mostly Bya does the talking for all of them. I crouched down and held on for dear life, having no idea what was coming next.

Then my stomach turned inside out, my lungs went upside down, and my eyeballs tried to drill themselves into my skull as he *bamphed*. With me on him. He *bamphed*!

Not even the Masters had ever said they could *bamph* with a passenger. If I hadn't been fighting something a hundred times worse than vertigo and trying not to throw up, I might have been stunned from the shock.

We landed as if he was jumping over an obstacle, and I vaguely recognized that we'd gone line-of-sight for about a mile, when he gathered himself and did it again. And again. My inner ear and my gut were sure we were going to die, and my brain didn't want to register what my eyes thought they were seeing. Partly because I was still *seeing* things with my eyes squeezed tight shut.

Finally he stopped *bamphing* and held stock-still; I slid off and threw up—but I knew we were in Karly's territory, right by one of the storm sewer access hatches, and it was open, with one of her Hounds flat and dead beside it. I stumbled to my feet as soon as I stopped vomiting and ran for the sewer hatch, all my Hounds beside me. Bya and Shinje *bamphed* down ahead of me as I grabbed for the top of the ladder. I could already tell there was something badly wrong, because the lights were out. I did something risky, put my insteps on the outside of the ladder and slid down instead of climbing down.

Ahead of me, I could hear my Hounds growling; the kind of high-pitched growl that means they'd come across something really nasty and dangerous. I couldn't see anything, and I wasn't going in there with no lights, even though I could *smell* blood. But Dazzle was a good teacher and I'm a fast learner; before I even took time to think about what I was doing, my hand shot out and a ball of light like a tiny sun hurtled from it, hit the ceiling, stuck there, and blazed.

Below it, something big and spiderlike screeched and cowered away from the light.

A Vampire.

Oh, Vampires are *not* the pretty things from some of the old books and vids before the Diseray—they can look that way if they want, but it's all illusion, part of their mind-powers. They're about seven feet tall, bald, with long, skinny legs and long, skinny, dangly arms with claws on their hands, and they look like that picture *The Scream*. I sometimes wonder if the artist hadn't got a glimpse into Otherside when he was painting that. Except Vamps have mouths full of needle teeth. They don't make two neat little holes in their victim's neck, they tear it open and drink that way.

He was crouching over someone on the ground, and I already knew it was Karly, another Hound dead beside her. I yelled with fury, and before the Hounds could do anything, I gathered in more manna, and formed the spell for a levin bolt, and a second later it left my hand like a tiny meteor and smashed into him with a *thwock* and a splash of light.

In fact, it hit him so hard, it knocked him up in the air and he came down about ten feet away from Karly. He hadn't even landed when I had the next spell lined up, and I smashed it down on top of him, the way I'd smashed the Gazer. Only harder.

Much harder.

I could hear the sound of bones snapping—but that wasn't going to keep a Vamp down for long. Only one thing would, and as I hit the monster a third time, I felt Bya shoving what I needed into my hand. My fingers closed around a piece of wood broken off so it had a pointed end, and then the Hounds and I closed in.

They got to the Vamp before I did, each one grabbing a limb and pulling back, so he was spread-eagled among them, like puppies playing tug-of-war with a rag doll. I straddled the obscene creature, so angry I could scarcely see, and rammed the point of the wood down at his chest, aiming for a spot between ribs on the left side. He howled with rage and pain, but of course, I hadn't pierced the heart, not yet, and that was the only thing that would kill him. I took my pistol and reversed it, using the grip like a hammer, and pounded on the flat end of the stake, driving it a little deeper with each hit, until I finally forced it through the ribs and into the chest cavity. Then, with a final blow, I pierced the heart.

The thing screamed. The death-scream of a Vamp is one of the worst things you can ever hear. It pierces your head; it's like having nails driven into your ears. I clapped both hands over my ears, but it didn't do any good. He was trying to writhe, trying to get his hands on me and kill me, too, but my Hounds had their teeth clamped hard on his wrists and ankles, and their feet dug in, and all he could do was vibrate and scream until finally, *finally*, he gave a last convulsion, threw his head back, and died.

The Hounds let go. I stumbled back to Karly's body, already crying so hard I could barely see.

The thing had completely torn her throat out. She must have bled out in seconds.

I . . . lost it. I threw back my head and howled like a dog.

There's a big blank spot then, because the next thing I knew, there were two of the older Hunters, some of the ones I'd been trading stories and watching the Hunt vids with a couple of days ago, helping me up the ladder. Big dark-skinned guys, all muscle, like statues. Steel and Hammer were their nicknames. They were saying the things you say, but they weren't in much better shape than me, just holding it together better. There was a chopper on the ground, and a couple of medics were putting a body bag in it. I started weeping again, and Steel just folded his arms around me and pulled me into his chest and let me rage and pound on him and cry until my throat was raw, I was coughing and wheezing, and my nose was so snotted up I couldn't breathe.

Then there was another big blank spot, and the next thing I knew, Knight had one arm around me while he was getting the door to my room open. He shoved me gently at the doorway, but I grabbed his hand, and begged him, "Don't leave me," so he came inside, and we sat down on the couch and I cried some more.

Only this time it was with plenty of handkerchiefs, and Mark giving me fruit juice and not saying anything, just letting me cry. And blubbering all the stupid stuff like "It's not *fair!*" as if the world actually cared about being fair, and finally, "Why *Karly*? She was smart! How could she—"

And at that moment, Mark went very, very quiet. So still and quiet that I stopped blubbering. The kind of still and quiet that happens when someone knows something, something horrible, and isn't sure how he's going to say it, or even if he should.

"*What?*" I demanded, sharply, now more scared than grieving, all my alarm instincts going into overdrive. Because that kind of silence and that hint at horrible generally means you need to be scared.

"You were supposed to be in that territory, Joy," he said slowly.

I knew exactly what he was not saying.

And I went cold all over.

The Vamp had help getting in there. It had to have; there was no way it could have gotten there otherwise. Vamps couldn't cross the Barriers; they had to go over with help or under by finding a hole. And it wasn't supposed to be Karly it killed.

It was supposed to be me.

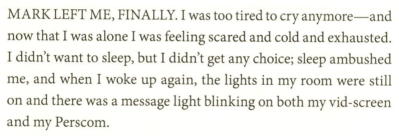

# 19

MARK LEFT ME, FINALLY. I was too tired to cry anymore—and now that I was alone I was feeling scared and cold and exhausted. I didn't want to sleep, but I didn't get any choice; sleep ambushed me, and when I woke up again, the lights in my room were still on and there was a message light blinking on both my vid-screen and my Perscom.

Answering was reflex now, and I did it without thinking. I answered the one on the Perscom first. It was an automated message, saying that Medical had given me a day off Hunting because of my "loss." Great, one day to hide in my room—and did they have that many Hunters that they could *afford* to give me a day off? And I wanted to Hunt! It wasn't enough that I'd killed the thing that got her, I wanted to kill the thing that had sent it!

I had this surge of pure, white-hot anger that wiped everything out and pushed how scared I was into the background. Karly deserved more than that! She was a *Hunter,* and maybe she'd been a little cynical and maybe she hadn't been a ranker, but she was tough and competent and she never just sat back and coasted, she *Hunted.* And she was my friend, and like the big sister I'd never had. I wasn't going to hide in my room, dammit. I was going to find out who it was that had murdered Karly.

One of the first things my Masters ever taught us was how to solve problems. *Not every problem needs to be attacked head-on,* they'd tell me. And then they showed us, over and over until we got it.

*Blind rondori*—that was one of the ways they showed us. It was a martial-arts exercise where we were blindfolded and attacked from all sides. Single attacks when we were beginners, multiple when we got better. *Start from what you know. The answer will unfold.*

The lights had been shut off. The Vamp could never have gotten into FF-12 alone. FF-12 was too far from the Barrier for a Vamp to walk between sundown and sunup. And it would have had to have gotten in the same way the one Ace killed had—by a hole under the Barrier—and if it got in through a hole, so would swarms of other things. Yet there hadn't been anything but that Vamp. *Some-one* had helped it get to FF-12 and then down into the sewers, and then shut off the lights for it so it could lie in wait.

So I closed my eyes, took a lot of deep, shuddering breaths, held back sobs, and waited for something I knew to float toward me out of the dark. When I let it happen, something did, something important. Which was that whoever had brought in that fang-face that killed Karly hadn't known we'd swapped territories.

Why not? Well, the simplest answer? He hadn't watched

the feeds. He'd depended on what our schedules said. If he had watched the feeds, he hadn't paid that much attention—and FF-12 and F-22 looked a lot alike if you were just glancing through the feeds and not paying attention to the commentary or who was in the zone. Especially if you didn't know the outlying districts well.

He probably wouldn't have had a lot of time to work in either. Unless he had a job that gave him a lot of freedom of movement, he'd have to do his shift, *then* find the time to set up his ambush.

Who could possibly persuade or coerce—or even encounter!— a Vamp?

A handful of people. No ordinary Cit, for sure. An army Magus, a Psimon, or a Hunter. Anyone else would be the fang's next entrée.

Yeah, I think fast. Especially when something or someone is trying to kill me. But I was concentrating so hard on all of this that I didn't notice the itch in the back of my head until it suddenly turned into a burn—and a matching burn on the Mandala scars on the backs of my hands.

*What?* The Hounds had only demanded to come through without being summoned a handful of times, and all of them had been urgent. This was something I didn't bother to think about. I clapped my hands over my eyes and opened the Way the quick-and-dirty way, just *calling* to the Hounds and letting the Mandalas on the backs of my hands serve as the Glyphs for the Portal.

The familiar surge of pain in my hands hit me twice; so, only two of the Hounds had come over. When I uncovered my eyes, I saw Bya, who I expected . . . but also Dusana, who almost filled the room.

When Bya was in a hurry, he never bothered to talk to me.

Instead, he showed me things, like vids in my head. And what I saw were the other pair of Karly's Hounds, the two we hadn't seen dead. They were badly wounded, down in that sewer tunnel. . . . If someone didn't get to them soon, they were going to die.

Dusana knelt, and it was clear that *soon* was not going to mean *wait for a pod.*

Not that I had any intention of calling a pod. Who'd look for me if I left my Perscom here, especially if I was supposed to be crying my eyes out in my room?

I pulled my Perscom off and threw it on the bed, climbed onto Dusana's back, and held on, feeling grateful I hadn't eaten.

Three *bamphs* got us to the sewer entrance, and I slid off to throw up. Seriously? Given the choice of *bamphing* and walking? I'll walk. . . .

Not an option this time, though.

Once my stomach stopped trying to exit through my mouth, I wiped my face and staggered for the sewer system. I went down the ladder and it all hit me again. The lump in my throat grew and I clenched my fists. The anger was overwhelming. Because there was someone out there who had murdered Karly by proxy, and that someone was probably a Hunter. Yeah, a Psimon or a Magician could do it—but the most logical was a Hunter. I think that was the moment I decided that whoever it was, he was going to pay. Murder was horrid if it was a Psimon or Magus, but if it was a fellow Hunter? There are no words filthy enough for the piece of dung who would do that.

The sewer tunnel was a patchwork of light and dark. Looked as if when there wasn't a Hunter down here, about two-thirds of the overhead lights were turned off, which only made sense. That might have been how Karly had gotten ambushed. Karly had probably gotten down here, tried to turn on the lights, and when they wouldn't light up, figured that there had been a glitch in the system and just decided to go on ahead anyway. I probably would have done the same thing.

Bya ran ahead, turning his head to make sure I was following. Dusana trotted at my side, and I understood he was guarding me, taking Bya's usual spot. We went about half a mile before we finally found the Hounds.

They were horribly torn up. Hounds . . . well they aren't exactly built like "real" animals. They don't seem to have any internal organs, for one thing. In this case that probably prevented them from dying instantly instead of by inches. So they were lying there, the wolves made of shadow, shadows in tatters, in pools of what passes for blood for them, with huge, terrible gashes where the fang had raked them with its talons.

This required some very special magic.

I layered both of them with Glyphs, three deep, stopping the blood flow, but fixing them needed more than that. I knelt between them, put a hand on each of them, and gathered my own manna. Then, with my eyes closed and my head bowed, I let my manna flow into them.

I wasn't sure it would work, actually. Every Hunter can heal her own Hounds by virtue of the connection between them. I knew *some* Hunters could heal other peoples' Hounds, but until that moment, I didn't know if I was one of them.

But I was. I felt the manna flowing out of me, into the two Hounds, and sighed with relief. I didn't need to look to know that those awful slashes were closing, that their flesh was knitting, their skin zipping shut. It all took place in moments, and I opened my eyes to see them whole.

Now they looked as they had when I had first seen them: beefy, thick-boned, heavily muscled shadow-wolves, whose golden-eyed heads would have been about level with my hip. But they were very weak, and there was no way I could give them enough manna to get back to strength without endangering myself and *my* Hounds. They couldn't cross back to their Otherside in this weakened state; they'd be prey for stuff over there if they did. So my—or rather *our*—work wasn't done.

I could feel Bya's assent as I cast the Glyphs and brought over the rest of the pack.

"Is there anything in the tunnels here we can Hunt?" I asked him, and showed him what I had in mind; the rest of the pack driving something toward where I would lie in ambush, so Karly's Hounds could feed on the kill.

He raised his head and sniffed the air; so did the rest. Given that Karly Hunted this territory every day, and presumably found kills every day, I figured the odds were good. . . .

They peeled off down the tunnel, a good sign that Bya thought he had detected something. He didn't say anything, though, and I didn't jiggle his elbow. He had felt determined, in a way I hadn't sensed from him before. Oh, he was focused when we Hunted, but ever since I was thirteenish, there'd been a sense from all the Hounds that no matter what got thrown at us, we could handle it. This time was different. Things had happened that we hadn't trained for, terrible things had happened to our friends, and our world was now unpredictable with enemies we couldn't recognize, and they didn't like it one bit.

Well, I liked it even less. I was just glad they were driven to help Karly's Hounds.

As I waited with them, the poor things so weak all they could do was raise their heads a little, guilt crept over me. Because in a way, this was my fault. Maybe I should have talked to Karly and swapped territories with her until things got properly sorted out. *We* would have been able to handle a Vamp. I'm not saying he wouldn't have given us some trouble—he would have. Vamps are crazy fast and as strong as six or seven humans put together. But he wasn't as fast or strong as that Wyvern, and we'd handled that solo. Plus, my Hounds would have *bamphed* down into the sewer ahead of me, and sniffed him out. Karly had to wait for her Hounds to jump down to join her—that was probably when she'd gotten ambushed.

I mean, maybe the person who had smuggled the Vamp down here had known that. He'd have known I would just get a good scare. Except it wasn't me who came down that ladder. . . .

The more I thought about it, the worse I felt, sick and grieving at the same time. All I could think of now was that it *should* have been me, and if it had been, Karly would still be alive. I squeezed my eyes shut and choked on a sob.

That was when I felt something heavy and warm shove under my hand, and I looked down and saw that one of Karly's Hounds had inched over to me and pushed his head underneath my palm.

I hadn't quite processed that when I heard my lot bellow out their Hunting cries in the far distance. The sounds echoed down through the tunnels, and were enough like the cries of a dog pack that it was clear why these Othersiders had been named Hounds in the first place. At the same time, I got a brief flash from Bya.

They'd found some Knockers. Only a few—probably some strays that hadn't followed along with the horde that had attacked us, and so had escaped for a time. But my crew had nosed them out, and now they were herding the little horrors toward us.

Perfect.

I got to my feet and moved a little distance off, making use of the shadows between where the lights fell to cloak my presence. I didn't have any weapons, but I was far from unarmed.

Back home, you had to save your ammo and had weapons that weren't always reliable. Back home, what I depended on was magic.

I won't say I didn't *need* a gun, but I will say I never counted on having one. Which was a good thing right now.

I readied the spell for the snare. Karly's Hounds couldn't move much, so the timing on this would have to be just right. Close enough for the Hounds to consume the manna, far enough away that the Knockers couldn't reach them to hurt them.

I heard the clatter of their rock-hard feet on the concrete; my fingers tingled with the power I had coiled up and waiting. Then I spotted movement in the distance, a sort of flicker as the running Knockers moved in and out of pools of light from the overhead lamps. Behind them was another sort of flicker—the flicker of flame as my Hounds spat their fires to keep the Knockers running.

I brought my hands up close to my chest; I could feel the scars on the backs of them warming, and the tingle in my fingers ramped up until it felt as if my hands were vibrating. The Knockers were running as fast as their horrid bandy little legs would carry them—there were six or eight of them, so not nearly enough to challenge my Hounds. And they were in a panic, paying no attention to anything except the Hounds at their heels. I could have been standing right in the middle of the light and they probably wouldn't have seen me.

They reached the spot I had marked in my mind, and I keyed the spell and dropped the net on them. With so few, it was a nice, tight one; the interstitial spaces were far too small to let anything but an arm or a leg through.

Then, as I held the net down on them, I began to have doubts. This wasn't Hunting—this was going to be just plain cruel. The Knockers were completely outnumbered, and netted like this there was no way they could harm us. And what I proposed to do to them...

My Hounds skidded to a halt as the Knockers began to screech. Bya sauntered over to me and looked up at me.

*They have blood on them,* he said. *We can smell it.*

Now, Bya wouldn't have bothered to tell me this if it was animal blood he smelled. All my reservations vanished.

One or more of the Hounds would seize an arm or a leg from the pile. I would withdraw the net from that particular Knocker, and they would drag it, screaming and screeching, to Karly's Hounds. They'd wait until one of the two got its jaws locked on some part of the creature. Then they'd kill it, and let the wounded Hound absorb all the manna for itself. After the first four Knockers were dead, Karly's Hounds had revived enough to join the pack at the net, and do the killing themselves. When all of the Knockers were bloody meat on the concrete, Karly's Hounds were looking much more like their normal selves. Certainly doing well enough to cross over to the Otherside without worrying if something there would attack them.

I felt a little guilt easing. At least I'd managed to save them.

They padded ponderously over to me, and I opened the Way for them. But they didn't step through it. Instead, they sat down, looked at each other, then looked at Bya.

Bya gazed back, then swung his head to look at me. *They want to join our pack,* he said.

I felt stunned. I'd never *heard* of this happening before. Everything I knew about Hounds said that when their Hunter died, if they were still alive, they went back Otherside. I answered with the first thing that came into my head.

*Do you want them in your pack?* I asked him, or rather, thought at him.

*They are not our kind, but they will do,* he replied with a bit of a swagger. Well, small wonder, he was pack leader, the alpha, and the bigger your pack, the more prestige among Hounds you had. I looked at the two Hounds—so unlike my gaudy lot—which were about to become mine.

"You are welcome in our pack," I said gravely.

Both of them bowed their heads, first to me, then to Bya. One of them got up, walked to me, and opened his mouth. I knew without prompting what he wanted and put my hand in it. He closed his mouth gently around it, and I could feel a small part of the backs of my hands within the Mandala burning. He let go, and I pulled my hand back and looked at it. Sure enough, where I'd felt the burning spot, there was a fresh scar. Same on the other hand.

The second came over and did the same, with the same result; another new patch of scar pattern in the Mandalas.

Bya padded up to me and looked up into my face gravely. *Their names are Hold and Strike,* he said. Not terribly imaginative, I suppose, but Karly was pretty much what you see is what you get.

Was ...

I felt my throat closing up, and my eyes burning, and I just knelt down between Hold and Strike and put my arms around their shoulders and sobbed. I felt them shaking beneath my arms, and little whines came from their throats that sounded just like crying. So we all three cried together for the friend we had lost, and the rest of the pack closed around us protectively. I finally stopped only when my eyes hurt too much to keep on, rubbed them dry with the tail of my shirt, and stood up. I didn't say anything, but I didn't have to. I just cast the Glyphs and opened the Way, and all the Hounds except Dusana passed through to the Otherside. Dusana looked at me expectantly, and I groaned a little. If I was going to keep *bamphing* with him, I was going to have to find a solution to barfing my toenails up when the ride was over. But I didn't have any other way to get back to headquarters, and it was a long, long walk that I would have to explain. ...

I climbed up onto his back, squeezed my eyes tight, and held on for dear life.

It didn't help. But at least we made it back to my room in one piece.

I didn't so much throw myself onto the bed as collapse there; I fumbled for my Perscom and strapped it back on, checked the time—it was only mid-morning, impossible as that seemed—then lay there in a sort of stupor until my stomach recovered enough to decide it was empty and should be filled. There had been a text message from Josh, but I hadn't felt like reading it when I got back, and I still didn't feel like reading it now.

Feeling as limp as a wrung-out cloth, I made some tea and drank it, ate some fruit, then checked that text message. It was

simple enough. *If you need me, call me.* But it made me feel a little
... a very little ... better. I still didn't feel up to answering it, so I
dropped back into my stupor. Maybe I even dozed a little. It was
the vid chiming that broke me out of it.

I half expected another text from Josh or one from Mark, but
it was just an impersonal message noting that I hadn't appeared
in the mess hall for breakfast and offering me a lunch menu for
a robot to bring to the room. My brain was a mess and nothing
looked good, but I picked some stuff at random so the system
wouldn't nag at me to eat.

Before the food turned up, I realized that I was going to have
to pull myself together, at least to the point where I could think.
The best way I knew to do that was to meditate, so I sat myself
zazen—in what they call lotus position—on the messy bed. And
I know you might find this hard to believe, but once you're really
trained in meditation, you can meditate under just about any cir-
cumstance. Meditation lets you clear out your thoughts and let
your subconscious go to work on problems. You might not have
answers when you come out of it, but at least you'll get the problem
sorted out into manageable bits.

That's pretty much what happened when the robot turned up
at my door and it chimed to let me know it was there. I didn't have
a plan, but I at least had some idea what I shouldn't do.

While sitting there, my memory had turned out the useful bit
that the armorer could make vids go away. Now, whoever had set
up the ambush might have been caught on vid, or might worry that
he would be, which would mean he'd want to make sure someone
who could make vid footage go away would be someone he would
want to be friendly with.

So for right now I had better not go to the armorer with any of this, even though Uncle had said I could ask him things. Not yet, anyway. Not until I was sure.

As the list I was tallying up of who I couldn't trust started to get longer and longer, I realized two things. The first was that it was a good thing I had picked soup for lunch, because I don't think I could have gotten anything else past the cold lump of fear in my throat. And the second was that the list of people I could probably trust was a lot shorter than the other one.

Three people, in fact: Uncle, Josh, and Mark. That was more or less by default; if I couldn't trust my uncle and the Psimon *he* trusted, I was already in deep kimchee, and if I couldn't trust White Knight, all my instincts were off.

I can't tell you how tempting it was at that moment to sneak down to the armory, grab some weapons, pack up my old clothing and some survival supplies, call Dusana, and *bamph* out of there. Once we got outside the city Barriers, we could live off the land as we made our way home. . . .

But that wouldn't be getting justice for Karly. It would definitely trigger a hunt for me that would *start* at the Mountain, and that was the last place I wanted anyone snooping right now. And it wouldn't make things easier on Uncle; in fact, that would pretty much play into the hands of whoever was threatening him. I knew for certain-sure my Masters would say, if I were to ask them for advice, that I should stay here and face things.

My Masters would tell me that there were seldom coincidences where Hunters and magic were concerned, and would remind me that if I needed a sign I had to stay here, I'd just gotten two—Dusana *bamphing* with me, and Karly's Hounds joining my pack.

So where to go from here?

I thought about Mark...but he wasn't any better off than I was. Worse in some ways. He had relatives of his own—and a sweetheart—who could easily be threatened, at least until they moved out to the Springs. That left me with one person who might be in a position to find out things for me. Well, two, but I didn't want to call *more* attention down on Uncle by doing anything to hint that I was beginning to get wind of what was going on. That left Josh. I left him a text—just, *I really need to talk to you right now,* which was what anyone who'd just lost a good friend would say. And then I waited.

# 20

AND WAITED. Not that I really expected an answer right away, but ... it seemed like the minutes just crawled by. I knew what I couldn't do. I knew what I wouldn't do. Neither was a lot of help just now. I still had no good idea of how to protect myself from whoever was out there trying to get me, much less how to get some rough justice for Karly. And yeah, I was still scared.

That was when my Perscom went off again, and I grabbed for it.

But it wasn't Josh. It was Mark ... and his message was awfully peculiar.

*Work will do you more good than crying in your room. Come join me.* Of course, the message came with his location on the map.

That just didn't *sound* like Mark. Was this some kind of trap? Had someone gotten hold of his Perscom, or cloned it, and was setting me up? I thought about texting him back, then I thought better of it and tried voice.

He answered almost as soon as I pinged him. "Good, you're awake. You should come out here to work."

Then, a *completely* different voice added, "Absolutely. Get some sun."

Josh's voice.

Either whoever was trying to get me had managed to get to both of them, or else this was Josh's answer to my not calling him.

I felt Bya poking at my brain, so I brought him through, just as Mark spoke up again. "You really should get out here, Joy. The sooner, the better. Got to go."

I looked at Bya. Bya looked at me, then nudged my wrist, the one with the Perscom on it. I showed it to him—I don't know why I did, it just seemed like the thing to do. The Perscom was still showing Mark's location, and even though I'd never had any indication that the Hounds could get a read off of a Perscom, in the next moment, Bya had *bamphed* out.

I think this might have been the moment I stopped being surprised at my Hounds. I mean, I'd always thought of them more as my partners than anything else, but this was when I started thinking of them as being like a bunch of *human* partners.

I waited, deliberately keeping myself from fidgeting by concentrating on what I was doing, one little thing at a time. This time I wasn't going to go out half prepared. I didn't have access to the armory weapons, but I did have knives, a crossbow, and a short spear, all of which I had brought with me, and all of which were among my old things. I didn't put on one of my city Hunting outfits; I dressed myself in my old Hunting gear. And a few minutes later, I got a vague, distant feeling from Bya that everything was fine.

I took my Perscom with me, intending to use it to get a pod, but there was already an unmanned pod waiting for me, door open invitingly. I got in, and since the door closed and it took off immediately, I was obviously the person it was waiting for.

It left me at one of the Barrier pylons, one of the ones with a door in it. The door answered to my thumbprint and Perscom, and I crossed through into Spillover and followed my map.

I didn't have to go too far.

I noticed the little dot that represented Mark coming toward me, Bya with him. I stopped long enough to cast the Glyphs and bring the rest of the Hounds over, with Strike and Hold milling with the rest of them. I didn't want to be caught unaware by anything. It looked as if the two new Hounds had settled right in with mine.

We moved quickly but cautiously toward Mark. The first sign I had of him was one of his Hounds flying by overhead, obviously looking for us. It did a quick turn and circled overhead, then flew back in the direction where Mark was. We all met in an area between two rows of what had once been houses, in the middle of a cracked and broken-up street. He didn't say anything, just waved to me and turned around without waiting for me, and Bya trotted over to me.

I was going through so many emotions it was almost making me sick. I had to get myself under better control, because right now I couldn't afford to *lose* control, not for a moment.

It was a struggle. It's one I am not sure I would have won if it hadn't been for Bya on one side of me and Dusana on the other. But by the time we got to this ... *forest* of buildings all tumbled against each other, I had my Hunt face back on, and my control was mostly back.

There was a camera hovering above Mark. I took a quick glance around. I didn't have one. Had I somehow escaped notice? When I looked back at Mark, he made this little *stay there* motion, so I did, backing off into the shadows of some walls that looked like they were probably going to stay put.

"All clear!" That was Josh's voice, and I didn't need Mark waving me over to know I should go to meet them. Josh was actually *in* that warren, and he led us deeper in, down some stairs and into a basement—or maybe it was one of those old shelters, because there was what was left of metal bunk beds bolted to the floor inside. All the Hounds crowded in with us. The camera stayed outside. Josh had a light with him and put it up on top of one of the upper bunks.

"Did Uncle send you?" I asked.

He shook his head. "I volunteered. The prefect couldn't think of any way to get to you without being monitored. But I have a hacker friend in the Hunter-vid department who owes me a favor, and I figured it was worth the risk to come myself."

That was the moment I knew I could trust him completely. Because he had just risked *everything.* If whoever was after me found out about *him*, he'd have an even bigger target on his back than I did. And he was a Psimon and part of PsiCorps; he could be ordered back to the Corps and not even Uncle could countermand that, because Uncle didn't run the Corps. Once he was back in the Corps, he would just disappear—and could *be* "disappeared," and no one would be the wiser.

"How long have we got?" Mark was asking as I wiggled into the room among the Hounds.

"Half an hour at worst, an hour and a half at best." Josh turned to me. "My friend is glitching the system for us. You're still showing as in your rooms. Knight's camera is reporting itself as offline, but they won't bother sending a new one for a while, because he's not a top-ranker when you aren't around."

"Has Uncle got any idea who was behind the attack on Karly?" I asked a bit desperately. "At all?"

Josh shook his head silently. "The prefect obviously didn't tell me everything he knows; that's way above my pay grade. But ... okay, he knew that people would probably try to get to him through you if he showed you any kind of favoritism. But he told me he never, ever thought anyone was going to try to actually *hurt* you. That's—" Josh shook his head.

"It's stupid, is what it is," Mark rumbled. "I don't care what political crap you're getting into, we need all the Hunters we can get." He ran a hand through his hair, looking as if he was thinking about pulling some of it out.

"It's insane," Josh agreed. "By *our* standards. But remember, it might not have been intended to hurt Joy, at least not badly. She's ... she's crazy good, and so are her Hounds. So ..." He shrugged, looking distressed.

"Or maybe not," Mark said darkly. "I mean, think about it. Maybe at the beginning, before she actually got here ... but after that save at the train, it was obvious she was not just another turnip like me, who might be useful as leverage one day. Once it was clear that her abilities were *that* good, she might have gone from being 'useful leverage' to being 'too potentially dangerous to leave alive.'"

"Why?" I asked aloud. "I mean ... what would be the point?" Just because something looks like a conspiracy doesn't mean there actually is one. "Besides, what if most of this is coincidence, except for the Vamp? We know the Othersiders have been hitting us with increasing frequency and nastier critters for the past year. If it's an exponential increase, the way I think it is—I could just have been unlucky enough to turn up when the curve shot up into the sky like a rocket. Ace hit a Vamp too, remember, and a bunch of the others had some pretty nasty things pop up on their territories in the last two weeks."

Knight and Josh looked at each other. "She's right. We can't be sure of anything," Josh said, finally. "But if someone is coming after Joy, the likeliest reason is to try to put pressure on the prefect and blackmail him into favors, or into taking sides."

"Could gambling factor in too?" I asked, voicing the thought that had occurred to me—gods, it seemed like years ago now.

"There *is* a lot of money changing hands," Josh said slowly. "Any time there's money flowing, things can get nasty. So that might be one more complication."

"She's Ace's chief rival now," Mark said, his expression darkening. "And Ace just got knocked out of the top spot. That could make a whole lot of folks unhappy."

"I don't know a *lot* about high-level politics, because everyone wears Psi-shields, but there's no reason why it couldn't be all three things," Josh agreed. "Gamblers backing Ace, somebody wanting favors from the prefect, *and* somebody wanting the prefect to take sides. They could be working separately or in any combination."

I looked from Josh to Mark and back again. Both seemed to think that actually *was* likely. I swallowed. Suddenly my uncle's warnings took on a much darker tone.

"Let's just concentrate on who got that Vamp in. I don't know how that could be coincidence," I said finally. "I don't know how it could possibly have been Ace. Hasn't he had eyeballs on him every single minute since his brother was killed?"

Josh looked at Mark. Mark grimaced. "He's got the psych-techs watching him like hawks for signs of a breakdown. I know that for a fact. That means face-recognition running on every single passive cam in and around the HQ, just in case he tries something clever, like ditching his Perscom."

I nodded. "An ordinary Mage probably couldn't have held him for long enough to persuade him, and then when the Magic Bindings were off, why would the Vamp cooperate? And the same goes for a Psimon...."

"That makes sense." Josh nodded. "There's a lot fewer Psimons powerful enough to control a Vamp than there are Hunters, and—well, they're pretty much monitored day and night." He made a face. I knew why. *No one* trusts the really powerful Psimons. I mean, seriously, someone who can get into your head and make you do anything he wants? You can't blame people for not trusting them. Even I had been glad for the Psi-shield I had in my Perscom when I was around Josh.

Mark sucked on his lower lip. "I suppose," he admitted reluctantly. "There are a lot more Hunters, and with Hounds, you can corner a Vamp and herd it where you want it, basically. I mean, between the ones under the prefect and the ones in the army, there are a couple hundred Hunters in Apex alone, and it pretty much could be any of them." He laughed mirthlessly. "Even me."

Josh ran a hand through his hair and grimaced just the tiniest bit. "The prefect wouldn't have sent me to talk to you if you weren't trustworthy." At that moment, Kalachakra decided to go over and wrap herself around Josh's ankles. He scratched her absentmindedly and she sighed with happiness.

Mark looked at that gesture of trust sourly. He knew what it meant. When Hounds have a bond with their Hunter the way mine do with me, well, they have fine-tuned instincts for people who can't be trusted. So no matter what Mark wanted to think, Josh was here for exactly the reason he claimed: to try to help me figure out how I could defend myself. It was the skulking around that was the worst. The not knowing. "If I could just drive him into the open—" I muttered between clenched teeth. "If I could just figure out a way to find him out—" I pounded my knee with my fist. "If only I were home!" I snarled. "I could challenge him, no matter who he was, even if I couldn't *prove* he was the one that killed Karly. Or if I could just get myself into a position where I was *too* valuable to mess with, I could—" I stopped, because suddenly ... was it possible? Was *that* the way? Make myself too important to touch?

"What?" Josh and Mark demanded together, seeing the look on my face.

"How do you become Elite?" I asked.

They were silent for a moment. "Good Lord, that's risky—" Josh said slowly.

Mark nodded. "But she's right. If she can pull this off—"

"No one will ever be able to touch her afterward," Josh finished.

"So there *is* a way!" I said.

Finally it was Mark who turned to me. "Yes. It's actually pretty simple. You petition the armorer for Hunter Elite."

Josh nodded. "You can petition to take the trials and no one will question if you're good enough. You *are* that good. You faced down a Folk Mage. You took out a Wyvern and a Vamp solo. You're a seven-Hound team—" He looked around and did a double take. "Wait a minute—"

"Nine Hounds," I corrected him weakly.

*"Nine?"* They both gaped at me.

"Hold and Strike—Karly's Hounds—asked to join my pack." I shook my head. "Never mind that. Tell me more."

Mark scratched his head. "I can almost bet no one is going to see this coming. Most Hunters won't go for Elite. We have regular shifts. Elites are on call twenty-four-seven. No regular shifts, no regular territories, and they don't have channels like the regular Hunters do, because they're going after things we don't want the Cits to think about, or Hunting in places we don't want the Cits to know Othersiders can get into. We get to go do fan-service, which even Karly thought was fun. They don't. Every six months or so, you get some upgrades, if you're a ranker, based on your rankings. Bigger quarters, nicer things, a little more time off. Elites don't get any of that, because they're not in the quarters long enough to do more than sleep, and they never get time off unless they're hurt and recovering."

"Never mind that," I interrupted. "How do I make Elite after I petition?"

"To get Elite you have to pass Combat Trials. Nobody has passed in at least a year—and it's risky, because these are full-combat, no-holding-back trials that end with you versus another Hunter, and even though the trials stop cold if the Hunter gets hurt, there can be accidents." He waited to see if I got it.

"So, you can get hurt, which really sucks, and you could be out and not on your channel, and—" I raised my eyebrow.

"And no one will know why, because the Trials aren't broadcast until after they are over, and only if you passed." Mark nodded. "So you aren't Hunting or on your channel, which means your rankings fall while you recover."

I thought that over. It made sense. It would be humiliating enough to go for Elite only to fail—why humiliate the Hunter further by making that failure public? And why crater the Cits' estimation of him? But if you got hurt, no one would know that either. They'd only know your channel was showing old vid and, people being people, would figure you were slacking.

"So . . . I'm guessing at least a couple of Hunters have been worse than just hurt?" I continued.

"Years ago, but yeah, there's been at least one death that I know of." Mark confirmed my guess. "Now, they *will* stop the trial if you get hurt, because we can't afford to lose Hunters; that was something everyone agreed to after the last death. But you are absolutely right. Once you're Elite, you're practically untouchable."

"And once you've passed the Trials, not only will it not be possible for someone to come after you, not even the prefect's worst enemy in the world would try to use you as a pawn," Josh concluded. "That would be insane. If we can't afford to lose Hunters, we doubly can't afford to lose an Elite. From everything I've seen or heard, the Elites are *tight*. If they thought someone was messing with one of their own . . . they'd do something about it, and whatever it was, it wouldn't be anything anyone would be happy about."

I felt resolution build. "It doesn't help me figure out who killed Karly. But what it *does* do is clear the way for me and Uncle to work to find that out ourselves. That makes sense. I get off the chessboard. *Then* we can figure out what's going on and who's pulling the strings where."

"And Elites report directly to the prefect too," Mark pointed out. "That not only makes you and your uncle safer, it makes it possible for you to talk whenever you need to. I won't lie, Joy, this is going to be hard, but I think you can do it. I've seen you in combat. You'll be doing this without your Hounds, but that's not a handicap for you."

Well, I had to agree with them. I looked at Bya. He nodded solemnly, and I stood up, my nine Hounds with me. "Right, then." I looked at Mark. "So, how do I apply?"

# 21

I STOOD IN something they called a "Sky Box"—which was more like a luxurious apartment with lots of windows in it—and looked down at the Rayne Stadium. This stadium was a new construction, so far as Apex was concerned; it wasn't more than twenty years old. Before that, the idea of gathering that many Cits together in one place would have been insane—laying out a giant buffet Othersiders simply could not resist. Today, no one would be watching except other Hunters, and not from the stadium itself.

No one else would see this until *after* the Trials were over.

It turned out that applying for Hunter Elite had been astoundingly simple. And in the few days it had taken for them to schedule the Trials . . . no one and nothing had made a try at me. It had been in the back of my mind after I proposed the idea that this might actually *push* whoever was after my hide—if, in fact, anyone was—into making one more attempt. But nothing happened.

Mind, every time I had gone out Hunting, I had been so much on alert that I actually shot two cams out of the air . . . and at least one of my Hounds slept with me every night . . . so maybe, just maybe, they had given it up as a lost cause.

"You're absolutely sure about this, Joy?" the armorer murmured from just behind me. "You can say you've changed your mind, even now. But once you set foot on the turf down there, you're committed."

"Absolutely," I said firmly.

"All right then." I heard him turn; I kept looking down at the field. "She's all yours, Citizen Pierce."

Now I turned to find myself facing a woman I had seen on the vid channels a lot. Gayle Pierce; I remembered the name. She was wearing an outfit that was *impossibly* stylish, and she was surrounded by cams.

"Joyeaux!" she exclaimed, as if we were old friends—which, I suppose, she certainly wanted everyone to think we were. "I can't say I ever anticipated interviewing you like this when you first arrived here!"

I smiled very slightly and nodded. "I can't say I ever expected to have this much attention paid to me," I replied, trying to sound modest. "It's an unexpected and overwhelming honor." The cams were vidding, of course. This was going to be part of the broadcast that would be played before they showed my Trials. *Not* live, of course. So far as my fans were concerned, I was getting a training day. Still, I'd have to tread carefully.

"Well, what everyone wants to know is this: why did you decide to apply for Hunter Elite *now*?" she asked. "You're the fastest trender *ever*. Why give all that up to become Elite?"

"Well, Gayle, when I first got here, they asked me what I wanted," I replied, using her first name, implying that same "special relationship" she was banking on. "I told them that my reason for being here is to serve and protect the Citizens. Now that I'm here, now that I've seen how the Hunters here in civilization work, I *know* the best way I can do that is to try to join the Elite. The Elite take on the creatures beyond the Barriers, making sure they never come near Apex, so our Cits remain safe."

"But what if you fail the Trials?" she asked breathlessly.

"Then I'll work harder, learn more, and apply again," I told her.

"But what made you decide you were ready *now*?" she persisted.

I took a deep breath. "I'll show you," I said, and right then and there, I formed the Glyphs and cast them, and my Hounds came through.

All nine of them.

I have to say, she counted—did a faint double take and counted again—and the look on her face was worth gold. "I'd like you to meet my pack," I said into the silence and to the cameras. "Bya, Dusana, Begtse, Chenresig, Shinje, Kalachakra, and Hevajra all came with me. But Hold and Strike have just joined my pack in the last few days. They are the survivors of my mentor Hunter Karly's pack. And because they chose to join me, making our pack the strongest that has ever existed in the history of the Hunters, I decided that the best way to honor Karly's memory was to try for Elite until I won it."

This was quite the bombshell; I hadn't told anyone other than Mark and Josh about how Karly's Hounds had joined mine, so no one but us knew until this point. Josh had been the one who had advised me to keep it quiet until the last minute. He figured that it would make a big impression at the inevitable interview. Josh also said it might rattle whoever our enemy was, and make him slip up, revealing himself. I thought, why not? It was worth trying.

"Hunter Karly's Hounds—" Gayle was as close to stammering as her training and composure would allow. She put her left hand up to her left ear. "Well, Joy, you certainly know how to drop a bomb on an interview!"

I shrugged, gesturing at the Hounds. "I guess they're like Hunter Karly herself was; they are as focused on protecting the Citizens as she was, and they know I am too."

"Your Hounds will not be allowed to participate in the Trials; does that make any difference to you?" Pierce said, getting her composure back.

I shook my head. "Being Elite means you can take care of yourself in case you and the pack get separated. Besides, it's not a trial for *them*—we already know how good they are. It's a trial of *my* abilities."

"And whatever surprises you can bring to the table!" Gayle giggled. "Well, I predicted you would be full of surprises for us the first time I introduced you on vid!"

"And obviously you were right, Gayle," I said with a little smile.

She actually simpered. I guess reporters respond to flattery just like about everyone else. "Well, I hope the rest of your surprises are all good ones for you, Hunter Joyeaux! Good Hunting in your Trials! This has been an interview with Hunter Joyeaux Charmand; Gayle Pierce for Apex News."

The cams all zipped away, and Pierce turned off the high-intensity charm. "Good interview, Hunter, and thank you for keeping your little surprise until I could get to you," she said.

I hadn't saved it for *her*, but I wasn't about to tell her that.

"I'm glad I could help," was all I said. She looked at me curiously.

"You really mean that, don't you?" she said, sounding surprised.

"It's what we do," I told her, in all seriousness. "Hunters, that is. Help."

She blinked at me, for once at a loss for words. Finally she found some. "You are *very* like your uncle." The way she said that, it was clearly not a compliment—more like a statement of something that baffled her. But I chose to take it as a compliment.

"I certainly hope so," I replied, and checked my Perscom. "Looks to be just about time."

"So it is." She snatched the last remaining cam out of the air and stuck it in her bag. "Good luck in the Trials. I think Apex could use an Elite like you." And she sounded a little surprised at herself for saying it.

◄◊►

A few minutes later, I followed the directions on my Perscom, which took me through a locker room and out into a tunnel that would dump me onto the manicured turf of the stadium. Well, what used to be the manicured turf of the stadium. I was wearing Hunt gear and carrying a full load-out. Josh and Mark and I had been going over the Trials documents practically word by word, so we had made sure of two things. The first was that every bit of my load-out was waterproofed, because the documents had specified a certain amount of swimming. The second was that I had little packs, about a mouthful each, of very dense energy food, sugar and protein combined. Wasn't the best thing I had ever eaten, but I knew I was going to need it.

I came out of the tunnel into the light. I knew in general what I was about to face, and there were a limited number of obstacles that could be presented. But I wasn't going to have *any* time to think about what I saw. I was going to have to take everything on the fly and react to it immediately. The speaker system that I guessed they used for big events here came to life. *"When you are ready, Hunter,"* someone said. I didn't recognize the voice. In front of me was—a gauntlet.

The "series of dangerous obstacles" sort of gauntlet, of course. And timed. All the Trials were timed. The moment I started, the clock started ticking, and if I didn't finish before that clock ran out...I failed.

This first of the Trials was a path I was going to run along that spiraled into a safe zone in the middle. And this was why I was going to need those energy packs. I was going to be spending energy. A *lot* of energy.

And there was something else going on here, something I had not told Josh or Mark, because they'd never have gone along with this plan if I had.

There was every chance that someone would be able to booby-trap these tests. Whoever'd been able to sneak a Vamp into the sewers could just as easily have the access to make one or more of the things I was going to face deadly.

Ahead of me was a green path with tree and bush stand-ins on either side. This part of the Trials was all evasive, but it was going to be pretty showy, and I had no doubt there were cams *everywhere*. I tried not to think too much about how many of the things I was going to be evading could have been tampered with. *Right,* I told myself. *How different is this from Hunting? It's not. You just have to be sharp.* I took a deep breath and started running.

And I brought up my Shield. Except my Shield, like that Folk Mage's, wasn't just tuned against magic.

My Shield probably wouldn't stop a *real* gunshot, but what I was supposed to be coming up against were nerfed arrows and spears and rubber bullets. They'd hurt if they hit me, but between my Wall and the dodging I was going to be doing, I was pretty sure there wasn't going to be a lot that got through.

Right at the first jag on the trail, I caught a hint of movement and flung myself sideways. A nerfed spear zinged out of the "brush" and glanced off my Shield. I kept right on going at the same speed.

All my nerves felt on fire. Arrows and spears, even real ones, I could deflect, no problem. But bullets . . . *Just keep that Shield tight. And keep dodging.*

I felt the path rising under my feet and I knew I was about to hit the next part of the Trials. The reason why my load-out was waterproofed. I didn't have a lot of time when I hit the top of the ramp and saw it—the long stretch of water between me and the next part of the path.

I was going full speed, and I didn't hesitate. At the edge of the water I pushed off into a long, flat dive. The requirement was that I swim underwater for a hundred and fifty feet. Soon my fingers hit the end of the tank, and I grabbed the rungs of the ladder I found there, hauled myself up and out, and hit the trail running again.

I was met by blasts of literally freezing air, so frigid it made fog and had little ice crystals in it. In seconds I was bone cold. *Is there someone counting on the cold to slow me down?* I forced myself to push through the cold and kept going.

Then I *did* come to a screeching halt, right at the edge of the next obstacle.

Ahead of me was another tank, this time full of something that might *look* just like mud, but which I knew was going to be more like quicksand. Dotted across this tank were little green islands just a bit bigger than my foot. Some of them were supported. Some of them were not, and would sink right under me, leaving me floundering in the mud.

But I wasn't a city-raised Hunter. . . .

I had the tank in seconds and tested my theory as to which lump of stuff was safe by trying the nearest tussock to me. Some of them had moss and some had grass. It was almost the same length, but if you are raised out in turnip land, you know moss from grass at a glance. I got mud-splashed, which only added to the fun of wet, freezing clothes, but I made it to the other side without slipping but once. Then I lit out running again.

Then came a short stretch of hilly, rocky terrain where it would be far too easy to turn an ankle. And I was being shot at now.

I felt something *zing* past me! Just a rubber bullet that I somehow hadn't deflected? Or a *real* bullet? I didn't have time to even think about it. The clock was running! Was I behind, or ahead? Then another water obstacle, this time a stretch I had to cross on floating logs.

A rope hanging down into the trail warned me before I fell into the pit trap. I made a leap for the rope as the trap opened up underneath me, caught it, and swung myself over to the other side. Then came a three-rope bridge to get across as fast as possible while being shot at—I got hit twice by rubber bullets on that. I was just happy they hadn't been real ones.

Then a pit too wide to jump—I had to drop down into it, discover it was full of snakes and big bugs, recognize that they were harmless, and climb out on the other side.

Then a single-rope traverse across another pit. Also while being shot at. Magic, this time, so nothing got through, though I got knocked around on the line a lot. By this time my breath was burning in my lungs, my hands were scraped up from the rope, I was bruised and battered, the clock was running, and I had no idea how long it was going to take me to get to the end.

And dropping down off the rope was when I found myself on the edge of another drop, down into a round, flat area covered in nothing but sand. But it was ringed with people and guns, and on the other side was the flat, red, concrete slab that marked the end. It was surrounded by Elite Hunters. *Oh, crap.* This would be a great place to take me out. As in, permanently.

Obviously, I was meant to run straight across there, under a hail of rubber bullets and magic. And probably there were all sorts of ankle-turning objects hidden under all that soft sand. Or maybe the sand was knee-deep.

I launched myself off to the left, dropping down within inches of the Elite Hunter nearest me. Startled, he jumped back, then had to jump again and put up *his* Shield as all the guns started to fire in our direction. I drop-rolled, jumped to my feet, ran a few steps, still skirting along the edge of the sand where I was pretty sure the footing was good, drop-rolled again, shouldered one of the Elites aside when he got in my way, ran the last few steps full-out, and stumbled onto the red concrete—

—where I bent over double, panting and exhausted. The clock was stopped . . . for now.

The Elites all filed out of doors that opened up in the wall behind them, a door opened behind me, and the voice in the speakers said, *"Trial One complete: Hunter Joyeaux passes."*

But there was a tear along the top of my pack. Either I'd snagged it on something—or one of those rounds had been live.

I ATE TWO of those food packets in the tunnel, and hoped like anything that I wasn't going to need my Shield for a while. Now that it was over, I could hardly believe I'd gotten through that with as little damage as I had. I don't think I'd ever gone full-out for that long before, and that was just the first Trial. I hoped the second one would be something that would at least let me catch my breath. And I tried not to think of the damage to my pack and what it might mean.

I came out into another part of the stadium field. Ahead of me was a flat stretch of faux turf boxed in by walls.

Then I knew what the next Trial was. And in this one, depending on who my opponent was, I might or might not have to be on guard for treachery. This was hand-to-hand combat, and the first opportunity for someone to arrange an "accident."

Now this *was* one of the Trials where I could be in trouble, besides being a chance for our unknown enemy to get his licks in. I could definitely fail out here, putting us back to square one.

Hey, there was nothing in the rules that said I had to fight in my full pack, so I shrugged out of it, left it at the side, and stepped out onto the field. Or, more properly, into the field of combat. And that was when the armorer stepped out onto the other side himself, and I knew all I had to concentrate on was my performance.

So the last time we did this little dance, I'd been caught off guard, and we were in a relatively small room. Nothing in the rules said I had to *win* this thing, either. I just had to avoid defeat for fifteen minutes. That might not work so well for someone who was strictly trained in offensive arts, but my Masters taught defense *first*.

The speaker said, *"Begin,"* and the armorer came right at me, as I had figured he would.

As far as the observers were concerned, I just stood there and let the armorer rush me. Then, somehow, I completely avoided his foot to my face, lightly brushed at his leg, and he ended up having to scramble to save himself from going arse-over-teakettle.

It's all energy and leverage. Your opponent supplies all the energy, you get off the line of attack and apply leverage at exactly the right time and place, and they send *themselves* flying.

The difference between our first bout and this one was pretty simple; I was ready for him this time. I had plenty of time, and could give myself plenty of distance to see what he was going to do. And—and this is the important thing—remember, I wasn't trying to beat him. When you are trying to beat an opponent, it puts you in an entirely different headspace, where you start to act instead of react, and where you start taking risks.

The plan was working. The armorer was working up a heck of a sweat; I was actually getting some of my energy back.

Finally a horn sounded, and the armorer aborted his attack, turning it into a deep bow, which I returned.

"Well fought," he said—then muttered under his breath, "You were holding back the first time!" Then he winked.

I shook my head no, but I wasn't given a chance to follow up on that, as one of the doors into the fighting space opened up and the speakers said, *"Trial Two: Hunter Joyeaux passes."*

I picked up my pack and headed for the door.

This time it was only a door, leading into yet another section of the stadium floor, where the clock started again. I went cold, because I figured I was about to be shot at. There was a very good chance one or more of the things shooting at me was going to have a lethal load this time. Now was the time to get really scared. If someone was going to take me out, this was the time to do so.

I did get scared; and then I used it. Fear is a natural instinct, and anyone who says it isn't, and that you can get past fear, is lying. You can never eliminate it or get past it. But you can make it work for you.

They called it the "Shooting Gallery," which it kind of was.

The speakers said, *"Trial Three: begin."*

I figured that I stood a better chance of *not* getting in the way of bruises or a lethal load if I took my time. But running would also leave me exhausted for the fourth and final Trial, the Magic Duel, which was going to need everything I had. Whatever other skills the Elites had, they had to be masters of magic.

So I would be steady. Deliberate. Methodical. And above all, focused.

I started my run between the two long lines of pop-up targets. The targets popped up and back down again a lot faster than I liked. *Enemy, enemy, enemy—friendly!* It was in no pattern at all, but I had to shoot every enemy or it would shoot *me*, and I had to avoid shooting *any* friendlies. By the time I exhausted the ammo for my rifle and moved on to my pistol, I had two more bruises to show. I tried not to think too hard about the fact that every time I missed an enemy target, the bullet that came at me could be a live round. I only got one more bruise when I finished the crossbow bolts, and the last target got my knife right between the eyes, and it was over.

I stopped where I was. The clock stopped. The left-hand part of the Gallery parted, another door opened up beyond it, and the speakers said, *"Trial Three: Hunter Joyeaux passes."*

Was I going to be lucky? Were Josh and Mark right? Was it just too risky to make a try at me during the Trials? Had our enemies given up?

Were these enemies only things that existed in our heads?

I didn't want to have to deal with this. I was all cold and knotted up inside. I wanted to call the whole thing off, wanted to call Dusana to me and *bamph* out of there. But I couldn't, because if I did, not only would I always be running, but the Mountain would be endangered, Uncle would still be vulnerable to whoever was using me against him, and I'd never get justice for Karly. Maybe Mark and Josh would be in danger too, since they had associated with me. This wasn't just about me. It never had been, actually.

I managed, somehow, to get myself moving. I shrugged out of my pack and left it with my discarded weapons. Nothing could go on to the fourth Trial but me and the clothing I stood up in. The only weapons I was allowed were those I already had inside myself. I forced myself to take those hard, hard steps through that door, into the dark tunnel, and finally, out into the light again.

It was another sort of space of the kind where I had met with the armorer—but this time it was ringed with Hunters. Twelve of them, evenly spaced around the bounds of a circle defined by a band of red turf. Of them, I recognized only the armorer.

Behind them, in another ring, were the packs, including mine. No distracting shapes and colors for my Hounds today; they were still holding to the greyhound and wolf shapes, with only the shifting shadows and glowing eyes to show what they were.

But waiting for me in the center of the ring was someone I *did* recognize.

Ace.

I felt shocked—and oddly, not shocked. I knew Ace was something hot in the way of a Mage, and the rules said that the Elite—or anyone who was as good as Elite—could be the challenger in both the hand-to-hand and the magic rounds. Here I had assumed it would be one of the Elite. I really hadn't considered that Ace would be good enough, but I should have. He wouldn't have made it to number one on the leader boards and kept that position for so long on looks and flash alone.

But *why* was he here? Was this a chance for him to exercise a purely personal grudge, because he thought my neglect had killed his brother, Paules? He could do that just by defeating me. Was he actually the enemy, the one who had slipped in the Vamp, or was it someone else? Or was he here because someone else was using him and his personal grudge?

I planted all of my attention on him, and then the only thing I knew for sure was that, judging by the glare Ace was giving me, he really did wish me dead. Even surrounded by cameras and Elite, he looked as if he wanted to try to put me in the ground rather than on it.

But he didn't move, and neither did I, because a guy with slicked-back hair in a suit so white it glowed was stepping into the middle of the ring.

*"This is the last of the four Trials that will determine if Hunter Joyeaux Charmand attains Elite Hunter status,"* he said, his voice coming amplified through the stadium speakers. Well, now I had a face to match to the voice. *"This is the Trial of Combat by Magic."* Well, duh, everyone here knew that—but I guess that it had been long enough since the last Trials that the Cits' little carp brains had reset and they wouldn't remember, so for the benefit of the later viewing audience, it had to be said. Sure I had *used* magic in the other trials, but it had been entirely defensive. This would be offensive magic.

*"The rules are simple; each of you will expend his and her magic weapons on each other. You may not use any other form of weapon. If one of you should break the other's Shield, you may use non-lethal hand-to-hand. You may not call in your Hounds for help or support. You may not get help or support from outside this ring. Do you both understand these rules?"*

"Aye," I said first. Ace's glare practically skinned me.

"Yes," he snapped.

*"The conflict will be over when one of you is unconscious, disabled, or unable to continue,"* the referee—I guessed that was what he was—concluded. He walked out of the ring, and the twelve Elite formed their own personal Shields into one big Shield that

covered the entire circle like a dome. Smart move; no point in letting a ricochet or a missed bolt take out five or six rows of seats.

This was a fight with live, and living, weapons. There was no other way to fight a magic duel. There was no way to hold back, no way to abort a strike, and no way to use the equivalent of rubber bullets. That's why it was so important for Hunters to get proper training. Your magic only had an *on* and an *off* switch. There was nothing in between.

So this Trial would have had a slight chance of being lethal to one of us even if it was being fought over nothing more than my right to enter the Elite ranks.

All I could see in Ace's face was hate.

I put up my Shield. He did the same.

The referee walked off the field and the loudspeakers came to life.

*"Trial Four: begin."*

# 23

WE CIRCLED AROUND each other, warily, neither of us ready to make the first move. I didn't trust that what I'd seen of Ace was all that he could do. I also didn't trust that he was assuming he knew all *I* could do. Magic is so very situational, and the problem with using it on the Othersiders is that you might not know what they are or are not going to be affected by. And of course, no sane Hunter would just take on a Folk Mage with straight-on magic. Our best weapons against Othersiders are, in some ways, the crudest: bullets, fire, arrows, artillery, missiles. So far I hadn't yet demonstrated more than a third of what I actually knew. The big question mark, so far as what he knew of me, was—how much of what we were taught of magic on the Mountain was the same as was taught down here?

Best to assume that everything was, I figured. My one and

only advantage was Ace's rage. It would make him impatient. The one thing I did know about him was that he really did not have a handle on how to channel his feelings, and giving in to all that anger was going to make him waste energy. Provided we were equal in strength, this fight might well come down to who ran out of steam first.

There was something terribly unreal about this. Part of me was screaming away, deep inside. Sure, Ace was in a red rage, but would he *really* try to kill me? It's one thing to want to kill someone, it's something else to rain hell down on someone you know and see him start to bleed. It's one thing to kill monsters, and quite another thing to kill a man. Happens, I have done both. And he might have too, and he might be ready to kill me. But that seemed totally impossible. This was someone I knew. Okay, we hadn't gotten along all that well, but this wasn't a Folk Mage, this wasn't some shadowy unknown, this wasn't even a scruffy misfit outside in Spillover. This was a fellow Hunter. I'd eaten alongside him, fought alongside him. We slept in the same building, did the same things. And part of me was *convinced*, even as the other part of me was shrieking inside, that Ace was only going to try to bully and humiliate me, maybe hurt me.

And I couldn't pay attention to either of those parts of me. Focus was all that was going to save me. Whether he was planning to murder me or not, this was still deadly serious, not a game, and I had to win it. I had to make Elite. That was the only thing that would buy me and Uncle more time to figure out together how to handle his enemies and mine, how to uncover who had killed Karly.

Ace began the fight, as I figured he would, but he surprised me a little by doing something subtle. Subtle was not what I expected out of Ace, particularly not replicating my little "grinding" spell on the front of my Shield. I almost laughed—though it was more hysteria than confidence. Did he think I was *that* stupid that I wouldn't notice? The moment it touched my Shield, to my Magic senses, he might just as well have painted a big red blotch there.

And it was my spell, so I knew how to unravel it, which I did.

Actually I am pretty good at unraveling spells; remember, they are processes, and not *things*, so all you have to do is find the place where all the components are meshed together, and give a little yank or a push, and the energy that makes the spell work in the first place then pushes on the wrong places, and that same energy makes it all fall apart. The Masters taught us how to do that, because often we found spells set out in fields and forests to work mischief on whatever human ran across them. Unraveling them was part of our job on the Mountain.

Did Ace know how to do that? Was there any chance he'd run across a spell trap, *ever*, inside the Barriers?

I figured I would find out.

Because I was also going to find the answer to a second question: did he know that you could put a temporary binding on a transient spell and an ongoing spell, link them, and fire them off both together? This was complicated magic, something you usually didn't have to use against a mere Monster.

I set up a barrage of three levin bolts in quick succession, and attached a little gift of my own on the second one. I had more than one way to get through a Shield or a Wall beyond grinding it or battering it down.

With the bound spells set up for the left hand, pure transients to the right, I thrust out my hands at him, *bam, bam, bam!* in rapid succession. And the three levin bolts fired from my palms, like little meteors hitting his Shield squarely. The two from the right hand hit at the level of his face—meant to rattle him, since it was wildly unlikely anything would get through the Shield—but the one from the right hand "appeared" to glance off the top of his Shield. "Appeared," because the real purpose of the levin bolt was to deposit its passenger on the top of his Shield, where he might not notice it working.

There's only one way to make Shields, and they are all alike. The only difference between a Shield a human makes, a Shield a Hound makes, and a Shield a Folk Mage makes is that sometimes—so I was taught—a very powerful Folk Mage layers several Shields, one inside the other.

That didn't matter here. Neither of us could do that.

Now if, like the Masters, you have studied the processes intensively, you can introduce other spells to change a Shield. And you can teach your Hunters how to do the same.

In this case, my little passenger was attaching itself to the process that created Ace's Shield and changing it, so that the Shield would become harder—and more brittle. When I finally hit that Shield with a blow that shattered it—provided Ace didn't detect my work and unravel it—I'd have an instant or two of time when I could get to him before he got another Shield spell working.

He fired back three fire bolts, and sure enough, the third one had a grinding spell attached, which I unraveled.

He still hadn't noticed the little saboteur. I guess he thought *I* didn't know how to piggyback. Noted. *Don't get cocky.*

He'd barely gotten back his balance from firing his three fire bolts when I hit back. But not with a direct barrage.

I couldn't get through the Shield yet, but I could make things uncomfortable for him in there.

Obviously, Shields are not completely impervious; if they were, you would never be able to see out, because light wouldn't get through, and you wouldn't be able to breathe, because air wouldn't get through.

I recognized what the faux turf was: real grass woven like a carpet and dyed. We used that stuff ourselves sometimes, when we got shipments of scraps no one in the cities wanted to bother with. It made good paths on the snow and over mud. It was nicely flammable and I set fire to it in a ring right up against his Shield, and fed the fire with more energy bound into the spell so the flames roared up all around, licking at the Shield. It was hot, scary, and put out a *lot* of smoke.

He put it out almost immediately—that's not hard if you know anything about fire—but there was still a lot of smoke inside the Shield with him, and he was coughing and red-eyed and even angrier. He countered with cold; intense cold that made my breath smoke and instantly coated all the turf around me and inside my Shield with frost.

*Cold? Really? That's all you have?*

*Do NOT get cocky!* I ordered myself. Overconfidence could kill me too.

But I needed to keep fueling his anger, because anger means a loss of control, and that was a weapon in my hand. I wanted to goad him some more, so I wrinkled my nose with contempt and let him have a stink bomb. That's right, pure skunk essence, manifested in that burned ring around him. Just to show that if this wasn't "just a Trial," I could have planted something lethal around him. And while he was coughing, wiping his watering eyes, and choking and running away from the spot, I was taking my time in unraveling his cold spell.

Oh, and at least half the Elites were sniggering.

I hoped he hadn't been too careful about where he stepped, because that was real skunk spray I created—and if any of it transferred to those pretty boots of his, it would still be oh, so very much with him.

A moment after he moved, though, the stink stopped. I guess one of the Elites or the referee did something about it.

A little disappointing, but of course, I couldn't blame them. Pretty much everyone was going to be getting the "benefit" of it if they'd just let it be.

We circled for a while; I was concentrating hard on keeping my focus. He still hadn't noticed my brittle spell working, so I reckoned I would give him something else to think about. *His* turn to feel the cold.

I encased him in ice.

Ice is a spell we use a lot on the Mountain. Othersiders just cannot handle the cold, and if you have about half a minute, you can significantly slow down their reflexes by ice-casing them. Again, this is only good when you are going one-on-one and you have some distance on them, because it does take about thirty seconds for the process, start to finish. But if you catch them unaware, plenty of times you'll have them stopped dead. And then literally dead, because once they are slowed, no matter what they are, or how good their Shields are, the cold disrupts their ability to keep the Shield up, and bullets take them out just fine.

And I caught him by surprise. I almost got him completely closed in, and if I'd had a chance to thicken the ice wall around him to the point he couldn't break it, I'd have won the Trial painlessly—

But, alas, no. He figured out what I was doing at about the point where the ice wall was closing in the top of his Shield, and he figured out the right response.

He flexed his Shield outward, shattering the ice wall. With nothing to work on, the spell unraveled by itself.

That broke his temper as well, and for the next while, it was an exchange of direct attacks—levin bolts of pure electrical energy, like lightning; fire bolts, ice bolts—that battered at our Shields. His were sheer, brute force, trying to bring my Shield down. Mine were all underpowered—testing his Shield, waiting for it to have gotten brittle enough to smash, although I did vary what he was forced to deal with by attacking the ground right where his Shield met it, chewing away at the turf and dirt underneath it, and forcing him to move when I threatened to dig under the edge of the Shield.

All of this was exhausting and I was just hemorrhaging energy. Gnawing hunger nagged at me, and if it hadn't been for the reserves I had built up for this, I'd have been in trouble. I caught a good look at his face, and it sent a chill down my back and finally silenced that nagging little voice.

He wanted me *dead*. My insides just went to water. And then, as we maneuvered around the circle a little more, my insides froze, because that murderous glare turned to a murderous grin of pure triumph.

There was just a split second of warning, a tiny wink of light up in what should have been empty stands, just over Ace's shoulder.

I flung up my hands to shield my eyes in pure instinct, otherwise I would have been blinded by the flash that hit my face. Someone had used a purely mechanical, powerful light source and shone it right into my eyes!

And something dark, big, and fur-covered hit me and knocked me to the ground.

It was off me in a second—falling away from me with a heart-rending yelp of pain. A Hound!

But it wasn't one of *my* Hounds. It was one of Ace's.

And I hadn't been the one that hurt it.

It writhed on the ground in agony, and I looked up to see Ace standing there, his mouth dropping open in shock, with something held in his outstretched hand, something he could have hidden easily in his sleeve. I hadn't been inspected and neither had he. So much for the honor system.

I knew what it was immediately, and why he was using it instead of a gun.

A laser. Because I'd hardened my Shield against solid objects, but light would go right through a Shield. . . .

He had tried to kill me by *cheating*, and it had been *his* Hound who saved me, *bamphing* across my Shield and intercepting the lethal laser beam that Ace had fired at me at the moment I was blinded.

I snapped.

A monumental rage erupted inside me, and I had just enough control and sense left to grab the reins of that horse and ride it because I could not have *stopped* myself, even if there had been a helpless child between me and that miserable *bastard*.

I hit his Shield with everything I had, a powerful physical blow like the one I had used on the Gazer's Shield, and it shattered as he stood there with a stunned look on his face.

Then I ran straight for him.

Launched myself into the air at the last minute in a flying side kick.

Felt my foot hit his chin with the most satisfying *thwack* I have ever felt in my life. It was a moment in breathless slow motion, my foot hitting his face, his feet coming up off the ground as mine came down in a "ready" stance.

Ace went *flying* backward, already unconscious before he hit the turf.

But I wasn't going to stand there and gloat. Not while there was a wonderful, self-sacrificing Hound I could still save.

I whirled and ran back to where the Hound was still keening in pain, a smoking wound in its shoulder. It had not, thank whatever gods you choose, taken what *would* have been a lethal shot to *me* in any part of it that would kill it immediately. But it was in desperate bad shape. I dropped to my knees beside it and began pouring every bit of healing I could into it.

There was a lot of shouting and carrying on behind me, but I was concentrating, eyes closed, because there wasn't a lot in me left, and I needed all of it to get into that Hound.

I felt the big Shield go down, and then I felt my pack surround me, and more energy poured from them into me, and then into Ace's Hound.

The Hound's keening turned to a whimper, from a whimper to a whine, and then, at last, into a long sigh of relief and release from the pain. And I opened my eyes as he struggled to his feet.

My pack parted as he staggered a few steps forward. I saw that two of the Elites had hauled Ace, finally coming around, to his feet, while the rest of them and their Hounds were swarming up to that spot in the stands where the flash of light had come from that had nearly blinded me.

Ace's other Hound, mane bristling with anger, stalked toward its master, while the wounded Hound did the same. I had no idea what was going on with them, and clearly, neither did the Elites. Were the Hounds about to attack the two men that held their master prisoner?

But my Hounds were all calm—and so were the Hounds packed up behind the two Elites.

Ace's Hounds reached him, and closed their mouths around his hands.

Ace—screamed. Screamed as if someone had just gut-stabbed him. His entire body arced backward, and the two Elites could barely hold him.

Then the Hounds dropped his hands, and he went limp in their grasp.

We all just stopped for a moment, and my eyes went straight to Ace's hands.

The backs were blank. No scars. No tattoos.

Ace was no longer a Hunter, because he no longer had any Hounds.

The two Hounds turned and stared at Bya. Bya stared back at them.

A moment later, the wounded one transferred his gaze from Bya to me, and I heard a brand-new voice in my head.

*By your leave, honest Hunter, we would join your pack. Your alpha has given consent, and we will follow him.*

I felt my mouth fall open.

But what could I say but yes? I mean, Bya had already agreed—heckfire, I would never hear the end of it from him if I said no.

I nodded, and Bya left my side to help the other support the wounded one over to me, where I was still kneeling on the turf. Like Karly's Hounds, they each took one of my hands in their mouths, and I felt that red-hot burning that meant two more Glyphs had been added to my Mandalas.

I was going to have to get a lot of tattooing done now. I still hadn't gotten Hold and Strike's scars overwritten.

When the burning stopped, they let go of my hands and looked into my eyes.

Their eyes were silver, and they looked like two enormous, dark-silver gargoyles. Their heads were kind of a cross between a wolf and a big cat, with blunt muzzles and huge fangs.

Well, at least I wouldn't have any trouble telling them from Karly's Hounds, or mine.

*I am Myrrdhin,* said the wounded one.

*I am Gwalchmai,* said the other.

"Myrrdhin," I nodded, speaking aloud into a very strange and uncanny silence. "Gwalchmai. You are welcome to my pack."

The silence stretched on for what seemed like forever. Then, finally, there was a strange-sounding cough from the loudspeakers. And the referee spoke, almost apologetically.

*"Fourth and final Trial is concluded. Hunter Joyeaux passes. Hunter Joyeaux Charmand and pack, welcome as the fifteenth member of Apex Hunter Elite."*

# 24

YOU WOULD THINK that would be the end of the drama.

Oh no. There was still one more surprise.

Before the Elites could come down out of the grandstand empty-handed, before the two who held Ace prisoner could cart him away, we were literally descended on by—

—an Army helichopper. A *big* one, one of the troop carriers.

A group of soldiers in black uniforms of a sort I had never seen before, with an officer with more gold on him than I had ever seen in my life, descended on the two Elite Hunters and their prisoner.

There followed a lot of shouting and arguing, as I sat, largely ignored, on the turf, surrounded by my pack and slowly trickling more manna into Myrrdhin. My head was pounding, I was famished and dry-mouthed and, frankly, a bit light-headed as I tried to make sense of what they were carrying on about. I had thought the confrontation with the Folk Magician had taken a lot out of me. That was nothing compared to how I felt now. The longer I sat there, the worse my head got. I couldn't get my brain wrapped around how *insane* Ace had been, trying to kill me with a weapon. With magic, he might have pulled it off as a regrettable accident in the Trials, but like this? This was *nuts*. It just didn't add up.

The Elite Hunters, of course, were shouting at the tops of their lungs, and making no doubt that they were adamant that Ace was going to be taken off, investigated, questioned, and then put on trial for trying to murder me. Which seemed entirely sensible to *me*, obviously. . . . Except—Ace hadn't been working alone. Someone up in the stands had set me up for him to kill me. And whoever was behind him had used him and was unlikely to leave him alive. He was more likely to survive to be questioned if the army had him now. Ace was an Elite-level Mage, and without his Hounds that meant he was army property. As far as they were concerned, that he was a criminal was all the better. Criminals have no rights. They could do whatever they wanted to with him, with little or no consequences. They wouldn't have to coax him or reward him. He'd do what they wanted, or find himself tossed into a deep, dark hole. Heck, they might even stick him in that dark hole and *only* let him out to do what they wanted.

Along with the shouting, there was a lot of frantic calling on Perscoms, requests streaking up the chain of command on both sides, until at last an answer came back that silenced the Hunter Elites, direct from Premier Rayne's office and countersigned by my uncle.

They hauled Ace off in restraints, and it was pretty clear as far as they were concerned, that he was tried and convicted and they had him by the short hairs. He was not going to have an easy time of it, much less the sort of life he had become accustomed to.

You might think I would be angry, but I wasn't. I was just tired, worried, and once again had way more questions than answers. The only *answer* I had was that there definitely *had been* someone out to kill me.

But mostly I was tired, and my head was pounding as if someone was using it for a fancy-dance drum. So when the rest of the Elite descended on me to take me back off to headquarters—I didn't fight it. I was just relieved that they all understood that right now, I didn't need or want some sort of initiation or celebration or anything else.

All I wanted was a big meal, my bed, and Bya.

And that was what I got.

The next day I woke up to a message from Uncle. Directly from him, too, and not through Josh. The message light was flashing when I woke, and when I brought up the lights, the message started playing on my vid-screen.

"Congratulations, Niece," said Uncle—not "Prefect Charmand." I could tell he was being Uncle by the broad, relieved smile he was wearing. "I never doubted you'd make Elite, but I am astonished and pleased you did so in so short a time. I'll be sending a pod for you at eleven thirty for lunch."

And that was all.

When the pod came around, I was wearing an outfit I hadn't

yet worn, something I hoped would be fancy enough to go to luncheon with the prefect, but not so fancy that I'd feel foolishly overdressed. This was one of those asymmetrical outfits that the people around here seemed to like so much, although it didn't go so far as having only one sleeve and one short leg and one long. It was a tunic with a slanty hem, half charcoal and half silver-gray; charcoal leggings; a black, corsetlike belt; and black boots. I'd done some business Karly had shown me how to do—pulling the pony-tail under my right ear and stringing beads on three strands of hair behind my left ear—but my makeup was minimal.

The pod rolled up right on the dot, and I was already outside waiting for it. But to my surprise, when the door opened, Uncle was waiting in it.

It had a driver of course, who probably doubled as a body-guard. Now that I knew Uncle had *deadly* enemies, plus there were rebels, that just made sense. I got in, very formal and all, but as soon as the door dropped, the decorum got thrown out, as Uncle grabbed me and *hugged* me as hard as can be! I hugged back, of course.

"I am so incredibly proud of you!" Uncle said, holding me at arm's length and beaming at me. Which told me that *this* pod must have been taken apart piece by piece and gone over for listening bugs. "Joy, I want you to know I never, ever thought that anyone would cause you serious harm when I brought you here. I will admit I did so with the intention of seeing who might try to use you. I never thought things would go *this* far."

"Well, now we know they're ruthless and they're stupid," I replied as bravely as I could. "Ruthless, that's obvious. And *stupid* because they clearly didn't bother studying either of us."

"I wish I had warned you more explicitly and I had done it while you were still back home," he said.

Well, I've said before that one of the things I've studied at the Monastery is *The Art of War* and *The Book of Five Rings*. Not a lot, but I've studied them. So, I wasn't like all *how could you!* I just shrugged. "'Let your plans be dark and impenetrable as night, and when you move, fall like a thunderbolt.'" I quoted. He smiled so broadly I thought his face might split in two.

"You sound *just* like my brother, and I see you have gotten an excellent education." He hesitated a moment. "There is a great deal going on that—"

"You can't tell me about," I finished for him. "You're the general, Uncle. I'm just the soldier." I figured I would leave it at that. And that seemed to satisfy him.

"We won't be as much strangers now," he said, changing the subject—or maybe not. "There can be no question in anyone's mind about favoritism now that you've earned Elite." And that made me almost giggle I was so happy.

He picked a place to eat at random and didn't have to explain to me why: it would be impossible for anyone to have set up spy-ears that way. We made a big stir among the patrons when we came in, but no one was daring or bad-mannered enough to try to come up to us. We got a little private alcove, and I couldn't tell you what we ate, because I was just too busy *finally* being with *my uncle*, and not the Prefect Charmand. Finally I had family, all of my own.

And I was never going to let anyone take that away from me.

We probably burned two hours, although most of what we talked about was personal, and maybe that was just in case someone had managed to sneak some sort of spy-ear in once they knew where we were. Or maybe it wasn't. He told me more in that two hours about my parents than I had ever known before. Nothing like biographies, of course, because I already knew that—it was the little things, like how my mom *killed* in chess, and my dad could not stand the taste of fish, that both of them had been big fans of old fantasy vids and books, and things like that. He told me what a joker my dad had been when the two of them were growing up, and the kind of pranks he pulled, like completely disassembling an old junked tractor and reassembling it on the roof of the police station without the police having any idea until they saw it the next morning. So the people I only knew as a couple of photos started to become ... people to me.

He hugged me again when we were done, kissed the top of my head, and sent me back to headquarters in my own pod with a promise that this was only the first of many more times we'd get to be together. And a promise that those times together would be a whole lot longer than just two hours.

Which was a better reward than anything I'd gotten since I arrived here.

"So, I'll ask what no one else is asking," Josh said as the driverless car whisked us off to the Strauss Palais. "How much free time are you going to have *now?*"

Besides Uncle taking me out to lunch, Josh had asked me out again. This time my gown was all silver lace over a dark charcoal lining, with a kind of fan collar, and I had lacy silver hair ornaments that matched a lacy silver necklace.

They'd had other outfits for me too; I didn't need any lessons in dancing this time, so while the gown was being made, I had—a photo session. It was for those posters and splash-screens you saw everywhere, the ones that featured an Elite and said "Your Hunter Elite, making the Allied Territories *safe!*" Yes, like some sort of vidster or rockster, I was set up to pose against a green background with and without my pack, with and without weapons, wearing various examples of the design team's imagination.

Part of the job . . . part of the deception. For now, I had to put up with the deception.

"It's so *weird,*" I had told Josh after I'd described the session to him. "When I look at newsvids, it looks like something out of pre-Diseray. So many people in gray and black and silver—even that reporter Gayle!"

"Well, what do you expect?" Josh had asked archly. "I'll bet a lot of those people used to be wearing Ace's colors, and they can't exactly do that anymore, now can they?"

I was afraid Josh was going to ask me about Ace now. And I didn't know anything about him, beyond what everyone else knew—mostly, it was things I didn't know. The army hadn't let him talk to anyone that wasn't them. And, come on, that was some craziness even for a guy whose brother had been killed . . . because even if he'd killed *me,* the result would have been the same! His Hounds would have left him, and he'd have been hauled off and taken away, so he had thrown *everything* away no matter whether I lived or died. And I still didn't know if he was the one responsible for Karly's death, or if it had been someone else. And that was fairly crazy too. It just didn't match with the Hunter who had held the number one spot all this time. Crazy people can't do that. Had he just snapped? Or had someone given him a push down the wacko slide? The more I thought about it, the more it seemed likely he'd been led into nutter-land.

I did know this much: I had asked Myrrdhin and Gwalchmai about the Vamp in the sewer. They had looked at each other, then solemnly at me, and said, *It was not something we knew, nothing we helped with,* which at first had suggested rather strongly it hadn't been Ace. And I don't think even he would have been good enough to plant the Vamp without his Hounds. But *then* they had said, *But he kept much of his mind closed to us,* which opened up all sorts of possibilities.

Apex couldn't afford to lose me now, and no matter how highly placed Uncle's enemies were, I was now considered so necessary, even though I would literally be *less* visible, that everyone in the city was going to be aware of me. And no one was going to forget me. Not when I was the only Hunter, *ever*, to have a pack of eleven.

"So. You've been very quiet. Are you still going to have time to see me?" Josh asked, relieving me, since he hadn't asked me anything I couldn't answer honestly.

"I asked Armorer Kent about that before I left the building tonight," I said, not mentioning how surreal it was to have *all the Hunter Elite* on speed-call on my Perscom. "He said I'd have to be prepared to drop a date right in the middle, but yes. 'All work and no play makes a burned-out Elite,' is what he said exactly."

"Well," Josh said ruefully, "this isn't going to be as much of a date as I had hoped, I am afraid. I've been given my orders, which I am to relay to you. We're only allowed one dance together per set."

I sighed. Of course, I should have expected something of the sort. "So . . . I guess that everyone at the Palais tonight is going to be some sort of notable notable? And dancing with me is the prize they've won." I made a little face, but really, it wasn't so bad. "If it'll help Uncle, how could I say no?"

It wasn't bad. In fact, it was kind of fun.

And when Josh leaned toward me in the pod on the way home, I hesitated for just a second, wondering if he had another note to pass or some other ulterior motive. But no. It was a completely lovely, toe-curling, thrilling kiss; it made a whole flock of butterflies erupt and fill my insides. And just as I was thinking it was a good thing this pod was nice and roomy—and driverless— the darn thing pulled up at HQ and popped the door, which pretty much put an end to it.

So Josh pulled away, reluctantly, and helped me out—which I needed in that ridiculous dress, to make sure I didn't catch it on something. He held me for just a few seconds, then his Perscom beeped and we both jumped.

He swore, looking at it. "No rest for the wicked," he said, and smiled. "Let's do this again soon, Joy."

I smiled. "Good. Maybe we can even do it incognito."

He laughed at that. "I doubt it, but who knows? You have a habit of surprising people."

The pod door closed before he could say anything more. I waved as it rolled off, then picked up the trailing end of my dress and went back inside.

*Sometimes I wish I was stupid,* I thought, as I undressed and got into something comfortable. *If I was stupider, I'd be happier.* After all, I had a life people in Spillover could only fantasize about—heck, a life regular Cits could only daydream about. I had rockster fame. I had my pack. I'd won myself some peace. There was Mark, who was certainly the best friend I had here, and there was Josh.

Okay, granted, I had a job that could easily get me dead if I wasn't careful—but I'd had that job since I was knee-high to a goat, and I was kind of used to it.

I fed power to the vid-screen and discovered to my embarrassment that someone had thought it would be a great idea to put one of the photo-shoot pieces up as wallpaper. There was this—girl. Someone I scarcely recognized. She was wearing a mostly silver outfit that was so tight it left absolutely nothing to the imagination. She was bracing a big-ass rifle on one hip, and staring out over the head of the observer, with her pack ranged alertly behind her. The background was the cityscape of Apex—the nice part of it, anyway. I guess she looked sexy. She didn't look like me, even though I remembered that exact shot being taken.

Part of me thought that I would have traded every fancy outfit, every gourmet meal, Mark, Josh, and my personal bathroom to go home again. I'd have traded an awful lot of it just to be able to talk to my Masters. I wanted to talk to people who knew *me*. Even a letter would be wonderful, but I didn't dare send one, because the Monastery and everything in it were not supposed to exist. I wanted that so badly it was an ache in my throat.

Oh, how I wished I was a Psimon, or that there was some magical way to carry message—

I felt my eyes widen as an idea hit me. I scrambled to my feet, then drew and cast the Glyphs.

Bya came through and stood there, looking at me.

He was laughing.

At me.

Of course he was. It had certainly taken me long enough to figure this out.

"You can take messages to the Masters, can't you?" It was more of a demand than a question.

*Of course.* No apology. No explanation of why he hadn't offered. I knew, of course. This was one of those things I was supposed to figure out for myself. After all, I knew they could *bamph*. I also now knew they could carry things with them—like me—when they did it. So, I was the idiot for not figuring it out until now.

"I've been a little preoccupied, you know," I said a bit crossly.

*Well, you're not now.* Bya jumped up on the couch next to me and settled down. *So write your letter.*

I knew it was going to be more than a letter, of course. I was going to have to tell them everything that had happened to me and around me, before I could start asking for advice. But everything has to begin somewhere, so I got a pen and some paper and sat myself down beside Bya, and began to write.

TURN THE PAGE FOR A SNEAK PEEK

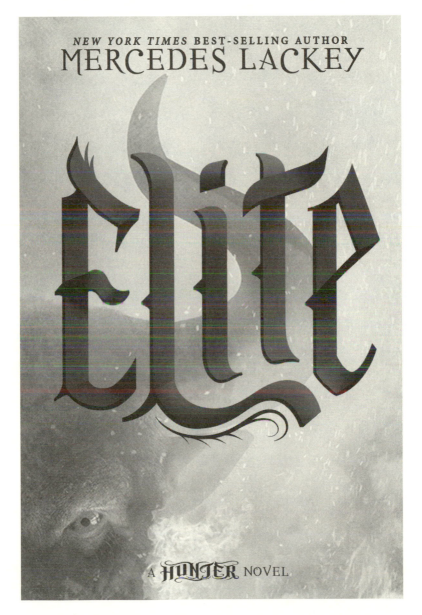

NEW YORK TIMES BEST-SELLING AUTHOR
MERCEDES LACKEY

Elite

A HUNTER NOVEL

1

I LOOKED OVER MY shoulder, and fear hit me like a bolt of frozen lightning because all I could see were teeth.

Hundreds and hundreds of white, shining teeth, the smallest of them as long as my hand, the biggest as long as my whole arm, and all of them thin and needle-sharp. The mouths holding those teeth were much too close.

Dusana and I were running at Dusana's top speed, and it didn't seem anywhere near fast enough. I made myself as small as I could on Dusana's back and tried to tell myself that I didn't actually feel the Drakken's hot, bitter breath on my neck.

Dusana could do more than run away from this horror chasing us; he could bamph both of us right out of there, leaving the Drakken frustrated and confused. But we didn't want the Drakken frustrated and confused because the thing would just turn right back around to the agro-station and take out that frustration on the station and the handful of people inside it. Their power was out because the Drakken had destroyed first the transformer linking the station to the main grid, then the backup solar panels and their wiring. Now the electrocution field that would have protected them was gone, and we were their last hope for getting out of the situation alive. Drakken can and do tear entire concrete or reinforced metal buildings apart. All they need is a little seam or crack to get their claws into, and they dig and claw until they pull the toughest wall down.

So we were playing bait. We were a bit of meat on a string, and we were pulling the Drakken toward a trap.

Dusana's run was a lot smoother than a horse, even as he jumped over obstacles in the agri-field we were running through. I looked back over my shoulder again. I'd never been this close to a Drakken before, not even when one had been ravening alongside the train I was in. I hadn't known they had three mouths; the mouth you see, then another mouth inside of that coming out on a stalk, then another mouth inside of that one coming out on another stalk, the whole thing darting at what it wants to catch like a frog tongue. A tongue that's about half as long as the Drakken. Except instead of being sticky like a frog tongue, the end, the middle, and the beginning are all razor-sharp teeth. No wonder they were top predators among the Othersiders. No wonder they were able to drag victims right out of any shelter they'd found.

The mouth-tongue darted straight at me just as I looked, and I couldn't help myself, I meeped with stark terror and made myself even smaller as the last mouth snapped a few feet behind Dusana's hindquarters. That's not a view anyone ever wants to see, ever. My insides were so knotted up with panic that I felt sick, and I was shaking like I had a fever. But I was still thinking, still watching, still calculating, and still readying spells; that never goes away. I'm a Hunter: I can be throwing up with fear and still be ready to throw a dazzle spell or put up a Shield. I had both of those ready, just in case.

I had to be on Dusana's back, because while the Drakken might chase him, it would go over chasms and through buildings to get to me. Dusana was just another Othersider, probably something like the thing's normal prey, but Drakken on this side don't want normal prey—they want humans. Humans were the best things on the buffet to Drakken, and a magic wielder like me was a tightly-packed, nutrient-dense bomb of manna.

We had to stay close, because if we got too far out ahead of him, the Drakken would start to lose interest and his attention would start to waver. I was only one tasty morsel. There were a dozen yummy bites back in the station. If we couldn't keep his focus on us, he'd remember that and go back for them.

Obviously, there was no way I was going to be able to take on a Drakken alone, not even with a pack of Hounds eleven strong. But I was heading right for some people who could do what I couldn't.

I spotted the markers they'd set out on the tops of two bushes at the same time Dusana did: two bandanas tied to branches. He somehow put on a burst of speed to get out of the smash zone, and I hung on for all I was worth, and just as we got past, right behind us I felt a blast of air shove us forward and heard a huge, concussive thump.

Dusana skidded to a halt and pivoted on his forelegs at the same time so we could both see what was happening. The Drakken was frozen in midleap. I averted my eyes and opened up with the light-dazzling spells I'd had ready, hitting the Drakken right in the eyes with the brightest and most powerful ones in my arsenal.

I looked back up as soon as the light show was over. The Drakken, with the front part of him looking strangely thinner and oddly flatter, seemed to be hanging in midair, its forefeet dangling, the claws as long as I was tall just brushing the ground. To people who could see magic, like me, it looked like he'd been flattened in a giant tortilla press, two huge disks of magic slammed together. Then one of the disks evaporated, and he started to slide down on the stationary one, when another disk came out of nowhere and slammed into the first again. I hit it in the front of the head with a hammer blow myself, but what I did was just icing on a devastation cake. This happened three more times, and then the two Elite that were responsible for this phenomena decided the thing was good and dead, and the stationary disk evaporated too.

The Drakken dropped bonelessly down into the blueberry bushes. Bonelessly because at this point whatever it had that passed for bones had been shattered, at least in the front half.

An avalanche of meat, tons and tons and tons of it, crashed down onto the ground in front of me and Dusana, crushing the bushes underneath it. A shock wave carrying dust and leaves smacked us. Dusana jumped back in reaction, even though we both knew we were too far away for the dead Drakken to hit us. The earth shook, and the sound...like the time I'd been way too close when lightning hit a tree near me. It all struck me and Dusana with a physical blow that left us both trembling.

And Hammer and Steel came out of the rows of thick blueberry bushes where they'd been lying in wait, and walked over to examine their target.

It oozed greenish liquids from all its orifices. That horrible three-sectioned mouth-tongue lolled on the ground, limp, in two loops of flesh, and the flattened head looked somehow worse than when it had been alive. All those teeth…they still looked terrifying. Something inside me was waiting for that tongue thing to suddenly leap to life and lash out at me. It was going to take a while to get my jumpy nerves calmed down.

I'd expected it to stink, but it didn't. It just smelled like hot valerian tea: a bit bitter, but not intolerable.

My two partners snagged their bandanas, then leaned on each other, breathing hard. They were sweat-drenched and exhausted, as you'd expect, from doing a feat of magic that impressive. Both of them had fumbled out energy squares and were chewing on them, and even the movements of their jaws looked tired.

Hammer and Steel were brothers. Both had perfectly sculpted faces, like amazing statues, and deep mahogany skin, darker than what I was used to seeing on the Mountain, where people with ancestors from all over had been partnering up ever since the Diseray. At Anston's Well, Safehaven, and the Monastery, we're all sort of tan with brown-to-black hair, and only rarely do you see a blond or ginger. In fact, I was pretty sure that the influx of Mark Knight's people into the area was the biggest concentration of blonds in forever. Both brothers kept their hair at little more than a fuzz on their skulls. Most Hunters either keep their hair very short or get it all tied up and pinned down for Hunting because you don't want to give any Othersider something to grab for. Hammer was a bit shorter than Steel, and a bit broader in the muscular sense. Both of them smiled a lot when they weren't in the middle of a Hunt. They were smiling very broadly now, as well they should, for a job well done. As tired as they were, the mere fact of such a tremendous accomplishment was giving them back energy. They were the first two Elite I had ever met, outside of Armorer Kent. That had been back when I first got out of my probation period. They'd come as fast as they could when the "Hunter down" call went out for my friend Karly, though I got there first because Dusana bamphed me there, and…well, they were just really, really kind and did what they could for me while I was falling apart. Now that I was an Elite and worked with them, I knew that was just how they were: kindhearted, solid, and steady.

Hammer is the implacable force, and Steel is the immovable object, and whatever gets between them is going to end up very dead. They only have the one offensive trick, which is a manipulation of their Walls, but really, when you can use that to squash a Drakken, what else do you need?

Their colors were gold and brown, and they are the only Hunters in or out of the Elite that share colors. Their outfits are exactly the same pattern and cut, but with the colors reversed from Hammer to Steel. Today, for instance, they both wore sleeveless tunics and trousers tucked into boots. Hammer had a brown tunic, gold pants, and brown boots. Steel had a gold tunic, brown pants, and gold boots.

My legs were still feeling too shaky to get down off Dusana, so I asked my Hound to walk up to where they were. Even on Dusana's back, I was just barely as tall as Steel. He looked up from his examination of the dead Drakken, saw us coming, straightened, and grinned. "Well, that worked out just fine. Maybe we oughta make your call sign 'Bait,' Joy." He pulled his brown bandana out of the pocket he'd stuffed it into, and wiped his head and neck down with it.

I shuddered. "This isn't something I really want to get into the habit of doing."

"May not have a choice, kiddo," said his brother, gently, mopping his own head with his gold bandana. "You're the only one of us with a Hound you can ride."

I swallowed hard, but I could see his point.

"You said when we were in the chopper that this was a small Drakken!" I countered. We'd come up with this idea on the fly, on the helichopper ride in to the site. It was a very, very, effective strategy, and unless we did it within sight of one of the Folk, not one that the Drakken would ever learn to avoid.

"It was," Steel replied, his mouth quirking as he tried not to laugh at me. "We've never seen anything smaller than that."

I had no good reply for that, so I got down off Dusana and let him join my pack. The Hounds—my pack of eleven, and the six belonging to Steel and Hammer—all clustered around the dead Drakken. It looked as if all they were doing was breathing hard, but what they were really doing was inhaling manna, which is a sort of magical energy, a force that they live on, and what puts the power behind Hunters' magic. Everything alive has manna, but humans, even non-magic ones, have more of it than anything that comes from Otherside. Mind, something the size of a Drakken has loads and loads and loads, as much as all the Hounds together could "eat."

Hammer was on his Perscom. "Drakken down. Need disposal crew," he was saying.

"Disposal crew dispatched, Elite Team HSJ. ETA fifteen minutes," came over all three of the radios on our Perscoms. He probably hadn't needed to call that in, since the little ubiquitous cameras that hung around every Hunter were hovering discretely in the background, but it was better to be sure. Something like a Drakken carcass might attract more Othersiders if it didn't get disposed of quickly.

"What are they going to do with that thing?" I asked, a little queasy and a lot curious. Hammer looked at Steel, and they both shrugged, as a breeze blew the oddly mingled scents of crushed blueberries, crushed greenery, and valerian tea over all of us.

"Never asked. Probably goes into the soup for the vat farms, or gets made into fertilizer," said Hammer. "There's a market for things like skin, claws, teeth, horns, and tusks, though. Rich people have books bound in Drakken skin or make boots and shoes out of it. They get decorators to make display pieces out of bones, teeth, claws ,and all. Sometimes have artists carve stuff out of them or make composite works."

"I was at a reception at Premier Rayne's palace once," Steel offered. "There was a chair made out of teeth and bones. People were taking their selfies sitting in it."

I shuddered again, this time revulsion mixing with fear. Hammer nodded. "I know, right? Sure, we have the Barriers but...if anything ever comes through the Barriers, I'm thinking you might as well paint targets on all those fancy apartments with dead Othersider knickknacks in them."

Our Hounds began drifting back toward us, now gleaming and prosperous-looking with all the manna they'd taken in. Hammer and Steel's were pretty typical for Hounds; they looked like oversize mastiffs with heavy coats; Hammer's were ebony and Steel's were chocolate. Mine are a disparate bunch. There are the two that I "inherited" from Karly that look like wolves, except wolves made out of shadow. That's Hold and Strike. Then there's the two that abandoned their previous Hunter, Ace, when he betrayed everything about being a Hunter by trying to murder me during my last Elite Trial. That's Myrrdhin and Gwalchmai. Their heads look a bit like a cross between a wolf and a big cat, almost exactly like some of the French gargoyles I've seen pictures of. They're an all-over silvery gray.

And then there's my original pack: Bya, Dusana, Begtse, Chenresig, Shinje, Kalachakra, and Hevajra. They're...not like any Hounds anyone here at Apex City has ever seen before. In fact, the only other person I know of who has Hounds like mine is my mentor back on the Mountain, Master Kedo Patli.

For one thing, they can choose what they want to look like. Right now they were in their "normal" forms, which is to say, like something out of a psychedelic vision. They ranged in size from pack-alpha Bya, whose head was just about at my rib cage, to Dusana, who was big enough to ride on, to Begtse, who was about as big as the shed you'd put Dusana in, they were covered in multiple patterns picked out in multiple eye-watering colors, and sprouted horns, tusks, teeth, spikes, and ridges in ways that made no sense or logic. But when we weren't Hunting, they were generally a pack of black greyhounds with fiery eyes.

Their ability to change form was one big difference between them and the other Hounds around here. For another, they'd accepted other peoples' Hounds into their pack. Nobody had ever heard of that happening before. Normally when a Hunter dies or somehow makes his Hounds desert him, they just go back Otherside. But these four hadn't, giving me the biggest pack anyone had ever heard of, a pack of eleven. I think that huge pack was why Hammer, Steel, and I had been sent out after a Drakken, instead of a bigger team. My Hounds had been the safeguard; while Dusana and I had been leading the Drakken away, they had been coursing silently alongside, just in case something went wrong. And they had been prepared to jump in and start harrying the Drakken in case Hammer and Steel hadn't been able to kill it right away.

The last difference between my Hounds and every other Hunter's was that they were doing things with me and for me that I'd never even read about Hounds doing before. Like Dusana bamphing me along with him.

That would mostly likely give me an edge over whoever was trying to kill me. Besides Ace, that is. Because although the former Hunter Ace was currently in army custody (and locked up when he wasn't out under guard to use his magic against the Othersiders the army deals with), Ace had been working with someone else, someone who had never been caught.

Steel cocked his head to the side; listening hard, I could hear the heavy whomp whomp whomp of a couple of cargo helichoppers. "That's the disposal crew," he said. "We might want to move back to the station and the landing pad."

Since I had no particular wish to watch and maybe get splattered with yuck, I nodded, and we all backtracked along the path between the blueberry bushes I'd taken leading the Drakken away. The guys started helping themselves to berries as we walked, which was all the invitation I needed to do the same. Sure, we get whatever we want to eat at HQ, and Hunters get fed really, really well, but working magic makes you hungry.

Fruit off the bush is always the best, anyway. The berries weren't the same as wild blueberries; they didn't have the same intense, slightly tart flavor, but they were bigger and sweeter than the ones back home, and I liked them better than the so-called "blueberry jam" they served at HQ.

The guys were slowly recovering as we walked. The bushes were as tall as Steel's head, and the ground between the rows had some sort of dense, small-leaved ground cover growing over it, to discourage weeds. The stuff was hardy; it didn't really even seem bruised by us walking on it.

"Good Hunt," Steel said, around a mouthful of berries. He was the strategist of the two brothers, as I'd learned on the chopper ride into the drop zone. This was the first time I'd worked with them alone, rather than being in a full six- or eight-man Elite team.

His brother grunt-laughed. "Any Hunt you can walk away from is a good Hunt." He and Steel fist-bumped. The helichoppers must have landed because there were no more sounds from their blades, but there were other noises behind us now. A breeze carried the sound of chain saws revving up, so the cleanup crew was already at work. Otherwise the only thing you could hear out here was the sound of wind in the bushes and the songs of birds and beneficial insects. That was part of the job of the ag-station, growing bugs that ate other bugs and releasing them at the proper time, and maintaining food stations that attracted bug-eating birds. There's a lot of farming stuff we don't do that they did before the Diseray, and spraying poison all over everything is one of them.

When we got to the station, some of the techs were already outside, fixing the transformer and jury-rigging a link to the wind array, and the rest were looking at the deep scores in the concrete of the building. They kept glancing at us rather shyly, as if they wanted to thank us but were diffident about it. Steel solved that by walking up to them as casually as if we had not just flattened a Drakken.

"Everyone all right?" he asked. They seemed to take that as the cue that it was okay for them to flock around us and ask for autographs. Crazy, right? But believe it or not, Steel and Hammer both reached into thigh pockets and pulled out little palm-size cards with their pictures on them. Right there, after just having killed a Drakken, they were signing their names, as if they weren't ready to drop, as if they were in a club or a bar. I was hanging back, but Steel beckoned me forward and pulled out another set of cards from his other thigh-pocket. This lot had the whole Elite unit on it, including me. I didn't remember posing for that, but I suppose that someone had pasted the picture together from our individual shots. So I signed those. And our Hounds milled around and accepted attention from anyone who'd give it to them. Mine reverted to greyhound shape as soon as they saw the crowd, maybe to keep from scaring anyone, although at this point you'd think all those people who'd watched my channel would know what they looked like.

So weird. So very, very surreal. Back home, Hunters were just not idolized like this. But then, back home, we weren't entertainers. And I swear, even with these people who should have known better because they'd nearly become lunch for a Drakken, they reverted to being fans as soon as they saw us.

But playing along was part of the job, as I kept being reminded at every turn. "Fan service" it was called, and it was another way to make the Cits believe they were safe, no matter what. So I signed cards and imitated Hammer and Steel. Eventually the supervisor realized they should actually be working, and chased everyone inside except the techs fixing the transformer, and we went over to the landing pad to wait for the helichopper that would pick us up. Hammer and Steel were still keeping up the façade of being indestructible, but I could tell they were fading.

"How long have you been Elite?" I asked, to keep their minds off how tired they were and not trying at all to keep the admiration out of my voice. I hadn't had much chance to talk with them since I joined the Elite ranks. Actually, I hadn't had much chance to talk with anyone. We worked really hard; when we weren't drilling under Armorer Kent's eye, we were either deployed against something big or running patrols in some places in and around Apex that I hadn't even known existed.

"Maybe not as long as you're thinking," Hammer mused, with a raised eyebrow. "Just four years."

"We became Hunters a lot later than you, kiddo," said Steel. "Powers popped at eighteen, full Hunter at eighteen and a half, got sick of the posturing and went for Elite together at twenty-one, and we're twenty-five now." He glanced as his brother as if to suggest he should say something.

"We decided that we had to apply together. My trick doesn't work without my brother," Hammer said modestly. "We did the Trials separately, though. I guess we kind of cheated on the last one."

Steel threw back his head and laughed. "It's not cheating if it works!" he retorted. "Our Walls are so strong, we actually never needed to go on the offensive. It was pretty funny, to tell you the truth. I got Kent; he tapped out and surrendered when he just ran out of energy after beating against my Wall to the point that he couldn't even produce a light-flash."

"I got Archer. I kind of hated to flatten him the way I did, he's such a nice guy, but…" Hammer shrugged. "Playing nice doesn't win the Trials. I just shoved, shoved his own Shield right up against him and squashed him against the big containment Shield. He was at the point of getting the air pushed out of his lungs when he tapped out."

They both laughed. "Joy, you've got to look that up. The look on Archer's face!" Steel chortled. I'd never heard a laugh I could have described as a chortle before. It surprised me into laughing too.

"I will," I promised. And that was when the helichopper for our ride back came cruising in just above the berry bushes.

We opened the Way for our Hounds, who went back Otherside, looking sleek and contented. Then we loaded in, with me going last; there was a limited amount of room in the chopper, and the two big guys had to arrange themselves first because I could just squeeze in anywhere. They strapped in, leaned back in their seats, fastened chin straps to keep their heads from lolling about, and closed their eyes as the tough fight caught up with them. They were asleep within a minute; the chopper had just turned around and was starting back for home while they dozed off. They looked weirdly younger when asleep.

It had been a grueling fight for them, no matter how easy it had looked. Doing things with magic isn't effortless, far from it. It takes energy to move magical energy, and that energy has to come from inside the Hunter. Those two had been working like champion weight lifters the entire time they'd been bashing that Drakken. I was amazed they had managed to stay on their feet and look perfectly normal for the station crew.

But that was part of the mythos we were trying to project, I guess. We can never do anything that might make the Cits lose confidence in us or think they were anything less than completely safe.

But although I'd done some to help, I was still at about 90 percent charge. I keyed my Perscom, and called up HQ.

"Hunter Joy," I said when I got the handshake.

"Go, Hunter Joy."

"Put me back in rotation. I hardly did anything this run," I said. Because I hadn't, and if we got another callout, it could be that one more Hunter would make the difference between handling it ourselves, and having to call in the army. One thing I'd learned, the Elite hate having to call in the army. Calling in an artillery barrage or some of the attack choppers is one thing, but having to call in troops or army Mages or army Hunters makes everyone feel like they fell down on the job somehow. Right now, I was pretty sure most of us didn't want to get within a mile of an army group that had a Mage with it because that Mage might be Ace. The army took him, and the army tends to want to use what it takes. So Ace was probably out there, somewhere, supervised, sure, but not in a prison cell as long as he was "working."

It would be even worse if we had to call in Psimons from Psi-Corps, the people with Powers that worked on the mind like telepathy, psychokinesis, mind-control, and that sort of thing. But they never worked outside the Barriers unless they were working with the army. Hunters don't much like Psimons, but then, no one really does. How can you like someone who can rummage around inside your head anytime he pleases? Psimons, though, they have this cold arrogance every time they look at Hunters, like they're thinking, I can do more than you can, and I don't need Hounds to do it.

"Roger, Hunter Joy. Noted back in rotation." That was another change from being a plain old Hunter and being Elite. HQ assumed you knew your own strength, and if you figured you were good to go back on call, they didn't argue with you. Only the medics could override that, and the medics would know from my vitals that I was just fine.

So I watched the fields roll by about six feet below the skids of the chopper, and change from blueberries to tomatoes, to corn, to things I didn't recognize, I thought about Hammer and Steel and their call signs; there was something about that combination of Hammer and Steel that was hitting a note of familiarity but not strongly enough that I was getting the connection.

Oh, well. I'll just tuck it in my subconscious, and it'll wake me up in the middle of the night, probably.

We raced toward the huge, conical silver towers that created the Barrier; if I craned my neck, I could see them through the pilot's windshield. The helichoppers, like the trains, have a field around them that cancels out some of the Barrier effects, but I braced myself anyway. Hitting the Barrier feels for a human a lot like breaking the surface of water, except you feel it all through you instead of just at your skin. Of course, most Othersiders would be disintegrated if they tried to pass it.

But now that I knew what I did…I had to wonder, just how many Othersiders had managed to learn how to pass Barriers somehow. Because an awful lot of them were getting on the city side these days. More than Apex admitted, except to the Hunters, from whom it could not be hidden.

As if in answer to my thoughts, my Perscom beeped. "Hunter Joy, do you copy?"

"I copy, HQ," I said instantly.

"You're to bounce when you hit the landing pad. Your old friend White Knight's turned up another Gazer nest. You and Archer are to rendezvous with him."

"Copy that, HQ," I replied. "Out."

I was already so focused on the Gazer nest that the jolts when we passed through the Secondary and Prime Barriers barely registered. I had one hand on my harness release as we came in hot to the landing pad, and the skids weren't even on the ground when I was out and sprinting for the second chopper, where I could see Archer beckoning to me from the door. Then we were in the air, and he and I were neck-deep in strategy as the chopper sped off.

056022862

CHASE BRANCH LIBRARY
17731 W. SEVEN MILE RD.
DETROIT, MI  48235
313-481-1580